TALES OF MYSTERY
AND IMAGINATION

TALES OF MYSTERY AND IMAGINATION

Edgar Allan Poe

WORDSWORTH CLASSICS

This edition published 1993 by
Wordsworth Editions Limited
Cumberland House, Crib Street
Ware, Hertfordshire SG12 9ET

ISBN 1 85326 013 4

Wordsworth® is a registered trade mark of
Wordsworth Editions Ltd

Typeset by Antony Gray
Printed and bound in Great Britain by
Mackays of Chatham plc, Chatham, Kent

INTRODUCTION

It has never been easy to give biographical details of Edgar Allan Poe's life because he frequently fantasised (lied) about dates and places, and he suffered from possibly the worst literary executor in history, Rufus Griswold, who sought every opportunity to blacken Poe's name. Poe was born in Boston in 1809 to actor parents who very soon died, whereupon the infant was taken in by John Allan, a merchant in Richmond, Virginia. He lived with the Allans, including a lengthy spell in England, until he was seventeen, and this left him with a lifelong conception of himself as a Southern gentleman. A brief period as a student at the University of Virginia was followed by the publication, in 1827, of *Tamerlane and Other Poems*, a two-year spell in the army and the publication of *Al Aaraaf, Tamerlane and Minor Poems* in 1829. A brief time at West Point came in 1830–1 (he was expelled) and a third volume of *Poems* in 1831. The years in Baltimore (1831–5) were characterised by poverty, marriage to his thirteen-year-old cousin, Virginia Clemm, the friendship of the writer John Pendleton Kennedy and the commencement, with 'Metzengerstein' in the Philadelphia *Saturday Courier* in 1832, of the publication of his tales (the term 'short story' did not come into use until the 1880s). In 1833 he won $50 from the *Baltimore Saturday Visitor* for 'MS. Found in a Bottle'.

Poe became an assistant editor on the *Southern Literary Messenger* in Richmond, from 1835–7, and published *The Narrative of Arthur Gordon Pym* in 1838, though, because he pretended only to be its editor, a typical Gothic trick, he earned no money from it. This failure was hard, for he and his family were extremely poor by this time. In 1839 he found a job as co-editor of *Burton's Gentleman's Magazine* in Philadelphia, where he continued his reputation as a brilliant but acerbic reviewer and literary theorist, and published *Tales of the Grotesque and Arabesque*, which was not a success. Fired from *Burton's* because he would not stop drinking, he became a co-editor of *Graham's Magazine* and his powers as a writer were at their height. During the next few years he published steadily. 'The Raven', a collection of a dozen of his stories and *The Raven and Other Poems* all appeared in 1845, the year he also became sole owner of the *Broadway Journal*, a move which, like so many in his benighted life, turned out to be a failure. His drinking and ill-health increased in 1847, following the death of his wife, who had been a semi-invalid for a number of years. He managed to publish 'Ulalume' in 1847 and his remarkable work, *Eureka*, the following year. Amid a number of attachments to women, and following a temporary attachment to the Temperance Movement, he died in mysterious circumstances in Baltimore on 7 October 1849.

Despite his properly considerable literary reputation (something he always felt he should have), Poe was a racist (witness *Arthur Gordon Pym*); a supporter of slavery; a snob (his detestation of mobs seems at times to edge over into a dislike of people); a user of drugs; an alcoholic; a paranoiac (while some of his feuds had substance, others did not) and a hysteric. None of this alters his literary value one jot, but it does give strength to D. H. Lawrence's dictum : 'An artist is usually a damned liar, but his art, if it be art, will tell you the truth of his day.' [1]

Since the 1950s, Edgar Allan Poe has, like so many classic American writers, become an academic industry. A visit to a university library will reveal volumes examining French criticism of Poe; Poe in Russia; the image of Poe in American poetry; Poe and the British magazine tradition; the Scandinavian response to Poe; Poe, Lacan and Derrida; and one 'simply' called *Poe Poe Poe Poe Poe Poe Poe* (presumably because the author, like his subject, believed in the powers of incantation). Yet for most people it surely remains the case that Poe has two great claims to fame. The first is that, in his three Dupin stories ('The Murders in the Rue Morgue', 'The Mystery of Marie Rogêt' and 'The Purloined Letter'), as well as the cipher tale, 'The Gold Bug', and the least-likely-suspect story, 'Thou Art The Man', he laid the foundations for the subsequent development of the detective story. Poe can be credited with the creation or very early refinements of the locked-room convention; the Olympian detective; the less-than-brilliant associate and chronicler; the linguistic and visual puzzle; the easily dismissed police force; the murder as disruption of a small town and the solving of crime as an intellectual exercise.

The second claim to fame is as one of the greatest of all writers of horror stories; not merely because he made more sophisticated the elements he took from the European Gothic tradition, such as subterranean dangers, the *femme fatale* (literally so in 'The Fall of the House

[1] D. H. Lawrence, *Studies in Classic American Literature*, Garden City, New York 1951, p. 12

of Usher'), burial alive, ghosts, excessive curiosity, the curse from the past and exotic locales, but because he fashioned those elements into a remarkable investigation of abnormal psychological states and obsessional behaviour (what he chose to call 'the imp of the perverse'). In his Preface to the original edition of *Tales of the Grotesque and Arabesque* (1840), Poe asserted that ' . . . terror is not of Germany, but of the soul . . . ', thus immediately distancing himself from what he saw as outdated Gothic paraphernalia. The Gothic novel served as a major model for the early development of fiction in America. In an interesting British collection of American short stories published in 1930,[2] I find that in the first two stories, 'Peter Rugg, The Missing Man' by William Austin (1824) and 'Rip Van Winkle' by Washington Irving (1819), both use the old Gothic notion of the man who defies a higher power and loses his place in the normal flow of time and in each case misses the change from colonies to new nation; an excellent example of the way in which a popular literary formula was used to air the stresses and nostalgias of contemporary life. One of the earliest published American novelists, Charles Brockden Brown, was a fully-fledged Gothic novelist, whose works substitute Indians for the demons of European Gothic; where humble two-storey wooden edifices, far from crumbling ruins, still hold terrors from the European past, and where the chaos of the plot mirrors the chaos of the first decades after the War of Revolution, when there seemed to be little tradition and few recognised moral and political codes to work with. Similarly, one does not have to read far into the tales and novels of a much greater American nineteenth-century writer, Nathaniel Hawthorne, to see how heavy was the influence of the European Gothic on his writing.[3]

'The Tell-Tale Heart' is a very good example of Gothic elements narrowed down to the smallest possible compass in order to emphasise the narrator's horrifying descent into madness. The castle becomes two small rooms; the subterranean caverns become the small space under a few floorboards; the cast of characters is limited to two (of whom one could, just possibly, be a figment of the other's imagination) and the past is discounted as any explanation of the narrator's obsession:

> It is impossible to say how the idea entered my brain, but once conceived, it haunted me day and night.

[2] John Cournos (ed.), *American Short Stories of the Nineteenth Century*, London 1930

[3] See Jane Lundblad, *Nathaniel Hawthorne and European Literary Tradition*, New York 1947

Even when he seems to be more obviously indebted to European models, as in 'The Fall of the House of Usher', the Gothic drama is soon internalised, since the allegorical links between Gothic architecture and the structure of the human consciousness, always lurking less or more plainly in earlier narratives, are here made manifest, both by the description of the house itself and the rather intrusive poem, 'The Haunted Palace', as well as in the small cast of three, allowing for a reading which sees Roderick as the human intellect torn between rationality (the narrator) and ideality (Madeline), a struggle which is far from equal. Poe can also leave the reader poised between psychological and 'Gothic' readings, as in 'Ligeia', where it is likely that the narrator has created a milieu where it is possible for him to hallucinate the presence of his first wife, even by killing his second; but where it is equally possible that Ligeia, through the sheer force of her will, returns from the dead to take over Rowena's body. It is the 'Gothic' readings, of course, which so appealed to Roger Corman.

It has often been asserted that there are therefore two Poes: the writer of tales of imagination, where the irrational reigns supreme, and the writer of mystery tales whose cardinal emphasis is on the operations of the reasoning faculties. This seems to me to be the same kind of simplification as saying that there are two John Donnes, the writer of love poems and the composer of religious poetry. Just as Donne takes an attitude of jokey adoration towards his beloved(s), so his devotion to God is frequently couched in the passion, wit and startling wordplay of his more material relationships. There is only *one* John Donne and all his work shares in his struggles towards what he conceives as an ideal state; so it is with the work of Edgar Allan Poe. Perhaps the best way to understand this is to start with Poe's least accessible work, *Eureka*, a Romantic prose-poem-cum-philosophical-and-mathematical treatise on the nature of the universe, first published in 1848. This long work is impossible to summarise in the brief space of this introduction: suffice it to say that Poe's view of the universe is at once highly sophisticated and profoundly simple. The reason for this paradox is that, although Poe is familiar with recent theories of cosmogony and, not being satisfied with the basic regularity of the Newtonian universe, he anticipates Einstein in discussing the finiteness of space and time, his insistence on the original *unity* of the universe is really the final gesture of the Romantic imagination. Just as Wordsworth could talk about that which we half-perceive and half-create and Coleridge could argue that the outside world only becomes alive through the shaping spirit of the poet's imagination, so Poe felt that the prime impulse of the artist must be towards restoring an original unity to the chaos which seems to surround the poetic spirit. Thus, at the very beginning of *Eureka*, he likens the artistic impulse to a person spinning round on his heel at the top of Mount Etna so as to obtain a dizzy blending of the formally disparate elements of the scene into a vertiginous whole. He repeatedly insists on the need for a leap of imagination (or 'faith') to understand the operations of the universe and this insistence is demonstrated in the texture of his prose:

> Does not so evident a brotherhood among the atoms point to a common parentage? Does not a sympathy so omniprevalent, so ineradicable, and so thoroughly irrespective, suggest a common paternity as its source? Does not one extreme impel the reason to the other? Does not the infinitude of division refer to the utterness of individuality? Does not the entireness of the complex hint at the perfection of the simple? It is *not* that the atoms, as we see them, are divided or that they are complex in their relations – but that they are inconceivably divided and unutterably complex – it is the extreme-ness of the conditions to which I now allude, rather than to the conditions themselves. In a word, not because the atoms were, at some remote epoch of time, even *more than together* – is it not because originally, and therefore normally, they were *One* that now, in all circumstances – at all points – in all directions – by all modes of approach – in all relations and through all conditions – they struggle *back* to this absolutely, this irrelatively, this unconditionally *One*?[4]

Note how the reader is lulled here by the familial references, by the balance of words (' . . . entireness . . . perfection . . . ') but, most of all, by the insistence, in both the thought and language of this passage, of the *extremeness* of Poe's imaginative creations (an orang-utan; whirl-pools; plagues; wind machines which make the curtains move; journeys into strange and irregular lands; premature burials). There is, then, an extreme *oneness* involved in the stories: the vampire-seeming Madeline Usher literally falls on top of her brother, Roderick, and they both expire at the same moment (followed immediately by the house crumbling into its inverted image in the tarn); the magical conditions of a pentagonal chamber create a situation where the 'hyacinthine'-haired Ligeia merges with the fair-haired Lady Rowena; the coat of arms of the Montresors, in 'The Cask of Amontillado' ('A huge human foot d'or, in a field azure; the foot crushes a serpent rampant whose fangs are imbedded in the heel'), suggests enticingly that the narrator, a

[4] H. Beaver (ed.), *The Science Fiction of Edgar Allan Poe*, Harmondsworth 1976, p. 237

Montresor, is, in getting rid of Fortunato (also, presumably a part of the 'treasure'), wiping out a part of himself, like William Wilson.[5] And, finally, premature burial approaches as close to a oneness with death as is humanly possible (without dying). Thus Poe, like Shelley, recorded the 'desire of the moth for a star', the effort of the Romantic artist to create the journey towards, and sometimes the arrival at, a supernal realm of the imagination; but, for Poe, the search is very dangerous and the result might well be horrific. Keats longed for death, but Poe was less sure. The end of the search might be the Domain of Arnheim:

> There is a gush of entrancing melody . . . there is a dream-like intermingling to the eye of tall slender Eastern trees, bosky shrubberies, flocks of golden and crimson birds, lily-fringed lakes, meadows of violets, tulips, poppies . . .

but is more likely to be a plunge into an abyss; a drop into a pit containing who knows what horrors; incarceration in some dreadful darkness; or even, in 'The Facts in the Case of M. Valdemar', merely 'detestable putrescence'.

The oneness is as applicable to the detective stories as to the horror tales. In *Eureka*, Poe, despite a good deal of scorn aimed at the philosophers who deal only in *facts* (' . . . a more intolerable set of bigots and tyrants never existed on the face of the earth'),[6] seeks to combine scientific observation with poetic leaps of the imagination. Similarly, Dupin, Poe's great detective, makes such a leap with no difficulty. In 'The Murders in the Rue Morgue' he remembers the great French thief-taker/detective, Vidocq, and his limitations:

> He impaired his vision by holding the object too close. He might see, perhaps, one or two points with unusual clearness, but in so doing, he necessarily lost sight of the matter as a whole.

This could also be said of the French police in 'The Purloined Letter', who search the apartment with absolute thoroughness but fail to see the letter in the letter-rack because they have not obtained any conception of the *room*. They are easily outdone by Dupin, who finds the letter because he has a notion of the room as a whole; he sees the

---

[5] Herman Melville seems to have had a similar notion in 'Benito Cereno' in describing the stern-piece of the slave-ship: ' . . . uppermost and central of which was a dark satyr in a mask, holding his foot on the prostrate neck of a writhing figure, likewise masked'. See H. Beaver (ed.), *Billy Budd, Sailor & Other Stories*, Harmondsworth 1967, p.220

[6] *The Science Fiction of Edgar Allan Poe*, p. 215

oneness of the room. One is reminded here of Mark Twain's view of Sherlock Holmes's success rate:

> Anybody that knows him the way I do knows he can't detect a crime except where he plans it all out beforehand and arranges the clues and hires some fellow to commit it according to instructions . . . [7]

There is a real sense in these stories that the world goes according to Dupin's view of how it should go.

Oneness, in Poe's stories, comes often from a rapacious curiosity. In this, Poe adapted a borrowing from the European Gothic tradition. In that kind of literature, curiosity is both the motor force of the plot and the Achilles' heel of the central protagonist. In *The Monk* (1796) such a desire to know hands the hero into the clutches of the Devil and a grisly end; in *Caleb Williams* (1794) the hero's quest for the truth about his employer, Falkland, is compared to Pandora's opening of the dreaded box; and Vathek's quest for knowledge, in William Beckford's novella of that name (1786), leads to damnation because

> Such shall be the chastisement of that blind curiosity, which would transgress those bounds the wisdom of the Creator has prescribed to human knowledge . . . [8]

For Poe, curiosity fits much less easily into any pattern of transgression and punishment. No condemnation of the narrator of 'Ligeia' occurs, despite the possibility that he has murdered his wife; the narrator of 'The Pit and the Pendulum', despite his semi-conscious desire to merge with whatever horrors exist at the bottom of the pit, is given a last-minute, tongue-in-cheek rescue by *deus ex machina*; the narrator of most of 'A Descent into the Maelström' emerges from the abyss with his hair changed from 'raven-black' to 'white' but with a strong ability to tell his tale. To *know* can lead to horror, just like the desire for oneness (at its limit, this merging can only come through death), but it can also lead to an escape from this humdrum world of *facts*.

I have already mentioned that Poe is revered as a great *American* writer, but that estimate raises obvious problems, for how far *can* Poe be seen as American? His stories are usually set in some imaginary or at least unnamed land. Where is the House of Usher? Perhaps it were best to say that most of his tales and poems occur in a place he locates (in 'Dream-Land') 'Out of SPACE – out of TIME'. When he wishes to use an actual place for the location of memory, he uses the 'old world'

---

[7] C. Neider (ed.), *The Complete Short Stories of Mark Twain*, New York 1958, p. 451

[8] P. Fairclough (ed.), *Three Gothic Novels*, Harmondsworth 1968, p. 254

of England ('William Wilson'); when he wants to create a city detective he invents a Frenchman and places him in Paris, even making mistakes when he transposes the events of a real American murder case to France in 'The Mystery of Marie Rogêt', and on the rare occasion when he wants to use a story to illuminate a growing problem of anomie and identity in the growing cityscape, he chooses London (in 'The Man of the Crowd'). In the present volume, the only stories which set foot in the United States are 'The Gold Bug' which almost immediately leaves Charleston for an island off the coast of South Carolina and 'The Oblong Box' which very soon sets sail for the open sea. Mention might be made, however, of the last tale in the volume, 'Some Words with a Mummy', which turns out to be an arch and half-hearted satiric allegory of Poe's view of American politics. The subject matter of the last-named tale thus makes it very unusual among Poe's works; for the reader scans his writings almost in vain for references to American history or biography or politics or, indeed, American literature (we are reminded of Poe's wranglings with the East Coast *literati* and the fact that Walt Whitman was the only American writer to attend his funeral, and he refused to say anything).

Yet perhaps the very fact of Poe's isolation from American society and culture may be most important. The period in which he wrote (the 1830s and '40s) was a disputatious, bustling period, probably like many other periods in American history, and the artist seems to have needed persistently to justify his/her existence. In 1844, Ralph Waldo Emerson had firmly enunciated the authority of the poet:

> The poet is the person in whom these powers are in balance, the man without impediment, who sees and handles that which others dream of, traverses the whole scale of experience, and is representative of man, in virtue of being the largest power to receive and to impart.[9]

But in the 'Custom-House' introduction to *The Scarlet Letter*, Hawthorne (only partly as a joke) fears the reaction of his Puritan forebears to his literary calling:

> A writer of story-books! What kind of a business in life – what mode of glorifying God, or being serviceable to mankind in his day and generation – may that be? Why, the degenerate fellow might as well have been a fiddler![10]

[9] L. Ziff (ed.), *Ralph Waldo Emerson: Selected Essays*, Harmondsworth 1982, p. 261

[10] B. Harding (ed.), *The Scarlet Letter*, Oxford 1990, p.10

It was hard to be a writer in America, not least financially, since the lack of an international copyright agreement between the United States and Great Britain meant that large quantities of cheap, pirated copies of British works flooded the American market. Moreover, in a time of a rapidly expanding economy, individualism might too often mean opportunism and greed; scientific achievements and the expansion of American society across the continent bolstered a progressive and aggressive epoch. The public, political voice of America was, therefore, one of boundless optimism. A piece in the *Democratic Review* in 1839 believed that, since the War of Revolution, the United States had achieved 'progress in all the substantial elements of national grandeur which is believed to have had scarce a parallel in the annals of mankind'.[11] Writers, as they are wont to do, tended to show the darker side of this optimism. James Fenimore Cooper remarked, in *Home As Found* (1838):

> . . . the mass has become so consolidated that it no longer has any integral parts . . . the individual is fast losing his individuality in a common identity.[12]

Emerson found, in 'The American Scholar' (1837), that:

> The state of society is one in which the members have suffered amputation from the trunk, and strut about so many walking monsters – a good finger, a neck, a stomach, an elbow, but never a man.[13]

and Thoreau, in *Walden* (1954), felt that, 'The mass of men lead lives of quiet desperation.'[14]

Poe, too, showed an alternative to the optimism and complacency and materialism of his age, a dream of beauty and primal unity which always contained the probability of terror and darkness. Few people at the time heeded him, but since his death, and particularly in the twentieth century, his voice has been widely heard and recognised, like that meaningful shape from the past so beloved of Gothic writers.

JOHN S. WHITLEY
School of English and American Studies
University of Sussex

---

[11] Quoted in M. Cunliffe, *The Nation Takes Shape*, Chicago, p. 2
[12] Lewis Leary, Introduction to *Home As Found*, New York 1961, p. VI
[13] *Selected Essays*, p. 84
[14] H. D. Thoreau, *Walden*, New York 1962, p. 10

FURTHER READING

Poe's other writings

R. L. Hough (ed.), *Literary Criticism of Edgar Allan Poe*, Lincoln, Nebraska 1965

J .W. Ostrom (ed.), *Letters of Edgar Allan Poe* (2 vols.), New York 1966

Biography

J. C. Miller, *Building Poe Biography*, Baton Rouge, Louisiana 1977

S. P. Moss, *Poe's Literary Battles*, Durham, North Carolina 1963

A. H. Quinn, *Edgar Allan Poe: A Critical Biography*, New York 1941

K. Silverman, *Edgar Allan Poe: Mournful and Never-Ending Remembrance*, London 1992

Collections of critical essays

H. Bloom (ed.), *Edgar Allan Poe: Modern Critical Views*, New York 1985

R. Regan (ed.), *Poe: A Collection of Critical Essays*, Englewood Cliffs, New Jersey 1967

K. Silverman (ed.), *New Essays on Poe's Major Tales*, Cambridge 1993

Critical studies

M. L. Burdick, *Grim Phantasms*, New York 1992

J. Dayan, *Fables of Mind*, New York 1987

D. Halliburton, *Edgar Allan Poe: A Phenomenological View*, Princeton 1973

D. G. Hoffman, *Poe Poe Poe Poe Poe Poe Poe*, London 1973

D. Ketterer, *The Rationale of Deception in Poe*, Baton Rouge 1979

B. R. Pollin, *Discoveries in Poe*, Notre Dame, Indiana 1970

G. R. Thompson, *Poe's Fiction: Romantic Irony in the Gothic Tales*, Madison, Wisconsin 1973

CONTENTS

The Gold Bug

What ho! what ho! this fellow is dancing mad!
He hath been bitten by the Tarantula.[1]

All in the Wrong

MANY YEARS AGO I contracted an intimacy with a Mr William Legrand.[2] He was of an ancient Huguenot family, and had once been wealthy; but a series of misfortunes had reduced him to want. To avoid the mortification consequent upon his disasters, he left New Orleans, the city of his forefathers, and took up his residence at Sullivan's Island,[3] near Charleston, South Carolina.

This island is a very singular one. It consists of little else than the sea sand, and is about three miles long. Its breadth at no point exceeds a quarter of a mile. It is separated from the main land by a scarcely perceptible creek, oozing its way through a wilderness of reeds and slime, a favourite resort of the marsh-hen. The vegetation, as might be supposed, is scant, or at least dwarfish. No trees of any magnitude are to be seen. Near the western extremity, where Fort Moultrie[4] stands, and where are some miserable frame buildings, tenanted, during summer, by the fugitives from Charleston dust and fever, may be found, indeed, the bristly palmetto; but the whole island, with the exception of this western point, and a line of hard, white beach on the sea-coast, is covered with a dense undergrowth of the sweet myrtle, so much prized by the horticulturists of England. The shrub here often attains the height of fifteen or twenty feet, and forms an almost impenetrable coppice, burdening the air with its fragrance.

In the inmost recesses of this coppice, not far from the eastern or more remote end of the island, Legrand had built himself a small hut, which he occupied when I first, by mere accident, made his acquaintance. This soon ripened into friendship – for there was much in the recluse to excite interest and esteem. I found him well educated, with unusual powers of mind, but infected with misanthropy, and subject to perverse moods of alternate enthusiasm and melancholy. He had with him many books, but rarely employed them. His chief amusements were gunning and fishing, or sauntering along the beach and through the myrtles, in quest of shells or entomological specimens; – his collection of the latter might have been envied by a Swammerdamm.[5] In these excursions he was usually accompanied by an old negro, called Jupiter, who had been manumitted[6] before the reverses of the family, but who could be induced, neither by threats nor by promises, to abandon what he considered his right of attendance upon the footsteps of his young 'Massa Will.' It is not improbable that the relatives of Legrand, conceiving him to be somewhat unsettled in intellect, had contrived to instil this obstinacy into Jupiter, with a view to the supervision and guardianship of the wanderer.

The winters in the latitude of Sullivan's Island are seldom very severe, and in the fall of the year it is a rare event indeed when a fire is considered necessary. About the middle of October, 18—, there occurred, however, a day of remarkable chilliness. Just before sunset I scrambled my way through the evergreens to the hut of my friend, whom I had not visited for several weeks – my residence being, at that time, in Charleston, a distance of nine miles from the island, while the facilities of passage and re-passage were very far behind those of the present day. Upon reaching the hut I rapped, as was my custom, and getting no reply, sought for the key where I knew it was secreted, unlocked the door and went in. A fine fire was blazing upon the hearth. It was a novelty, and by no means an ungrateful one. I threw off an overcoat, took an arm-chair by the crackling logs, and awaited patiently the arrival of my hosts.

Soon after dark they arrived, and gave me a most cordial welcome. Jupiter, grinning from ear to ear, bustled about to prepare some marsh-hens for supper. Legrand was in one of his fits – how else shall I term them? – of enthusiasm. He had found an unknown bivalve,[7] forming a new genus, and, more than this, he had hunted down and secured, with Jupiter's assistance, a *scarabæus*[8] which he believed to be totally new, but in respect to which he wished to have my opinion on the morrow.

'And why not tonight?' I asked, rubbing my hands over the blaze, and wishing the whole tribe of *scarabæi* at the devil.

'Ah, if I had only known you were here!' said Legrand, 'but it's so long since I saw you; and how could I foresee that you would pay me a visit this very night of all others? As I was coming home I met Lieutenant G—, from the fort, and, very foolishly, I lent him the bug; so it will be impossible for you to see it until the morning. Stay here tonight, and I will send Jup down for it at sunrise. It is the loveliest thing in creation.'

'What? – sunrise?'

'Nonsense! no! – the bug. It is of a brilliant gold colour – about the size of a large hickory-nut – with two jet-black spots near one extremity of the back, and another, somewhat longer, at the other. The *antennæ* are – '

'Dey aint *no* tin in him, Massa Will, I keep a-tellin on you,' here interrupted Jupiter; 'de bug is a goole bug, solid, ebery bit of him, inside and all, sep him wing – neber feel half so hebby a bug in my life.'

'Well, suppose it is, Jup,' replied Legrand, somewhat more earnestly, it seemed to me, than the case demanded, 'is that any reason for your letting the birds burn? The colour' – here he turned to me – 'is really almost enough to warrant Jupiter's idea. You never saw a more brilliant metallic lustre than the scales emit – but of this you cannot judge till tomorrow. In the meantime I can give you some idea of the shape.' Saying this, he seated himself at a small table, on which were a pen and ink, but no paper. He looked for some in a drawer, but found none.

'Never mind,' said he at length, 'this will answer;' and he drew from his waistcoat pocket a scrap of what I took to be very dirty foolscap, and made upon it a rough drawing with the pen. While he did this, I retained my seat by the fire, for I was still chilly. When the design was complete, he handed it to me without rising. As I received it, a loud growl was heard, succeeded by a scratching at the door. Jupiter opened it, and a large Newfoundland, belonging to Legrand, rushed in, leaped upon my shoulders, and loaded me with caresses; for I had shown him much attention during previous visits. When his gambols were over, I looked at the paper, and, to speak the truth, found myself not a little puzzled at what my friend had depicted.

'Well!' I said, after contemplating it for some minutes, 'this *is* a strange *scarabæus*, I must confess: new to me: never saw anything like it before – unless it was a skull, or a death's-head – which it more nearly resembles than anything else that has come under *my* observation.'

'A death's-head!' echoed Legrand. 'Oh – yes – well, it has something of that appearance upon paper, no doubt. The two upper black spots look like eyes, eh? and the longer one at the bottom like a mouth – and then the shape of the whole is oval.'

'Perhaps so,' said I; 'but, Legrand, I fear you are no artist. I must wait until I see the beetle itself, if I am to form any idea of its personal appearance.'

'Well, I don't know,' said he, a little nettled, 'I draw tolerably – *should* do it at least – have had good masters, and flatter myself that I am not quite a blockhead.'

'But, my dear fellow, you are joking then,' said I, 'this is a very passable *skull* – indeed, I may say that it is a very *excellent* skull, according to the vulgar notions about such specimens of physiology – and your *scarabæus* must be the queerest *scarabæus* in the world if it resembles it. Why, we may get up a very thrilling bit of superstition upon this hint. I presume you will call the bug *scarabæus caput hominis*,[9] or something of that kind – there are many similar titles in the Natural Histories. But where are the *antennæ* you spoke of?'

'The *antennæ*!' said Legrand, who seemed to be getting unaccountably warm upon the subject; 'I am sure you must see the *antennæ*. I made them as distinct as they are in the original insect, and I presume that is sufficient.'

'Well, well,' I said, 'perhaps you have – still I don't see them;' and I handed him the paper without additional remark, not wishing to ruffle his temper; but I was much surprised at the turn affairs had taken; his ill humour puzzled me – and, as for the drawing of the beetle, there were positively *no antennæ* visible, and the whole *did* bear a very close resemblance to the ordinary cuts of a death's-head.

He received the paper very peevishly, and was about to crumple it, apparently to throw it in the fire, when a casual glance at the design seemed suddenly to rivet his attention. In an instant his face grew violently red – in another as excessively pale. For some minutes he continued to scrutinise the drawing minutely where he sat. At length he arose, took a candle from the table, and proceeded to seat himself upon a sea-chest in the farthest corner of the room. Here again he made an anxious examination of the paper, turning it in all directions. He said nothing, however, and his conduct greatly astonished me; yet I thought it prudent not to exacerbate the growing moodiness of his temper by any comment. Presently he took from his coat pocket a wallet, placed the paper carefully in it, and deposited both in a writing-desk, which he locked. He now grew more composed in his demeanour; but his original air of enthusiasm had quite disappeared. Yet he seemed not so much sulky as abstracted. As the evening wore away he became more and more absorbed in reverie, from which no sallies of mine could arouse him. It had been my intention to pass the night at the hut, as I had frequently done before, but, seeing my host in this mood, I deemed it proper to take leave. He did not press me to remain, but, as I departed, he shook my hand with even more than his usual cordiality.

It was about a month after this (and during the interval I had seen nothing of Legrand) when I received a visit, at Charleston, from his man, Jupiter. I had never seen the good old negro look so dispirited, and I feared that some serious disaster had befallen my friend.

'Well, Jup,' said I, 'what is the matter now? – how is your master?'

'Why, to speak de troof, massa, him not so berry well as mought be.'

'Not well! I am truly sorry to hear it. What does he complain of ?'

'Dar! dat's it! – him neber plain of notin – but him bery sick for all dat.'

'*Very* sick, Jupiter! – why didn't you say so at once! Is he confined to bed?'

'No, dat he aint! – he aint find nowhar – dat's just whar de shoe pinch. My mind is got to be berry hebby bout poor Massa Will.'

'Jupiter, I should like to understand what it is you are talking about. You say your master is sick. Hasn't he told you what ails him?'

'Why, massa, taint worf while for to git mad about de matter – Massa Will say noffin at all aint de matter wid him – but den what make him go about looking dis here way, wid he head down and he soldiers up, and as white as a gose? And den he keep a syphon[10] all de time –'

'Keeps a what, Jupiter?'

'Keeps a syphon wid de figgurs on de slate – de queerest figgurs I ebber did see. Ise gittin to be skeered, I tell you. Hab for to keep mighty tight eye pon him noovers. Todder day he gib me slip fore de sun up and was gone de whole ob de blessed day. I had a big stick ready cut for to gib him deuced good beating when he did come – but Ise sich a fool dat I hadn't de heart arter all – he look so berry poorly.'

'Eh? – what? – ah yes! – upon the whole I think you had better not be too severe with the poor fellow – don't flog him, Jupiter – he can't very well stand it – but can you form no idea of what has occasioned this illness, or rather this change of conduct? Has anything unpleasant happened since I saw you?'

'No, massa, dey aint bin noffin onpleasant *since* den – 'twas *fore* den I'm feared – 'twas de berry day you was dare.'

'How? what do you mean?'

'Why, massa, I mean de bug – dare now.'

'The what?'

'De bug – I'm berry sartain dat Massa Will bin bit somewhere bout de head by dat goole-bug.'

'And what cause have you, Jupiter, for such a supposition?'

'Claws enuff, massa, and mouff too. I nebber did see sich a deuced bug – he kick and he bite ebery ting what cum near him. Massa Will cotch him fuss, but had for to let him go gin mighty quick, I tell you – den was de time he must ha got de bite. I didn't like de look ob de bug mouff, myself, no how, so I wouldn't take hold ob him wid my finger, but I cotch him wid a piece ob paper dat I found. I wrap him up in de paper and stuff piece ob it in he mouff – dat was de way.'

'And you think, then, that your master was really bitten by the beetle, and that the bite made him sick?'

'I don't tink noffin about it – I nose it. What make him dream bout de goole so much, if taint cause he bit by de goole-bug? Ise heerd bout dem goole-bugs fore dis.'

'But how do you know he dreams about gold?'

'How I know? why, cause he talk about it in he sleep – dat's how I nose.'

'Well, Jup, perhaps you are right; but to what fortunate circumstance am I to attribute the honour of a visit from you today?'

'What de matter, massa?'

'Did you bring any message from Mr Legrand?'

'No, massa, I bring dis here pissel;' and here Jupiter handed me a note which ran thus:

MY DEAR — ,   Why have I not seen you for so long a time? I hope you have not been so foolish as to take offence at any little *brusquerie* of mine; but no, that is improbable.

'Since I saw you I have had great cause for anxiety. I have something to tell you, yet scarcely know how to tell it, or whether I should tell it at all.

'I have not been quite well for some days past, and poor old Jup annoys me, almost beyond endurance, by his well-meant attentions. Would you believe it? – he had prepared a huge stick, the other day, with which to chastise me for giving him the slip, and spending the day, *solus*, among the hills on the mainland. I verily believe that my ill looks alone saved me a flogging.

'I have made no addition to my cabinet since we met.

'If you can, in any way, make it convenient, come over with Jupiter. *Do* come. I wish to see you *tonight*, upon business of importance. I assure you that it is of the *highest* importance.

– Ever yours,

WILLIAM LEGRAND.

There was something in the tone of this note which gave me great uneasiness. Its whole style differed materially from that of Legrand. What could he be dreaming of? What new crotchet[11] possessed his excitable brain? What 'business of the highest importance' could *he* possibly have to transact? Jupiter's account of him boded no good. I dreaded lest the continued pressure of misfortune had, at length, fairly unsettled the reason of my friend. Without a moment's hesitation, therefore, I prepared to accompany the negro.

Upon reaching the wharf, I noticed a scythe and three spades, all apparently new, lying in the bottom of the boat in which we were to embark.

'What is the meaning of all this, Jup?' I inquired.

'Him syfe, massa, and spade.'

'Very true; but what are they doing here?'

'Him de syfe and de spade what Massa Will sis pon my buying for him in de town, and de debbil's own lot of money I had to gib for em.'

'But what, in the name of all that is mysterious, is your "Massa Will" going to do with scythes and spades?'

'Dat's more dan *I* know, and debbil take me if I don't believe 'tis more dan he know, too. But it's all cum ob de bug.'

Finding that no satisfaction was to be obtained of Jupiter, whose whole intellect seemed to be absorbed by 'de bug,' I now stepped into the boat and made sail. With a fair and strong breeze we soon ran into the little cove to the northward of Fort Moultrie, and a walk of some two miles brought us to the hut. It was about three in the afternoon when we arrived. Legrand had been awaiting us in eager expectation. He grasped my hand with a nervous *empressement* which alarmed me and strengthened the suspicions already entertained. His countenance was pale even to ghastliness, and his deep-set eyes glared with unnatural lustre. After some inquiries respecting his health, I asked him, not knowing what better to say, if he had yet obtained the *scarabæus* from Lieutenant G—.

'Oh yes,' he replied, colouring violently, 'I got it from him the next morning. Nothing should tempt me to part with that *scarabæus*. Do you know that Jupiter is quite right about it?'

'In what way?' I asked, with a sad foreboding at heart.

'In supposing it to be a bug of *real gold*!' He said this with an air of profound seriousness, and I felt inexpressibly shocked.

'This bug is to make my fortune,' he continued, with a triumphant smile, 'to reinstate me in my family possessions. Is it any wonder, then, that I prize it? Since Fortune has thought fit to bestow it upon me, I have only to use it properly and I shall arrive at the gold of which it is the index. Jupiter, bring me that *scarabæus*!'

'What! de bug, massa? I'd rudder not go fer trubble dat bug – you mus git him for your own self.' Hereupon Legrand arose, with a grave and stately air, and brought me the beetle from a glass case in which it was enclosed. It was a beautiful *scarabæus*, and, at that time, unknown to naturalists – of course a great prize in a scientific point of view. There were two round black spots near one extremity of the back, and a long one near the other. The scales were exceedingly hard and glossy, with all the appearance of burnished gold. The weight of the insect was very remarkable, and, taking all things into consideration, I could hardly blame Jupiter for his opinion respecting it; but what to make of Legrand's concordance with that opinion, I could not, for the life of me, tell.

'I sent for you,' said he, in a grandiloquent tone, when I had completed my examination of the beetle, 'I sent for you, that I might have your counsel and assistance in furthering the views of Fate and of the bug – '

'My dear Legrand,' I cried, interrupting him, 'you are certainly unwell, and had better use some little precautions. You shall go to bed, and I will remain with you a few days, until you get over this. You are feverish and – '

'Feel my pulse,' said he.

I felt it, and, to say the truth, found not the slightest indication of fever.

'But you may be ill and yet have no fever. Allow me this once to prescribe for you. In the first place, go to bed. In the next – '

'You are mistaken,' he interposed, 'I am as well as I can expect to be under the excitement which I suffer. If you really wish me well, you will relieve this excitement.'

'And how is this to be done?'

'Very easily. Jupiter and myself are going upon an expedition into the hills, upon the mainland, and, in this expedition, we shall need the aid of some person in whom we can confide. You are the only one we can trust. Whether we succeed or fail, the excitement which you now perceive in me will be equally allayed.'

'I am anxious to oblige you in any way,' I replied; 'but do you mean to say that this infernal beetle has any connection with your expedition into the hills?'

'It has.'

'Then, Legrand, I can become a party to no such absurd proceeding.'

'I am sorry – very sorry – for we shall have to try it by ourselves.'

'Try it by yourselves! The man is surely mad! – but stay! – how long do you propose to be absent?'

'Probably all night. We shall start immediately, and be back, at all events, by sunrise.'

'And will you promise me, upon your honour, that when this freak of yours is over, and the bug business (good God!) settled to your satisfaction, you will then return home and follow my advice implicitly, as that of your physician?'

'Yes; I promise; and now let us be off, for we have no time to lose.'

With a heavy heart I accompanied my friend. We started about four o'clock – Legrand, Jupiter, the dog, and myself. Jupiter had with him the scythe and spades – the whole of which he insisted upon carrying – more through fear, it seemed to me, of trusting either of the implements within reach of his master, than from any excess of industry or complaisance. His demeanour was dogged in the extreme, and 'dat deuced bug' were the sole words which escaped his lips during the journey. For my own part, I had charge of a couple of dark lanterns, while Legrand contented himself with the *scarabæus*, which he carried attached to the end of a bit of whip-cord; twirling it to and fro, with the air of a conjuror, as he went. When I observed this last, plain evidence of my friend's aberration of mind, I could scarcely refrain from tears. I thought it best, however, to humour his fancy, at least for the present, or until I could adopt some more energetic measures with a chance of success. In the meantime I endeavoured, but all in vain, to sound him in regard to the object of the expedition. Having succeeded in inducing me to accompany him, he seemed unwilling to hold conversation upon any topic of minor importance, and to all my questions vouchsafed no other reply than 'we shall see!'

We crossed the creek at the head of the island by means of a skiff, and, ascending the high grounds on the shore of the mainland, proceeded in a northwesterly direction, through a tract of country excessively wild and desolate, where no trace of a human footstep was to be seen. Legrand led the way with decision; pausing only for an instant, here and there, to consult what appeared to be certain landmarks of his own contrivance upon a former occasion.

In this manner we journeyed for about two hours, and the sun was just setting when we entered a region infinitely more dreary than any yet seen. It was a species of tableland, near the summit of an almost inaccessible hill, densely wooded from base to pinnacle, and interspersed with huge crags that appeared to lie loosely upon the soil, and in many cases were prevented from precipitating themselves into the valleys below, merely by the support of the trees against which they reclined. Deep ravines, in various directions, gave an air of still sterner solemnity to the scene.

The natural platform to which we had clambered was thickly overgrown with brambles, through which we soon discovered that it would have been impossible to force our way but for the scythe; and Jupiter, by direction of his master, proceeded to clear for us a path to the foot of an enormously tall tulip-tree, which stood, with some eight or ten oaks, upon the level, and far surpassed them all, and all other trees which I had then ever seen, in the beauty of its foliage and form, in the wide spread of its branches, and in the general majesty of its appearance. When we reached this tree, Legrand turned to Jupiter, and asked him if he thought he could climb it. The old man seemed a little staggered by the question, and for some moments made no reply. At length he approached the huge trunk, walked slowly around it, and examined it with minute attention. When he had completed his scrutiny, he merely said –

'Yes, massa, Jup climb any tree he ebber see in he life.'

'Then up with you as soon as possible, for it will soon be too dark to see what we are about.'

'How far mus go up, massa?' inquired Jupiter.

'Get up the main trunk first, and then I will tell you which way to go – and here – stop! take this beetle with you.'

'De bug, Massa Will! – de goole bug!' cried the negro, drawing back in dismay – 'what for mus tote de bug way up de tree? – d—n if I do!'

'If you are afraid, Jup, a great big negro like you, to take hold of a harmless little dead beetle, why you can carry it up by this string – but, if you do not take it up with you in some way, I shall be under the necessity of breaking your head with this shovel.'

'What de matter now, massa?' said Jup, evidently shamed into compliance; 'always want for to raise fuss wid old nigger. Was only funnin any how. *Me* feered de bug! what I keer for de bug?' Here he took cautiously hold of the extreme end of the string, and, maintaining the insect as far from his person as circumstances would permit, prepared to ascend the tree.

In youth, the tulip-tree, or *Liriodendron Tulipiferum*, the most magnificent of American foresters, has a trunk peculiarly smooth, and often rises to a great height without lateral branches; but, in its riper age, the bark becomes gnarled and uneven, while many short limbs make their appearance on the stem. Thus the difficulty of ascension, in the present case, lay more in semblance than in reality. Embracing the huge cylinder, as closely as possible, with his arms and knees, seizing with his hands some projections, and resting his naked toes upon others, Jupiter, after one or two narrow escapes from falling, at length wriggled himself into the first great fork, and seemed to consider the whole business as virtually accomplished. The *risk* of the achievement was, in fact, now over, although the climber was some sixty or seventy feet from the ground.

'Which way mus go now, Massa Will?' he asked.

'Keep up the largest branch – the one on this side,' said Legrand. The negro obeyed him promptly, and apparently with but little trouble; ascending higher and higher, until no glimpse of his squat figure could be obtained through the dense foliage which enveloped it. Presently his voice was heard in a sort of halloo:

'How much fudder is got for go?'

'How high up are you?' asked Legrand.

'Ebber so fur,' replied the negro; 'can see de sky fru de top ob de tree.'

'Never mind the sky, but attend to what I say. Look down the trunk and count the limbs below you on this side. How many limbs have you passed?'

'One, two, tree, four, fibe – I done pass fibe big limb, massa, pon dis side.'

'Then go one limb higher.'

In a few minutes the voice was heard again, announcing that the seventh limb was attained.

'Now, Jup,' cried Legrand, evidently much excited, 'I want you to work your way out upon that limb as far as you can. If you see anything strange, let me know.'

By this time what little doubt I might have entertained of my poor friend's insanity was put finally at rest. I had no alternative but to conclude him stricken with lunacy, and I became seriously anxious about getting him home. While I was pondering upon what was best to be done, Jupiter's voice was again heard.

'Mos feerd for to ventur pon dis limb berry far – tis dead limb putty much all de way.'

'Did you say it was a *dead* limb, Jupiter?' cried Legrand in a quavering voice.

'Yes, massa, him dead as de door-nail – done up for sartain – done departed dis here life.'

'What in the name of heaven shall I do?' asked Legrand, seemingly in the greatest distress.

'Do!' said I, glad of an opportunity to interpose a word, 'why, come home and go to bed. Come now! that's a fine fellow. It's getting late, and besides, you remember your promise.'

'Jupiter,' cried he, without heeding me in the least, 'do you hear me?'

'Yes, Massa Will, hear you ebber so plain.'

'Try the wood well, then, with your knife, and see if you think it *very* rotten.'

'Him rotten, massa, sure nuff,' replied the negro in a few moments, 'but not so berry rotten as mought be. Mought ventur out leetle way pon de limb by myself, dat's true.'

'By yourself! – what do you mean?'

'Why, I mean de bug. 'Tis *berry* hebby bug. Spose I drop him down fuss, and den de limb won't break wid just de weight ob one nigger.'

'You infernal scoundrel!' cried Legrand, apparently much relieved, 'what do you mean by telling me such nonsense as that? As sure as you drop that beetle I'll break your neck. Look here, Jupiter, do you hear me?'

'Yes, massa, needn't hollo at poor nigger dat style.'

'Well! now listen! – if you will venture out on the limb as far as you think safe, and not let go the beetle, I'll make you a present of a silver dollar as soon as you get down.'

'I'm gwine, Massa Will – deed I is,' replied the negro very promptly – 'mos out to the eend now.'

'*Out to the end*!' here fairly screamed Legrand, 'do you say you are out to the end of that limb?'

'Soon be to de eend, massa – o-o-o-o-oh! Lor-gol-a-marcy! what *is* dis here pon de tree?'

'Well!' cried Legrand, highly delighted, 'what is it?'

'Why, taint nuffin but a skull – somebody bin lef him head up de tree, and de crows done gobble ebery bit ob de meat off.'

'A skull, you say! – very well! – how is it fastened to the limb? – what holds it on?'

'Sure nuff, massa; mus look. Why, dis berry curous sarcumstance, pon my word – dare's a great big nail in de skull, what fastens ob it on to de tree.'

'Well now, Jupiter, do exactly as I tell you – do you hear?'

'Yes, massa.'

'Pay attention, then! – find the left eye of the skull.'

'Hum! hoo! dat's good! why, dare aint no eye lef at all.'

'Curse your stupidity! do you know your right hand from your left?'

'Yes, I nose dat – nose all bout dat – tis my lef hand what I chops de wood wid.'

'To be sure! you are left-handed; and your left eye is on the same side as your left hand. Now, I suppose, you can find the left eye of the skull, or the place where the left eye has been. Have you found it?'

Here was a long pause. At length the negro asked –

'Is de lef eye of de skull pon de same side as de lef hand of de skull, too? – cause de skull aint got not a bit ob a hand at all – nebber mind! I got de lef eye now – here de lef eye! what mus do wid it?'

'Let the beetle drop through it, as far as the string will reach – but be careful and not let go your hold of the string.'

'All dat done, Massa Will; mighty easy ting for to put de bug fru de hole – look out for him dare below!'

During this colloquy no portion of Jupiter's person could be seen; but the beetle, which he had suffered to descend, was now visible at the end of the string, and glistened like a globe of burnished gold, in the last rays of the setting sun, some of which still faintly illumined the eminence upon which we stood. The *scarabæus* hung quite clear of any branches, and, if allowed to fall, would have fallen at our feet. Legrand immediately took the scythe, and cleared with it a circular space, three or four yards in diameter, just beneath the insect, and, having accomplished this, ordered Jupiter to let go the string and come down from the tree.

Driving a peg, with great nicety, into the ground, at the precise spot where the beetle fell, my friend now produced from his pocket a tape-measure. Fastening one end of this at that point of the trunk of the tree which was nearest the peg, he unrolled it till it reached the peg, and thence farther unrolled it, in the direction already established by the two points of the tree and the peg, for the distance of fifty feet – Jupiter clearing away the brambles with the scythe. At the spot thus attained a second peg was driven, and about this, as a centre, a rude circle, about four feet in diameter, described. Taking now a spade himself, and giving one to Jupiter and one to me, Legrand begged us to set about digging as quickly as possible.

To speak the truth, I had no especial relish for such amusement at any time, and, at that particular moment, would most willingly have declined it; for the night was coming on, and I felt much fatigued with the exercise already taken; but I saw no mode of escape, and was fearful of disturbing my poor friend's equanimity by a refusal. Could I have depended, indeed, upon Jupiter's aid, I would have had no hesitation in attempting to get the lunatic home by force; but I was too well assured of the old negro's disposition, to hope that he would assist me, under any circumstances, in a personal contest with his master. I made no doubt that the latter had been infected with some of the innumerable Southern superstitions about money buried, and that his fantasy had received confirmation by the finding of the *scarabæus*, or, perhaps, by Jupiter's obstinacy in maintaining it to be 'a bug of real gold.' A mind disposed to lunacy would readily be led away by such suggestions – especially if chiming in with favourite preconceived ideas – and then I called to mind the poor fellow's speech about the beetle's being 'the index of his fortune.' Upon the whole, I was sadly vexed and puzzled, but, at length, I concluded to make a virtue of necessity – to dig with a good will, and thus the sooner to convince the visionary, by ocular demonstration, of the fallacy of the opinions he entertained.

The lanterns having been lit, we all fell to work with a zeal worthy a more rational cause; and, as the glare fell upon our persons and implements, I could not help thinking how picturesque a group we composed, and how strange and suspicious our labours must have appeared to any interloper who, by chance, might have stumbled upon our whereabouts.

We dug very steadily for two hours. Little was said; and our chief embarrassment lay in the yelpings of the dog, who took exceeding interest in our proceedings. He at length became so obstreperous that we grew fearful of his giving the alarm to some stragglers in the vicinity – or, rather, this was the apprehension of Legrand – for myself, I should have rejoiced at any interruption which might have enabled me to get the wanderer home. The noise was, at length, very effectually silenced by Jupiter, who, getting out of the hole with a dogged air of deliberation, tied the brute's mouth up with one of his suspenders, and then returned, with a grave chuckle, to his task.

When the time mentioned had expired, we had reached a depth of five feet, and yet no signs of any treasure became manifest. A general pause ensued, and I began to hope that the farce was at an end. Legrand, however, although evidently much disconcerted, wiped his brow thoughtfully and recommenced. We had excavated the entire circle of four feet diameter, and now we slightly enlarged the limit, and went to the farther depth of two feet. Still nothing appeared. The gold-seeker, whom I sincerely pitied, at length clambered from the pit, with the bitterest disappointment imprinted upon every feature, and proceeded, slowly and reluctantly, to put on his coat, which he had thrown off at the beginning of his labour. In the meantime I made no remark. Jupiter, at a signal from his master, began to gather up his tools. This done, and the dog having been unmuzzled, we turned in profound silence towards home.

We had taken, perhaps, a dozen steps in this direction, when, with a loud oath, Legrand strode up to Jupiter, and seized him by the collar. The astonished negro opened his eyes and mouth to the fullest extent, let fall the spades, and fell upon his knees.

'You scoundrel!' said Legrand, hissing out the syllables from between his clenched teeth – 'you infernal black villain! – speak, I tell you! – answer me this instant, without prevarication! – which – which is your left eye?'

'Oh, my golly, Massa Will! aint dis here my lef eye for sartain?' roared the terrified Jupiter, placing his hand upon his *right* organ of vision, and holding it there with a desperate pertinacity, as if in immediate dread of his master's attempt at a gouge.

'I thought so! – I knew it! hurrah!' vociferated Legrand, letting the negro go, and executing a series of curvets and caracoles,[12] much to the astonishment of his valet, who, arising from his knees, looked mutely from his master to myself, and them from myself to his master.

'Come! we must go back,' said the latter; 'the game's not up yet;' and he again led the way to the tulip-tree.

'Jupiter,' said he, when we reached its foot, 'come here! Was the skull nailed to the limb with the face outwards, or with the face to the limb?'

'De face was out, massa, so dat de crows could get at de eyes good, widout any trouble.'

'Well, then, was it this eye or that through which you dropped the beetle?' – here Legrand touched each of Jupiter's eyes.

' 'Twas dis eye, massa – de lef eye – jis as you tell me,' and here it was his right eye that the negro indicated.

'That will do – we must try it again.'

Here my friend, about whose madness I now saw, or fancied that I saw, certain indications of method, removed the peg which marked the spot where the beetle fell, to a spot about three inches to the westward of its former position. Taking, now, the tape-measure from the nearest point of the trunk to the peg, as before, and continuing the extension in a straight line to the distance of fifty feet, a spot was indicated, removed, by several yards, from the point at which we had been digging.

Around the new position a circle, somewhat larger than in the former instance, was now described, and we again set to work with the spades. I was dreadfully weary, but, scarcely understanding what had occasioned the change in my thoughts, I felt no longer any great aversion from the labour imposed. I had become most unaccountably interested – nay, even excited. Perhaps there was something, amid all the extravagant demeanour of Legrand – some air of forethought, or of deliberation, which impressed me. I dug eagerly, and now and then caught myself actually looking, with something that very much resembled expectation, for the fancied treasure, the vision of which had demented my unfortunate companion. At a period when such vagaries of thought most fully possessed me, and when we had been at work perhaps an hour and a half, we were again interrupted by the violent howlings of the dog. His uneasiness in the first instance, had been, evidently, but the result of playfulness or caprice, but he now assumed a bitter and serious tone. Upon Jupiter's again attempting to muzzle him, he made furious resistance, and, leaping into the hole, tore up the mould frantically with his claws. In a few seconds he had uncovered a mass of human bones, forming two complete skeletons, intermingled with several buttons of metal, and what appeared to be the dust of decayed woollen. One or two strokes of a spade upturned the blade of a large Spanish knife, and, as we dug farther, three or four loose pieces of gold and silver coin came to light.

At sight of these the joy of Jupiter could scarcely be restrained, but the countenance of his master wore an air of extreme disappointment. He urged us, however, to continue our exertions, and the words were hardly uttered when I stumbled and fell forward, having caught the toe of my boot in a large ring of iron that lay half buried in the loose earth.

We now worked in earnest, and never did I pass ten minutes of more intense excitement. During this interval we had fairly unearthed an oblong chest of wood, which, from its perfect preservation and wonderful hardness, had plainly been subjected to some mineralising process – perhaps that of the bichloride of mercury. This box was three feet and a half long, three feet broad, and two and a half feet deep. It was firmly secured by bands of wrought iron, riveted, and forming a kind of open trellis-work over the whole. On each side of the chest, near the top, were three rings of iron – six in all – by means of which a firm hold could be obtained by six persons. Our utmost united endeavours served only to disturb the coffer very slightly in its bed. We at once saw the impossibility of removing so great a weight. Luckily, the sole fastenings of the lid consisted of two sliding bolts. These we drew back – trembling and panting with anxiety. In an instant, a treasure of incalculable value lay gleaming before us. As the rays of the lanterns fell within the pit, there flashed upwards a glow and a glare, from a confused heap of gold and of jewels, that absolutely dazzled our eyes.

I shall not pretend to describe the feelings with which I gazed. Amazement was, of course, predominant. Legrand appeared exhausted with excitement, and spoke very few words. Jupiter's countenance wore, for some minutes, as deadly a pallor as it is possible, in the nature of things, for any negro's visage to assume. He seemed stupefied – thunderstricken. Presently he fell upon his knees in the pit, and, burying his naked arms up to the elbows in gold, let them there remain, as if enjoying the luxury of a bath. At length, with a deep sigh, he exclaimed, as if in a soliloquy –

'And dis all come ob de goole-bug! de putty goole-bug! de poor little goole-bug, what I boosed in dat sabage kind ob style! Aint you shamed ob yourself, nigger? – answer me dat!'

It became necessary, at last, that I should arouse both master and valet to the expediency of removing the treasure. It was growing late, and it behoved us to make exertion, that we might get everything housed before daylight. It was difficult to say what should be done, and much time was spent in deliberation – so confused were the ideas of all. We, finally, lightened the box by removing two-thirds of its contents, when we were enabled, with some trouble, to raise it from the hole. The articles taken out were deposited among the brambles, and the dog left to guard them, with strict orders from Jupiter, neither, upon any pretence, to stir from the spot, nor to open his mouth until our return. We then hurriedly made for home with the chest; reaching the hut in safety, but after excessive toil, at one o'clock in the morning.

Worn out as we were, it was not in human nature to do more immediately. We rested until two, and had supper; starting for the hills immediately afterwards, armed with three stout sacks, which, by good luck, were upon the premises. A little before four we arrived at the pit, divided the remainder of the booty, as equally as might be, among us, and, leaving the holes unfilled, again set out for the hut, at which, for the second time, we deposited our golden burdens, just as the first faint streaks of the dawn gleamed from over the tree-tops in the east.

We were now thoroughly broken down; but the intense excitement of the time denied us repose. After an unquiet slumber of some three or four hours' duration, we arose, as if by preconcert, to make examination of our treasure.

The chest had been full to the brim, and we spent the whole day, and the greater part of the next night, in a scrutiny of its contents. There had been nothing like order or arrangement. Everything had been heaped in promiscuously. Having assorted all with care, we found ourselves possessed of even vaster wealth than we had at first supposed. In coin there was rather more than four hundred and fifty thousand dollars – estimating the value of the pieces, as accurately as we could, by the tables of the period. There was not a particle of silver. All was gold of antique date and of great variety – French, Spanish, and German money, with a few English guineas, and some counters, of which we had never seen specimens before. There were several very large and heavy coins, so worn that we could make nothing of their inscriptions. There was no American money. The value of the jewels we found more difficulty in estimating. There were diamonds – some of them exceedingly large and fine – a hundred and ten in all, and not one of them small; eighteen rubies of remarkable brilliancy; three hundred and ten emeralds, all very beautiful; and twenty-one sapphires, with an opal. These stones had all been broken from their settings and thrown loose in the chest. The settings themselves, which we picked out from among the other gold, appeared to have been beaten up with hammers, as if to prevent identification. Besides all this, there was a vast quantity of solid gold ornaments – nearly two hundred massive finger- and ear-rings; rich chains – thirty of these, if I remember; eighty-three very large and heavy crucifixes; five gold censers of great value; a prodigious golden punch-bowl, ornamented with richly-chased vine-leaves and Bacchanalian figures;[13] with two sword handles exquisitely embossed, and many other smaller articles which I cannot recollect. The weight of these valuables exceeded three hundred and fifty pounds avoirdupois;[14] and in this estimate I have not included one hundred and ninety-seven superb gold watches; three of the number being worth each five hundred dollars, if one. Many of them were very old, and as time-keepers valueless; the works having suffered, more or less, from corrosion – but all were richly jewelled and in cases of great worth. We estimated the entire contents of the chest, that night, at a million and a half of dollars; and upon the subsequent disposal of the trinkets and jewels (a few being retained for our own use), it was found that we had greatly undervalued the treasure.

When, at length, we had concluded our examination, and the intense excitement of the time had, in some measure, subsided, Legrand, who saw that I was dying with impatience for a solution of this most extraordinary riddle, entered into a full detail of all the circumstances connected with it.

'You remember,' said he, 'the night when I handed you the rough sketch I had made of the *scarabæus*. You recollect also, that I became quite vexed at you for insisting that my drawing resembled a death's-head. When you first made this assertion I thought you were jesting; but afterwards I called to mind the peculiar spots on the back of the insect, and admitted to myself that your remark had some little foundation in fact. Still, the sneer at my graphic powers irritated me – for I am considered a good artist – and, therefore, when you handed me the scrap of parchment, I was about to crumple it up and throw it angrily into the fire.'

'The scrap of paper, you mean,' said I.

'No; it had much of the appearance of paper, and at first I supposed it to be such, but when I came to draw upon it, I discovered it, at once, to be a piece of very thin parchment. It was quite dirty, you remember. Well, as I was in the very act of crumpling it up, my glance fell upon the sketch at which you had been looking, and you may imagine my astonishment when I perceived in fact, the figure of a death's-head just where, it seemed to me, I had made the drawing of the beetle. For a moment I was too much amazed to think with accuracy. I knew that my design was very different in detail from this – although there was a certain similarity in general outline. Presently I took a candle, and seating myself at the other end of the room, proceeded to scrutinise the parchment more closely. Upon turning it over, I saw my own sketch upon the reverse, just as I had made it. My first idea, now, was mere surprise at the really remarkable similarity of outline – at the singular coincidence involved in the fact, that unknown to me, there should have been a skull upon the other side of the parchment, immediately beneath my figure of the *scarabæus*, and that this skull, not only in outline, but in size, should so closely resemble my drawing. I say the singularity of this coincidence absolutely stupefied me for a time. This is the usual effect of such coincidences. The mind struggles to establish a connection – a sequence of cause and effect – and, being unable to do so, suffers a species of temporary paralysis. But, when I recovered from this stupor, there dawned upon me gradually a conviction which startled me even far more than the coincidence. I began distinctly, positively, to remember that there had been *no* drawing upon the parchment when I made my sketch of the *scarabæus*. I became perfectly certain of this; for I recollected turning up first one side and then the other, in search of the cleanest spot. Had the skull been then there, of course I could not have failed to notice it. Here was indeed a mystery which I felt it impossible to explain; but even at that early moment, there seemed to glimmer, faintly, within the most remote and secret chambers of my intellect, a glow-worm-like conception of that truth which last night's adventure brought to so magnificent a demonstration. I arose at once, and putting the parchment securely away, dismissed all further reflection until I should be alone.

'When you had gone, and when Jupiter was fast asleep, I betook myself to a more methodical investigation of the affair. In the first place I considered the manner in which the parchment had come into my possession. The spot where we discovered the *scarabæus* was on the coast of the mainland, about a mile eastward of the island, and but a short distance above high-water mark. Upon my taking hold of it, it gave me a sharp bite, which caused me to let it drop. Jupiter, with his accustomed caution, before seizing the insect, which had flown towards him, looked about him for a leaf, or something of that nature, by which to take hold of it. It was at this moment that his eyes, and mine also, fell upon the scrap of parchment, which I then supposed to be paper. It was lying half buried in the sand, a corner sticking up. Near the spot where we found it, I observed the remnants of the hull of what appeared to have been a ship's long-boat. The wreck seemed to have been there for a very great while; for the resemblance to boat timbers could scarcely be traced.

'Well, Jupiter picked up the parchment, wrapped the beetle in it, and gave it to me. Soon afterwards we turned to go home, and on the way met Lieutenant G—. I showed him the insect, and he begged me to let him take it to the fort. Upon my consenting, he thrust it forthwith into his waistcoat pocket, without the parchment in which it had been wrapped, and which I had continued to hold in my hand during his inspection. Perhaps he dreaded my changing my mind, and thought it best to make sure of the prize at once – you know how enthusiastic he is on all subjects connected with Natural History. At the same time, without being conscious of it, I must have deposited the parchment in my own pocket.

'You remember that when I went to the table, for the purpose of making a sketch of the beetle, I found no paper where it was usually kept. I looked in the drawer, and found none there. I searched my pockets, hoping to find an old letter, when my hand fell upon the parchment. I thus detail the precise mode in which it came into my possession; for the circumstances impressed me with peculiar force.

'No doubt you will think me fanciful – but I had already established a kind of *connection*. I had put together two links of a great chain. There was a boat lying upon a sea-coast, and not far from the boat was a parchment – *not a paper* – with a skull depicted upon it. You will, of course, ask "where is the connection?" I reply, that the skull, or death's-head, is the well-known emblem of the pirate. The flag of the death's-head is hoisted in all engagements.

'I have said that the scrap was parchment, and not paper. Parchment is durable – almost imperishable. Matters of little moment are rarely consigned to parchment; since, for the mere ordinary purposes of drawing or writing, it is not nearly so well adapted as paper. This reflection suggested some meaning – some relevancy – in the death's-head. I did not fail to observe, also, the *form* of the parchment. Although one of its corners had been, by some accident, destroyed, it could be seen that the original form was oblong. It was just such a slip, indeed, as might have been chosen for a memorandum – for a record of something to be long remembered and carefully preserved.'

'But,' I interposed, 'you say that the skull was *not* upon the parchment when you made the drawing of the beetle. How then do you trace any connection between the boat and the skull – since this latter, according to your own admission, must have been designed (God only knows how or by whom) at some period subsequent to your sketching the *scarabæus*?'

'Ah, hereupon turns the whole mystery; although the secret, at this point, I had comparatively little difficulty in solving. My steps were sure, and could afford but a single result. I reasoned, for example, thus: When I drew the *scarabæus*, there was no skull apparent upon the parchment. When I had completed the drawing I gave it to you, and observed you narrowly until you returned it. *You*, therefore, did not design the skull, and no one else was present to do it. Then it was not done by human agency. And nevertheless it was done.

'At this stage of my reflections I endeavoured to remember, and *did* remember, with entire distinctness, every incident which occurred about the period in question. The weather was chilly (oh, rare and happy accident!), and a fire was blazing upon the hearth. I was heated with exercise and sat near the table. You, however, had drawn a chair close to the chimney. Just as I placed the parchment in your hand, and as you were in the act of inspecting it, Wolf, the Newfoundland, entered, and leaped upon your shoulders. With your left hand you caressed him and kept him off, while your right, holding the parchment, was permitted to fall listlessly between your knees, and in close proximity to the fire. At one moment I thought the blaze had caught it, and was about to caution you, but before I could speak you had withdrawn it, and were engaged in its examination. When I considered all these particulars, I doubted not for a moment that *heat* had been the agent in bringing to light, upon the parchment, the skull which I saw designed upon it. You are well aware that chemical preparations exist, and have existed time out of mind, by means of which it is possible to write upon either paper or vellum, so that the characters shall become visible only when subjected to the action of fire. Zaffre,[15] digested in *aqua regia*,[16] and diluted with four times its weight of water, is sometimes employed; a green tint results. The regulus[17] of cobalt, dissolved in spirit of nitre,[18] gives a red. These colours disappear at longer or shorter intervals after the material written upon cools, but again become apparent upon the reapplication of heat.

'I now scrutinised the death's-head with care. Its outer edges – the edges of the drawing nearest the edge of the vellum – were far more *distinct* than the others. It was clear that the action of the caloric had been imperfect or unequal. I immediately kindled a fire, and subjected every portion of the parchment to a glowing heat. At first, the only effect was the strengthening of the faint lines in the skull; but, upon persevering in the experiment, there became visible, at the corner of the slip, diagonally opposite to the spot in which the death's-head was delineated, the figure of what I at first supposed to be a goat. A closer scrutiny, however, satisfied me that it was intended for a kid.'

'Ha! ha!' said I, 'to be sure I have no right to laugh at you – a million and a half of money is too serious a matter for mirth – but you are not about to establish a third link in your chain – you will not find any special connection between your pirates and a goat – pirates, you know, have nothing to do with goats; they appertain to the farming interest.'

'But I have just said that the figure was *not* that of a goat.'

'Well, a kid, then – pretty much the same thing.'

'Pretty much, but not altogether,' said Legrand. 'You may have heard of one *Captain* Kidd. I at once looked upon the figure of the animal as a kind of punning or hieroglyphical signature. I say signature; because its position upon the vellum suggested this idea. The death's-head at the corner diagonally opposite, had, in the same manner, the air of a stamp, or seal. But I was sorely put out by the absence of all else – of the body to my imagined instrument – of the text for my context.'

'I presume you expected to find a letter between the stamp and the signature.'

'Something of that kind. The fact is, I felt irresistibly impressed with a presentiment of some vast good fortune impending. I can scarcely say why. Perhaps, after all, it was rather a desire than an actual belief; but do you know that Jupiter's silly words, about the bug being of solid gold, had a remarkable effect upon my fancy? And then the series of accidents and coincidences – these were so *very* extraordinary. Do you observe how mere an accident it was that these events should have occurred upon the *sole* day of all the year in which it has been, or may be, sufficiently cool for fire, and that without the fire, or without the intervention of the dog at the precise moment in which he appeared, I should never have become aware of the death's-head, and so never the possessor of the treasure?'

'But proceed – I am all impatience.'

'Well; you have heard, of course, the many stories current – the thousand vague rumours afloat, about money buried, somewhere upon the Atlantic coast, by Kidd and his associates. These rumours must have had some foundation in fact. And that the rumours have existed so long and so continuous, could have resulted, it appeared to me, only from the circumstance of the buried treasure still *remaining* entombed. Had Kidd concealed his plunder for a time, and afterwards reclaimed it, the rumours would scarcely have reached us in their present unvarying form. You will observe that the stories told are all about money-seekers, not about money-finders. Had the pirate recovered his money, there the affair would have dropped. It seemed to me that some accident – say the loss of a memorandum indicating its locality – had deprived him of the means of recovering it, and that this accident had become known to his followers, who otherwise might never have heard that treasure had been concealed at all, and who, busying themselves in vain, because unguided attempts, to regain it, had given first birth, and then universal currency, to the reports which are now so common. Have you ever heard of any important treasure being unearthed along the coast?'

'Never.'

'But that Kidd's accumulations were immense, is well known. I took it for granted, therefore, that the earth still held them; and you will scarcely be surprised when I tell you that I felt a hope, nearly amounting to certainty, that the parchment so strangely found, involved a lost record of the place of deposit.'

'But how did you proceed?'

'I held the vellum again to the fire, after increasing the heat; but nothing appeared. I now thought it possible that the coating of dirt might have something to do with the failure; so I carefully rinsed the parchment by pouring warm water over it, and, having done this, I placed it in a tin pan, with the skull downwards, and put the pan upon a furnace of lighted charcoal. In a few minutes, the pan having become thoroughly heated, I removed the slip, and, to my inexpressible joy, found it spotted, in several places, with what appeared to be figures arranged in lines. Again I placed it in the pan, and suffered it to remain another minute. Upon taking it off, the whole was just as you see it now.'

Here Legrand, having reheated the parchment, submitted it to my inspection. The following characters were rudely traced, in a red tint, between the death's-head and the goat:

53‡‡†305))6*;4826)4‡.)4;806*;48†8¶60))85;1‡(;:
‡*8†83(88)5*†;46(;88*96*?;8)*‡(;485);5*†2:*‡(;
4956*2(5*—4)8¶8*;4069285);)6†8)4‡‡;1(‡9;480
81;8:8‡1;48†85;4)485†528806*81(‡9;48;(88;4(‡?34;48)
4‡;161;:188;‡?;

'But,' said I, returning him the slip, 'I am as much in the dark as ever. Were all the jewels of Golconda awaiting me upon my solution of this enigma, I am quite sure that I should be unable to earn them.'

'And yet,' said Legrand, 'the solution is by no means so difficult as you might be led to imagine from the first hasty inspection of the characters. These characters, as any one might readily guess, form a cipher – that is to say, they convey a meaning; but then, from what is known of Kidd, I could not suppose him capable of constructing any of the more abstruse cryptographs. I made up my mind, at once, that this was of a simple species – such, however, as would appear, to the crude intellect of the sailor, absolutely insoluble without the key.'

'And you really solved it?'

'Readily; I have solved others of an abstruseness ten thousand times greater. Circumstances, and a certain bias of mind, have led me to take interest in such riddles, and it may well be doubted whether human ingenuity can construct an enigma of the kind which human ingenuity may not, by proper application, resolve. In fact, having once established connected and legible characters, I scarcely gave a thought to the mere difficulty of developing their import.

'In the present case – indeed in all cases of secret writing – the first question regards the *language* of the cipher; for the principles of solution, so far, especially, as the more simple ciphers are concerned, depend upon, and are varied by, the genius of the particular idiom. In general there is no alternative but experiment (directed by probabilities) of every tongue known to him who attempts the solution, until the true one be attained. But, with the cipher now before us, all difficulty was removed by the signature. The pun upon the word "Kidd" is appreciable in no other language than the English. But for this consideration I should have begun my attempts with the Spanish and French, as the tongues in which a secret of this kind would most naturally have been written by a pirate of the Spanish main. As it was, I assumed the cryptograph to be English.

'You observe there are no divisions between the words. Had there been divisions, the task would have been comparatively easy. In such case I should have commenced with a collation and analysis of the shorter words, and had a word of a single letter occurred, as is most likely (*a* or *I* for example), I should have considered the solution as assured. But, there being no division, my first step was to ascertain the predominant letters, as well as the least frequent. Counting all, I constructed a table, thus:

'Of the character 8 there are 33.

;	"	26.
4	"	19.
‡)	"	16.
*	"	13.
5	"	12.
6	"	11.
†1	"	8.
0	"	6.
92	"	5.
:3	"	4.
?	"	3.
¶	"	2.
—.	"	1.

'Now, in English, the letter which most frequently occurs is *e*. Afterwards, the succession runs thus: *a o i d h n r s t u y c f g l m w b k p q x z*. *E* predominates so remarkably that an individual sentence of any length is rarely seen, in which it is not the prevailing character.

'Here, then, we have, in the very beginning, the groundwork for something more than a mere guess. The general use which may be made of the table is obvious – but in this particular cipher we shall only very partially require its aid. As our predominant character is 8, we will commence by assuming it as the *e* of the natural alphabet. To verify the supposition, let us observe if the 8 be seen often in couples – for *e* is doubled with great frequency in English – in such words, for example, as "meet", "fleet", "speed", "seen", "been", "agree", &c. In the present instance we see it doubled no less than five times, although the cryptograph is brief.

'Let us assume 8, then, as *e*. Now, of all *words* in the language "the" is the most usual; let us see, therefore, whether there are not repetitions of any three characters, in the same order of collocation, the last of them being 8. If we discover repetitions of such letters, so arranged, they will most probably represent the word "the". Upon inspection, we find no less than seven such arrangements, the characters being ;48. We may therefore assume that ; represents *t*, 4 represents h, and 8 represents *e* – the last being now well confirmed. Thus a great step has been taken.

'But, having established a single word, we are enabled to establish a vastly important point; that is to say, several commencements and terminations of other words. Let us refer, for example, to the last instance but one, in which the combination ;48 occurs – not far from the end of the cipher. We know that the ; immediately ensuing is the commencement of a word, and of the six characters succeeding this "the", we are cognisant of no less than five. Let us set these characters down, thus, by the letters we know them to represent, leaving a space for the unknown –

t eeth.

'Here we are enabled, at once, to discard the "*th*", as forming no portion of the word commencing with the first *t*; since, by experiment of the entire alphabet for a letter adapted to the vacancy, we perceive that no word can be formed of which this *th* can be a part. We are thus narrowed into

t ee,

and, going through the alphabet, if necessary, as before, we arrive at the word "tree", as the sole possible reading. We thus gain another letter, *r*, represented by (, with the words "the tree" in juxtaposition.

'Looking beyond these words, for a short distance, we again see the combination ;48, and employ it by way of *termination* to what immediately precedes. We have thus this arrangement –

the tree ;4(‡?34 the,

or, substituting the natural letters, where known, it reads thus —

the tree thr‡?3h the.

'Now if, in place of the unknown characters, we leave blank spaces, or substitute dots, we read thus —

the tree thr. . .h the,

when the word "*through*" makes itself evident at once. But this discovery gives us three new letters, *o*, *u*, and *g*, represented by ‡? and 3.

'Looking now, narrowly, through the cipher for combinations of known characters, we find, not very far from the beginning, this arrangement —

83(88, or egree,

which, plainly, is the conclusion of the word "degree", and gives us another letter, *d*, represented by †.

'Four letters beyond the word "degree", we perceive the combination

;(48;88.

'Translating the known characters, and representing the unknown by dots, as before, we read thus —

th rtee,

an arrangement immediately suggestive of the word "thirteen", and again furnishing us with two new characters, *i* and *n*, represented by 6 and *.

'Referring, now, to the beginning of the cryptograph, we find the combination

53‡‡†.

'Translating, as before, we obtain

.good,

which assures us that the first letter is *A*, and that the first two words are "A good".

'It is now time that we arrange our key, as far as discovered, in a tabular form, to avoid confusion. It will stand thus –

5	represents	a
†	"	d
8	"	e
3	"	g
4	"	h
6	"	i
*	"	n
‡	"	o
(	"	r
;	"	t

'We have, therefore, no less than ten of the most important letters represented, and it will be unnecessary to proceed with the details of the solution. I have said enough to convince you that ciphers of this nature are readily soluble, and to give you some insight into the *rationale* of their development. But be assured that the specimen before us appertains to the very simplest species of cryptograph. It now only remains to give you the full translation of the characters upon the parchment, as unriddled. Here it is:

' "*A good glass in the bishop's hostel in the devil's seat forty-one degrees and thirteen minutes north-east and by north main branch seventh limb east side shoot from the left eye of the death's-head a bee line from the tree through the shot fifty feet out.*" '

'But,' said I, 'the enigma seems still in as bad a condition as ever. How is it possible to extort a meaning from all this jargon about "devil's seats", "death's-heads", and "bishop's hotels"?'

'I confess,' replied Legrand, 'that the matter still wears a serious aspect, when regarded with a casual glance. My first endeavour was to divide the sentence into the natural division intended by the cryptographist.'

"You mean to punctuate it?'

'Something of that kind.'

'But how was it possible to effect this?'

'I reflected that it had been a *point* with the writer to run his words together without division, so as to increase the difficulty of solution. Now, a not over-acute man, in pursuing such an object, would be nearly certain to overdo the matter. When, in the course of his composition, he arrived at a break in his subject which would naturally require a pause, or a point, he would be exceedingly apt to run his characters, at this place, more than usually close together. If you will observe the MS., in the present instance, you will easily detect five such cases of unusual crowding. Acting upon this hint, I made the division thus:

' "*A good glass in the Bishop's hostel in the Devil's seat – forty-one degrees and thirteen minutes – north-east and by north – main branch seventh limb east side – shoot from the left eye of the death's-head – a bee-line from the tree through the shot fifty feet out.*" '

'Even this division,' said I, 'leaves me still in the dark.'

'It left me also in the dark,' replied Legrand, 'for a few days; during which I made diligent inquiry, in the neighbourhood of Sullivan's Island, for any building which went by the name of the "Bishop's Hotel"; for, of course, I dropped the obsolete word "hostel". Gaining no information on the subject, I was on the point of extending my sphere of search, and proceeding in a more systematic manner, when, one morning, it entered into my head, quite suddenly, that this "Bishop's Hostel" might have some reference to an old family, of the name of Bessop, which, time out of mind, had held possession of an ancient manor-house, about four miles to the northward of the island. I accordingly went over to the plantation, and re-instituted my inquiries among the older negroes of the place. At length one of the most aged of the women said that she had heard of such a place as *Bessop's Castle*, and thought that she could guide me to it, but that it was not a castle, nor a tavern, but a high rock.

'I offered to pay her well for her trouble, and after some demur, she consented to accompany me to the spot. We found it without much difficulty, when, dismissing her, I proceeded to examine the place. The "castle" consisted of an irregular assemblage of cliffs and rocks – one of the latter being quite remarkable for its height as well as for its insulated and artificial appearance. I clambered to its apex, and then felt much at a loss as to what should be next done.

'While I was busied in reflection, my eyes fell upon a narrow ledge in the eastern face of the rock, perhaps a yard below the summit upon which I stood. This ledge projected about eighteen inches, and was not more than a foot wide, while a niche in the cliff just above it, gave it a rude resemblance to one of the hollow-backed chairs used by our ancestors. I made no doubt that here was the "devil's-seat" alluded to in the MS., and now I seemed to grasp the full secret of the riddle.

'The "good glass", I knew, could have reference to nothing but a telescope; for the word "glass" is rarely employed in any other sense by seamen. Now here, I at once saw, was a telescope to be used, and a definite point of view, *admitting no variation*, from which to use it. Nor did I hesitate to believe that the phrases, "forty-one degrees and thirteen minutes," and "northeast and by north," were intended as directions for the levelling of the glass. Greatly excited by these discoveries, I hurried home, procured a telescope, and returned to the rock.

'I let myself down to the ledge, and found that it was impossible to retain a seat upon it except in one particular position. This fact confirmed my preconceived idea. I proceeded to use the glass. Of course, the "forty-one degrees and thirteen minutes" could allude to nothing but elevation above the visible horizon, since the horizontal direction was clearly indicated by the words, "north-east and by north", This latter direction I at once established by means of a pocket-compass; then, pointing the glass as nearly at an angle of forty-one degrees of elevation as I could do it by guess, I moved it cautiously up or down, until my attention was arrested by a circular rift or opening in the foliage of a large tree that overtopped its fellows in the distance. In the centre of this rift I perceived a white spot, but could not, at first, distinguish what it was. Adjusting the focus of the telescope, I again looked, and now made it out to be a human skull.

'Upon this discovery I was so sanguine as to consider the enigma solved; for the phrase "main branch, seventh limb, east side", could refer only to the position of the skull upon the tree, while "shoot from the left eye of the death's-head" admitted, also, of but one interpretation, in regard to a search for buried treasure. I perceived that the design was to drop a bullet from the left eye of the skull, and that a bee-line, or, in other words, a straight line, drawn from the nearest point of the trunk through "the shot" (or the spot where the bullet fell), and thence extended to a distance of fifty feet, would indicate a definite point – and beneath this point I thought it at least *possible* that a deposit of value lay concealed.'

'All this,' I said, 'is exceedingly clear, and, although ingenious, still simple and explicit. When you left the Bishop's Hotel, what then?'

'Why, having carefully taken the bearings of the tree, I turned homewards. The instant that I left "the devil's seat", however, the circular rift vanished; nor could I get a glimpse of it afterwards, turn as I would. What seems to me the chief ingenuity in this whole business, is the fact (for repeated experiment has convinced me it *is* a fact) that the circular opening in question is visible from no other attainable point of view than that afforded by the narrow ledge upon the face of the rock.

'In this expedition to the "Bishop's Hotel" I had been attended by Jupiter, who had, no doubt, observed, for some weeks past, the abstraction of my demeanour, and took especial care not to leave me alone. But, on the next day, getting up very early, I contrived to give him the slip, and went into the hills in search of the tree. After much toil I found it. When I came home at night my valet proposed to give me a flogging. With the rest of the adventure I believe you are as well acquainted as myself.'

'I suppose,' said I, 'you missed the spot, in the first attempt at digging, through Jupiter's stupidity in letting the bug fall through the right instead of through the left eye of the skull.'

'Precisely. This mistake made a difference of about two inches and a half in the "shot" – that is to say, in the position of the peg nearest the tree; and had the treasure been *beneath* the "shot", the error would have been of little moment; but the "shot", together with the nearest point of the tree, were merely two points for the establishment of a line of direction; of course the error, however trivial in the beginning, increased as we proceeded with the line, and by the time we had gone fifty feet, threw us quite off the scent. But for my deep-seated impressions that treasure was here somewhere actually buried, we might have had all our labour in vain.'

'But your grandiloquence, and your conduct in swinging the beetle – how excessively odd! I was sure you were mad. And why did you insist upon letting fall the bug, instead of a bullet from the shell?'

'Why, to be frank, I felt somewhat annoyed by your evident suspicions touching my sanity, and so resolved to punish you quietly, in my own way, by a little bit of sober mystification. For this reason I swung the beetle, and for this reason I let it fall from the tree. An observation of yours about its great weight suggested the latter idea.'

'Yes, I perceive; and now there is only one point which puzzles me. What are we to make of the skeletons found in the hole?'

'That is a question I am no more able to answer than yourself. There seems, however, only one plausible way of accounting for them – and yet it is dreadful to believe in such atrocity as my suggestion would imply. It is clear that Kidd – if Kidd indeed secreted this treasure, which I doubt not – it is clear that he must have had assistance in the labour. But this labour concluded, he may have thought it expedient to remove all participants in his secret. Perhaps a couple of blows with a mattock were sufficient, while his coadjutors were busy in the pit; perhaps it required a dozen – who shall tell?'

The Facts in the Case of M. Valdemar

OF COURSE I shall not pretend to consider it any matter for wonder that the extraordinary case of M. Valdemar has excited discussion. It would have been a miracle had it not – especially under the circumstances. Through the desire of all parties concerned to keep the affair from the public, at least for the present, or until we had further opportunities for investigation – through our endeavours to effect this – a garbled or exaggerated account made its way into society, and became the source of many unpleasant misrepresentations; and, very naturally, of a great deal of disbelief.

It is now rendered necessary that I give the *facts* – as far as I comprehend them myself. They are, succinctly, these:

My attention, for the last three years, had been repeatedly drawn to the subject of mesmerism;[1] and, about nine months ago, it occurred to me, quite suddenly, that in the series of experiments made hitherto, there had been a very remarkable and most unaccountable omission – no person had as yet been mesmerised *in articulo mortis.*[2] It remained to be seen, first, whether, in such condition, there existed in the patient any susceptibility to the magnetic influence; secondly, whether, if any existed, it was impaired or increased by the condition; thirdly, to what extent, or for how long a period, the encroachments of Death might be arrested by the process. There were other points to be ascertained, but these most excited my curiosity – the last in especial, from the immensely important character of its consequences.

In looking around me for some subject by whose means I might test these particulars, I was brought to think of my friend, M. Ernest Valdemar, the well-known compiler of the 'Bibliotheca Forensica,' and author (under the *nom de plume* of Issachar Marx) of the Polish versions of 'Wallenstein' and 'Gargantua'. M. Valdemar, who has resided principally at Harlem, N.Y., since the year 1839, is (or was) particularly noticeable for the extreme spareness of his person – his lower limbs much resembling those of John Randolph;[3] and, also, for the whiteness of his whiskers, in violent contrast to the blackness of his hair – the latter, in consequence, being very generally mistaken for a wig. His temperament was markedly nervous, and rendered him a good subject for mesmeric experiment. On two or three occasions I had put him to sleep with little difficulty, but was disappointed in other results which his peculiar constitution had naturally led me to anticipate. His will was at no period positively, or thoroughly, under my control; and in regard to *clairvoyance*, I could accomplish with him nothing to be relied upon. I always attributed my failure at these points to the disordered state of his health. For some months previous to my becoming acquainted with him, his physicians had declared him in a confirmed phthisis.[4] It was his custom, indeed, to speak calmly of his approaching dissolution, as of a matter neither to be avoided nor regretted.

When the ideas to which I have alluded first occurred to me, it was of course very natural that I should think of M. Valdemar. I knew the steady philosophy of the man too well to apprehend any scruples from *him*; and he had no relatives in America who would be likely to interfere. I spoke to him frankly upon the subject; and, to my surprise, his interest seemed vividly excited. I say to my surprise; for, although he had always yielded his person freely to my experiments, he had never before given me any tokens of sympathy with what I did. His disease was of that character which would admit of exact calculation in respect to the epoch of its termination in death; and it was finally arranged between us that he would send for me about twenty-four hours before the period announced by his physicians as that of his decease.

It is now rather more than seven months since I received, from M. Valdemar himself, the subjoined note:

My dear P—, You may as well come *now*. D— and F— are agreed that I cannot hold out beyond tomorrow midnight; and I think they have hit the time very nearly.

Valdemar.

I received this note within half-an-hour after it was written, and in fifteen minutes more I was in the dying man's chamber. I had not seen him for ten days, and was appalled by the fearful alteration which the brief interval had wrought in him. His face wore a leaden hue; the eyes were utterly lustreless; and the emaciation was so extreme, that the skin had been broken through by the cheek-bones. His expectoration was excessive. The pulse was barely perceptible. He retained, nevertheless, in a very remarkable manner both his mental power and a certain degree of physical strength. He spoke with distinctness – took some palliative medicines without aid – and, when I entered the room, was occupied in pencilling memoranda in a pocket-book. He was propped up in the bed by pillows. Doctors D— and F— were in attendance. After pressing Valdemar's hand, I took these gentlemen aside, and obtained from them a minute account of the patient's condition. The left lung had been for eighteen months in a semi-osseous[5] or cartilaginous[6] state, and was, of course, entirely useless for all purposes of vitality. The right, in its upper portion, was also partially, if not thoroughly, ossified, while the lower region was merely a mass of purulent tubercles, running one into another. Several extensive perforations existed; and, at one point, permanent adhesion to the ribs had taken place. These appearances in the right lobe were of comparatively recent date. The ossification had proceeded with very unusual rapidity; no sign of it had been discovered a month before, and the adhesion had only been observed during the three previous days. Independently of the phthisis, the patient was suspected of aneurism[7] of the aorta;[8] but on this point the osseous symptoms rendered an exact diagnosis impossible. It was the opinion of both physicians that M. Valdemar would die about midnight on the morrow (Sunday). It was then seven o'clock on Saturday evening.

On quitting the invalid's bedside to hold conversation with myself, Doctors D— and F— had bidden him a final farewell. It had not been their intention to return; but, at my request, they agreed to look in upon the patient about ten the next night.

When they had gone, I spoke freely with M. Valdemar on the subject of his approaching dissolution, as well as, more particularly, of the experiment proposed. He still professed himself quite willing and even anxious to have it made, and urged me to commence it at once. A male and a female nurse were in attendance; but I did not feel myself altogether at liberty to engage in a task of this character with no more reliable witnesses than these people, in case of sudden accident, might prove. I therefore postponed operations until about eight the next night, when the arrival of a medical student, with whom I had some acquaintance (Mr Theodore L—l), relieved me from further embarrassment. It had been my design, originally, to wait for the physicians; but I was induced to proceed, first, by the urgent entreaties of M. Valdemar, and secondly, by my conviction that I had not a moment to lose, as he was evidently sinking fast.

Mr L—l was so kind as to accede to my desire that he would take notes of all that occurred; and it is from his memoranda that what I now have to relate is, for the most part, either condensed or copied *verbatim*.

It wanted about five minutes of eight when, taking the patient's hand, I begged him to state, as distinctly as he could, to Mr L—l, whether he (M. Valdemar) was entirely willing that I should make the experiment of mesmerising him in his then condition.

He replied feebly, yet quite audibly, 'Yes, I wish to be mesmerised' –

adding immediately afterwards, 'I fear you have deferred it too long.'

While he spoke thus, I commenced the passes which I had already found most effectual in subduing him. He was evidently influenced with the first lateral stroke of my hand across his forehead; but although I exerted all my powers, no further perceptible effect was induced until some minutes after ten o'clock, when Doctors D— and F— called, according to appointment. I explained to them, in a few words, what I designed, and as they opposed no objection, saying that the patient was already in the death agony, I proceeded without hesitation – exchanging, however, the lateral passes for downward ones, and directing my gaze entirely into the right eye of the sufferer.

By this time his pulse was imperceptible and his breathing was stertorous, and at intervals of half a minute.

This condition was nearly unaltered for a quarter of an hour. At the expiration of this period, however, a natural, although a very deep sigh, escaped the bosom of the dying man, and the stertorous breathing ceased – that is to say, its stertorousness was no longer apparent; the intervals were undiminished. The patient's extremities were of an icy coldness.

At five minutes before eleven I perceived unequivocal signs of the mesmeric influence. The glassy roll of the eye was changed for that expression of uneasy *inward* examination which is never seen except in cases of sleep-waking, and which it is quite impossible to mistake. With a few rapid lateral passes I made the lids quiver, as in incipient sleep, and with a few more I closed them altogether. I was not satisfied, however, with this, but continued the manipulations vigorously, and with the fullest exertion of the will, until I had completely stiffened the limbs of the slumberer, after placing them in a seemingly easy position. The legs were at full length; the arms were nearly so, and reposed on the bed at a moderate distance from the loins. The head was very slightly elevated.

When I had accomplished this, it was fully midnight, and I requested the gentlemen present to examine M. Valdemar's condition. After a few experiments, they admitted him to be in an unusually perfect state of mesmeric trance. The curiosity of both the physicians was greatly excited. Dr D— resolved at once to remain with the patient all night, while Dr F— took leave with a promise to return at daybreak. Mr L—l and the nurses remained.

We left M. Valdemar entirely undisturbed until about three o'clock in the morning, when I approached him, and found him in precisely the same condition as when Dr F— went away – that is to say, he lay in the same position. The pulse was imperceptible; the breathing was gentle (scarcely noticeable, unless through the application of a mirror to the lips); the eyes were closed naturally; and the limbs were as rigid and as cold as marble. Still, the general appearance was certainly not that of death.

As I approached M. Valdemar I made a kind of half effort to influence his right arm into pursuit of my own, as I passed the latter gently to and fro above his person. In such experiments with this patient I had never perfectly succeeded before, and assuredly I had little thought of succeeding now; but to my astonishment, his arm very readily, although feebly, followed every direction I assigned it with mine. I determined to hazard a few words of conversation.

'M. Valdemar,' I said, 'are you asleep?' He made no answer, but I perceived a tremor about the lips, and was thus induced to repeat the question, again and again. At its third repetition, his whole frame was agitated by a very slight shivering; the eyelids unclosed themselves so far as to display a white line of a ball; the lips moved sluggishly, and from between them, in a barely audible whisper, issued the words –

'Yes; asleep now. Do not wake me! – let me die so!'

I here felt the limbs and found them as rigid as ever. The right arm, as before, obeyed the direction of my hand. I questioned the sleep-waker again –

'Do you still feel pain in the breast, M. Valdemar?'

The answer now was immediate, but even less audible than before –

'No pain – I am dying.'

I did not think it advisable to disturb him further just then, and nothing more was said or done until the arrival of Dr F—, who came a little before sunrise, and expressed unbounded astonishment at finding the patient still alive. After feeling the pulse and applying a mirror to the lips, he requested me to speak to the sleep-waker again. I did so, saying –

'M. Valdemar, do you still sleep?'

As before, some minutes elapsed ere a reply was made; and during the interval the dying man seemed to be collecting his energies to speak. At my fourth repetition of the question, he said very faintly, almost inaudibly –

'Yes; still asleep – dying.'

It was now the opinion, or rather the wish, of the physicians, that M. Valdemar should be suffered to remain undisturbed in his present apparently tranquil condition, until death should supervene – and this, it was generally agreed, must now take place within a few minutes. I concluded, however, to speak to him once more, and merely repeated my previous question.

While I spoke, there came a marked change over the countenance of the sleep-waker. The eyes rolled themselves slowly open, the pupils disappearing upwardly; the skin generally assumed a cadaverous hue, resembling not so much parchment as white paper; and the circular hectic spots which, hitherto, had been strongly defined in the centre of each cheek, *went out* at once. I use this expression, because the suddenness of their departure put me in mind of nothing so much as the extinguishment of a candle by a puff of the breath. The upper lip, at the same time, writhed itself away from the teeth, which it had previously covered completely; while the lower jaw fell with an audible jerk, leaving the mouth widely extended, and disclosing in full view the swollen and blackened tongue. I presume that no member of the party then present had been unaccustomed to death-bed horrors; but so hideous beyond conception was the appearance of M. Valdemar at this moment, that there was a general shrinking back from the region of the bed.

I now feel that I have reached a point of this narrative at which every reader will be startled into positive disbelief. It is my business, however, simply to proceed.

There was no longer the faintest sign of vitality in M. Valdemar; and concluding him to be dead, we were consigning him to the charge of the nurses, when a strong vibratory motion was observable in the tongue. This continued for perhaps a minute. At the expiration of this period, there issued from the distended and motionless jaws a voice – such as it would be madness in me to attempt describing. There are, indeed, two or three epithets which might be considered as applicable to it in part; I might say, for example, that the sound was harsh, and broken, and hollow; but the hideous whole is indescribable, for the simple reason that no similar sounds have ever jarred upon the ear of humanity. There were two particulars, nevertheless, which I thought then, and still think, might fairly be stated as characteristic of the intonation – as well adapted to convey some idea of its unearthly peculiarity. In the first place, the voice seemed to reach our ears – at least mine – from a vast distance, or from some deep cavern within the earth. In the second place, it impressed me (I fear, indeed, that it will be impossible to make myself comprehended) as gelatinous or glutinous matters impress the sense of touch.

I have spoken both of 'sound' and of 'voice.' I mean to say that the sound was one of distinct – of even wonderfully, thrillingly distinct – syllabification. M. Valdemar *spoke* – obviously in reply to the question I had propounded to him a few minutes before. I had asked him, it will be remembered, if he still slept. He now said –

'Yes – no – I *have been* sleeping – and now – now – *I am dead.*'

No person present even affected to deny, or attempted to repress, the unutterable, shuddering horror which these few words, thus uttered, were so well calculated to convey. Mr L—l (the student) swooned. The nurses immediately left the chamber, and could not be induced to return. My own impressions I would not pretend to render intelligible to the reader. For nearly an hour, we busied ourselves, silently – without the utterance of a word – in endeavours to revive Mr L—l. When he came to himself, we addressed ourselves again to an investigation of M. Valdemar's condition.

It remained in all respects as I have last described it, with the exception that the mirror no longer afforded evidence of respiration. An attempt to draw blood from the arm failed. I should mention, too, that this limb was no further subject to my will. I endeavoured in vain to make it follow the direction of my hand. The only real indication, indeed, of the mesmeric influence was now found in the vibratory movement of the tongue, whenever I addressed M. Valdemar a question. He seemed to be making an effort to reply, but had no longer sufficient volition. To queries put to him by any other person than myself he seemed utterly insensible – although I endeavoured to place each member of the company in mesmeric *rapport* with him. I believe that I have now related all that is necessary to an understanding of the sleep-waker's state at this epoch. Other nurses were procured; and at ten o'clock I left the house in company with the two physicians and Mr L—l.

In the afternoon we all called again to see the patient. His condition remained precisely the same. We had now some discussion as to the propriety and feasibility of awakening him; but we had little difficulty in agreeing that no good purpose would be served by so doing. It was evident that, so far, death (or what is usually termed death) had been arrested by the mesmeric process. It seemed clear to us all that to awaken M. Valdemar would be merely to insure his instant, or at least his speedy dissolution.

From this period until the close of last week – *an interval of nearly seven months* – we continued to make daily calls at M. Valdemar's house, accompanied, now and then, by medical and other friends. All this time the sleep-waker remained *exactly* as I have last described him. The nurses' attentions were continual.

It was on Friday last that we finally resolved to make the experiment of awakening, or attempting to awaken him; and it is the (perhaps) unfortunate result of this latter experiment which has given rise to so much discussion in private circles – to so much of what I cannot help thinking unwarranted popular feeling.

For the purpose of relieving M. Valdemar from the mesmeric trance, I made use of the customary passes. These for a time were unsuccessful. The first indication of revival was afforded by a partial descent of the iris. It was observed, as especially remarkable, that this lowering of the pupil was accompanied by the profuse outflowing of a yellowish ichor (from beneath the lids) of a pungent and highly offensive odour.

It was now suggested that I should attempt to influence the patient's arm as heretofore. I made the attempt and failed. Dr F— then intimated a desire to have me put a question. I did so, as follows –

'M. Valdemar, can you explain to us what are your feelings or wishes now?'

There was an instant return of the hectic circles on the cheeks; the tongue quivered, or rather rolled violently in the mouth (although the jaws and lips remained rigid as before); and at length the same hideous voice which I have already described, broke forth –

'For God's sake! – quick! – quick – put me to sleep – or quick! – waken me! – quick! – *I say to you that I am dead!*'

I was thoroughly unnerved, and for an instant remained undecided what to do. At first I made an endeavour to re-compose the patient; but, failing in this through total abeyance of the will, I retraced my steps, and as earnestly struggled to awaken him. In this attempt I soon saw that I should be successful – or at least I soon fancied that my success would be complete – and I am sure that all in the room were prepared to see the patient awaken.

For what really occurred, however, it is quite impossible that any human being could have been prepared.

As I rapidly made the mesmeric passes, amid ejaculations of 'Dead! dead!' absolutely *bursting* from the tongue and not from the lips of the sufferer, his whole frame at once – within the space of a single minute, or even less, shrunk – crumbled – absolutely *rotted* away beneath my hands. Upon the bed, before that whole company, there lay a nearly liquid mass of loathsome – of detestable putrescence.

MS. Found in a Bottle

Qui n'a plus qu'un moment à vivre
N'a plus rien à dissimuler.[1]

QUINAULT, *Atys*

OF MY COUNTRY and of my family I have little to say. Ill usage and length of years have driven me from the one, and estranged me from the other. Hereditary wealth afforded me an education of no common order, and a contemplative turn of mind enabled me to methodise the stories which early study diligently garnered up. Beyond all things, the works of the German moralists gave me a great delight; not from my ill-advised admiration of their eloquent madness, but from the ease with which my habits of rigid thought enabled me to detect their falsities. I have often been reproached with the aridity of my genius; a deficiency of imagination has been imputed to me as a crime; and the Pyrrhonism[2] of my opinions has at all times rendered me notorious. Indeed, a strong relish for physical philosophy has, I fear, tinctured my mind with a very common error of this age – I mean the habit of referring occurrences, even the least susceptible of such reference, to the principles of that science. Upon the whole, no person could be less liable than myself to be led away from the severe precincts of truth by the *ignes fatui*[3] of superstition. I have thought proper to premise thus much, lest the incredible tale I have to tell should be considered rather the raving of a crude imagination, than the positive experience of a mind to which the reveries of fancy have been a dead letter and a nullity.

After many years spent in foreign travel, I sailed in the year 18—, from the port of Batavia, in the rich and populous island of Java, on a voyage to the Archipelago of the Sunda[4] Islands. I went as passenger – having no other inducement than a kind of nervous restlessness which haunted me as a fiend.

Our vessel was a beautiful ship of about four hundred tons, copper-fastened, and built at Bombay of Malabar teak. She was freighted with cotton-wool and oil, from the Lachadive Islands.[5] We had also on board coir,[6] jaggeree,[7] ghee,[8] cocoa-nuts, and a few cases of opium. The stowage was clumsily done, and the vessel consequently crank.

We got under way with a mere breath of wind, and for many days stood along the eastern coast of Java, without any other incident to beguile the monotony of our course than the occasional meeting with some of the small grabs[9] of the Archipelago to which we were bound.

One evening, leaning over the taffrail, I observed a very singular isolated cloud, to the N.W. It was remarkable, as well for its colour, as from its being the first we had seen since our departure from Batavia. I watched it attentively until sunset, when it spread all at once to the eastward and westward, girting in the horizon with a narrow strip of vapour, and looking like a long line of low beach. My notice was soon afterwards attracted by the dusky-red appearance of the moon, and the peculiar character of the sea. The latter was undergoing a rapid change, and the water seemed more than usually transparent. Although I could distinctly see the bottom, yet, heaving the lead, I found the ship in fifteen fathoms. The air now became intolerably hot, and was loaded with spiral exhalations similar to those arising from heated iron. As night came on, every breath of wind died away, and a more entire calm it is impossible to conceive. The flame of a candle burned upon the poop without the least perceptible motion, and a long hair, held between the finger and thumb, hung without the possibility of detecting a vibration. However, as the captain said he could perceive no indication of danger, and as we were drifting in bodily to shore, he ordered the sails to be furled, and the anchor let go. No watch was set, and the crew, consisting principally of Malays, stretched themselves deliberately upon deck. I went below – not without a full presentiment of evil. Indeed, every appearance warranted me in apprehending a simoom.[10] I told the captain my fears; but he paid no attention to what I said, and left me without deigning to give a reply. My uneasiness, however, prevented me from sleeping, and about midnight I went upon deck. As I placed my foot upon the upper step of the companion-ladder, I was startled by a loud, humming noise, like that occasioned by the rapid revolution of a mill-wheel, and before I could ascertain its meaning, I found the ship quivering to its centre. In the next instant, a wilderness of foam hurled us upon our beam-ends, and, rushing over us fore and aft, swept the entire decks from stem to stern.

The extreme fury of the blast proved, in a great measure, the salvation of the ship. Although completely waterlogged, yet, as her masts had gone by the board, she rose, after a minute, heavily from the sea, and, staggering awhile beneath the immense pressure of the tempest, finally righted.

By what miracle I escaped destruction, it is impossible to say. Stunned by the shock of the water, I found myself, upon recovery, jammed in between the stern-post and rudder. With great difficulty I gained my feet, and looking dizzily around, was at first struck with the idea of our being among breakers; so terrific, beyond the wildest imagination, was the whirlpool of mountainous and foaming ocean within which we were engulfed. After a while, I heard the voice of an old Swede, who had shipped with us at the moment of leaving port. I hallooed to him with all my strength, and presently he came reeling aft. We soon discovered that we were the sole survivors of the accident. All on deck, with the exception of ourselves, had been swept overboard; the captain and mates must have perished as they slept, for the cabins were deluged with water. Without assistance, we could expect to do little for the security of the ship, and our exertions were at first paralysed by the momentary expectation of going down. Our cable had, of course, parted like pack-thread,[11] at the first breath of the hurricane, or we should have been instantaneously overwhelmed. We scudded with frightful velocity before the sea, and the water made clear breaches over us. The framework of our stern was shattered excessively, and, in almost every respect, we had received considerable injury; but to our extreme joy we found the pumps unchoked, and that we had made no great shifting of our ballast. The main fury of the blast had already blown over, and we apprehended little danger from the violence of the wind; but we looked forward to its total cessation with dismay, well believing, that in our shattered condition, we should inevitably perish in the tremendous swell which would ensue. But this very just apprehension seemed by no means likely to be soon verified. For five entire days and nights – during which our only subsistence was a small quantity of jaggeree, procured with great difficulty from the forecastle – the hulk flew at a rate defying computation, before rapidly succeeding flaws of wind, which without equalling the first violence of the simoom, were still more terrific than any tempest I had before encountered. Our course for the first four days was, with trifling variations, S.E. and by S.; and we must have run down the coast of New Holland. On the fifth day the cold became extreme, although the wind had hauled round a point more to the northward. The sun arose with a sickly yellow lustre, and clambered a very few degrees above the horizon – emitting no decisive light. There were no clouds apparent, yet the wind was upon the increase, and blew with a fitful and unsteady fury. About noon, as nearly as we could guess, our attention was again arrested by the appearance of the sun. It gave out no light, properly so called, but a dull and sullen glow without reflection, as if all its rays were polarised. Just before sinking within the turgid sea, its central fires suddenly went out, as if hurriedly extinguished by some unaccountable power. It was a dim, silver-like rim, alone, as it rushed down the unfathomable ocean.

We waited in vain for the arrival of the sixth day – that day to me has

not arrived – to the Swede, never did arrive. Thenceforward we were
enshrouded in pitchy darkness, so that we could not have seen an object
at twenty paces from the ship. Eternal night continued to envelop us, all
unrelieved by the phosphoric sea-brilliancy to which we had been
accustomed in the tropics. We observed, too, that, although the tempest
continued to rage with unabated violence, there was no longer to be
discovered the usual appearance of surf, or foam, which had hitherto
attended us. All around were horror, and thick gloom, and a black
sweltering desert of ebony. Superstitious terror crept by degrees into the
spirit of the old Swede, and my own soul was wrapped up in silent
wonder. We neglected all care of the ship, as worse than useless, and
securing ourselves, as well as possible, to the stump of the mizzen-mast,
looked out bitterly into the world of ocean. We had no means of
calculating time, nor could we form any guess of our situation. We were,
however, well aware of having made farther to the southward than any
previous navigators, and felt great amazement at not meeting with the
usual impediments of ice. In the meantime every moment threatened to
be our last – every mountainous billow hurried to overwhelm us. The
swell surpassed anything I had imagined possible, and that we were not
instantly buried is a miracle. My companion spoke of the lightness of our
cargo, and reminded me of the excellent qualities of our ship; but I could
not help feeling the utter hopelessness of hope itself, and prepared
myself gloomily for that death which I thought nothing could defer
beyond an hour, as with every knot of way the ship made, the swelling of
the black stupendous seas became more dismally appalling. At times we
gasped for breath at an elevation beyond the albatross – at times became
dizzy with the velocity of our descent into some watery hell, where the
air grew stagnant, and no sound disturbed the slumbers of the kraken.[12]

We were at the bottom of one of these abysses, when a quick scream
from my companion broke fearfully upon the night. 'See! see!' cried he,
shrieking in my ears, 'Almighty God! see! see!' As he spoke, I became
aware of a dull, sullen glare of red light which streamed down the sides
of the vast chasm where we lay, and threw a fitful brilliancy upon our
deck. Casting my eyes upwards, I beheld a spectacle which froze the
current of my blood. At a terrific height directly above us, and upon the
very verge of the precipitous descent, hovered a gigantic ship, of
perhaps four thousand tons. Although upreared upon the summit of a
wave more than a hundred times her own altitude, her apparent size
still exceeded that of any ship of the line or East Indiaman in existence.
Her huge hull was of a deep dingy black, unrelieved by any of the
customary carvings of a ship. A single row of brass cannon protruded
from her open ports, and dashed from their polished surfaces the fires

of innumerable battle-lanterns which swung to and fro about her rigging. But what mainly inspired us with horror and astonishment, was that she bore up under a press of sail in the very teeth of that supernatural sea, and of that ungovernable hurricane. When we first discovered her, her bows were alone to be seen, as she rose slowly from the dim and horrible gulf beyond her. For a moment of intense terror she paused upon the giddy pinnacle, as if in contemplation of her own sublimity, then trembled and tottered, and – came down.

At this instant, I know not what sudden self-possession came over my spirit. Staggering as far aft as I could, I awaited fearlessly the ruin that was to overwhelm. Our own vessel was at length ceasing from her struggles, and sinking with her head to the sea. The shock of the descending mass struck her, consequently, in that portion of her frame which was nearly under water, and the inevitable result was to hurl me, with irresistible violence, upon the rigging of the stranger.

As I fell, the ship hove in stays, and went about; and to the confusion ensuing I attributed my escape from the notice of the crew. With little difficulty I made my way, unperceived, to the main hatchway, which was partially open, and soon found an opportunity of secreting myself in the hold. Why I did so I can hardly tell. An indefinite sense of awe, which at first sight of the navigators of the ship had taken hold of my mind, was perhaps the principle of my concealment. I was unwilling to trust myself with a race of people who had offered to the cursory glance I had taken, so many points of vague novelty, doubt, and apprehension. I therefore thought proper to contrive a hiding-place in the hold. This I did by removing a small portion of the shifting-boards, in such a manner as to afford me a convenient retreat between the huge timbers of the ship.

I had scarcely completed my work, when a footstep in the hold forced me to make use of it. A man passed by my place of concealment with a feeble and unsteady gait. I could not see his face, but had an opportunity of observing his general appearance. There was about it an evidence of great age and infirmity. His knees tottered beneath a load of years, and his entire frame quivered under the burthen. He muttered to himself, in a low broken tone, some words of a language which I could not understand, and groped in a corner among a pile of singular-looking instruments, and decayed charts of navigation. His manner was a wild mixture of the peevishness of second childhood and the solemn dignity of a god. He at length went on deck, and I saw him no more.

A feeling, for which I have no name, has taken possession of my soul – a sensation which will admit of no analysis, to which the lessons of bygone time are inadequate, and for which I fear futurity itself will offer me no key. To a mind constituted like my own, the latter consideration is an evil. I shall never – I know that I shall never – be satisfied with regard to the nature of my conceptions. Yet it is not wonderful that these conceptions are indefinite, since they have their origin in sources so utterly novel. A new sense – a new entity is added to my soul.

It is long since I first trod the deck of this terrible ship, and the rays of my destiny are, I think, gathering to a focus. Incomprehensible men! Wrapped up in meditations of a kind which I cannot divine, they pass me by unnoticed. Concealment is utter folly on my part, for the people *will not* see. It was but just now that I passed directly before the eyes of the mate; it was no long while ago that I ventured into the captain's own private cabin, and took thence the materials with which I write, and have written. I shall from time to time continue this journal. It is true that I may not find an opportunity of transmitting it to the world, but I will not fail to make the endeavour. At the last moment I will enclose the MS. in a bottle, and cast it within the sea.

An incident has occurred which has given me new room for meditation. Are such things the operation of ungoverned chance? I had ventured upon deck and thrown myself down, without attracting any notice, among a pile of ratlin-stuff and old sails, in the bottom of the yawl. While musing upon the singularity of my fate, I unwittingly daubed with a tar-brush the edges of a neatly-folded studding-sail which lay near me on a barrel. The studding-sail is now bent upon the ship, and the thoughtless touches of the brush are spread out into the word Discovery.

I have made many observations lately upon the structure of the vessel. Although well armed, she is not, I think, a ship of war. Her rigging, build, and general equipment, all negative a supposition of this kind. What she *is not*, I can easily perceive; what she *is*, I fear it is impossible to say. I know not how it is, but in scrutinising her strange model and singular cast of spars, her huge size and overgrown suits of canvas, her severely simple bow and antiquated stern, there will occasionally flash across my mind a sensation of familiar things, and there is always mixed up with such indistinct shadows of recollection, an unaccountable memory of old foreign chronicles and ages long ago.

I have been looking at the timbers of the ship. She is built of a material to which I am a stranger. There is a peculiar character about the wood which strikes me as rendering it unfit for the purpose to which it has been applied. I mean its extreme *porousness*, considered independently of the worm-eaten condition which is a consequence of navigation in these seas, and apart from the rottenness attendant upon age. It will appear, perhaps, an observation somewhat over-curious, but this wood would have every characteristic of Spanish oak, if Spanish oak were distended by any unnatural means.

In reading the above sentence, a curious apothegm of an old weather-beaten Dutch navigator comes full upon my recollection. 'It is as sure,' he was wont to say, when any doubt was entertained of his veracity, 'as sure as there is a sea where the ship itself will grow in bulk like the living body of the seaman.'

About an hour ago I made bold to trust myself among a group of the crew. They paid me no manner of attention, and, although I stood in the very midst of them all, seemed utterly unconscious of my presence. Like the one I had at first seen in the hold, they all bore about them the marks of a hoary old age. Their knees trembled with infirmity; their shoulders were bent double with decrepitude; their shrivelled skins rattled in the wind; their voices were low, tremulous, and broken; their eyes glistened with the rheum of years; and their grey hairs streamed terribly in the tempest. Around them, on every part of the deck, lay scattered mathematical instruments of the most quaint and obsolete construction.

I mentioned, some time ago, the bending of a studding-sail. From that period, the ship, being thrown dead off the wind, has continued her terrific course due south, with every rag of canvas packed upon her, from her truck to her lower studding-sail booms, and rolling every moment her top-gallant yard-arms into the most appalling hell of water which it can enter into the mind of man to imagine. I have just left the deck, where I find it impossible to maintain a footing, although the crew seem to experience little inconvenience. It appears to me a miracle of miracles that our enormous bulk is not swallowed up at once and for ever. We are surely doomed to hover continually upon the brink of eternity, without taking a final plunge into the abyss. From billows a thousand times more stupendous than any I have ever seen, we glide away with the facility of the arrowy sea-gull; and the colossal waters rear their heads above us like demons of the deep, but like demons confined to simple threats, and forbidden to destroy. I am led to attribute these frequent escapes to the only natural cause which can account for such effect. I must suppose the ship to be within the influence of some strong current, or impetuous under-tow.

I have seen the captain face to face, and in his own cabin – but, as I expected, he paid me no attention. Although in his appearance there is, to a casual observer, nothing which might bespeak him more or less than man, still a feeling of irrepressible reverence and awe mingled with the sensation of wonder with which I regarded him. In stature, he is nearly my own height; that is, about five feet eight inches. He is of a well-knit and compact frame of body, neither robust nor remarkable otherwise. But it is the singularity of the expression which reigns upon the face – it is the intense, the wonderful, the thrilling evidence of old age so utter, so extreme, which excites within my spirit a sense – a sentiment ineffable. His forehead, although little wrinkled, seems to bear upon it the stamp of a myriad of years. His grey hairs are records of the past, and his greyer eyes are sibyls of the future. The cabin floor was thickly strewn with strange, iron-clasped folios, and mouldering instruments of science, and obsolete long-forgotten charts. His head was bowed down upon his hands, and he pored, with a fiery, unquiet eye, over a paper which I took to be a commission, and which, at all events, bore the signature of a monarch. He muttered to himself – as did the first seaman whom I saw in the hold – some low peevish syllables of a foreign tongue; and although the speaker was close at my elbow, his voice seemed to reach my ears from the distance of a mile.

The ship and all in it are imbued with the spirit of Eld.[13] The crew glide to and fro like the ghosts of buried centuries; their eyes have an eager and uneasy meaning; and when their fingers fall athwart my path in the wild glare of the battle-lanterns, I feel as I have never felt before, although I have been all my life a dealer in antiquities, and have imbibed the shadows of fallen columns at Balbec,[14] and Tadmor,[15] and Persepolis,[16] until my very soul has become a ruin.

When I look around me, I feel ashamed of my former apprehensions. If I trembled at the blast which has hitherto attended us, shall I not stand aghast at a warring of wind and ocean, to convey any idea of which, the words tornado and simoom are trivial and ineffective? All in the immediate vicinity of the ship is the blackness of eternal night, and a chaos of foamless water; but, about a league on either side of us, may be seen, indistinctly, and at intervals, stupendous ramparts of ice, towering away into the desolate sky, and looking like the walls of the universe.

As I imagined, the ship proves to be in a current – if that appellation can properly be given to a tide which, howling and shrieking by the white ice, thunders on to the southward with a velocity like the headlong dashing of a cataract.

To conceive the horror of my sensations is, I presume, utterly impossible; yet a curiosity to penetrate the mysteries of these awful regions predominates even over my despair, and will reconcile me to the most hideous aspect of death. It is evident that we are hurrying onwards to some exciting knowledge – some never-to-be-imparted secret, whose attainment is destruction. Perhaps this current leads us to the southern pole itself. It must be confessed that a supposition apparently so wild has every probability in its favour.

The crew pace the deck with unquiet and tremulous step; but there is upon their countenance an expression more of the eagerness of hope than of the apathy of despair.

In the meantime the wind is still in our poop, and, as we carry a crowd of canvas, the ship is at times lifted bodily from out the sea! Oh, horror upon horror! – the ice opens suddenly to the right, and to the left, and we are whirling dizzily, in immense concentric circles, round and round the borders of a gigantic amphitheatre, the summit of whose walls is lost in the darkness and the distance. But little time will be left me to ponder upon my destiny! The circles rapidly grow small – we are plunging madly within the grasp of the whirlpool – and amid a roaring, and bellowing, and thundering of ocean and tempest, the ship is quivering – O God! and – going down!

Note – 'MS. Found in a Bottle' was originally published in 1831; and it was not until many years afterwards that I became acquainted with the maps of Mercator, in which the ocean is represented as rushing, by four mouths, into the (northern) Polar Gulf, to be absorbed into the bowels of the earth; the Pole itself being represented by a black rock, towering to a prodigious height.

A Descent into the Maelström

The ways of God in Nature, as in Providence, are not as *our* ways;
nor are the models that we frame any way commensurate to the
vastness, profundity, and unsearchableness of His works, *which
have a depth in them greater than the well of Democritus.*[1]

JOSEPH GLANVILL

WE HAD NOW reached the summit of the loftiest crag. For some
minutes the old man seemed too much exhausted to speak.

'Not long ago,' said he at length, 'and I could have guided you on
this route as well as the youngest of my sons; but, about three years
past, there happened to me an event such as never happened before to
mortal man – or at least such as no man ever survived to tell of – and
the six hours of deadly terror which I then endured have broken me up
body and soul. You suppose me a *very* old man – but I am not. It took
less than a single day to change these hairs from a jetty black to white,
to weaken my limbs, and to unstring my nerves, so that I tremble at the
least exertion, and am frightened at a shadow. Do you know I can
scarcely look over this little cliff without getting giddy?'

The 'little cliff,' upon whose edge he had so carelessly thrown
himself down to rest, that the weightier portion of his body hung over
it, while he was only kept from falling by the tenure of his elbow on its
extreme and slippery edge – this 'little cliff' arose, a sheer unobstructed
precipice of black shining rock, some fifteen or sixteen hundred feet
from the world of crags beneath us. Nothing would have tempted me
to within half-a-dozen yards of its brink. In truth, so deeply was I
excited by the perilous position of my companion, that I fell at full
length upon the ground, clung to the shrubs around me, and dared not
even glance upward at the sky – while I struggled in vain to divest
myself of the idea that the very foundations of the mountain were in
danger from the fury of the winds. It was long before I could reason
myself into sufficient courage to sit up and look out into the distance.

'You must get over these fancies,' said the guide, 'for I have brought
you here that you might have the best possible view of the scene of that
event I mentioned – and to tell you the whole story with the spot just
under your eye.'

'We are now,' he continued, in that particularising manner which
distinguished him – 'we are now close upon the Norwegian coast – in
the sixty-eighth degree of latitude – in the great province of Nordland[2]
– and in the dreary district of Lofoden.[3] The mountain upon whose top

we sit is Helseggen, the Cloudy. Now raise yourself up a little higher – hold on to the grass if you feel giddy – so – and look out, beyond the belt of vapour beneath us, into the sea.'

I looked dizzily, and beheld a wide expanse of ocean, whose waters wore so inky a hue as to bring at once to my mind the Nubian geographer's[4] account of the *Mare Tenebrarum*.[5] A panorama more deplorably desolate no human imagination can conceive. To the right and left, as far as the eye could reach, there lay out-stretched, like ramparts of the world, lines of horribly black and beetling cliff, whose character of gloom was but the more forcibly illustrated by the surf which reared high up against it its white and ghastly crest, howling and shrieking for ever. Just opposite the promontory upon whose apex we were placed, and at a distance of some five or six miles out at sea, there was visible a small, bleak-looking island; or, more properly, its position was discernible through the wilderness of surge in which it was enveloped. About two miles nearer the land, arose another of smaller size, hideously craggy and barren, and encompassed at various intervals by a cluster of dark rocks.

The appearance of the ocean, in the space between the more distant island and the shore, had something very unusual about it. Although, at the time, so strong a gale was blowing landward that a brig in the remote offing lay to under a double-reefed trysail, and constantly plunged her whole hull out of sight, still there was here nothing like a regular swell, but only a short, quick, angry cross dashing of water in every direction – as well in the teeth of the wind as otherwise. Of foam there was little except in the immediate vicinity of the rocks.

'The island[6] in the distance,' resumed the old man, 'is called by the Norwegians Vurrgh. The one midway is Moskoe. That a mile to the northward is Ambaaren. Yonder are Islesen, Hotholm, Keildhelm, Suarven, and Buckholm. Farther off – between Moskoe and Vurrgh – are Otterholm, Flimen, Sandflesen, and Stockholm. These are the true names of the places – but why it has been thought necessary to name them at all, is more than either you or I can understand. Do you hear anything? Do you see any change in the water?'

We had now been about ten minutes upon the top of Helseggen, to which we had ascended from the interior of Lofoden, so that we had caught no glimpse of the sea until it had burst upon us from the summit. As the old man spoke, I became aware of a loud and gradually increasing sound, like the moaning of a vast herd of buffaloes upon an American prairie; and at the same moment I perceived what seamen term the *chopping* character of the ocean beneath us, was rapidly changing into a current which set to the eastward. Even while I gazed, this current acquired a monstrous velocity. Each moment added to its speed – to its headlong impetuosity. In five minutes the whole sea, as far as Vurrgh, was lashed into ungovernable fury; but it was between Moskoe and the coast that the main uproar held its sway. Here the vast bed of the waters, seamed and scarred into a thousand conflicting channels, burst suddenly into frenzied convulsion – heaving, boiling, hissing – gyrating in gigantic and innumerable vortices, and all whirling and plunging on to the eastward with a rapidity which water never elsewhere assumes, except in precipitous descents.

In a few minutes more, there came over the scene another radical alteration. The general surface grew somewhat more smooth, and the whirlpools, one by one, disappeared, while prodigious streaks of foam became apparent where none had been seen before. These streaks, at length, spreading out to a great distance, and entering into combination, took unto themselves the gyratory motion of the subsided vortices, and seemed to form the germ of another more vast. Suddenly – very suddenly – this assumed a distinct and definite existence, in a circle of more than a mile in diameter. The edge of the whirl was represented by a broad belt of gleaming spray; but no particle of this slipped into the mouth of the terrific funnel, whose interior, as far as the eye could fathom it, was a smooth, shining, and jet-black wall of water, inclined to the horizon at an angle of some forty-five degrees, speeding dizzily round and round with a swaying and sweltering motion, and sending forth to the winds an appalling voice, half-shriek, half-roar, such as not even the mighty cataract of Niagara ever lifts up in its agony to Heaven.

The mountain trembled to its very base, and the rock rocked. I threw myself upon my face, and clung to the scant herbage in an excess of nervous agitation.

'This,' said I at length, to the old man – 'this *can* be nothing else than the great whirlpool of the Maelström.'[7]

'So it is sometimes termed,' said he. 'We Norwegians call it the Moskoe-ström, from the island of Moskoe in the midway.'

The ordinary accounts of this vortex had by no means prepared me for what I saw. That of Jonas Ramus,[8] which is perhaps the most circumstantial of any, cannot impart the faintest conception either of the magnificence, or of the horror of the scene – or of the wild bewildering sense of *the novel* which confounds the beholder. I am not sure from what point of view the writer in question surveyed it, nor at what time; but it could neither have been from the summit of Helseggen, nor during a storm. There are some passages of his description, nevertheless, which may be quoted for their details, although their effect is exceedingly feeble in conveying an impression of the spectacle.

'Between Lofoden and Moskoe,' he says, 'the depth of the water is between thirty-six and forty fathoms; but on the other side, toward Ver (Vurrgh), this depth decreases so as not to afford a convenient passage for a vessel, without the risk of splitting on the rocks, which happens even in the calmest weather. When it is flood, the stream runs up the country between Lofoden and Moskoe with a boisterous rapidity; but the roar of its impetuous ebb to the sea is scarce equalled by the loudest and most dreadful cataracts, the noise being heard several leagues off; and the vortices or pits are of such an extent and depth, that if a ship comes within its attraction, it is inevitably absorbed and carried down to the bottom, and there beat to pieces against the rocks; and when the water relaxes, the fragments thereof are thrown up again. But these intervals of tranquillity are only at the turn of the ebb and flood, and in calm weather, and last but a quarter of an hour, its violence gradually returning. When the stream is most boisterous, and its fury heightened by a storm, it is dangerous to come within a Norway mile of it. Boats, yachts, and ships have been carried away by not guarding against it before they were within its reach. It likewise happens frequently, that whales come too near the stream, and are overpowered by its violence; and then it is impossible to describe their howlings and bellowings in their fruitless struggles to disengage themselves. A bear once, attempting to swim from Lofoden to Moskoe, was caught by the stream and borne down, while he roared terribly, so as to be heard on shore. Large stocks of firs and pine trees, after being absorbed by the current, rise again broken and torn to such a degree as if bristles grew upon them. This plainly shows the bottom to consist of craggy rocks, among which they are whirled to and fro. This stream is regulated by the flux and reflux of the sea – it being constantly high and low water every six hours. In the year 1645, early in the morning of Sexagesima Sunday, it raged with such noise and impetuosity that the very stones of the houses on the coast fell to the ground.'

In regard to the depth of the water, I could not see how this could have been ascertained at all in the immediate vicinity of the vortex. The 'forty fathoms' must have reference only to portions of the channel close upon the shore either of Moskoe or Lofoden. The depth in the centre of the Moskoe-ström must be immeasurably greater; and no better proof of this fact is necessary than can be obtained from even the sidelong glance into the abyss of the whirl which may be had from the highest crag of Helseggen. Looking down from this pinnacle upon the howling Phlegethon[9] below, I could not help smiling at the simplicity with which the honest Jonas Ramus records, as a matter difficult of belief, the anecdotes of the whales and the bears; for it appeared to me, in fact, a self-evident thing, that the largest ship of the line in existence, coming within the influence of that deadly attraction, could resist it as little as a feather the hurricane, and must disappear bodily and at once.

The attempts to account for the phenomenon – some of which, I remember, seemed to me sufficiently plausible in perusal – now wore a very different and unsatisfactory aspect. The idea generally received is that this, as well as three smaller vortices among the Faroe Islands, 'have no other cause than the collision of waves rising and falling, at flux and reflux, against a ridge of rocks and shelves, which confines the water so that it precipitates itself like a cataract; and thus the higher the flood rises, the deeper must the fall be, and the natural result of all is a whirlpool or vortex, the prodigious suction of which is sufficiently known by lesser experiments.' – These are the words of the Encyclopædia Britannica. Kircher [10] and others imagine that in the centre of the channel of the Maelström is an abyss penetrating the globe, and issuing in some very remote part – the Gulf of Bothnia [11] being somewhat decidedly named in one instance. This opinion, idle in itself, was the one to which, as I gazed, my imagination most readily assented; and, mentioning it to the guide, I was rather surprised to hear him say that, although it was the view almost universally entertained of the subject by the Norwegians, it nevertheless was not his own. As to the former notion, he confessed his inability to comprehend it; and here I agreed with him – for, however conclusive on paper, it becomes altogether unintelligible, and even absurd, amid the thunder of the abyss.

'You have had a good look at the whirl now,' said the old man, 'and if you will creep round this crag, so as to get in its lee, and deaden the roar of the water, I will tell you a story that will convince you I ought to know something of the Moskoe-ström.'

I placed myself as desired, and he proceeded.

'Myself and my two brothers once owned a schooner-rigged smack of about seventy tons burden, with which we were in the habit of fishing among the islands beyond Moskoe, nearly to Vurrgh. In all violent eddies at sea there is good fishing, at proper opportunities, if one has only the courage to attempt it; but among the whole of the Lofoden coastmen, we three were the only ones who made a regular business of going out to the islands, as I tell you. The usual grounds are a great way lower down to the southward. There fish can be got at all hours, without much risk, and therefore these places are preferred. The choice spots over here among the rocks, however, not only yield the finest variety, but in far greater abundance; so that we often got in a single day, what the more timid of the craft could not scrape together in a week. In fact, we made it a matter of desperate speculation – the risk of life standing instead of labour, and courage answering for capital.

'We kept the smack in a cove about five miles higher up the coast than this; and it was our practice, in fine weather, to take advantage of the fifteen minutes' slack to push across the main channel of the Moskoe-ström, far above the pool, and then drop down upon anchorage somewhere near Otterholm, or Sandflesen, where the eddies are not so violent as elsewhere. Here we used to remain until nearly time for slack-water again, when we weighed and made for home. We never set out upon this expedition without a steady side wind for going and coming – one that we felt sure would not fail us before our return – and we seldom made a miscalculation upon this point. Twice, during six years, we were forced to stay all night at anchor on account of a dead calm, which is a rare thing indeed just about here; and once we had to remain on the grounds nearly a week, starving to death, owing to a gale which blew up shortly after our arrival, and made the channel too boisterous to be thought of. Upon this occasion we should have been driven out to sea in spite of everything (for the whirlpools threw us round and round so violently, that, at length, we fouled our anchor and dragged it), if it had not been that we drifted into one of the innumerable cross currents – here today and gone tomorrow – which drove us under the lee of Flimen, where, by good luck, we brought up.

'I could not tell you the twentieth part of the difficulties we encountered "on the grounds" – it is a bad spot to be in, even in good weather – but we made shift always to run the gauntlet of the Moskoe-ström itself without accident; although at times my heart has been in my mouth when we happened to be a minute or so behind or before the slack. The wind sometimes was not as strong as we thought it at starting, and then we made rather less way than we could wish, while the current rendered the smack unmanageable. My eldest brother had a son eighteen years old, and I had two stout boys of my own. These would have been of great assistance at such times, in using the sweeps, as well as afterwards in fishing – but, somehow, although we ran the risk ourselves, we had not the heart to let the young ones get into danger – for, after all said and done, it *was* a horrible danger, and that is the truth.

'It is now within a few days of three years since what I am going to tell you occurred. It was on the 10th of July 18—, a day which the people of this part of the world will never forget – for it was one in which blew the most terrible hurricane that ever came out of the heavens. And yet all the morning, and indeed until late in the afternoon, there was a gentle and steady breeze from the south-west, while the sun shone brightly, so that the oldest seamen among us could not have foreseen what was to follow.

'The three of us – my two brothers and myself – had crossed over to the islands about two o'clock P.M., and soon nearly loaded the smack with fine fish, which, we all remarked, were more plenty that day than we had ever known them. It was just seven, *by my watch*, when we weighed and started for home, so as to make the worst of the Ström at slack water, which we knew would be at eight.

'We set out with a fresh wind on our starboard quarter, and for some time spanked along at a great rate, never dreaming of danger, for indeed we saw not the slightest reason to apprehend it. All at once we were taken aback by a breeze from over Helseggen. This was most unusual – something that had never happened to us before – and I began to feel a little uneasy, without exactly knowing why. We put the boat on the wind, but could make no headway at all for the eddies, and I was upon the point of proposing to return to the anchorage, when, looking astern, we saw the whole horizon covered with a singular copper-coloured cloud that rose with the most amazing velocity.

'In the meantime the breeze that had headed us off fell away, and we were dead becalmed, drifting about in every direction. This state of things, however, did not last long enough to give us time to think about it. In less than a minute the storm was upon us – in less than two the sky was entirely overcast – and what with this and the driving spray, it became suddenly so dark that we could not see each other in the smack.

'Such a hurricane as then blew it is folly to attempt describing. The oldest seamen in Norway never experienced anything like it. We had let our sails go by the run before it cleverly took us; but, at the first puff, both our masts went by the board as if they had been sawed off – the mainmast taking with it my youngest brother, who had lashed himself to it for safety.

'Our boat was the lightest feather of a thing that ever sat upon water. It had a complete flush deck, with only a small hatch near the bow, and this hatch it had always been our custom to batten down when about to cross the Ström, by way of precaution against the chopping seas. But for this circumstance we should have foundered at once – for we lay entirely buried for some moments. How my elder brother escaped destruction I cannot say, for I never had an opportunity of ascertaining. For my part, as soon as I had let the foresail run, I threw myself flat on deck, with my feet against the narrow gunwale of the bow, and with my hands grasping a ring-bolt near the foot of the foremast. It was mere instinct that prompted me to do this – which was undoubtedly the very best thing I could have done – for I was too much flurried to think.

'For some moments we were completely deluged, as I say, and all this time I held my breath, and clung to the bolt. When I could stand it no longer, I raised myself upon my knees, still keeping hold with my hands, and thus got my head clear. Presently our little boat gave herself a shake, just as a dog does in coming out of the water, and thus rid herself, in some measure, of the seas. I was now trying to get the better of the stupor that had come over me, and to collect my senses, so as to see what was to be done, when I felt somebody grasp my arm. It was my elder brother, and my heart leaped for joy, for I had made sure that he was overboard; but the next moment all this joy was turned into horror, for he put his mouth close to my ear, and screamed out the word "*Moskoe-ström!*"

'No one ever will know what my feelings were at that moment. I shook from head to foot as if I had the most violent fit of the ague. I knew what he meant by that one word well enough – I knew what he wished to make me understand. With the wind that now drove us on, we were bound for the whirl of the Ström, and nothing could save us!

'You perceive that in crossing the Ström *channel*, we always went a long way up above the whirl, even in the calmest weather, and then had to wait and watch carefully for the slack – but now we were driving right upon the pool itself, and in such a hurricane as this! "To be sure," I thought, "we shall get there just about the slack – there is some little hope in that" – but in the next moment I cursed myself for being so great a fool as to dream of hope at all. I knew very well that we were doomed, had we been ten times a ninety-gun ship.

'By this time the first fury of the tempest had spent itself, or perhaps we did not feel it so much, as we scudded before it, but at all events the seas, which at first had been kept down by the wind, and lay flat and frothing, now got up into absolute mountains. A singular change, too, had come over the heavens. Around in every direction it was still as black as pitch, but nearly overhead there burst out, all at once, a circular rift of clear sky – as clear as I ever saw – and of a deep bright blue – and through it there blazed forth the full moon with a lustre that I never before knew her to wear. She lit up everything about us with the greatest distinctness – but, O God, what a scene it was to light up!

'I now made one or two attempts to speak to my brother – but in some manner which I could not understand, the din had so increased that I could not make him hear a single word, although I screamed at the top of my voice in his ear. Presently he shook his head, looking as pale as death, and held up one of his fingers, as if to say *"listen!"*

'At first I could not make out what he meant – but soon a hideous thought flashed upon me. I dragged my watch from its fob. It was not going. I glanced at its face by the moonlight, and then burst into tears as I flung it far away into the ocean. *It had run down at seven o'clock! We were behind the time of the slack, and the whirl of the Ström was in full fury!*

'When a boat is well built, properly trimmed, and not deep laden, the waves in a strong gale, when she is going large, seem always to slip from beneath her – which appears very strange to a landsman – and this is what is called *riding*, in sea phrase.

'Well, so far we had ridden the swells very cleverly; but presently a gigantic sea happened to take us right under the counter, and bore us with it as it rose up – up – as if into the sky. I would not have believed that any wave could rise so high. And then down we came with a sweep, a slide, and a plunge, that made me feel sick and dizzy, as if I was falling from some lofty mountain-top in a dream. But while we were up I had thrown a quick glance around – and that one glance was all sufficient. I saw our exact position in an instant. The Moskoe-Ström whirlpool was about a quarter of a mile dead ahead – but no more like the every-day Moskoe-Ström, than the whirl as you now see it, is like a mill-race. If I had not known where we were, and what we had to expect, I should not have recognised the place at all. As it was, I involuntarily closed my eyes in horror. The lids clenched themselves together as if in a spasm.

'It could not have been more than two minutes afterwards until we suddenly felt the waves subside, and were enveloped in foam. The boat made a sharp half turn to larboard, and then shot off in its new direction like a thunderbolt. At the same moment the roaring noise of the water was completely drowned in a kind of shrill shriek – such a sound as you might imagine given out by the waste-pipes of many thousand steam-vessels, letting off their steam all together. We were now in the belt of surf that always surrounds the whirl; and I thought, of course, that another moment would plunge us into the abyss – down which we could only see indistinctly on account of the amazing velocity with which we were borne along. The boat did not seem to sink into the water at all, but to skim like an air-bubble upon the surface of the surge. Her starboard side was next the whirl, and on the larboard arose the world of ocean we had left. It stood like a huge writhing wall between us and the horizon.

'It may appear strange, but now, when we were in the very jaws of the gulf, I felt more composed than when we were only approaching it. Having made up my mind to hope no more, I got rid of a great deal of that terror which unmanned me at first. I suppose it was despair that strung my nerves.

'It may look like boasting – but what I tell you is truth – I began to reflect how magnificent a thing it was to die in such a manner, and how foolish it was in me to think of so paltry a consideration as my own individual life, in view of so wonderful a manifestation of God's power. I do believe that I blushed with shame when this idea crossed my mind. After a little while I became possessed with the keenest curiosity about the whirl itself. I positively felt a *wish* to explore its depths, even at the sacrifice I was going to make; and my principal grief was that I should never be able to tell my old companions on shore about the mysteries I should see. These, no doubt, were singular fancies to occupy a man's mind in such extremity – and I have often thought since, that the revolutions of the boat around the pool might have rendered me a little light-headed.

'There was another circumstance which tended to restore my self-possession; and this was the cessation of the wind, which could not reach us in our present situation – for, as you saw yourself, the belt of surf is considerably lower than the general bed of the ocean, and this latter now towered above us, a high, black, mountainous ridge. If you have never been at sea in a heavy gale, you can form no idea of the confusion of mind occasioned by the wind and spray together. They blind, deafen, and strangle you, and take away all power of action or reflection. But we were now, in a great measure, rid of these annoyances – just as death-condemned felons in prison are allowed petty indulgences, forbidden them while their doom is yet uncertain.

'How often we made the circuit of the belt it is impossible to say. We careered round and round for perhaps an hour, flying rather than floating, getting gradually more and more into the middle of the surge, and then nearer and nearer to its horrible inner edge. All this time I had never let go of the ring-bolt. My brother was at the stern, holding on to a small empty water-cask, which had been securely lashed under the coop of the counter, and was the only thing on deck that had not been swept overboard when the gale first took us. As we approached the brink of the pit he let go his hold upon this, and made for the ring, from which, in the agony of his terror, he endeavoured to force my hands, as it was not large enough to afford us both a secure grasp. I never felt deeper grief than when I saw him attempt this act – although I knew he was a madman when he did it – a raving maniac through sheer fright. I did not care, however, to contest the point with him. I knew it could make no difference whether either of us held on at all; so I let him have the bolt, and went astern to the cask. This there was no great difficulty in doing; for the smack flew round steadily enough, and upon an even keel – only swaying to and fro, with the immense sweeps and swelters of the whirl. Scarcely had I secured myself in my new position, when we gave a wild lurch to starboard, and rushed headlong into the abyss. I muttered a hurried prayer to God, and thought all was over.

'As I felt the sickening sweep of the descent, I had instinctively tightened my hold upon the barrel, and closed my eyes. For some seconds I dared not open them – while I expected instant destruction, and wondered that I was not already in my death-struggles with the water. But moment after moment elapsed. I still lived. The sense of falling had ceased; and the motion of the vessel seemed much as it had been before, while in the belt of foam, with the exception that she now lay more along. I took courage and looked once again upon the scene.

'Never shall I forget the sensations of awe, horror, and admiration with which I gazed about me. The boat appeared to be hanging, as if by magic, midway down, upon the interior surface of a funnel, vast in circumference, prodigious in depth, and whose perfectly smooth sides might have been mistaken for ebony, but for the bewildering rapidity with which they spun around, and for the gleaming and ghastly radiance they shot forth, as the rays of the full moon, from that circular rift amid the clouds which I have already described, streamed in a flood of golden glory along the black walls, and far away down into the inmost recesses of the abyss.

'At first I was too much confused to observe anything accurately. The general burst of terrific grandeur was all that I beheld. When I recovered myself a little, however, my gaze fell instinctively downward. In this direction I was able to obtain an unobstructed view, from the manner in which the smack hung on the inclined surface of the pool. She was quite upon an even keel – that is to say, her deck lay in a plane parallel with that of the water – but this latter sloped at an angle of more than forty-five degrees, so that we seemed to be lying upon our beam-ends. I could not help observing, nevertheless, that I had scarcely more difficulty in maintaining my hold and footing in this situation, than if we had been upon a dead level; and this, I suppose, was owing to the speed at which we revolved.

'The rays of the moon seemed to search the very bottom of the profound gulf; but still I could make out nothing distinctly, on account of a thick mist in which everything there was enveloped, and over which there hung a magnificent rainbow, like that narrow and tottering bridge which Mussulmans say is the only pathway between Time and Eternity. This mist, or spray, was no doubt occasioned by the clashing of the great walls of the funnel, as they all met together at the bottom – but the yell that went up to the heavens from out of that mist, I dare not attempt to describe.

'Our first slide into the abyss itself, from the belt of foam above, had carried us to a great distance down the slope; but our farther descent was by no means proportionate. Round and round we swept – not with any uniform movement – but in dizzying swings and jerks, that sent us sometimes only a few hundred yards – sometimes nearly the complete circuit of the whirl. Our progress downward, at each revolution, was slow, but very perceptible.

'Looking about me upon the wide waste of liquid ebony on which we were thus borne, I perceived that our boat was not the only object in the embrace of the whirl. Both above and below us were visible fragments of vessels, large masses of building timber and trunks of trees, with many smaller articles, such as pieces of house furniture, broken boxes, barrels and staves. I have already described the unnatural curiosity which had taken the place of my original terrors. It appeared to grow upon me as I drew nearer and nearer to my dreadful doom. I now began to watch, with a strange interest, the numerous things that floated in our company. I *must* have been delirious – for I even sought *amusement* in speculating upon the relative velocities of their several descents toward the foam below. "This fir tree," I found myself at one time saying, "will certainly be the next thing that takes the awful plunge and disappears," and then I was disappointed to find that the wreck of a Dutch merchant ship overtook it and went down before. At length, after making several guesses of this nature, and being deceived in all – this fact – the fact of my invariable miscalculation, set me upon a train of reflection that made my limbs again tremble, and my heart beat heavily once more.

'It was not a new terror that thus affected me, but the dawn of a more exciting *hope*. This hope arose partly from memory and partly from present observation. I called to mind the great variety of buoyant matter that strewed the coast of Lofoden, having been absorbed and then thrown forth by the Moskoe-ström. By far the greater number of the articles were shattered in the most extraordinary way – so chafed and roughened as to have the appearance of being stuck full of splinters – but then I distinctly recollected that there were *some* of them which were not disfigured at all. Now I could not account for this difference except by supposing that the roughened fragments were the only ones which had been *completely absorbed* – that the others had entered the whirl at so late a period of the tide, or, from some reason, had descended so slowly after entering, that they did not reach the bottom before the turn of the flood came, or of the ebb as the case might be. I conceived it possible, in either instance, that they might thus be whirled up again to the level of the ocean, without undergoing the fate of those which had been drawn in more early or absorbed more rapidly. I made, also, three important observations. The first was, that as a general rule, the larger the bodies were, the more rapid their descent – the second, that, between two masses of equal extent, the one spherical, and the other *of any other shape*, the superiority in speed of descent was with the sphere – the third, that, between two masses of equal size, the one cylindrical, and the other of any other shape, the cylinder was absorbed the more slowly. Since my escape, I have had several conversations on this subject with an old schoolmaster of the district; and it was from him that I learned the use of the words "cylinder" and "sphere", He explained to me – although I have forgotten the explanation – how what I observed was, in fact, the natural consequence of the forms of the floating fragments – and showed me how it happened that a cylinder, swimming in a vortex, offered more resistance to its suction, and was drawn in with greater difficulty than an equally bulky body of any form whatever.*

'There was one startling circumstance which went a great way in enforcing these observations, and rendering me anxious to turn them to account, and this was that, at every revolution, we passed something like a barrel, or else the yard or the mast of a vessel, while many of these things, which had been on our level when I first opened my eyes upon the wonders of the whirlpool, were now high up above us, and seemed to have moved but little from their original station.

'I no longer hesitated what to do. I resolved to lash myself securely to the water cask upon which I now held, to cut it loose from the counter, and to throw myself with it into the water. I attracted my brother's attention by signs, pointed to the floating barrels that came near us, and did everything in my power to make him understand what I was about to do. I thought at length that he comprehended my design – but whether this was the case or not, he shook his head despairingly, and refused to move from his station by the ring-bolt. It was impossible to reach him; the emergency admitted of no delay; and so, with a bitter struggle, I resigned him to his fate, fastened myself to the cask by means of the lashings which secured it to the counter, and precipitated myself with it into the sea, without another moment's hesitation.

'The result was precisely what I had hoped it might be. As it is myself who now tell you this tale – as you see that I *did* escape – and as you are already in possession of the mode in which this escape was effected, and must therefore anticipate all that I have further to say – I will bring my story quickly to conclusion. It might have been an hour, or thereabout,

* See Archimedes,[13] *De Incidentibus in Fluido*, lib. 2

after my quitting the smack, when, having descended to a vast distance beneath me, it made three or four wild gyrations in rapid succession, and, bearing my loved brother with it, plunged headlong, at once and for ever, into the chaos of foam below. The barrel to which I was attached sunk very little farther than half the distance between the bottom of the gulf and the spot at which I leaped overboard, before a great change took place in the character of the whirlpool. The slope of the sides of the vast funnel became momentarily less and less steep, the gyrations of the whirl grew gradually less and less violent. By degrees, the froth and the rainbow disappeared, and the bottom of the gulf seemed slowly to uprise. The sky was clear, the winds had gone down, and the full moon was setting radiantly in the west, when I found myself on the surface of the ocean, in full view of the shores of Lofoden, and above the spot where the pool of the Moskoe-ström *had been*. It was the hour of the slack – but the sea still heaved in mountainous waves from the effects of the hurricane. I was borne violently into the channel of the Ström, and in a few minutes, was hurried down the coast into the "grounds" of the fishermen. A boat picked me up – exhausted from fatigue – and (now that the danger was removed) – speechless from the memory of its horror. Those who drew me on board were my old mates and daily companions – but they knew me no more than they would have known a traveller from the spirit-land. My hair, which had been raven-black the day before, was as white as you see it now. They say, too, that the whole expression of my countenance had changed. I told them my story – they did not believe it. I now tell it to *you* – and I can scarcely expect you to put more faith in it than did the merry fishermen of Lofoden.'

The Murders in the Rue Morgue

What song the Syrens sang, or what name Achilles assumed when
he hid himself among women, although puzzling questions, are
not beyond *all* conjecture.[1]

THE MENTAL FEATURES discoursed of as the analytical, are, in
themselves, but little susceptible of analysis. We appreciate them only
in their effects. We know of them, among other things, that they are
always to their possessor, when inordinately possessed, a source of the
liveliest enjoyment. As the strong man exults in his physical ability,
delighting in such exercises as call his muscles into action, so glories the
analyst in that moral activity which *disentangles*. He derives pleasure
from even the most trivial occupations bringing his talent into play. He
is fond of enigmas, of conundrums, of hieroglyphics; exhibiting in his
solutions of each a degree of acumen which appears to the ordinary
apprehension preternatural. His results, brought about by the very soul
and essence of method, have, in truth, the whole air of intuition.

The faculty of re-solution is possibly much invigorated by mathematical study, and especially by that highest branch of it which,
unjustly, and merely on account of its retrograde operations, has been
called, as if *par excellence*, analysis. Yet to calculate is not in itself to
analyse. A chess-player, for example, does the one, without effort at the
other. It follows that the game of chess, in its effects upon mental
character, is greatly misunderstood. I am not now writing a treatise, but
simply prefacing a somewhat peculiar narrative by observations very
much at random; I will, therefore, take occasion to assert that the
higher powers of the reflective intellect are more decidedly and more
usefully tasked by the unostentatious game of draughts than by all the
elaborate frivolity of chess. In this latter, where the pieces have
different and bizarre motions, with various and variable values, what is
only complex, is mistaken (a not unusual error) for what is profound.
The *attention* is here called powerfully into play. If it flag for an instant,
an oversight is committed, resulting in injury or defeat. The possible
moves being not only manifold, but involute, the chances of such
oversights are multiplied; and in nine cases out of ten, it is the more
concentrative rather than the more acute player who conquers. In
draughts, on the contrary, where the moves are *unique* and have but
little variation, the probabilities of inadvertence are diminished,
and the mere attention being left comparatively unemployed, what

advantages are obtained by either party are obtained by superior acumen. To be less abstract – Let us suppose a game of draughts where the pieces are reduced to four kings, and where, of course, no oversight is to be expected. It is obvious that here the victory can be decided (the players being at all equal) only by some *recherché* movement, the result of some strong exertion of the intellect. Deprived of ordinary resources, the analyst throws himself into the spirit of his opponent, identifies himself therewith, and not unfrequently sees thus, at a glance, the sole methods (sometimes indeed absurdly simple ones) by which he may seduce into error or hurry into miscalculation.

Whist has long been noted for its influence upon what is termed the calculating power; and men of the highest order of intellect have been known to take an apparently unaccountable delight in it, while eschewing chess as frivolous. Beyond doubt there is nothing of a similar nature so greatly tasking the faculty of analysis. The best chess-player in Christendom *may* be little more than the best player of chess; but proficiency in whist implies capacity for success in all these more important undertakings where mind struggles with mind. When I say proficiency, I mean that perfection in the game which includes a comprehension of *all* the sources whence legitimate advantage may be derived. These are not only manifold, but multiform, and lie frequently among recesses of thought altogether inaccessible to the ordinary understanding. To observe attentively is to remember distinctly; and, so far, the concentrative chess-player will do very well at whist; while the rules of Hoyle[2] (themselves based upon the mere mechanism of the game) are sufficiently and generally comprehensible. Thus to have a retentive memory, and to proceed by 'the book,' are points commonly regarded as the sum total of good playing. But it is in matters beyond the limits of mere rule that the skill of the analyst is evinced. He makes, in silence, a host of observations and inferences. So, perhaps, do his companions; and the difference in the extent of the information obtained, lies not so much in the validity of the inference as in the quality of the observation. The necessary knowledge is that of *what* to observe. Our player confines himself not at all; nor, because the game is the object, does he reject deductions from things external to the game. He examines the countenance of his partner, comparing it carefully with that of each of his opponents. He considers the mode of assorting the cards in each hand; often counting trump by trump, and honour by honour, through the glances bestowed by their holders upon each. He notes every variation of face as the play progresses, gathering a fund of thought from the differences in the expression of certainty, of surprise, of triumph, or chagrin. From the manner of gathering up a trick he judges whether the person taking it can make another in the suit. He recognises what is played through feint, by the air with which it is thrown upon the table. A casual or inadvertent word; the accidental dropping or turning of a card, with the accompanying anxiety or carelessness in regard to its concealment; the counting of the tricks, with the order of their arrangement; embarrassment, hesitation, eagerness or trepidation – all afford, to his apparently intuitive perception, indications of the true state of affairs. The first two or three rounds having been played, he is in full possession of the contents of each hand, and thenceforward puts down his cards with as absolute a precision of purpose as if the rest of the party had turned outward the faces of their own.

The analytical power should not be confounded with simple ingenuity; for while the analyst is necessarily ingenious, the ingenious man is often remarkably incapable of analysis. The constructive or combining power, by which ingenuity is usually manifested, and to which the phrenologists (I believe erroneously) have assigned a separate organ, supposing it a primitive faculty, has been so frequently seen in those whose intellect bordered otherwise upon idiotcy, as to have attracted general observation among writers on morals. Between ingenuity and the analytic ability there exists a difference far greater, indeed, than that between the fancy and the imagination, but of a character very strictly analogous. It will be found, in fact, that the ingenious are always fanciful, and the *truly* imaginative never otherwise than analytic.

The narrative which follows will appear to the reader somewhat in the light of a commentary upon the propositions just advanced.

Residing in Paris during the spring and part of the summer of 18—, I there became acquainted with a Monsieur C. Auguste Dupin. This young gentleman was of an excellent – indeed of an illustrious family, but, by a variety of untoward events, had been reduced to such poverty that the energy of his character succumbed beneath it, and he ceased to bestir himself in the world, or to care for the retrieval of his fortunes. By courtesy of his creditors there still remained in his possession a small remnant of his patrimony; and, upon the income arising from this, he managed, by means of a rigorous economy, to procure the necessaries of life, without troubling himself about its superfluities. Books, indeed, were his sole luxuries, and in Paris these are easily obtained.

Our first meeting was at an obscure library in the Rue Montmartre, where the accident of our both being in search of the same very rare and very remarkable volume, brought us into closer communion. We saw each other again and again. I was deeply interested in the little family history which he detailed to me with all that candour which a Frenchman indulges whenever mere self is the theme. I was astonished, too, at the vast extent of his reading; and, above all, I felt my soul enkindled within me by the wild fervour, and the vivid freshness of his imagination. Seeking in Paris the objects I then sought, I felt that the society of such a man would be to me a treasure beyond price; and this feeling I frankly confided to him. It was at length arranged that we should live together during my stay in the city; and as my worldly circumstances were somewhat less embarrassed than his own, I was permitted to be at the expense of renting, and furnishing in a style which suited the rather fantastic gloom of our common temper, a time-eaten and grotesque[3] mansion, long deserted through superstitions into which we did not inquire, and tottering to its fall in a retired and desolate portion of the Faubourg St Germain.

Had the routine of our life at this place been known to the world, we should have been regarded as madmen – although, perhaps, as madmen of a harmless nature. Our seclusion was perfect. We admitted no visitors. Indeed the locality of our retirement had been carefully kept a secret from my own former associates; and it had been many years since Dupin had ceased to know or be known in Paris. We existed within ourselves alone.

It was a freak of fancy in my friend (for what else shall I call it?) to be enamoured of the night for her own sake; and into this *bizarrerie*,[4] as into all his others, I quietly fell, giving myself up to his wild whims with a perfect abandon. The sable divinity would not herself dwell with us always; but we could counterfeit her presence. At the first dawn of the morning we closed all the massy shutters of our old building; lighted a couple of tapers which, strongly perfumed, threw out only the ghastliest and feeblest of rays. By the aid of these we then busied our souls in dreams – reading, writing, or conversing, until warned by the clock of the advent of the true Darkness. Then we sallied forth into the streets, arm in arm, continuing the topics of the day, or roaming far and wide until a late hour, seeking, amid the wild lights and shadows of the populous city, that infinity of mental excitement which quiet observation can afford.

At such times I could not helping remarking and admiring (although from his rich ideality[5] I had been prepared to expect it) a peculiar analytic ability in Dupin. He seemed, too, to take an eager delight in its exercise – if not exactly in its display – and did not hesitate to confess the pleasure thus derived. He boasted to me, with a low chuckling laugh, that most men, in respect to himself, wore windows in their bosoms, and was wont to follow up such assertions by direct and very startling proofs of his intimate knowledge of my own. His manner at these moments was frigid and abstract; his eyes were vacant in expression; while his voice, usually a rich tenor, rose into a treble which would have sounded petulantly but for the deliberateness and entire distinctness of the enunciation. Observing him in these moods, I often dwelt meditatively upon the old philosophy of the Bi-Part Soul,[6] and amused myself with the fancy of a double Dupin – the creative and the resolvent.

Let it not be supposed, from what I have just said, that I am detailing any mystery, or penning any romance. What I have described in the Frenchman, was merely the result of an excited, or perhaps of a diseased intelligence. But of the character of his remarks at the periods in question an example will best convey the idea.

We were strolling one night down a long dirty street, in the vicinity of the Palais Royal. Being both, apparently, occupied with thought, neither of us had spoken a syllable for fifteen minutes at least. All at once Dupin broke forth with these words –

'He is a very little fellow, that's true, and would do better for the *Théâtre des Variétés.*'

'There can be no doubt of that,' I replied unwittingly, and not at first observing (so much had I been absorbed in reflection) the extraordinary manner in which the speaker had chimed in with my meditations. In an instant afterward I recollected myself, and my astonishment was profound.

'Dupin,' said I, gravely, 'this is beyond my comprehension. I do not hesitate to say that I am amazed, and can scarcely credit my senses. How was it possible you should know I was thinking of –?' Here I paused, to ascertain beyond a doubt whether he really knew of whom I thought.

'Of Chantilly,' said he; 'why do you pause? You were remarking to yourself that his diminutive figure unfitted him for tragedy.'

This was precisely what had formed the subject of my reflections. Chantilly was a quondam cobbler of the Rue St Denis, who, becoming stage-mad, had attempted the *rôle* of Xerxes,[7] in Crébillon's tragedy so called, and been notoriously pasquinaded for his pains.

'Tell me, for Heaven's sake,' I exclaimed, 'the method – if method there is – by which you have been enabled to fathom my soul in this matter.' In fact I was even more startled than I would have been willing to express.

'It was the fruiterer,' replied my friend, 'who brought you to the conclusion that the mender of soles was not of sufficient height for Xerxes *et id genus omne.*'[8]

'The fruiterer! – you astonish me – I know no fruiterer whomsoever.'

'The man who ran up against you as we entered the street – it may have been fifteen minutes ago.'

I now remembered that, in fact, a fruiterer, carrying upon his head a large basket of apples, had nearly thrown me down, by accident, as we passed from the Rue C— into the thoroughfare where we stood; but what this had to do with Chantilly I could not possibly understand.

There was not a particle of *charlatanerie*[9] about Dupin.

'I will explain,' he said, 'and that you may comprehend all clearly, we will first retrace the course of your meditations, from the moment in which I spoke to you until that of the *rencontre* with the fruiterer in question. The larger links of the chain run thus – Chantilly, Orion,[10] Dr Nichols,[11] Epicurus,[12] Stereotomy,[13] the street stones, the fruiterer.'

There are few persons who have not, at some period of their lives, amused themselves in retracing the steps by which particular conclusions of their own minds have been attained. The occupation is often full of interest; and he who attempts it for the first time is astonished by the apparently illimitable distance and incoherence between the starting-point and the goal. What, then, must have been my amazement when I heard the Frenchman speak what he had just spoken, and when I could not help acknowledging that he had spoken the truth! He continued –

'We had been talking of horses, if I remember aright, just before leaving the Rue C—. This was the last subject we discussed. As we crossed into the street, a fruiterer, with a large basket upon his head, brushing quickly past us, thrust you upon a pile of paving-stones collected at a spot where the causeway is undergoing repair. You stepped upon one of the loose fragments, slipped, slightly strained your ankle, appeared vexed or sulky, muttered a few words, turned to look at the pile, and then proceeded in silence. I was not particularly attentive to what you did; but observation has become with me, of late, a species of necessity.

'You kept your eyes upon the ground – glancing, with a petulant expression, at the holes and ruts in the pavement (so that I saw you were still thinking of the stones), until we reached the little alley called Lamartine, which has been paved, by way of experiment, with the overlapping and riveted blocks. Here your countenance brightened up, and, perceiving your lips move, I could not doubt that you murmured the word "stereotomy", a term very affectedly applied to this species of pavement. I knew that you could not say to yourself "stereotomy" without being brought to think of atomics, and thus of the theories of Epicurus; and since, when we discussed this subject not very long ago, I

mentioned to you how singularly, yet with how little notice, the vague
guesses of that noble Greek had met with confirmation in the late
nebular cosmogony, I felt that you could not avoid casting your eyes
upward to the great nebula in Orion, and I certainly expected that you
would do so. You did look up; and I was now assured that I had
correctly followed your steps. But in that bitter tirade upon Chantilly,
which appeared in yesterday's *Musée*, the satirist, making some
disgraceful allusions to the cobbler's change of name upon assuming
the buskin, quoted a Latin line about which we have often conversed. I
mean the line

Perdidit antiquum litera prima sonum.[14]

I had told you that this was in reference to Orion, formerly written
Urion; and, from certain pungencies connected with this explanation, I
was aware that you could not have forgotten it. It was clear, therefore,
that you would not fail to combine the two ideas of Orion and
Chantilly. That you did combine them I saw by the character of the
smile which passed over your lips. You thought of the poor cobbler's
immolation. So far, you had been stooping in your gait; but now I saw
you draw yourself up to your full height. I was then sure that you
reflected upon the diminutive figure of Chantilly. At this point I
interrupted your meditations to remark that as, in fact, he *was* a very
little fellow, that Chantilly, he would do better at the *Théâtre des
Variétés.*'

Not long after this, we were looking over an evening edition of the
Gazette des Tribunaux when the following paragraphs arrested our
attention:

'EXTRAORDINARY MURDERS – This morning, about three o'clock,
the inhabitants of the Quartier St Roch were aroused from sleep by a
succession of terrific shrieks, issuing, apparently, from the fourth story
of a house in the Rue Morgue, known to be in the sole occupancy of
one Madame L'Espanaye, and her daughter, Mademoiselle Camille
L'Espanaye. After some delay, occasioned by a fruitless attempt to
procure admission in the usual manner, the gateway was broken in with
a crowbar, and eight or ten of the neighbours entered, accompanied by
two gendarmes. By this time the cries had ceased; but, as the party
rushed up the first flight of stairs, two or more rough voices, in angry
contention, were distinguished, and seemed to proceed from the upper
part of the house. As the second landing was reached, these sounds,
also, had ceased, and everything remained perfectly quiet. The party
spread themselves, and hurried from room to room. Upon arriving at a
large back chamber in the fourth story (the door of which, being found

locked, with the key inside, was forced open), a spectacle presented itself which struck every one present not less with horror than with astonishment.

'The apartment was in the wildest disorder – the furniture broken and thrown about in all directions. There was only one bedstead; and from this the bed had been removed, and thrown into the middle of the floor. On a chair lay a razor, besmeared with blood. On the hearth were two or three long and thick tresses of grey human hair, also dabbled in blood, and seeming to have been pulled out by the roots. Upon the floor were found four napoleons, an earring of topaz, three large silver spoons, three smaller of *métal d'Alger*,[15] and two bags, containing nearly four thousand francs in gold. The drawers of a bureau, which stood in one corner, were open, and had been, apparently, rifled, although many articles still remained in them A small iron safe was discovered under the *bed* (not under the bedstead). It was open, with a key still in the door. It had no contents beyond a few old letters, and other papers of little consequence.

'Of Madame L'Espanaye no traces were here seen; but an unusual quantity of soot being observed in the fireplace, a search was made in the chimney, and (horrible to relate!) the corpse of the daughter, head downward, was dragged therefrom; it having been thus forced up the narrow aperture for a considerable distance. The body was quite warm. Upon examining it, many excoriations were perceived, no doubt occasioned by the violence with which it had been thrust up and disengaged. Upon the face were many severe scratches, and, upon the throat, dark bruises, and deep indentations of finger nails, as if the deceased had been throttled to death.

'After a thorough investigation of every portion of the house, without further discovery, the party made its way into a small paved yard in the rear of the building, where lay the corpse of the old lady, with her throat so entirely cut that, upon an attempt to raise her, the head fell off. The body, as well as the head, was fearfully mutilated – the former so much so as scarcely to retain any semblance of humanity.

'To this horrible mystery there is not as yet, we believe, the slightest clew.'

The next day's paper had these additional particulars:

'The Tragedy in the Rue Morgue – Many individuals have been examined in relation to this most extraordinary and frightful affair' [the word '*affaire*' has not yet in France that levity of import which it conveys with us], 'but nothing whatever has transpired to throw light upon it. We give below all the material testimony elicited.

'*Pauline Dubourg*, laundress, deposes that she has known both the deceased for three years, having washed for them during that period. The old lady and her daughter seemed on good terms – very affectionate towards each other. They were excellent pay. Could not speak in regard to their mode or means of living. Believed that Madame L. told fortunes for a living. Was reputed to have money put by. Never met any persons in the house when she called for the clothes or took them home. Was sure that they had no servant in employ. There appeared to be no furniture in any part of the building, except in the fourth story.

'*Pierre Moreau*, tobacconist, deposes that he has been in the habit of selling small quantities of tobacco and snuff to Madame L'Espanaye for nearly four years. Was born in the neighbourhood, and has always resided there. The deceased and her daughter had occupied the house in which the corpses were found for more than six years. It was formerly occupied by a jeweller, who under-let the upper rooms to various persons. The house was the property of Madame L. She became dissatisfied with the abuse of the premises by her tenant, and moved into them herself, refusing to let any portion. The old lady was childish. Witness had seen the daughter some five or six times during the six years. The two lived an exceedingly retired life – were reputed to have money. Had heard it said among the neighbours that Madame L. told fortunes – did not believe it. Had never seen any person enter the door except the old lady and her daughter, a porter once or twice, and a physician some eight or ten times.

'Many other persons, neighbours, gave evidence to the same effect. No one was spoken of as frequenting the house. It was not known whether there were any living connections of Madame L. and her daughter. The shutters of the front windows were seldom opened. Those in the rear were always closed, with the exception of the large back room, fourth story. The house was a good house – not very old.

'*Isidore Mustè*, gendarme, deposes that he was called to the house about three o'clock in the morning, and found some twenty or thirty persons at the gateway, endeavouring to gain admittance. Forced it open, at length, with a bayonet – not with a crowbar. Had but little difficulty in getting it open, on account of its being a double or folding gate, and bolted neither at bottom nor top. The shrieks were continued until the gate was forced – and then suddenly ceased. They seemed to be screams of some person (or persons) in great agony – were loud and drawn out, not short and quick. Witness led the way upstairs. Upon reaching the first landing, heard two voices in loud and angry contention – the one a gruff voice, the other much shriller – a very strange voice. Could distinguish some words of the former, which was that of a Frenchman. Was positive that it was not a woman's voice. Could distinguish the words "*sacré*" and "*diable.*" The shrill voice was that of a foreigner. Could not be sure whether it was the voice of a man or of a woman. Could not make out what was said, but believed the language to be Spanish. The state of the room and of the bodies was described by this witness as we described them yesterday.

'*Henri Duval*, a neighbour, and by trade a silversmith, deposes that he was one of the party who first entered the house. Corroborates the testimony of Mustè in general. As soon as they forced an entrance, they reclosed the door, to keep out the crowd, which collected very fast, notwithstanding the lateness of the hour. The shrill voice, this witness thinks, was that of an Italian. Was certain it was not French. Could not be sure that it was a man's voice. It might have been a woman's. Was not acquainted with the Italian language. Could not distinguish the words, but was convinced by the intonation that the speaker was an Italian. Knew Madame L. and her daughter. Had conversed with both frequently. Was sure that the shrill voice was not that of either of the deceased.

'— *Odenheimer*, restaurateur. This witness volunteered his testimony. Not speaking French, was examined through an interpreter. Is a native of Amsterdam. Was passing the house at the time of the shrieks. They lasted for several minutes – probably ten. They were long and loud – very awful and distressing. Was one of those who entered the building. Corroborated the previous evidence in every respect but one. Was sure that the shrill voice was that of a man – of a Frenchman. Could not distinguish the words uttered. They were loud and quick – unequal – spoken apparently in fear as well as in anger. The voice was harsh – not so much shrill as harsh. Could not call it a shrill voice. The gruff voice said repeatedly "*sacré*," "*diable*", and once "*mon Dieu*".

'*Jules Mignaud*, banker, of the firm of Mignaud et Fils, Rue Deloraine. Is the elder Mignaud. Madame L'Espanaye had some property. Had opened an account with his banking house in the spring of the year — (eight years previously). Made frequent deposits in small sums. Had checked for nothing until the third day before her death, when she took out in person the sum of 4000 francs. This sum was paid in gold, and a clerk sent home with the money.

'*Adolphe Le Bon*, clerk to Mignaud et Fils, deposes that on the day in question, about noon, he accompanied Madame L'Espanaye to her residence with the 4000 francs put up in two bags. Upon the door being opened, Mademoiselle L. appeared and took from his hands one of the bags, while the old lady relieved him of the other. He then bowed and departed. Did not see any person in the street at the time. It is a by-street – very lonely.

'*William Bird*, tailor, deposes that he was one of the party who entered the house. Is an Englishman. Has lived in Paris two years. Was one of the first to ascend the stairs. Heard the voices in contention. The gruff voice was that of a Frenchman. Could make out several words, but cannot now remember all. Heard distinctly "*sacré*" and "*mon Dieu*." There was a sound at the moment as if of several persons struggling – a scraping and scuffling sound. The shrill voice was very loud – louder than the gruff one. Is sure that it was not the voice of an Englishman. Appeared to be that of a German. Might have been a woman's voice. Does not understand German.

'Four of the above-named witnesses, being recalled, deposed that the door of the chamber in which was found the body of Mademoiselle L. was locked on the inside when the party reached it. Everything was perfectly silent – no groans or noises of any kind. Upon forcing the door no person was seen. The windows, both of the back and front room, were down and firmly fastened from within. A door between the two rooms was closed, but not locked. The door leading from the front room into the passage was locked, with the key on the inside. A small room in the front of the house, on the fourth story, at the head of the passage, was open, the door being ajar. This room was crowded with old beds, boxes, and so forth. These were carefully removed and searched. There was not an inch of any portion of the house which was not carefully searched. Sweeps were sent up and down the chimneys. The house was a four-story one, with garrets (*mansardes*). A trap-door on the roof was nailed down very securely – did not appear to have been opened for years. The time elapsing between the hearing of the voices in contention and the breaking open of the room door, was variously stated by the witnesses. Some made it as short as three minutes – some as long as five. The door was opened with difficulty.

'*Alfonzo Garcio*, undertaker, deposes that he resides in the Rue Morgue. Is a native of Spain. Was one of the party who entered the house. Did not proceed upstairs. Is nervous, and was apprehensive of the consequences of agitation. Heard the voices in contention. The gruff voice was that of a Frenchman. Could not distinguish what was said. The shrill voice was that of an Englishman – is sure of this. Does not understand the English language, but judges by the intonation.

'*Alberto Montani*, confectioner, deposes that he was among the first to ascend the stairs. Heard the voices in question. The gruff voice was that of a Frenchman. Distinguished several words. The speaker appeared to be expostulating. Could not make out the words of the shrill voice. Spoke quick and unevenly. Thinks it the voice of a Russian. Corroborates the general testimony. Is an Italian. Never conversed with a native of Russia.

'Several witnesses, recalled, here testified that the chimneys of all the rooms on the fourth story were too narrow to admit the passage of a human being. By "sweeps" were meant cylindrical sweeping-brushes, such as are employed by those who clean chimneys. These brushes were passed up and down every flue in the house. There is no back passage by which any one could have descended while the party proceeded upstairs. The body of Mademoiselle L'Espanaye was so firmly wedged in the chimney that it could not be got down until four or five of the party united their strength.

'*Paul Dumas*, physician, deposes that he was called to view the bodies about daybreak. They were both then lying on the sacking of the bedstead in the chamber where Mademoiselle L. was found. The corpse of the young lady was much bruised and excoriated. The fact that it had been thrust up the chimney would sufficiently account for these appearances. The throat was greatly chafed. There were several deep scratches just below the chin, together with a series of livid spots which were evidently the impression of fingers. The face was fearfully discoloured, and the eyeballs protruded. The tongue had been partially bitten through. A large bruise was discovered upon the pit of the stomach, produced, apparently, by the pressure of a knee. In the opinion of M. Dumas, Mademoiselle L'Espanaye had been throttled to death by some person or persons unknown. The corpse of the mother was horribly mutilated. All the bones of the right leg and arm were more or less shattered. The left tibia much splintered, as well as all the ribs of the left side. Whole body dreadfully bruised and discoloured. It was not possible to say how the injuries had been inflicted. A heavy club of wood, or a broad bar of iron – a chair – any large, heavy, and obtuse weapon would have produced such results, if wielded by the hands of a very powerful man. No woman could have inflicted the blows with any weapon. The head of the deceased, when seen by witness, was entirely separated from the body, and was also greatly shattered. The throat had evidently been cut with some very sharp instrument – probably with a razor.

'*Alexandre Etienne*, surgeon, was called with M. Dumas, to view the bodies. Corroborated the testimony, and the opinions of M. Dumas.

'Nothing further of importance was elicited, although several other persons were examined. A murder so mysterious, and so perplexing in all its particulars, was never before committed in Paris – if indeed a murder has been committed at all. The police are entirely at fault – an unusual occurrence in affairs of this nature. There is not, however, the shadow of a clew apparent.'

The evening edition of the paper stated that the greatest excitement still continued in the Quartier St Roch – that the premises in question had been carefully re-searched, and fresh examinations of witnesses instituted, but all to no purpose. A postscript, however, mentioned that Adolphe Le Bon had been arrested and imprisoned – although nothing appeared to criminate him, beyond the facts already detailed.

Dupin seemed singularly interested in the progress of this affair – at least so I judged from his manner, for he made no comments. It was only after the announcement that Le Bon had been imprisoned, that he asked me my opinion respecting the murders.

I could merely agree with all Paris in considering them an insoluble mystery. I saw no means by which it would be possible to trace the murderer.

'We must not judge of the means,' said Dupin, 'by this shell of an examination. The Parisian police, so much extolled for acumen, are cunning, but no more. There is no method in their proceedings, beyond the method of the moment. They make a vast parade of measures; but, not unfrequently, these are so ill adapted to the objects proposed, as to put us in mind of Monsieur Jourdain's calling for his *robe-de-chambre – pour mieux entendre la musique*. The results attained by them are not unfrequently surprising, but, for the most part, are brought about by simple diligence and activity. When these qualities are unavailing, their schemes fail. Vidocq,[16] for example, was a good guesser, and a persevering man. But, without educated thought, he erred continually by the very intensity of his investigations. He impaired his vision by holding the object too close. He might see, perhaps, one or two points with unusual clearness, but in so doing, he, necessarily, lost sight of the matter as a whole. Thus there is such a thing as being too profound. Truth is not always in a well. In fact, as regards the more important knowledge, I do believe that she is invariably superficial. The depth lies in the valleys where we seek her, and not upon the mountain-top where she is found. The modes and sources of this kind of error are well typified in the contemplation of the heavenly bodies. To look at a star by glances – to view it in a sidelong way, by turning toward it the exterior portions of the retina (more susceptible of feeble impressions of light than the interior), is to behold the star distinctly – is to have the best appreciation of its lustre – a lustre which grows dim just in proportion as we turn our vision *fully* upon it. A greater number of rays actually fall upon the eye in the latter case, but, in the former, there is the more refined capacity for comprehension. By undue profundity we perplex and enfeeble thought; and it is possible to make even Venus herself vanish from the firmament by a scrutiny too sustained, too concentrated, or too direct.

'As for these murders, let us enter into some examinations for ourselves, before we make up an opinion respecting them. An inquiry will afford us amusement' [I thought this an odd term, so applied, but said nothing], 'and, besides, Le Bon once rendered me a service for which I am not ungrateful. We will go and see the premises with our own eyes. I know G—, the Prefect of Police, and shall have no difficulty in obtaining the necessary permission.'

The permission was obtained, and we proceeded at once to the Rue Morgue. This is one of those miserable thoroughfares which intervene between the Rue Richelieu and the Rue St Roch. It was late in the afternoon when we reached it; as this quarter is at a great distance from that in which we resided. The house was readily found; for there were still many persons gazing up at the closed shutters, with an objectless curiosity, from the opposite side of the way. It was an ordinary Parisian house, with a gateway, on one side of which was a glazed watch-box, with a sliding panel in the window, indicating a *loge de concierge*.[17] Before going in we walked up the street, turned down an alley, and then, again turning, passed in the rear of the building – Dupin, meanwhile, examining the whole neighbourhood, as well as the house, with a minuteness of attention for which I could see no possible object.

Retracing our steps, we came again to the front of the dwelling, rang, and having shown our credentials, were admitted by the agents in charge. We went upstairs – into the chamber where the body of Mademoiselle L'Espanaye had been found, and where both the deceased still lay. The disorders of the room had, as usual, been suffered to exist. I saw nothing beyond what had been stated in the *Gazette des Tribunaux*. Dupin scrutinised everything – not excepting the bodies of the victims. We then went into the other rooms, and into the yard; a gendarme accompanying us throughout. The examination occupied us until dark, when we took our departure. On our way home my companion stepped in for a moment at the office of one of the daily papers.

I have said that the whims of my friend were manifold, and that *Je les ménagais*[18] – for this phrase there is no English equivalent. It was his humour, now, to decline all conversation on the subject of the murders, until about noon the next day. He then asked me, suddenly, if I had observed anything *peculiar* at the scene of the atrocity.

There was something in his manner of emphasising the word 'peculiar,' which caused me to shudder, without knowing why.

'No, nothing *peculiar*,' I said; 'nothing more, at least, than we both saw stated in the paper.'

'The *Gazette*,' he replied, 'has not entered, I fear, into the unusual horror of the thing. But dismiss the idle opinions of this print. It appears to me that this mystery is considered insoluble, for the very reason which should cause it to be regarded as easy of solution – I mean for the *outré* [19] character of its features. The police are confounded by the seeming absence of motive – not for the murder itself – but for the atrocity of the murder. They are puzzled, too, by the seeming impossibility of reconciling the voices heard in contention, with the facts that no one was discovered upstairs but the assassinated Mademoiselle L'Espanaye, and that there were no means of egress without the notice of the party ascending. The wild disorder of the room; the corpse thrust, with the head downward, up the chimney; the frightful mutilation of the body of the old lady; these considerations, with those just mentioned, and others which I need not mention, have sufficed to paralyse the powers, by putting completely at fault the boasted acumen of the government agents. They have fallen into the gross but common error of confounding the unusual with the abstruse. But it is by these deviations from the plane of the ordinary, that reason feels its way, if at all, in its search for the true. In investigations such as we are now pursuing, it should not be so much asked "what has occurred?" as "what has occurred that has never occurred before?" In fact, the facility with which I shall arrive, or have arrived, at the solution of this mystery, is in the direct ratio of its apparent insolubility in the eyes of the police.'

I stared at the speaker in mute astonishment.

'I am now awaiting,' continued he, looking toward the door of our apartment – 'I am now awaiting a person who, although perhaps not the perpetrator of these butcheries, must have been in some measure implicated in their perpetration. Of the worst portion of the crimes committed, it is probable that he is innocent. I hope that I am right in this supposition; for upon it I build my expectation of reading the entire riddle. I look for the man here – in this room – every moment. It is true that he may not arrive; but the probability is that he will. Should he come, it will be necessary to detain him. Here are pistols; and we both know how to use them when occasion demands their use.'

I took the pistols, scarcely knowing what I did, or believing what I heard, while Dupin went on, very much as if in a soliloquy. I have already spoken of his abstract manner at such times. His discourse was addressed to myself; but his voice, although by no means loud, had that intonation which is commonly employed in speaking to some one at a great distance. His eyes, vacant in expression, regarded only the wall.

'That the voices heard in contention,' he said, 'by the party upon the stairs, were not the voices of the women themselves, was fully proved by the evidence. This relieves us of all doubt upon the question whether the old lady could have first destroyed the daughter, and afterward have committed suicide. I speak of this point chiefly for the sake of method; for the strength of Madame L'Espanaye would have been utterly unequal to the task of thrusting her daughter's corpse up the chimney as it was found; and the nature of the wounds upon her own person entirely precludes the idea of self-destruction. Murder, then, has been committed by some third party; and the voices of this third party were those heard in contention. Let me now advert – not to the whole testimony respecting these voices – but to what was *peculiar* in that testimony. Did you observe anything peculiar about it?'

I remarked that, while all the witnesses agreed in supposing the gruff voice to be that of a Frenchman, there was much disagreement in regard to the shrill, or, as one individual termed it, the harsh voice.

'That was the evidence itself,' said Dupin, 'but it was not the peculiarity of the evidence. You have observed nothing distinctive. Yet there *was* something to be observed. The witnesses, as you remark, agreed about the gruff voice; they were here unanimous. But in regard to the shrill voice, the peculiarity is – not that they disagreed – but that, while an Italian, an Englishman, a Spaniard, a Hollander, and a Frenchman attempted to describe it, each one spoke of it as that *of a foreigner*. Each is sure that it was not the voice of one of his own countrymen. Each likens it – not to the voice of an individual of any nation with whose language he is conversant – but the converse. The Frenchman supposes it the voice of a Spaniard, and "might have distinguished some words *had he been acquainted with the Spanish*." The Dutchman maintains it to have been that of a Frenchman; but we find it stated that, "*not understanding French, this witness was examined through an interpreter*." The Englishman thinks it the voice of a German, and "*does not understand German*." The Spaniard "is sure" that it was that of an Englishman, but "judges by the intonation" altogether, "*as he has no knowledge of the English*." The Italian believes it the voice of a Russian, but "*has never conversed with a native of Russia*." A second Frenchman differs, moreover, with the first, and is positive that the voice was that of an Italian; but, *not being cognisant of that tongue*, is, like the Spaniard, "convinced by the intonation." Now, how strangely unusual must that voice have really been, about which such testimony as this *could* have been elicited! – in whose *tones*, even, denizens of the five great divisions of Europe could recognise nothing familiar! You will say that it might have been the voice of an Asiatic – of an African. Neither Asiatics nor Africans abound in Paris; but, without denying the inference, I will now merely call your attention to three points. The voice is termed by one witness "harsh rather than shrill." It is represented by two others to have been "quick and *unequal*." No words – no sounds resembling words – were by any witness mentioned as distinguishable.

'I know not,' continued Dupin, 'what impression I may have made, so far, upon your own understanding; but I do not hesitate to say that legitimate deductions even from this portion of the testimony – the portion respecting the gruff and shrill voices – are in themselves sufficient to engender a suspicion which should give direction to all further progress in the investigation of the mystery. I said "legitimate deductions"; but my meaning is not thus fully expressed. I designed to imply that the deductions are the *sole* proper ones, and that the suspicion arises *inevitably* from them as the single result. What the suspicion is, however, I will not say just yet. I merely wish you to bear in mind that, with myself, it was sufficiently forcible to give a definite form – a certain tendency – to my inquiries in the chamber.

'Let us now transport ourselves, in fancy, to this chamber. What shall we first seek here? The means of egress employed by the murderers. It is not too much to say that neither of us believe in preternatural events. Madame and Mademoiselle L'Espanaye were not destroyed by spirits. The doers of the deed were material, and escaped materially. Then how? Fortunately, there is but one mode of reasoning upon the point, and that mode *must* lead us to a definite decision. Let us examine, each by each, the possible means of egress. It is clear that the assassins were in the room where Mademoiselle L'Espanaye was found, or at least in the room adjoining, when the party ascended the stairs. It is, then, only from these two apartments that we have to seek issues. The police have laid bare the floors, the ceilings, and the masonry of the walls, in every direction. No *secret* issues could have escaped their vigilance. But, not trusting to *their* eyes, I examined with my own. There were, then, *no* secret issues. Both doors leading from the rooms into the passage were securely locked, with the keys inside. Let us turn to the chimneys. These, although of ordinary width for some eight or ten feet above the hearths, will not admit, throughout their extent, the body of a large cat. The impossibility of egress, by means already stated, being thus absolute, we are reduced to the windows. Through those of the front room no one could have escaped without notice from the crowd in the street. The murderers *must* have passed, then, through those of the back room. Now, brought to this conclusion in so unequivocal a manner as we are, it is not our part, as reasoners, to reject it on account of apparent impossibilities. It is only left for us to prove that these apparent "impossibilities" are, in reality, not such.

'There are two windows in the chamber. One of them is unobstructed by furniture, and is wholly visible. The lower portion of the other is hidden from view by the head of the unwieldy bedstead which is thrust close up against it. The former was found securely fastened from within. It resisted the utmost force of those who endeavoured to raise it. A large gimlet hole had been pierced in its frame to the left, and a very stout nail was found fitted therein, nearly to the head. Upon examining the other window, a similar nail was seen similarly fitted in it; and a vigorous attempt to raise this sash, failed also. The police were now entirely satisfied that egress had not been in these directions. And, *therefore*, it was thought a matter of supererogation to withdraw the nails and open the windows.

'My own examination was somewhat more particular, and was so for the reason I have just given – because here it was, I knew, that all apparent impossibilities *must* be proved to be not such in reality.

'I proceeded to think thus – *à posteriori*. The murderers *did* escape from one of these windows. This being so, they could not have re-fastened the sashes from the inside, as they were found fastened – the consideration which put a stop, through its obviousness, to the scrutiny of the police in this quarter. Yet the sashes *were* fastened. They *must*, then, have the power of fastening themselves. There was no escape from this conclusion. I stepped to the unobstructed casement, withdrew the nail with some difficulty, and attempted to raise the sash. It resisted all my efforts, as I had anticipated. A concealed spring must, I now knew, exist; and this corroboration of my idea convinced me that my premises, at least, were correct, however mysterious still appeared the circumstances attending the nails. A careful search soon brought to light the hidden spring. I pressed it, and, satisfied with the discovery, forbore to upraise the sash.

'I now replaced the nail and regarded it attentively. A person passing out through this window might have reclosed it, and the spring would have caught – but the nail could not have been replaced. The conclusion was plain, and again narrowed in the field of my investigations. The assassins *must* have escaped through the other window. Supposing, then, the springs upon each sash to be the same, as was probable, there *must* be found a difference between the nails, or at least between the modes of their fixture. Getting upon the sacking of the bedstead, I looked over the head-board minutely at the second casement. Passing my hand down behind the board, I readily discovered and pressed the spring, which was, as I had supposed, identical in character with its neighbour. I now looked at the nail. It was as stout as the other, and apparently fitted in the same manner – driven in nearly up to the head.

'You will say that I was puzzled; but, if you think so, you must have misunderstood the nature of the inductions. To use a sporting phrase, I had not been once "at fault". The scent had never for an instant been lost. There was no flaw in any link of the chain. I had traced the secret to its ultimate result – and that result was *the nail*. It had, I say, in every respect, the appearance of its fellow in the other window; but this fact was an absolute nullity (conclusive as it might seem to be) when compared with the consideration that here, at this point, terminated the clew. "There *must* be something wrong," I said, "about the nail." I touched it; and the head, with about a quarter of an inch of the shank, came off in my fingers. The rest of the shank was in the gimlet hole, where it had been broken off. The fracture was an old one (for its edges were incrusted with rust), and had apparently been accomplished by the blow of a hammer, which had partially embedded, in the top of the bottom sash, the head portion of the nail. I now carefully replaced this head portion in the indentation whence I had taken it, and the resemblance to a perfect nail was complete – the fissure was invisible. Pressing the spring, I gently raised the sash for a few inches; the head went up with it, remaining firm in its bed. I closed the window, and the semblance of the whole nail was again perfect.

'The riddle, so far, was now unriddled. The assassin had escaped through the window which looked upon the bed. Dropping of its own accord upon his exit (or perhaps purposely closed), it had become fastened by the spring; and it was the retention of this spring which had been mistaken by the police for that of the nail – further inquiry being thus considered unnecessary.

'The next question is that of the mode of descent. Upon this point I had been satisfied in my walk with you around the building. About five feet and a half from the casement in question there runs a lightning-rod. From this rod it would have been impossible for any one to reach the window itself, to say nothing of entering it. I observed, however, that the shutters of the fourth story were of the peculiar kind called by Parisian carpenters *ferrades* – a kind rarely employed at the present day, but frequently seen upon very old mansions at Lyons and Bordeaux. They are in the form of an ordinary door (a single, not a folding door), except that the lower half is latticed or worked in open trellis – thus affording an excellent hold for the hands. In the present instance these shutters are fully three feet and a half broad. When we saw them from the rear of the house, they were both about half open – that is to say, they stood off at right angles from the wall. It is probable that the police, as well as myself, examined the back of the tenement; but, if so, in looking at these *ferrades* in the line of their breadth (as they must have done), they did not perceive this great breadth itself, or, at all events, failed to take it into due consideration. In fact, having once satisfied themselves that no egress could have been made in this quarter, they would naturally bestow here a very cursory examination. It was clear to me, however, that the shutter belonging to the window at the head of the bed, would, if swung fully back to the wall, reach to within two feet of the lightning-rod. It was also evident that, by exertion of a very unusual degree of activity and courage, an entrance into the window, from the rod, might have been thus effected. By reaching to the distance of two feet and a half (we now suppose the shutter open to its whole extent) a robber might have taken a firm grasp upon the trellis-work. Letting go, then, his hold upon the rod, placing his feet securely against the wall, and springing boldly from it, he might have swung the shutter so as to close it, and, if we imagine the window open at the time, might even have swung himself into the room.

'I wish you to bear especially in mind that I have spoken of a *very* unusual degree of activity as requisite to success in so hazardous and so difficult a feat. It is my design to show you, first, that the thing might possibly have been accomplished; but, secondly and *chiefly*, I wish to impress upon your understanding the *very extraordinary* – the almost preternatural character of that agility which could have accomplished it.

'You will say, no doubt, using the language of the law, that "to make out my case," I should rather undervalue, than insist upon a full estimation of the activity required in this matter. This may be the practice in law, but it is not the usage of reason. My ultimate object is only the truth. My immediate purpose is to lead you to place in juxtaposition, that *very unusual* activity of which I have just spoken, with that *very peculiar* shrill (or harsh) and *unequal* voice, about whose nationality no two persons could be found to agree, and in whose utterance no syllabification could be detected.'

At these words a vague and half-formed conception of the meaning of Dupin flitted over my mind. I seemed to be upon the verge of comprehension, without power to comprehend – as men, at times, find themselves upon the brink of remembrance, without being able in the end, to remember. My friend went on with his discourse.

'You will see,' he said, 'that I have shifted the question from the mode of egress to that of ingress. It was my design to convey the idea that both were effected in the same manner, at the same point. Let us now revert to the interior of the room. Let us survey the appearances here. The drawers of the bureau, it is said, had been rifled, although many articles of apparel still remained within them. The conclusion here is absurd. It is a mere guess – a very silly one – and no more. How are we to know that the articles found in the drawers were not all these drawers had originally contained? Madame L'Espanaye and her daughter lived an exceedingly retired life – saw no company – seldom went out – had little use for numerous changes of habiliment. Those found were at least of as good quality as any likely to be possessed by these ladies. If a thief had taken any, why did he not take the best – why did he not take all? In a word, why did he abandon four thousand francs in gold to encumber himself with a bundle of linen? The gold *was* abandoned. Nearly the whole sum mentioned by Monsieur Mignaud, the banker, was discovered, in bags, upon the floor. I wish you, therefore, to discard from your thoughts the blundering idea of *motive*, engendered in the brains of the police by that portion of the evidence which speaks of money delivered at the door of the house. Coincidences ten times as remarkable as this (the delivery of the money, and murder committed within three days upon the party receiving it), happen to all of us every hour of our lives, without attracting even momentary notice. Coincidences, in general, are great stumbling-blocks in the way of that class of thinkers who have been educated to know nothing of the theory of probabilities – that theory to which the most glorious objects of human research are indebted for the most glorious of illustration. In the present instance, had the gold been gone, the fact of its delivery three days before would have formed something more than a coincidence. It would have been corroborative of this idea of motive. But, under the real circumstances of the case, if we are to suppose gold the motive of this outrage, we must also imagine the perpetrator so vacillating an idiot as to have abandoned his gold and his motive together.

'Keeping now steadily in mind the points to which I have drawn your attention – that peculiar voice, that unusual agility, and that startling absence of motive in a murder so singularly atrocious as this – let us glance at the butchery itself. Here is a woman strangled to death by manual strength, and thrust up a chimney, head downward. Ordinary assassins employ no such modes of murder as this. Least of all, do they thus dispose of the murdered. In the manner of thrusting the corpse up the chimney, you will admit that there was something *excessively outré* – something altogether irreconcilable with our common notions of human action, even when we suppose the actors the most depraved of men. Think, too, how great must have been that strength which could have thrust the body *up* such an aperture so forcibly that the united vigour of several persons was found barely sufficient to drag it *down!*

'Turn, now, to other indications of the employment of a vigour most marvellous. On the hearth were thick tresses – very thick tresses – of grey human hair. These had been torn out by the roots. You are aware of the great force necessary in tearing thus from the head even twenty or thirty hairs together. You saw the locks in question as well as myself. Their roots (a hideous sight!) were clotted with fragments of the flesh of the scalp – sure token of the prodigious power which had been exerted in uprooting perhaps half a million of hairs at a time. The throat of the old lady was not merely cut, but the head absolutely severed from the body: the instrument was a mere razor. I wish you also to look at the *brutal* ferocity of these deeds. Of the bruises upon the body of Madame L'Espanaye I do not speak. Monsieur Dumas, and his worthy coadjutor Monsieur Etienne, have pronounced that they were inflicted by some obtuse instrument; and so far these gentlemen are very correct. The obtuse instrument was clearly the stone pavement in the yard, upon which the victim had fallen from the window which looked in upon the bed. This idea, however simple it may now seem, escaped the police for the same reason that the breadth of the shutters escaped them – because, by the affair of the nails, their perceptions had been hermetically sealed against the possibility of the windows having ever been opened at all.

'If now, in addition to all these things, you have properly reflected upon the odd disorder of the chamber, we have gone so far as to combine the ideas of an agility astounding, a strength superhuman, a ferocity brutal, a butchery without motive, a *grotesquerie* in horror absolutely alien from humanity, and a voice foreign in tone to the ears of men of many nations, and devoid of all distinct or intelligible syllabification. What result, then, has ensued? What impression have I made upon your fancy?'

I felt a creeping of the flesh as Dupin asked me the question. 'A madman,' I said, 'has done this deed – some raving maniac escaped from a neighbouring *Maison de Santé*.'[20]

'In some respects,' he replied, 'your idea is not irrelevant. But the voices of madmen, even in their wildest paroxysms, are never found to tally with that peculiar voice heard upon the stairs. Madmen are of some nation, and their language, however incoherent in its words, has always the coherence of syllabification. Besides, the hair of a madman is not such as I now hold in my hand. I disentangled this little tuft from the rigidly clutched fingers of Madame L'Espanaye. Tell me what you can make of it.'

'Dupin,' I said, completely unnerved; 'this hair is most unusual – this is no *human* hair.'

'I have not asserted that it is,' said he; 'but, before we decide this point, I wish you to glance at the little sketch I have here traced upon this paper. It is a *fac-simile* drawing of what has been described in one portion of the testimony as "dark bruises, and deep indentations of finger nails," upon the throat of Mademoiselle L'Espanaye, and in another (by Messrs Dumas and Etienne), as a "series of livid spots, evidently the impression of fingers."

'You will perceive,' continued my friend, spreading out the paper upon the table before us, 'that this drawing gives the idea of a firm and fixed hold. There is no *slipping* apparent. Each finger has retained – possibly until the death of the victim – the fearful grasp by which it originally embedded itself. Attempt, now, to place all your fingers, at the same time, in the respective impressions as you see them.'

I made the attempt in vain.

'We are possibly not giving this matter a fair trial,' he said. 'The paper is spread out upon a plane surface; but the human throat is cylindrical. Here is a billet of wood, the circumference of which is about that of the throat. Wrap the drawing round it, and try the experiment again.'

I did so; but the difficulty was even more obvious than before. 'This,' I said, 'is the mark of no human hand.'

'Read now,' replied Dupin, 'this passage from Cuvier.'[21]

It was a minute anatomical and generally descriptive account of the large fulvous Ourang-Outang[22] of the East Indian Islands. The gigantic stature, the prodigious strength and activity, the wild ferocity, and the imitative propensities of these mammalia are sufficiently well known to all. I understood the full horrors of the murder at once.

'The description of the digits,' said I, as I made an end of reading, 'is in exact accordance with this drawing. I see that no animal but an Ourang-Outang, of the species here mentioned, could have impressed the indentations, as you have traced them. This tuft of tawny hair, too, is identical in character with that of the beast of Cuvier. But I cannot possibly comprehend the particulars of this frightful mystery. Besides, there were *two* voices heard in contention, and one of them was unquestionably the voice of a Frenchman.'

'True; and you will remember an expression attributed almost unanimously, by the evidence, to this voice the expression "*Mon Dieu!*" This, under the circumstances, has been justly characterised by one of the witnesses (Montani, the confectioner) as an expression of remonstrance or expostulation. Upon these two words, therefore, I have mainly built my hopes of a full solution of the riddle. A Frenchman was cognisant of the murder. It is possible – indeed it is far more than probable that he was innocent of all participation in the bloody transactions which took place. The Ourang-Outang may have escaped from him. He may have traced it to the chamber; but, under the agitating circumstances which ensued, he could never have re-captured it. It is still at large. I will not pursue these guesses – for I have no right to call them more- since the shades of reflection upon which they are based are scarcely of sufficient depth to be appreciable to my own intellect, and since I could not pretend to make them intelligible to the understanding of another. We will call them guesses, then, and speak of them as such. If the Frenchman in question is indeed, as I suppose, innocent of this atrocity, this advertisement, which I left last night, upon our return home, at the office of *Le Monde* (a paper devoted to the shipping interest, and much sought by sailors), will bring him to our residence.'

He handed me a paper, and I read thus:

CAUGHT – *In the Bois de Boulogne, early in the morning of the — inst.* [the morning of the murder], *a very large, tawny Ourang-Outang of the Bornese species. The owner (who is ascertained to be a sailor, belonging to a Maltese vessel), may have the animal again, upon identifying it satisfactorily, and paying a few charges arising from its capture and keeping. Call at No.—, Rue—, Faubourg St Germain – au troisième.*[23]

'How was it possible,' I asked, 'that you should know the man to be a sailor, and belonging to a Maltese vessel?'

'I do *not* know it,' said Dupin. 'I am not *sure* of it. Here, however, is a small piece of ribbon, which from its form, and from its greasy appearance, has evidently been used in tying the hair in one of those long *queues* of which sailors are so fond. Moreover, this knot is one which few besides sailors can tie, and is peculiar to the Maltese. I picked the ribbon up at the foot of the lightning-rod. It could not have belonged to either of the deceased. Now if, after all, I am wrong in my induction from this ribbon, that the Frenchman was a sailor belonging to a Maltese vessel, still I can have done no harm in saying what I did in the advertisement. If I am in error, he will merely suppose that I have been misled by some circumstance into which he will not take the trouble to inquire. But if I am right, a great point is gained. Cognisant although innocent of the murder, the Frenchman will naturally hesitate about replying to the advertisement – about demanding the Ourang-Outang. He will reason thus: "I am innocent; I am poor; my Ourang-Outang is of great value to one in my circumstances a fortune of itself – why should I lose it through idle apprehensions of danger? Here it is within my grasp. It was found in the Bois de Boulogne – at a vast distance from the scene of that butchery. How can it ever be suspected that a brute beast should have done the deed? The police are at fault – they have failed to procure the slightest clew. Should they even trace the animal, it would be impossible to prove me cognisant of the murder, or to implicate me in guilt on account of that cognisance. Above all, *I am known*. The advertiser designates me as the possessor of the beast. I am not sure to what limit his knowledge may extend. Should I avoid claiming a property of so great value, which it is known that I possess, I will render the animal at least liable to suspicion. It is not my policy to attract attention either to myself or to the beast. I will answer the advertisement, get the Ourang-Outang, and keep it close until this matter has blown over." '

At this moment we heard a step upon the stairs.

'Be ready,' said Dupin, 'with your pistols, but neither use them nor show them until at a signal from myself.'

The front door of the house had been left open, and the visitor had entered, without ringing, and advanced several steps upon the staircase. Now, however, he seemed to hesitate. Presently we heard him descending. Dupin was moving quickly to the door, when we again heard him coming up. He did not turn back a second time, but stepped up with decision, and rapped at the door of our chamber.

'Come in,' said Dupin, in a cheerful and hearty tone.

A man entered. He was a sailor, evidently – a tall, stout, and muscular-looking person, with a certain dare-devil expression of countenance, not altogether unprepossessing. His face, greatly sunburnt, was more than half hidden by whisker and mustachio. He had with him a huge oaken cudgel, but appeared to be otherwise unarmed. He bowed awkwardly, and bade us 'good-evening,' in French accents, which, although somewhat Neufchatelish,[24] were still sufficiently indicative of a Parisian origin.

'Sit down, my friend,' said Dupin. 'I suppose you have called about the Ourang-Outang. Upon my word, I almost envy you the possession of him; a remarkably fine, and no doubt a very valuable animal. How old do you suppose him to be?'

The sailor drew a long breath, with the air of a man relieved of some intolerable burden, and then replied, in an assured tone –

'I have no way of telling – but he can't be more than four or five years old. Have you got him here?'

'Oh no; we had no conveniences for keeping him here. He is at a livery stable in the Rue Dubourg, just by. You can get him in the morning. Of course you are prepared to identify the property?'

'To be sure I am, sir.'

'I shall be sorry to part with him,' said Dupin.

'I don't mean that you should be at all this trouble for nothing, sir,' said the man. 'Couldn't expect it. Am very willing to pay a reward for the finding of the animal – that is to say, anything in reason.'

'Well,' replied my friend, 'that is all very fair, to be sure. Let me think! – what should I have? Oh! I will tell you. My reward shall be this. You shall give me all the information in your power about these murders in the Rue Morgue.'

Dupin said the last words in a very low tone, and very quietly. Just as quietly, too, he walked toward the door, locked it, and put the key in his pocket. He then drew a pistol from his bosom, and placed it, without the least flurry, upon the table.

The sailor's face flushed up as if he were struggling with suffocation. He started to his feet and grasped his cudgel; but the next moment he fell back into his seat, trembling violently, and with the countenance of death itself. He spoke not a word. I pitied him from the bottom of my heart.

'My friend,' said Dupin, in a kind tone, 'you are alarming yourself unnecessarily – you are indeed. We mean you no harm whatever. I pledge you the honour of a gentleman, and of a Frenchman, that we intend you no injury. I perfectly well know that you are innocent of the atrocities in the Rue Morgue. It will not do, however, to deny that you are in some measure implicated in them. From what I have already said, you must know that I have had means of information about this matter – means of which you could never have dreamed. Now the thing stands thus. You have done nothing which you could have avoided – nothing, certainly, which renders you culpable. You were not even guilty of robbery, when you might have robbed with impunity. You have nothing to conceal. You have no reason for concealment. On the other hand, you are bound by every principle of honour to confess all you know. An innocent man is now imprisoned, charged with that crime of which you can point out the perpetrator.'

The sailor had recovered his presence of mind, in a great measure, while Dupin uttered these words; but his original boldness of bearing was all gone.

'So help me God,' said he, after a brief pause, 'I *will* tell you all I know about this affair; but I do not expect you to believe one half I say – I would be a fool indeed if I did. Still, I *am* innocent, and I will make a clean breast if I die for it.'

What he stated was, in substance, this. He had lately made a voyage to the Indian Archipelago. A party, of which he formed one, landed at Borneo, and passed into the interior on an excursion of pleasure. Himself and a companion had captured the Ourang-Outang. This companion dying, the animal fell into his own exclusive possession. After great trouble, occasioned by the intractable ferocity of his captive during the home voyage, he at length succeeded in lodging it safely at his own residence in Paris, where, not to attract toward himself the unpleasant curiosity of his neighbours, he kept it carefully secluded, until such time as it should recover from a wound in the foot, received from a splinter on board ship. His ultimate design was to sell it.

Returning home from some sailors' frolic on the night, or rather in the morning of the murder, he found the beast occupying his own bedroom, into which it had broken from a closet adjoining, where it had been, as was thought, securely confined. Razor in hand, and fully lathered, it was sitting before a looking-glass, attempting the operation of shaving, in which it had no doubt previously watched its master through the key-hole of the closet. Terrified at the sight of so dangerous a weapon in the possession of an animal so ferocious, and so well able to use it, the man, for some moments, was at a loss what to do. He had been accustomed, however, to quiet the creature, even in its fiercest moods, by the use of a whip, and to this he now resorted. Upon sight of it, the Ourang-Outang sprang at once through the door of the chamber, down the stairs, and thence, through a window, unfortunately open, into the street.

The Frenchman followed in despair; the ape, razor still in hand, occasionally stopping to look back and gesticulate at its pursuer, until the latter had nearly come up with it. It then again made off. In this manner the chase continued for a long time. The streets were profoundly quiet, as it was nearly three o'clock in the morning. In passing down an alley in the rear of the Rue Morgue, the fugitive's attention was arrested by a light gleaming from the open window of Madame L'Espanaye's chamber, in the fourth story of her house. Rushing to the building, it perceived the lightning-rod, clambered up with inconceivable agility, grasped the shutter, which was thrown fully back against the wall, and, by its means, swung itself directly upon the headboard of the bed. The whole feat did not occupy a minute. The shutter was kicked open again by the Ourang-Outang as it entered the room.

The sailor, in the meantime, was both rejoiced and perplexed. He had strong hopes of now recapturing the brute, as it could scarcely escape from the trap into which it had ventured, except by the rod, where it might be intercepted as it came down. On the other hand, there was much cause for anxiety as to what it might do in the house.

This latter reflection urged the man still to follow the fugitive. A lightning-rod is ascended without difficulty, especially by a sailor; but, when he had arrived as high as the window, which lay far to his left, his career was stopped; the most that he could accomplish was to reach over so as to obtain a glimpse of the interior of the room. At this glimpse he nearly fell from his hold through excess of horror. Now it was that those hideous shrieks arose upon the night, which had startled from slumber the inmates of the Rue Morgue. Madame L'Espanaye and her daughter, habited in their night clothes, had apparently been occupied in arranging some papers in the iron chest already mentioned, which had been wheeled into the middle of the room. It was open, and its contents lay beside it on the floor. The victims must have been sitting with their backs toward the window; and, from the time elapsing between the ingress of the beast and the screams, it seems probable that it was not immediately perceived. The flapping-to of the shutter would naturally have been attributed to the wind.

As the sailor looked in, the gigantic animal had seized Madame L'Espanaye by the hair (which was loose, as she had been combing it), and was flourishing the razor about her face, in imitation of the motions of a barber. The daughter lay prostrate and motionless; she had swooned. The screams and struggles of the old lady (during which the hair was torn from her head) had the effect of changing the probably pacific purposes of the Ourang-Outang into those of wrath. With one determined sweep of its muscular arm it nearly severed her head from her body. The sight of blood inflamed its anger into frenzy. Gnashing its teeth, and flashing fire from its eyes, it flew upon the body of the girl, and embedded its fearful talons in her throat, retaining its grasp until she expired. Its wandering and wild glances fell at this moment upon the head of the bed, over which the face of its master, rigid with horror, was just discernible. The fury of the beast, who no doubt bore still in mind the dreaded whip, was instantly converted into fear. Conscious of having deserved punishment, it seemed desirous of concealing its bloody deeds, and skipped about the chamber in an agony of nervous agitation; throwing down and breaking the furniture as it moved, and dragging the bed from the bedstead. In conclusion, it seized first the corpse of the daughter, and thrust it up the chimney, as it was found; then that of the old lady, which it immediately hurled through the window headlong.

As the ape approached the casement with its mutilated burden, the sailor shrank aghast to the rod, and rather gliding than clambering down it, hurried at once home – dreading the consequences of the butchery, and gladly abandoning, in his terror, all solicitude about the fate of the Ourang-Outang. The words heard by the party upon the staircase were the Frenchman's exclamations of horror and affright, commingled with the fiendish jabberings of the brute.

I have scarcely anything to add. The Ourang-Outang must have escaped from the chamber, by the rod, just before the breaking of the door. It must have closed the window as it passed through it. It was subsequently caught by the owner himself, who obtained for it a very large sum at the *Jardin des Plantes*.[25] Le Bon was instantly released upon our narration of the circumstances (with some comments from Dupin) at the bureau of the Prefect of Police. This functionary, however well disposed to my friend, could not altogether conceal his chagrin at the turn which affairs had taken, and was fain to indulge in a sarcasm or two, about the propriety of every person minding his own business.

'Let him talk,' said Dupin, who had not thought it necessary to reply. 'Let him discourse; it will ease his conscience. I am satisfied with having defeated him in his own castle. Nevertheless, that he failed in the solution of this mystery is by no means that matter for wonder which he supposes it; for, in truth, our friend the Prefect is somewhat too cunning to be profound. In his wisdom is no *stamen*.[26] It is all head and no body, like the pictures of the goddess Laverna[27] – or, at best, all head and shoulders, like a codfish. But he is a good creature after all. I like him especially for one master-stroke of cant, by which he has attained his reputation for ingenuity. I mean the way he has "*de nier ce qui est, et d'expliquer ce qui n'est pas.*" '*[28]

* Rousseau, *Nouvelle Héloïse*

The Mystery of Marie Rogêt*

A SEQUEL TO 'THE MURDERS IN THE RUE MORGUE'

Es giebt eine Reihe idealischer Begebenheiten, die der Wirklichkeit parallel lauft. Selten fallen sie zusammen. Menschen und zufalle modificiren gewohulich die idealische Begebenheit, so dass sie unvollkommen erscheint, und ihre Folgen gleichfalls unvollkommen sind. So bei der Reformation; statt des Protestantismus kam das Lutherthum hervor.

There are ideal series of events which run parallel with the real ones. They rarely coincide. Men and circumstances generally modify the ideal train of events, so that it seems imperfect, and its consequences are equally imperfect. Thus with the Reformation; instead of Protestantism came Lutheranism.

NOVALIS[1] (the *nom de plume* of Von Hardenburg), *Moral Ansichten*

THERE ARE FEW persons, even amongst the calmest thinkers, who have not occasionally been startled into a vague yet thrilling half-credence in the super-natural, by *coincidences* of so seemingly marvellous a character that, as *mere* coincidences, the intellect has been unable to receive them. Such sentiments – for the half credences of which I speak have never the full force of *thought* – such sentiments are seldom thoroughly stifled

---

* Upon the original publication of 'Marie Rogêt,' the footnotes now appended were considered unnecessary; but the lapse of several years since the tragedy upon which the tale is based, renders it expedient to give them, and also to say a few words in explanation of the general design. A young girl, Mary Cecilia Rogers, was murdered in the vicinity of New York; and although her death occasioned an intense and long-enduring excitement, the mystery attending it had remained unsolved at the period when the present paper was written and published (November 1842). Herein, under pretence of relating the fate of a Parisian *grisette*, the author has followed, in minute detail, the essential, while merely paralleling the unessential facts of the real murder of Mary Rogers. Thus all argument founded upon the fiction is applicable The 'Mystery of Marie Rogêt' was composed at a distance from the scene of the atrocity, and with no other means of investigation than the newspapers afforded. Thus much escaped the writer of which he could have availed himself had he been upon the spot, and visited the localities. It may not be improper to record, nevertheless, that the confessions of *two* persons (one of them the Madame Deluc of the narrative), made at different periods, long subsequent to the publication, confirmed, in full, not only the general conclusion, but absolutely *all* the chief hypothetical details by which that conclusion was attained.

unless by reference to the doctrine of chance, or, as it is technically termed, the Calculus of Probabilities. Now this Calculus is, in its essence, purely mathematical; and thus we have the anomaly of the most rigidly exact in science applied to the shadow and spirituality of the most intangible in speculation.to the truth: and the investigation of the truth was the object.

The extraordinary details which I am now called upon to make public, will be found to form, as regards sequence of time, the primary branch of a series of scarcely intelligible *coincidences*, whose secondary or concluding branch will be recognised by all readers in the late murder of MARY CECILIA ROGERS, at New York.

When, in an article entitled 'The Murders in the Rue Morgue,' I endeavoured, about a year ago, to depict some very remarkable features in the mental character of my friend, the Chevalier C. Auguste Dupin, it did not occur to me that I should ever resume the subject. The depicting of character constituted my design; and this design was thoroughly fulfilled in the wild train of circumstances brought to instance Dupin's idiosyncrasy. I might have adduced other examples, but I should have proven no more. Late events, however, in their surprising development, have startled me into some further details, which will carry with them the air of extorted confession. Hearing what I have lately heard, it would be indeed strange should I remain silent in regard to what I both heard and saw so long ago.

Upon the winding up of the tragedy involved in thc deaths of Madame L'Espanaye and her daughter, the Chevalier dismissed the affair at once from his attention, and relapsed into his old habits of moody reverie. Prone, at all times, to abstraction, I readily fell in with his humour; and continuing to occupy our chambers in the Faubourg Saint Germain, we gave the Future to the winds, and slumbered tranquilly in the Present, weaving the dull world around us into dreams.

But these dreams were not altogether uninterrupted. It may readily be supposed that the part played by my friend, in the drama at the Rue Morgue, had not failed of its impression upon the fancies of the Parisian police. With its emissaries, the name of Dupin had grown into a household word. The simple character of those inductions by which he had disentangled the mystery never having been explained even to the Prefect, or to any other individual than myself, of course it is not surprising that the affair was regarded as little less than miraculous, or that the Chevalier's analytical abilities acquired for him the credit of intuition. His frankness would have led him to disabuse every inquirer of such prejudice; but his indolent humour forbade all further agitation of a topic whose interest to himself had long ceased. It thus happened that he found himself the cynosure of the policial eyes; and the cases were not few in which attempt was made to engage his services at the Prefecture. One of the most remarkable instances was that of the murder of a young girl named Marie Rogêt.

This event occurred about two years after the atrocity in the Rue Morgue. Marie, whose Christian and family name will at once arrest attention from their resemblance to those of the unfortunate 'cigar-girl,' was the only daughter of the widow Estelle Rogêt. The father had died during the child's infancy, and from the period of his death, until within eighteen months before the assassination which forms the subject of our narrative, the mother and daughter had dwelt together in the Rue Pavée Saint Andrée;* Madame there keeping a *pension*, assisted by Marie. Affairs went on thus until the latter had attained her twenty-second year, when her great beauty attracted the notice of a perfumer, who occupied one of the shops in the basement of the Palais Royal, and whose custom lay chiefly among the desperate adventurers infesting that neighbourhood. Monsieur Le Blanc† was not unaware of the advantages to be derived from the attendance of the fair Marie in his perfumery; and his liberal proposals were accepted eagerly by the girl, although with somewhat more of hesitation by Madame.

The anticipations of the shopkeeper were realised, and his rooms soon became notorious through the charms of the sprightly *grisette*.[2] She had been in his employ about a year, when her admirers were thrown into confusion by her sudden disappearance from the shop. Monsieur Le Blanc was unable to account for her absence, and Madame Rogêt was distracted with anxiety and terror. The public papers immediately took up the theme, and the police were upon the point of making serious investigations, when, one fine morning, after the lapse of a week, Marie, in good health, but with a somewhat saddened air, made her reappearance at her usual counter in the perfumery. All inquiry, except that of a private character, was of course immediately hushed. Monsieur Le Blanc professed total ignorance, as before. Marie, with Madame, replied to all questions, that the last week had been spent at the house of a relation in the country. Thus the affair died away, and was generally forgotten; for the girl, ostensibly to relieve herself from the impertinence of curiosity, soon bade a final adieu to the perfumer, and sought the shelter of her mother's residence in the Rue Pavée Saint Andrée.

It was about five months after this return home, that her friends were alarmed by her sudden disappearance for the second time. Three days elapsed, and nothing was heard of her. On the fourth her corpse was found floating in the Seine,* near the shore which is opposite the Quartier of the Rue Saint Andrée, and at a point not very far distant from the secluded neighbourhood of the Barrière du Roule.†

The atrocity of this murder (for it was at once evident that murder had been committed), the youth and beauty of the victim, and, above all, her previous notoriety, conspired to produce intense excitement in the minds of the sensitive Parisians. I can call to mind no similar occurrence producing so general and so intense an effect. For several weeks, in the discussion of this one absorbing theme, even the momentous political topics of the day were forgotten. The Prefect made unusual exertions; and the powers of the whole Parisian police were, of course, tasked to the utmost extent.

Upon the first discovery of the corpse, it was not supposed that the murderer would be able to elude, for more than a very brief period, the inquisition which was immediately set on foot. It was not until the expiration of a week that it was deemed necessary to offer a reward; and even then this reward was limited to a thousand francs. In the meantime the investigation proceeded with vigour, if not always with judgment, and numerous individuals were examined to no purpose; while, owing to the continual absence of all clew to the mystery, the popular excitement greatly increased. At the end of the tenth day it was thought advisable to double the sum originally proposed; and, at length, the second week having elapsed without leading to any discoveries, and the prejudice which always exists in Paris against the police having given vent to itself in several serious *émeutes*,[3] the Prefect took it upon himself to offer the sum of twenty thousand francs 'for the conviction of the assassin,' or, if more than one should prove to have been implicated, 'for the conviction of any one of the assassins.' In the proclamation setting forth this reward, a full pardon was promised to any accomplice who should come forward in evidence against his fellow; and to the whole was appended, wherever it appeared, the private placard of a committee of citizens, offering ten thousand francs, in addition to the amount proposed by the Prefecture. The entire reward thus stood at no less than thirty thousand francs, which will be regarded as an extraordinary sum when we consider the humble condition of the girl, and the great frequency, in large cities, of such atrocities as the one described.

No one doubted now that the mystery of this murder would be immediately brought to light. But although, in one or two instances, arrests were made which promised elucidation, yet nothing was elicited which could implicate the parties suspected; and they were discharged

---

* The Hudson   † Weehawken

forthwith. Strange as it may appear, the third week from the discovery of the body had passed, and passed without any light being thrown upon the subject, before even a rumour of the events which had so agitated the public mind reached the ears of Dupin and myself. Engaged in researches which had absorbed our whole attention, it had been nearly a month since either of us had gone abroad, or received a visitor, or more than glanced at the leading political articles in one of the daily papers. The first intelligence of the murder was brought us by G—, in person. He called upon us early in the afternoon of the 13th of July 18—, and remained with us until late in the night. He had been piqued by the failure of all his endeavours to ferret out the assassins. His reputation – so he said, with a peculiarly Parisian air – was at stake. Even his honour was concerned. The eyes of the public were upon him; and there was really no sacrifice which he would not be willing to make for the development of the mystery. He concluded a somewhat droll speech with a compliment upon what he was pleased to term the *tact* of Dupin, and made him a direct, and certainly a liberal proposition, the precise nature of which I do not feel myself at liberty to disclose, but which has no bearing upon the proper subject of my narrative.

The compliment my friend rebutted as best he could, but the proposition he accepted at once, although its advantages were altogether provisional. This point being settled, the Prefect broke forth at once into explanations of his own views, interspersing them with long comments upon the evidence; of which latter we were not yet in possession. He discoursed much, and beyond doubt learnedly; while I hazarded an occasional suggestion as the night wore drowsily away. Dupin, sitting steadily in his accustomed arm-chair, was the embodiment of respectful attention. He wore spectacles during the whole interview; and an occasional glance beneath their green glasses sufficed to convince me that he slept not the less soundly, because silently, throughout the seven or eight leaden-footed hours which immediately preceded the departure of the Prefect.

In the morning I procured, at the Prefecture, a full report of all the evidence elicited, and, at the various newspaper offices, a copy of every paper in which, from first to last, had been published any decisive information in regard to this sad affair. Freed from all that was positively disproved, this mass of information stood thus:

Marie Rogêt left the residence of her mother, in the Rue Pavée St Andrée, about nine o'clock in the morning of Sunday, June the 22nd, 18—. In going out she gave notice to a Monsieur Jacques St Eustache,*

* Payne

and to him only, of her intention to spend the day with an aunt who resided in the Rue des Drômes. The Rue des Drômes is a short and narrow but populous thoroughfare, not far from the banks of the river, and at a distance of some two miles, in the most direct course possible from the *pension* of Madame Rogêt. St Eustache was the accepted suitor of Marie, and lodged, as well as took his meals, at the *pension*. He was to have gone for his betrothed at dusk, and to have escorted her home. In the afternoon, however, it came on to rain heavily; and, supposing that she would remain all night at her aunt's (as she had done under similar circumstances before), he did not think it necessary to keep his promise. As night drew on, Madame Rogêt (who was an infirm old lady, seventy years of age) was heard to express a fear 'that she should never see Marie again'; but this observation attracted little attention at the time.

On Monday, it was ascertained that the girl had not been to the Rue des Drômes; and when the day elapsed without tidings of her, a tardy search was instituted at several points in the city and its environs. It was not, however, until the fourth day from the period of her disappearance that anything satisfactory was ascertained respecting her. On this day (Wednesday, the 25th of June), a Monsieur Beauvais,* who, with a friend, had been making inquiries for Marie near the Barrière du Roule, on the shore of the Seine which is opposite the Rue Pavée St Andrée, was informed that a corpse had just been towed ashore by some fishermen, who had found it floating in the river. Upon seeing the body, Beauvais, after some hesitation, identified it as that of the perfumery girl. His friend recognised it more promptly.

The face was suffused with dark blood, some of which issued from the mouth. No foam was seen, as in the case of the merely drowned. There was no discoloration in the cellular tissue. About the throat were bruises and impressions of fingers. The arms were bent over on the chest, and were rigid. The right hand was clenched; the left partially open. On the left wrist were two circular excoriations, apparently the effect of ropes, or of a rope in more than one volution. A part of the right wrist, also, was much chafed, as well as the back throughout its extent, but more especially at the shoulder-blades. In bringing the body to the shore the fishermen had attached to it a rope, but none of the excoriations had been effected by this. The flesh of the neck was much swollen. There were no cuts apparent, or bruises which appeared the effect of blows. A piece of lace was found tied so tightly around the neck as to be hidden from sight; it was completely buried in the flesh, and was fastened by a knot which lay just under the left ear. This alone would have sufficed to

* Crommelin

produce death. The medical testimony spoke confidently of the virtuous character of the deceased. She had been subjected, it said, to brutal violence. The corpse was in such condition when found that there could have been no difficulty in its recognition by friends.

The dress was much torn and otherwise disordered. In the outer garment, a slip, about a foot wide, had been torn upward from the bottom hem to the waist, but not torn off. It was wound three times around the waist, and secured by a sort of hitch in the back. The dress immediately beneath the frock was of fine muslin; and from this a slip eighteen inches wide had been torn entirely out – torn very evenly and with great care. It was found around her neck, fitting loosely, and secured with a hard knot. Over this muslin slip and the slip of lace, the strings of a bonnet were attached, the bonnet being appended. The knot by which the strings of the bonnet were fastened, was not a lady's, but a slip or sailor's knot.

After the recognition of the corpse, it was not, as usual, taken to the Morgue (this formality being superfluous), but hastily interred not far from the spot at which it was brought ashore. Through the exertions of Beauvais the matter was industriously hushed up, as far as possible; and several days had elapsed before any public emotion resulted. A weekly paper,* however, at length took up the theme; the corpse was disinterred, and a re-examination instituted; but nothing was elicited beyond what has been already noted. The clothes, however, were now submitted to the mother and friends of the deceased, and fully identified as those worn by the girl upon leaving home.

Meantime, the excitement increased hourly. Several individuals were arrested and discharged. St Eustache fell especially under suspicion; and he failed, at first, to give an intelligible account of his whereabouts during the Sunday on which Marie left home. Subsequently, however, he submitted to Monsieur G—, affidavits, accounting satisfactorily for every hour of the day in question. As time passed and no discovery ensued, a thousand contradictory rumours were circulated, and journalists busied themselves in *suggestions*. Among these, the one which attracted the most notice, was the idea that Marie Rogêt still lived – that the corpse found in the Seine was that of some other unfortunate. It will be proper that I submit to the reader some passages which embody the suggestion alluded to. These passages are *literal* translations from *L'Etoile*,† a paper conducted, in general, with much ability:

Mademoiselle Rogêt left her mother's house on Sunday morning,

* The *N. Y. Mercury*   † The *N. Y. Brother Jonathon*, edited by H. Hastings Weld, Esq.

June the 22nd, 18—, with the ostensible purpose of going to see her aunt, or some other connection, in the Rue des Drômes. From that hour nobody is proved to have seen her. There is no trace or tidings of her at all . . . There has no person, whatever, come forward, so far, who saw her at all, on that day, after she left her mother's door . . . Now, though we have no evidence that Marie Rogêt was in the land of the living after nine o'clock on Sunday, June the 22nd, we have proof that, up to that hour, she was alive. On Wednesday noon, at twelve, a female body was discovered afloat on the shore of the Barrière du Roule. This was, even if we presume that Marie Rogêt was thrown into the river within three hours after she left her mother's house, only three days from the time she left her home – three days to an hour. But it is folly to suppose that the murder, if murder was committed on her body, could have been consummated soon enough to have enabled her murderers to throw the body into the river before midnight. Those who are guilty of such horrid crimes, choose darkness rather than light . . . Thus we see that if the body found in the river *was* that of Marie Rogêt, it could only have been in the water two and a half days, or three at the outside. All experience has shown that drowned bodies, or bodies thrown into the water immediately after death by violence, require from six to ten days for sufficient decomposition to take place to bring them to the top of the water. Even where a cannon is fired over a corpse, and it rises before at least five or six day's immersion, it sinks again, if let alone. Now, we ask, what was there in this case to cause a departure from the ordinary course of nature? . . . If the body had been kept in its mangled state on shore until Tuesday night, some trace would be found on shore of the murderers. It is a doubtful point, also, whether the body would be so soon afloat, even were it thrown in after having been dead two days. And, furthermore, it is exceedingly improbable that any villains who had committed such a murder as is here supposed, would have thrown the body in without weight to sink it, when such a precaution could have so easily been taken.

The editor here proceeds to argue that the body must have been in the water 'not three days merely, but, at least, five times three days,' because it was so far decomposed that Beauvais had great difficulty in recognising it. This latter point, however, was fully disproved. I continue the translation:

What, then, are the facts on which M. Beauvais says that he has no doubt the body was that of Marie Rogêt? He ripped up the gown sleeve, and says he found marks which satisfied him of the identity. The public generally supposed those marks to have consisted of some description of scars. He rubbed the arm and found *hair* upon it – something as indefinite, we think, as can readily be imagined – as little conclusive as finding an arm in the sleeve. M. Beauvais did not return that night, but sent word to Madame Rogêt, at seven o'clock on Wednesday evening, that an investigation was still in progress respecting her daughter. If we allow that Madame Rogêt, from her age and grief, could not go over (which is allowing a great deal), there certainly must have been some one who would have thought it worth while to go over and attend the investigation, if they thought the body was that of Marie. Nobody went over. There was nothing said or heard about the matter in the Rue Pavée St Andrée, that reached even the occupants of the same building. M. St Eustache, the lover and intended husband of Marie, who boarded in her mother's house, deposes that he did not hear of the discovery of the body of his intended until the next morning, when M. Beauvais came into his chamber and told him of it. For an item of news like this, it strikes us it was very coolly received.

In this way the journal endeavoured to create the impression of an apathy on the part of the relatives of Marie, inconsistent with the supposition that these relatives believed the corpse to be hers. Its insinuations amount to this – that Marie, with the connivance of her friends, had absented herself from the city for reasons involving a charge against her chastity; and that these friends, upon the discovery of a corpse in the Seine, somewhat resembling that of the girl, had availed themselves of the opportunity to impress the public with the belief of her death. But *L'Etoile* was again over-hasty. It was distinctly proved that no apathy, such as was imagined, existed; that the old lady was exceedingly feeble, and so agitated as to be unable to attend to any duty; that St Eustache, so far from receiving the news coolly, was distracted with grief, and bore himself so frantically, that M. Beauvais prevailed upon a friend and relative to take charge of him, and prevent his attending the examination at the disinterment. Moreover, although it was stated by *L'Etoile* that the corpse was reinterred at the public expense – that an advantageous offer of private sepulture was absolutely declined by the family – and that no member of the family attended the ceremonial – although, I say, all this was asserted by *L'Etoile* in furtherance of the impression it designed to convey – yet *all* this was satisfactorily disproved. In a subsequent number of the paper an attempt was made to throw suspicion upon Beauvais himself. The editor says:

Now, then, a change comes over the matter. We are told that, on one occasion, while a Madame B— was at Madame Rogêt's house, M. Beauvais, who was going out, told her that a gendarme was expected there, and that she, Madame B., must not say anything to the gendarme until he returned, but let the matter be for him . . . In the present posture of affairs, M. Beauvais appears to have the whole matter locked up in his head. A single step cannot be taken without M. Beauvais; for, go which way you will, you run against him . . . For some reason, he determined that nobody shall have anything to do with the proceedings but himself, and he has elbowed the male relatives out of the way, according to their representations, in a very singular manner. He seems to have been very much averse to permitting the relatives to see the body.

By the following fact, some colour was given to the suspicion thus thrown upon Beauvais. A visitor at his office, a few days prior to the girl's disappearance, and during the absence of its occupant, had observed *a rose* in the keyhole of the door, and the name '*Marie*' inscribed upon a slate which hung near at hand.

The general impression, so far as we were enabled to glean it from the newspapers, seemed to be, that Marie had been the victim of *a gang* of desperadoes – that by these she had been borne across the river, maltreated and murdered. *Le Commerciel*,* however, a print of extensive influence, was earnest in combating this popular idea. I quote a passage or two from its columns:

We are persuaded that pursuit has hitherto been on a false scent, so far as it has been directed to the Barrière du Roule. It is impossible that a person so well known to thousands as this young woman was, should have passed three blocks without some one having seen her; and any one who saw her would have remembered it, for she interested all who knew her. It was when the streets were full of people, when she went out . . . It is impossible that she could have gone to the Barrière du Roule, or to the Rue des Drômes, without being recognised by a dozen persons; yet no one has come forward who saw her outside of her mother's door, and there is no evidence, except the testimony concerning her expressed intentions, that she did go out at all. Her gown was torn, bound round her, and tied; and by that the body was carried as a bundle. If the murder had been committed at the Barrière du Roule, there would have been no necessity for any such arrangement. The fact that the body was found floating near the Barrière, is no proof as to where it was thrown into the water . . . A piece of one of the unfortunate girl's petticoats, two feet long and one foot wide, was torn out and tied under her chin around the back of her head, probably to prevent screams. This was done by fellows who had no pocket-handkerchief.

A day or two before the Prefect called upon us, however, some important information reached the police, which seemed to overthrow, at least, the chief portion of *Le Commerciel*'s argument. Two small boys, sons of a Madame Deluc, while roaming among the woods near the Barrière du Roule, chanced to penetrate a close thicket, within which were three or four large stones, forming a kind of seat, with a back and foot-stool. On the upper stone lay a white petticoat; on the second a silk scarf. A parasol, gloves, and a pocket-handkerchief were also here found. The handkerchief bore the name 'Marie Rogêt.' Fragments of dress were discovered on the brambles around. The earth was trampled, the bushes were broken, and there was every evidence of a struggle. Between the thicket and the river, the fences were found taken down, and the ground bore evidence of some heavy burden having been dragged along it.

A weekly paper, *Le Soleil*,* had the following comments upon this discovery – comments which merely echoed the sentiment of the whole Parisian press: –

The things had all evidently been there at least three or four weeks; they were all mildewed down hard with the action of the rain, and stuck together from mildew. The grass had grown around and over some of them. The silk on the parasol was strong, but the threads of it were run together within. The upper part, where it had been doubled and folded, was all mildewed and rotten, and tore on its being opened . . . The pieces of her frock torn out by the bushes were about three inches wide and six inches long. One part was the hem of the frock, and it had been mended; the other piece was part of the skirt, not the hem. They looked like strips torn off, and were on the thorn bush, about a foot from the ground . . . There can be no doubt, therefore, that the spot of this appalling outrage has been discovered.

Consequent upon this discovery, new evidence appeared. Madame Deluc testified that she keeps a roadside inn not far from the bank of the river, opposite the Barrière du Roule. The neighbourhood is

* *Phil. Sat. Evening Post*

secluded – particularly so. It is the usual Sunday resort of blackguards from the city, who cross the river in boats. About three o'clock, in the afternoon of the Sunday in question, a young girl arrived at the inn, accompanied by a young man of dark complexion. The two remained here for some time. On their departure, they took the road to some thick woods in the vicinity. Madame Deluc's attention was called to the dress worn by the girl on account of its resemblance to one worn by a deceased relative. A scarf was particularly noticed. Soon after the departure of the couple, a gang of miscreants made their appearance, behaved boisterously, ate and drank without making payment, followed in the route of the young man and girl, returned to the inn about dusk, and recrossed the river as if in great haste.

It was soon after dark, upon this same evening, that Madame Deluc, as well as her eldest son, heard the screams of a female in the vicinity of the inn. The screams were violent but brief. Madame D. recognised not only the scarf which was found in the thicket, but the dress which was discovered upon the corpse. An omnibus-driver, Valence,* now also testified that he saw Marie Rogêt cross a ferry on the Seine, on the Sunday in question, in company with a young man of dark complexion. He, Valence, knew Marie, and could not be mistaken in her identity. The articles found in the thicket were fully identified by the relatives of Marie.

The items of evidence and information thus collected by myself, from the newspapers, at the suggestion of Dupin, embraced only one more point – but this was a point of seemingly vast consequence. It appears that, immediately after the discovery of the clothes as above described, the lifeless, or nearly lifeless body of St Eustache, Marie's betrothed, was found in the vicinity of what all now supposed the scene of the outrage. A phial labelled 'laudanum,' and emptied, was found near him. His breath gave evidence of the poison. He died without speaking. Upon his person was found a letter, briefly stating his love for Marie, with his design of self-destruction.

'I need scarcely tell you,' said Dupin, as he finished the perusal of my notes, 'that this is a far more intricate case than that of the Rue Morgue; from which it differs in one important respect. This is an *ordinary*, although an atrocious instance of crime. There is nothing peculiarly *outré* about it. You will observe that, for this reason, the mystery has been considered easy, when, for this reason, it should have been considered difficult of solution. Thus, at first, it was thought unnecessary to offer a reward The myrmidons of G— were able at once to

* Adam

comprehend how and why such an atrocity *might have been* committed. They could picture to their imaginations a mode – many modes – and a motive – many motives; and because it was not impossible that either of these numerous modes and motives *could* have been the actual one, they have taken it for granted that one of them *must*. But the ease with which these variable fancies were entertained, and the very plausibility which each assumed, should have been understood as indicative rather of the difficulties than of the facilities which must attend elucidation. I have before observed that it is by prominences above the plane of the ordinary, that reason feels her way, if at all, in her search for the true, and that the proper question in cases such as this, is not so much "what has occurred?" as "what has occurred that has never occurred before?" In the investigations at the house of Madame L'Espanaye,* the agents of G— were discouraged and confounded by that very *unusualness* which, to a properly regulated intellect, would have afforded the surest omen of success; while this same intellect might have been plunged in despair at the ordinary character of all that met the eye in the case of the perfumery girl, and yet told of nothing but easy triumph to the functionaries of the Prefecture.

'In the case of Madame L'Espanaye and her daughter, there was, even at the beginning of our investigation, no doubt that murder had been committed. The idea of suicide was excluded at once. Here, too, we are freed, at the commencement, from all supposition of self-murder. The body found at the Barrière du Roule, was found under such circumstances as to leave us no room for embarrassment upon this important point. But it has been suggested that the corpse discovered is not that of the Marie Rogêt for the conviction of whose assassin, or assassins, the reward is offered, and respecting whom, solely, our agreement has been arranged with the Prefect. We both know this gentleman well. It will not do to trust him too far. If, dating our inquiries from the body found, and thence tracing a murderer, we yet discover this body to be that of some other individual than Marie; or if, starting from the living Marie, we find her, yet find her unassassinated – in either case we lose our labour; since it is Monsieur G— with whom we have to deal. For our own purpose, therefore, if not for the purpose of justice, it is indispensable that our first step should be the determination of the identity of the corpse with the Marie Rogêt who is missing.

'With the public the arguments of *L'Etoile* have had weight; and that the journal itself is convinced of their importance would appear from the manner in which it commences one of its essays upon the subject:

* See 'The Murders in the Rue Morgue'

"Several of the morning papers of the day," it says, "speak of the *conclusive* article in Monday's *Etoile*." To me, this article appears conclusive of little beyond the zeal of its inditer. We should bear in mind that, in general, it is the object of our newspapers rather to create a sensation – to make a point – than to further the cause of truth. The latter end is only pursued when it seems coincident with the former. The print which merely falls in with ordinary opinion (however well-founded this opinion may be) earns for itself no credit with the mob. The mass of the people regard as profound only him who suggests *pungent contradictions* of the general idea. In ratiocination, not less than in literature, it is the *epigram* which is the most immediately and the most universally appreciated. In both, it is of the lowest order of merit.

'What I mean to say is, that it is the mingled epigram and melodrame of the idea that Marie Rogêt still lives, rather than any true plausibility in this idea, which have suggested it to *L'Etoile*, and secured it a favourable reception with the public. Let us examine the heads of this journal's argument; endeavouring to avoid the incoherence with which it is originally set forth.

'The first aim of the writer is to show, from the brevity of the interval between Marie's disappearance and the finding of the floating corpse, that this corpse cannot be that of Marie. The reduction of this interval to its smallest possible dimension, becomes thus, at once, an object with the reasoner. In the rash pursuit of this object, he rushes into mere assumption at the outset. "It is folly to suppose," he says, "that the murder, if murder was committed on her body, could have been consummated soon enough to have enabled her murderers to throw the body into the river before midnight." We demand at once, and very naturally, *why*? Why is it folly to suppose that the murder was committed *within five minutes* after the girl's quitting her mother's house? Why is it folly to suppose that the murder was committed at any given period of the day? There have been assassinations at all hours. But, had the murder taken place at any moment between nine o'clock in the morning of Sunday, and a quarter before midnight, there would still have been time enough "to throw the body into the river before midnight." This assumption, then, amounts precisely to this – that the murder was not committed on Sunday at all – and, if we allow *L'Etoile* to assume this, we may permit it any liberties whatever. The paragraph beginning "It is folly to suppose that the murder," &c., however it appears as printed in *L'Etoile*, may be imagined to have existed actually *thus* in the brain of its inditer: "It is folly to suppose that the murder, if murder was committed on the body, could have been committed soon enough to have enabled her murderers to throw the body into the river before midnight; it is folly, we say, to suppose all this, and to suppose at the same time (as we are resolved to suppose), that the body was *not* thrown in until *after* midnight" – a sentence sufficiently inconsequential in itself, but not so utterly preposterous as the one printed.

'Were it my purpose,' continued Dupin, 'merely to *make out a case* against this passage of *L'Etoile*'s argument, I might safely leave it where it is. It is not, however, with *L'Etoile* that we have to do, but with the truth. The sentence in question has but one meaning, as it stands; and this meaning I have fairly stated: but it is material that we go behind the mere words for an idea which these words have obviously intended, and failed to convey. It was the design of the journalist to say that, at whatever period of the day or night of Sunday this murder was committed, it was improbable that the assassins would have ventured to bear the corpse to the river before midnight. And herein lies, really, the assumption of which I complain. It is assumed that the murder was committed at such a position, and under such circumstances that *the bearing it* to the river became necessary. Now, the assassination might have taken place upon the river's brink, or on the river itself; and, thus, the throwing the corpse in the water might have been resorted to, at any period of the day or night, as the most obvious and most immediate mode of disposal. You will understand that I suggest nothing here as probable, or as coincident with my own opinion. My design, so far, has no reference to the facts of the case. I wish merely to caution you against the whole tone of *L'Etoile*'s *suggestion*, by calling your attention to its *ex parte* [4] character at the outset.

'Having prescribed thus a limit to suit its own preconceived notions; having assumed that, if this were the body of Marie, it could have been in the water but a very brief time; the journal goes on to say:

'All experience has shown that drowned bodies, or bodies thrown into the water immediately after death by violence, require from six to ten days for sufficient decomposition to take place to bring them to the top of the water. Even when a cannon is fired over a corpse, and it rises before at least five or six days' immersion, it sinks again if let alone.

'These assertions have been tacitly received by every paper in Paris, with the exception of *Le Moniteur*.* This latter print endeavours to combat that portion of the paragraph which has reference to "drowned bodies" only, by citing some five or six instances in which the bodies of

* The *N. Y. Commercial Advertiser*

individuals known to be drowned were found floating after the lapse of less time than is insisted upon by *L'Etoile*. But there is something excessively unphilosophical in the attempt on the part of *Le Moniteur*, to rebut the general assertion of *L'Etoile*, by a citation of particular instances militating against that assertion. Had it been possible to adduce fifty instead of five examples of bodies found floating at the end of two or three days, these fifty examples could still have been properly regarded only as exceptions to *L'Etoile*'s rule, until such time as the rule itself should be confuted. Admitting the rule (and this *Le Moniteur* does not deny, insisting merely upon its exceptions), the argument of *L'Etoile* is suffered to remain in full force; for this argument does not pretend to involve more than a question of the *probability* of the body having risen to the surface in less than three days; and this probability will be in favour of *L'Etoile*'s position until the instances so childishly adduced shall be sufficient in number to establish an antagonistical rule.

'You will see at once that all argument upon this head should be urged, if at all, against the rule itself, and for this end we must examine the *rationale* of the rule. Now the human body, in general, is neither much lighter nor much heavier than the water of the Seine; that is to say, the specific gravity of the human body, in its natural condition, is about equal to the bulk of fresh water which it displaces. The bodies of fat and fleshy persons, with small bones, and of women generally, are lighter than those of the lean and large-boned, and of men; and the specific gravity of the water of a river is somewhat influenced by the presence of the tide from sea. But, leaving this tide out of the question, it may be said that *very* few human bodies will sink at all, even in fresh water, *of their own accord*. Almost any one, falling into a river, will be enabled to float, if he suffer the specific gravity of the water fairly to be adduced in comparison with his own – that is to say, if he suffer his whole person to be immersed with as little exception as possible. The proper position for one who cannot swim, is the upright position of the walker on land, with the head thrown fully back, and immersed; the mouth and nostrils alone remaining above the surface. Thus circumstanced, we shall find that we float without difficulty and without exertion. It is evident, however, that the gravities of the body, and of the bulk of water displaced, are very nicely balanced, and that a trifle will cause either to preponderate. An arm, for instance, uplifted from the water, and thus deprived of its support, is an additional weight sufficient to immerse the whole head, while the accidental aid of the smallest piece of timber will enable us to elevate the head so as to look about. Now, in the struggles of one unused to swimming, the arms are invariably thrown upwards, while an attempt is made to keep the head in its usual perpendicular position. The result is the immersion of the mouth and nostrils, and the inception, during efforts to breathe while beneath the surface, of water into the lungs. Much is also received into the stomach, and the whole body becomes heavier by the difference between the weight of the air originally distending these cavities, and that of the fluid which now fills them. This difference is sufficient to cause the body to sink, as a general rule; but it is insufficient in the cases of individuals with small bones and an abnormal quantity of flaccid or fatty matter. Such individuals float even after drowning.

'The corpse, being supposed at the bottom of the river, will there remain until, by some means, its specific gravity again becomes less than that of the bulk of water which it displaces. This effect is brought about by decomposition, or otherwise. The result of decomposition is the generation of gas, distending the cellular tissues and all the cavities, and giving the *puffed* appearance which is so horrible. When this distension has so far progressed that the bulk of the corpse is materially increased without a corresponding increase of *mass* or weight, its specific gravity becomes less than that of the water displaced, and it forthwith makes its appearance at the surface. But decomposition is modified by innumerable circumstances – is hastened or retarded by innumerable agencies; for example, by the heat or cold of the season, by the mineral impregnation or purity of the water, by its depth or shallowness, by its currency or stagnation, by the temperament of the body, by its infection or freedom from disease before death. Thus it is evident that we can assign no period, with anything like accuracy, at which the corpse shall rise through decomposition. Under certain conditions this result would be brought about within an hour; under others, it might not take place at all. There are chemical infusions by which the animal frame can be preserved *for ever* from corruption; the bi-chloride of mercury is one. But, apart from decomposition, there may be, and very usually is, generation of gas within the stomach, from the acetous fermentation of vegetable matter (or within other cavities from other causes) sufficient to induce a distension which will bring the body to the surface. The effect produced by the firing of a cannon is that of simple vibration. This may either loosen the corpse from the soft mud or ooze in which it is embedded, thus permitting it to rise when other agencies have already prepared it for so doing; or it may overcome the tenacity of some putrescent portions of the cellular tissue, allowing the cavities to distend under the influence of the gas.

'Having thus before us the whole philosophy of this subject, we can easily test by it the assertions of *L'Etoile*. "All experience shows," says this paper, "that drowned bodies, or bodies thrown into the water immediately after death by violence, require from six to ten days for sufficient decomposition to take place to bring them to the top of the water. Even when a cannon is fired over a corpse, and it rises before at least five or six days' immersion, it sinks again if let alone."

'The whole of this paragraph must now appear a tissue of inconsequence and incoherence. All experience does *not* show that "drowned bodies" *require* from six to ten days for sufficient decomposition to take place to bring them to the surface. Both science and experience show that the period of their rising is, and necessarily must be, indeterminate. If, moreover, a body has risen to the surface through firing of cannon, it will *not* "sink again if let alone," until decomposition has so far progressed as to permit the escape of the generated gas. But I wish to call your attention to the distinction which is made between "drowned bodies," and "bodies thrown into the water immediately after death by violence." Although the writer admits the distinction, he yet includes them all in the same category. I have shown how it is that the body of a drowning man becomes specifically heavier than its bulk of water, and that he would not sink at all, except for the struggles by which he elevates his arms above the surface, and his gasps for breath while beneath the surface – gasps which supply by water the place of the original air in the lungs. But these struggles and these gasps would not occur in the body "thrown into the water immediately after death by violence." Thus, in the latter instance, *the body, as a general rule, would not sink at all* – a fact of which *L'Etoile* is evidently ignorant. When decomposition had proceeded to a very great extent – when the flesh had in a great measure left the bones – then, indeed, but not *till* then, should we lose sight of the corpse.

'And now what are we to make of the argument, that the body found could not be that of Marie Rogêt, because three days only having elapsed, the body was found floating? If drowned, being a woman, she might never have sunk; or having sunk, might have reappeared in twenty-four hours, or less. But no one supposes her to have been drowned; and, dying before being thrown into the river, she might have been found floating at any period afterwards whatever.

' "But," says *L'Etoile*, "if the body had been kept in its mangled state on shore until Tuesday night, some trace would be found on shore of the murderers." Here it is at first difficult to perceive the intention of the reasoner. He means to anticipate what he imagines would be an objection to his theory – viz., that the body was kept on shore two days, suffering rapid decomposition – *more* rapid than if immersed in water. He supposes that, had this been the case, it *might* have appeared at the surface on the Wednesday, and thinks that *only* under such circumstances it could so have appeared. He is accordingly in haste to show that it *was not* kept on shore; for, if so, "some trace would be found on shore of the murderers." I presume you smile at the *sequitur*. You cannot be made to see how the mere *duration* of the corpse on the shore could operate to *multiply traces* of the assassins. Nor can I.

' "And furthermore, it is exceedingly improbable," continues our journal, "that any villains who had committed such a murder as is here supposed, would have thrown the body in without weight to sink it, when such a precaution could have so easily been taken." Observe, here, the laughable confusion of thought! No one – not even *L'Etoile* – disputes the murder committed *on the body found*. The marks of violence are too obvious. It is our reasoner's object merely to show that this body is not Marie's. He wishes to prove that *Marie* is not assassinated – not that the corpse was not. Yet his observation proves only the latter point. Here is a corpse without weight attached. Murderers, casting it in, would not have failed to attach a weight. Therefore it was not thrown in by murderers. This is all which is proved, if anything is. The question of identity is not even approached, and *L'Etoile* has been at great pains merely to gainsay now what it has admitted only a moment before. "We are perfectly convinced," it says, "that the body found was that of the murdered female."

'Nor is this the sole instance, even in this division of his subject, where our reasoner unwittingly reasons against himself. His evident object, I have already said, is to reduce, as much as possible, the interval between Marie's disappearance and the finding of the corpse. Yet we find him *urging* the point that no person saw the girl from the moment of her leaving her mother's house. "We have no evidence," he says, "that Marie Rogêt was in the land of the living after nine o'clock on Sunday, June the 22nd." As his argument is obviously an *ex parte* one, he should, at least, have left this matter out of sight; for had any one been known to see Marie, say on Monday, or on Tuesday, the interval in question would have been much reduced, and, by his own ratiocination, the probability much diminished of the corpse being that of the *grisette*. It is, nevertheless, amusing to observe that *L'Etoile* insists upon its point in the full belief of its furthering its general argument.

'Reperuse now that portion of this argument which has reference to the identification of the corpse by Beauvais. In regard to the *hair* upon the arm, *L'Etoile* has been obviously disingenuous. M. Beauvais, not being an idiot, could never have urged, in identification of the corpse, simply *hair upon its arm*. No arm is *without* hair. The *generality* of the expression of *L'Etoile* is a mere perversion of the witness's phraseology. He must have spoken of some *peculiarity* in this hair. It must have been a peculiarity of colour, of quantity, of length, or of situation.

' "Her foot," says the journal, "was small – so are thousands of feet. Her garter is no proof whatever – nor is her shoe – for shoes and garters are sold in packages. The same may be said of the flowers in her hat. One thing upon which M. Beauvais strongly insists is; that the clasp on the garter found had been set back to take it in. This amounts to nothing; for most women find it proper to take a pair of garters home and fit them to the size of the limbs they are to encircle, rather than to try them in the store where they purchase." Here it is difficult to suppose the reasoner in earnest. Had M. Beauvais, in his search for the body of Marie, discovered a corpse corresponding in general size and appearance to the missing girl, he would have been warranted (without reference to the question of habiliment at all) in forming an opinion that his search had been successful. If, in addition to the point of general size and contour, he had found upon the arm a peculiar hairy appearance which he had observed upon the living Marie, his opinion might have been justly strengthened; and the increase of positiveness might well have been in the ratio of the peculiarity, or unusualness, of the hairy mark. If, the feet of Marie being small, those of the corpse were also small, the increase of probability that the body was that of Marie would not be an increase in a ratio merely arithmetical, but in one highly geometrical, or accumulative. Add to all this, shoes such as she had been known to wear upon the day of her disappearance, and, although these shoes may be "sold in packages," you so far augment the probability as to verge upon the certain. What, of itself, would be no evidence of identity, becomes through its corroborative position, proof most sure. Give us, then, flowers in the hat corresponding to those worn by the missing girl, and we seek for nothing further. If only *one* flower, we seek for nothing further – what then if two or three, or more? Each successive one is multiple evidence – proof not *added* to proof, but *multiplied* by hundreds or thousands. Let us now discover, upon the deceased, garters such as the living used, and it is almost folly to proceed. But these garters are found to be tightened, by the setting back of a clasp, in just such a manner as her own had been tightened by Marie shortly previous to her leaving home. It is now madness or hypocrisy to doubt. What *L'Etoile* says in respect to this abbreviation of the garters being an usual occurrence, shows nothing beyond its own pertinacity in error. The elastic nature of the clasp-garter is self-demonstration of the *unusualness* of the abbreviation. What is made to adjust itself, must of necessity require foreign adjustment but rarely. It must have been by an accident, in its strictest sense, that these garters of Marie needed the tightening described. They alone would have amply established her identity. But it is not that the corpse was found to have the garters of the missing girl, or found to have her shoes, or her bonnet, or the flowers of her bonnet, or her feet, or a peculiar mark upon the arm, or her general size and appearance – it is that the corpse had each and *all collectively*. Could it be proved that the editor of *L'Etoile really* entertained a doubt, under the circumstances, there would be no need, in his case, of a commission *de lunatico inquirendo*.[5] He has thought it sagacious to echo the small-talk of the lawyers, who, for the most part, content themselves with echoing the rectangular precepts of the courts. I would here observe that very much of what is rejected as evidence by a court, is the best of evidence to the intellect. For the court, guiding itself by the general principles of evidence – the recognised and *booked* principles – is averse from swerving at particular instances. And this steadfast adherence to principle, with rigorous disregard of the conflicting exception, is a sure mode of attaining the *maximum* of attainable truth, in any long sequence of time. The practice, *en masse*, is therefore philosophical; but it is not the less certain that it engenders vast individual error.*

'In respect to the insinuations levelled at Beauvais, you will be willing to dismiss them in a breath. You have already fathomed the true character of this good gentleman. He is a *busybody*, with much of romance and little of wit. Any one so constituted will readily so conduct himself, upon occasion of *real* excitement, as to render himself liable to suspicion on the part of the over-acute, or the ill-disposed. M. Beauvais (as it appears from your notes) had some personal interviews with the editor of *L'Etoile*, and offended him by venturing an opinion that the corpse, notwithstanding the theory of the editor, was, in sober fact, that of Marie. "He persists," says the paper, "in asserting the corpse to be that of Marie, but cannot give a circumstance, in addition to those which we have commented upon, to make others believe." Now, without readverting to the fact that stronger evidence "to make others believe," could *never* have been adduced, it may be remarked that a man may very well be understood to believe, in a case of this kind, without the ability to advance a single reason for the belief of a

---

* 'A theory based on the qualities of an object, will prevent its being unfolded according to its objects; and he who arranges topics in reference to their causes, will cease to value them according to their results. Thus the jurisprudence of every nation will show that, when law becomes a science and a system, it ceases to be justice. The errors into which a blind devotion to *principles* of classification has led the common law, will be seen by observing how often the legislature has been obliged to come forward to restore the equity its scheme had lost.' – LANDOR [6]

second party. Nothing is more vague than impressions of individual identity. Each man recognises his neighbour, yet there are few instances in which any one is prepared to *give a reason* for his recognition. The editor of *L'Etoile* had no right to be offended at M. Beauvais' unreasoning belief.

'The suspicious circumstances which invest him will be found to tally much better with my hypothesis of *romantic busybodyism*, than with the reasoner's suggestion of guilt. Once adopting the more charitable interpretation, we shall find no difficulty in comprehending the rose in the keyhole; the "Marie" upon the slate; the "elbowing the male relatives out of the way"; the "aversion to permitting them to see the body"; the caution given to Madame B——, that she must hold no conversation with the gendarme until his return (Beauvais'); and, lastly, his apparent determination "that nobody should have anything to do with the proceedings except himself." It seems to me unquestionable that Beauvais was a suitor of Marie's; that she coquetted with him; and that he was ambitious of being thought to enjoy her fullest intimacy and confidence. I shall say nothing more upon this point; and, as the evidence fully rebuts the assertion of *L'Etoile*, touching the matter of *apathy* on the part of the mother and other relatives – an apathy inconsistent with the supposition of their believing the corpse to be that of the perfumery girl – we shall now proceed as if the question of *identity* were settled to our perfect satisfaction.'

'And what,' I here demanded, 'do you think of the opinions of *Le Commerciel*?'

'That, in spirit, they are far more worthy of attention than any which have been promulgated upon the subject. The deductions from the premises are philosophical and acute; but the premises, in two instances at least, are founded in imperfect observation. *Le Commerciel* wishes to intimate that Marie was seized by some gang of low ruffians not far from her mother's door. "It is impossible," it urges, "that a person so well known to thousands as this young woman was, should have passed three blocks without some one having seen her." This is the idea of a man long resident in Paris – a public man – and one whose walks to and fro in the city have been mostly limited to thc vicinity of the public offices. He is aware that *he* seldom passes so far as a dozen blocks from his own bureau, without being recognised and accosted. And, knowing the extent of his personal acquaintance with others, and of others with him, he compares his notoriety with that of the perfumery girl, finds no great difference between them, and reaches at once the conclusion that she, in her walks, would be equally liable to recognition with himself in his. This could only be the case were her walks of the same unvarying, methodical character, and within the same *species* of limited region as are his own. He passes to and fro, at regular intervals, within a confined periphery, abounding in individuals who are led to observation of his person through interest in the kindred nature of his occupation with their own. But the walks of Marie may, in general, be supposed discursive. In this particular instance, it will be understood as most probable, that she proceeded upon a route of more than average diversity from her accustomed ones. The parallel which we imagine to have existed in the mind of *Le Commerciel* would only be sustained in the event of the two individuals traversing the whole city. In this case, granting the personal acquaintances to be equal, the chances would be also equal that an equal number of personal rencounters would be made. For my own part, I should hold it not only as possible, but as very far more than probable, that Marie might have proceeded, at any given period, by any one of the many routes between her own residence and that of her aunt, without meeting a single individual whom she knew, or by whom she was known. In viewing this question in its full and proper light, we must hold steadily in mind the great disproportion between the personal acquaintances of even the most noted individual in Paris, and the entire population of Paris itself.

'But whatever force there may still appear to be in the suggestion of *Le Commerciel*, will be much diminished when we take into consideration *the hour* at which the girl went abroad. "It was when the streets were full of people," says *Le Commerciel*, "that she went out." But not so. It was at nine o'clock in the morning. Now at nine o'clock of every morning in the week, *with the exception of Sunday*, the streets of the city are, it is true, thronged with people. At nine on Sunday, the populace are chiefly within doors *preparing for church*. No observing person can have failed to notice the peculiarly deserted air of the town, from about eight until ten on the morning of every Sabbath. Between ten and eleven the streets are thronged, but not at so early a period as that designated.

'There is another point at which there seems a deficiency of *observation* on the part of *Le Commerciel*. "A piece," it says, "of one of the unfortunate girl's petticoats, two feet long, and one foot wide, was torn out and tied under her chin, and around the back of her head, probably to prevent screams. This was done by fellows who had no pocket-handkerchiefs." Whether this idea is, or is not well founded, we will endeavour to see hereafter; but by "fellows who have no pocket-handkerchiefs," the editor intends the lowest class of ruffians. These, however, are the very description of people who will always be found to have handkerchiefs even when destitute of shirts. You must have had occasion to observe how absolutely indispensable, of late years, to the thorough blackguard, has become the pocket-handkerchief.'

'And what are we to think,' I asked, 'of the article in *Le Soleil*?'

'That it is a vast pity its inditer was not born a parrot – in which case he would have been the most illustrious parrot of his race. He has merely repeated the individual items of the already published opinion; collecting them, with a laudable industry, from this paper and from that. "The things had all *evidently* been there," he says, "at least three or four weeks, and there can be *no doubt* that the spot of this appalling outrage has been discovered." The facts here re-stated by *Le Soleil*, are very far indeed from removing my own doubts upon this subject, and we will examine them more particularly hereafter in connection with another division of the theme.

'At present we must occupy ourselves with other investigations. You cannot fail to have remarked the extreme laxity of the examination of the corpse. To be sure the question of identity was readily determined, or should have been; but there were other points to be ascertained. Had the body been in any respect *despoiled*? Had the deceased any articles of jewellery about her person upon leaving home? if so, had she any when found? These are important questions utterly untouched by the evidence; and there are others of equal moment, which have met with no attention. We must endeavour to satisfy ourselves by personal inquiry. The case of St Eustache must be re-examined. I have no suspicion of this person; but let us proceed methodically. We will ascertain beyond a doubt the validity of the affidavits in regard to his whereabouts on the Sunday. Affidavits of this character are readily made matter of mystification. Should there be nothing wrong here, however, we will dismiss St Eustache from our investigations. His suicide, however corroborative of suspicion, were there found to be deceit in the affidavits, is, without such deceit, in no respect an unaccountable circumstance, or one which need cause us to deflect from the line of ordinary analysis.

'In that which I now propose, we will discard the interior points of this tragedy, and concentrate our attention upon its outskirts. Not the least usual error, in investigations such as this, is the limiting of inquiry to the immediate, with total disregard of the collateral or circumstantial events. It is the malpractice of the courts to confine evidence and discussion to the bounds of apparent relevancy. Yet experience has shown, and a true philosophy will always show, that a vast, perhaps the larger portion of truth, arises from the seemingly irrelevant. It is through the spirit of this principle, if not precisely through its letter, that modern science resolved to *calculate upon the unforeseen*. But perhaps you do not comprehend me. The history of human knowledge has so uninterruptedly shown that to collateral, or incidental, or accidental events we are indebted for the most numerous and most valuable discoveries, that it has at length become necessary, in any prospective view of improvement, to make not only large, but the largest allowances for inventions that shall arise by chance, and quite out of the range of ordinary expectation. It is no longer philosophical to base, upon what has been, a vision of what is to be. *Accident* is admitted as a portion of the substructure. We make chance a matter of absolute calculation. We subject the unlooked-for and unimagined, to the mathematical formulæ of the schools.

'I repeat that it is no more than fact, that the *larger* portion of all truth has sprung from the collateral; and it is but in accordance with the spirit of the principle involved in this fact, that I would divert inquiry, in the present case, from the trodden and hitherto unfruitful ground of the event itself, to the contemporary circumstances which surround it. While you ascertain the validity of the affidavits, I will examine the newspapers more generally than you have as yet done. So far, we have only reconnoitred the field of investigation; but it will be strange indeed if a comprehensive survey, such as I propose, of the public prints, will not afford us some minute points which shall establish a *direction* for inquiry.'

In pursuance of Dupin's suggestions, I made scrupulous examination of the affair of the affidavits. The result was a firm conviction of their validity, and of the consequent innocence of St Eustache. In the meantime my friend occupied himself, with what seemed to me a minuteness altogether objectless, in a scrutiny of the various newspaper files. At the end of a week he placed before me the following extracts:

About three years and a half ago, a disturbance very similar to the present was caused by the disappearance of this same Marie Rogêt, from the *parfumerie* of Monsieur Le Blanc in the Palais Royal. At the end of a week, however, she reappeared at her customary *comptoir*,[7] as well as ever, with the exception of a slight paleness not altogether usual. It was given out by Monsieur Le Blanc and her mother, that she had merely been on a visit to some friend in the country; and the affair was speedily hushed up. We presume that the present absence is a freak of the same nature, and that, at the expiration of a week, or perhaps of a month, we shall have her among us again. – *Evening Paper*, Monday, June 23.*

* *N. Y. Express*

An evening journal of yesterday, refers to a former mysterious disappearance of Mademoiselle Rogêt. It is well known that, during the week of her absence from Le Blanc's *parfumerie*, she was in the company of a young naval officer, much noted for his debaucheries. A quarrel, it is supposed, providentially led to her return home. We have the name of the Lothario in question, who is, at present, stationed in Paris, but, for obvious reasons, forbear to make it public. – *Le Mercurie*, Tuesday morning, June 24.*

An outrage of the most atrocious character was perpetrated near this city the day before yesterday. A gentleman, with his wife and daughter, engaged about dusk the services of six young men, who were idly rowing a boat to and fro near the banks of the Seine, to convey him across the river. Upon reaching the opposite shore, the three passengers stepped out, and had proceeded so far as to be beyond the view of the boat, when the daughter discovered that she had left in it her parasol. She returned for it, was seized by the gang, carried out into the stream, gagged, brutally treated, and finally taken to the shore at a point not far from that at which she had originally entered the boat with her parents. The villains have escaped for the time, but the police are upon their trail, and some of them will soon be taken. – *Morning Paper*, June 25.†

We have received one or two communications, the object of which is to fasten the crime of the late atrocity upon Mennais;‡ but as this gentleman has been fully exonerated by a legal inquiry, and as the arguments of our several correspondents appear to be more zealous than profound, we do not think it advisable to make them public. – *Morning Paper*, June 28.§

We have received several forcibly written communications, apparently from various sources, and which go far to render it a matter of certainty that the unfortunate Marie Rogêt has become a victim of one of the numerous bands of blackguards which infest the vicinity of the city upon Sunday. Our own opinion is decidedly in favour of this supposition. We shall endeavour to make room for some of these arguments hereafter. – *Evening Paper*, June 30.**

On Monday, one of the bargemen connected with the revenue service, saw an empty boat floating down the Seine. Sails were lying

---

* *N. Y. Herald*   † *N. Y. Courier and Inquirer*   ‡ Mennais was one of the parties originally suspected and arrested, but discharged through total lack of evidence.   § *N. Y. Courier and Inquirer*   ** *N. Y. Evening Post*

in the bottom of the boat. The bargemen towed it under the barge office. The next morning it was taken from thence, without the knowledge of any of the officers. The rudder is now at the barge office. – *Le Diligence*, Thursday, June 26.*

Upon reading these various extracts, they not only seemed to me irrelevant, but I could perceive no mode in which any one of them could be brought to bear upon the matter in hand. I waited for some explanation from Dupin.

'It is not my present design,' he said, 'to *dwell* upon the first and second of these extracts. I have copied them chiefly to show you the extreme remissness of the police, who, as far as I can understand from the Prefect, have not troubled themselves, in any respect, with an examination of the naval officer alluded to. Yet it is mere folly to say that between the first and second disappearance of Marie, there is no *supposable* connection. Let us admit the first elopement to have resulted in a quarrel between the lovers, and the return home of the betrayed. We are now prepared to view a second *elopement* (if we *know* that an elopement has again taken place) as indicating a renewal of the betrayer's advances, rather than as the result of new proposals by a second individual – we are prepared to regard it as a "making up" of the old amour, rather than as the commencement of a new one. The chances are ten to one, that he who had once eloped with Marie, would again propose an elopement, rather than that she to whom proposals of elopement had been made by one individual, should have them made to her by another. And here let me call your attention to the fact, that the time elapsing between the first ascertained, and the second supposed elopement, is a few months more than the general period of the cruises of our men-of-war. Had the lover been interrupted in his first villainy by the necessity of departure to sea, and had he seized the first moment of his return to renew the base designs not yet altogether accomplished – or not yet altogether accomplished *by him*? Of all these things we know nothing.

'You will say, however, that, in the second instance, there was *no* elopement as imagined. Certainly not – but are we prepared to say that there was not the frustrated design? Beyond St Eustache, and perhaps Beauvais, we find no recognised, no open, no honourable suitors of Marie. Of none other is there anything said. Who, then, is the secret lover, of whom the relatives (*at least most of them*) know nothing, but whom Marie meets upon the morning of Sunday, and who is so deeply in her confidence, that she hesitates not to remain with him until the shades of the evening descend, amid the solitary groves of the Barrière du Roule? Who is that secret lover, I ask, of whom, at least, *most* of the relatives know nothing? And what means the singular prophecy of Madame Rogêt on the morning of Marie's departure – "I fear that I shall never see Marie again"?

'But if we cannot imagine Madame Rogêt privy to the design of elopement, may we not at least suppose this design entertained by the girl? Upon quitting home, she gave it to be understood that she was about to visit her aunt in the Rue des Drômes, and St Eustache was requested to call for her at dark. Now, at first glance, this fact strongly militates against my suggestion; but let us reflect. That she *did* meet some companion, and proceed with him across the river, reaching the Barrière du Roule at so late an hour as three o'clock in the afternoon, is known. But in consenting so to accompany this individual (*for whatever purpose – to her mother known or unknown*), she must have thought of her expressed intention when leaving home, and of the surprise and suspicion aroused in the bosom of her affianced suitor, St Eustache, when, calling for her at the hour appointed, in the Rue des Drômes, he should find that she had not been there, and when, moreover, upon returning to the *pension* with this alarming intelligence, he should become aware of her continued absence from home. She must have thought of these things, I say. She must have foreseen the chagrin of St Eustache, the suspicion of all. She could not have thought of returning to brave this suspicion; but the suspicion becomes a point of trivial importance to her, if we suppose her *not* intending to return.

'We may imagine her thinking thus – "I am to meet a certain person for the purpose of elopement, or for certain other purposes known only to myself. It is necessary that there be no chance of interruption – there must be sufficient time given us to elude pursuit – I will give it to be understood that I shall visit and spend the day with my aunt at the Rue des Drômes – I will tell St Eustache not to call for me until dark – in this way, my absence from home for the longest possible period, without causing suspicion or anxiety, will be accounted for, and I shall gain more time than in any other manner. If I bid St Eustache call for me at dark, he will be sure not to call before; but, if I wholly neglect to bid him call, my time for escape will be diminished, since it will be expected that I return the earlier, and my absence will the sooner excite anxiety. Now, if it were my design to return *at all* – if I had in contemplation merely a stroll with the individual in question – it would not be my policy to bid St Eustache call; for, calling he will be *sure* to ascertain that I have played him false – a fact of which I might keep him for ever in ignorance, by leaving home without notifying him of my intention, by returning before dark, and by then stating that I had been to visit my aunt in the Rue des Drômes. But, as it is my design *never* to return – or not for some weeks – or not until certain concealments are effected – the gaining of time is the only point about which I need give myself any concern."

'You have observed, in your notes, that the most general opinion in relation to this sad affair is, and was from the first, that the girl had been the victim of *a gang* of blackguards. Now, the popular opinion, under certain conditions, is not to be disregarded. When arising of itself – when manifesting itself in a strictly spontaneous manner – we should look upon it as analogous with that *intuition* which is the idiosyncrasy of the individual man of genius. In ninety-nine cases from the hundred I would abide by its decision. But it is important that we find no palpable traces of *suggestion*. The opinion must be rigorously *the public's own*; and the distinction is often exceedingly difficult to perceive and to maintain. In the present instance, it appears to me that this "public opinion", in respect to *a gang*, has been superinduced by the collateral event which is detailed in the third of my extracts. All Paris is excited by the discovered corpse of Marie, a girl young, beautiful, and notorious. This corpse is found, bearing marks of violence, and floating in the river. But it is now made known that, at the very period, or about the very period, in which it is supposed that the girl was assassinated, an outrage similar in nature to that endured by the deceased, although less in extent, was perpetrated, by a gang of young ruffians, upon the person of a second young female. Is it wonderful that the one known atrocity should influence the popular judgment in regard to the other unknown? This judgment awaited direction, and the known outrage seemed so opportunely to afford it? Marie, too, was found in the river; and upon this very river was this known outrage committed. The connection of the two events had about it so much of the palpable, that the true wonder would have been a *failure* of the populace to appreciate and to seize it. But, in fact, the one atrocity, known to be so committed, is, if anything, evidence that the other, committed at a time nearly coincident, was *not* so committed. It would have been a miracle indeed, if, while a gang of ruffians were perpetrating, at a given locality, a most unheard-of wrong, there should have been another similar gang, in a similar locality, in the same city, under the same circumstances, with the same means and appliances, engaged in a wrong of precisely the same aspect, at precisely the same period of time! Yet in what, if not in this marvellous train of coincidence, does the accidentally *suggested* opinion of the populace call upon us to believe?

'Before proceeding farther, let us consider the supposed scene of the assassination, in the thicket at the Barrière du Roule. This thicket, although dense, was in the close vicinity of a public road. Within were three or four large stones, forming a kind of seat, with a back and footstool. On the upper stone was discovered a white petticoat; on the second, a silk scarf. A parasol, gloves, and a pocket-handkerchief, were also here found. The handkerchief bore the name, "Marie Rogêt". Fragments of dress were seen on the branches around. The earth was trampled, the bushes were broken, and there was every evidence of a violent struggle.

'Notwithstanding the acclamation with which the discovery of this thicket was received by the press, and the unanimity with which it was supposed to indicate the precise scene of the outrage, it must be admitted that there was some very good reason for doubt. That it *was* the scene, I may or I may not believe but there was excellent reason for doubt. Had the *true* scene been, as *Le Commerciel* suggested, in the neighbourhood of the Rue Pavée St Andrée, the perpetrators of the crime, supposing them still resident in Paris, would naturally have been stricken with terror at the public attention thus acutely directed into the proper channel; and, in certain classes of minds, there would have arisen, at once, a sense of the necessity of some exertion to redivert this attention. And thus, the thicket of the Barrière du Roule having been already suspected, the idea of placing the articles where they were found, might have been naturally entertained. There is no real evidence, although *Le Soleil* so supposes, that the articles discovered had been more than a very few days in the thicket; while there is much circumstantial proof that they could not have remained there, without attracting attention, during the twenty days elapsing between the fatal Sunday and the afternoon upon which they were found by the boys. "They were all *mildewed* down hard," says *Le Soleil*, adopting the opinions of its predecessors, "with the action of the rain, and stuck together from *mildew*. The grass had grown around and over some of them. The silk of the parasol was strong, but the threads of it were run together within. The upper part, where it had been doubled and folded, was all *mildewed* and rotten, and tore on being opened." In respect to the grass having "grown around and over some of them," it is obvious that the fact could only have been ascertained from the words, and thus from the recollections, of two small boys; for these boys removed the articles and took them home before they had been seen by a third party. But grass will grow, especially in warm and damp weather (such as was that of the period of the murder), as much as two or three inches in a single day. A parasol lying upon a newly turfed ground, might, in a single week, be entirely concealed from sight by the upspringing grass. And touching that *mildew* upon which the editor of

Le Soleil so pertinaciously insists that he employs the word no less than three times in the brief paragraph just quoted, is he really unaware of the nature of this *mildew*? Is he to be told that it is one of the many classes of fungus, of which the most ordinary feature is its upspringing and decadence within twenty-four hours?

'Thus we see, at a glance, that what has been most triumphantly adduced in support of the idea that the articles had been "for at least three or four weeks" in the thicket, is most absurdly null as regards any evidence of that fact. On the other hand, it is exceedingly difficult to believe that these articles could have remained in the thicket specified, for a longer period than a single week – for a longer period than from one Sunday to the next. Those who know anything of the vicinity of Paris, know the extreme difficulty of finding *seclusion* unless at a great distance from its suburbs. Such a thing as an unexplored, or even an unfrequently visited recess, amid its woods or groves, is not for a moment to be imagined. Let any one who, being at heart a lover of nature, is yet chained by duty to the dust and heat of this great metropolis – let any such one attempt, even during the week-days, to slake his thirst for solitude amid the scenes of natural loveliness which immediately surround us. At every second step, he will find the growing charm dispelled by the voice and personal intrusion of some ruffian or party of carousing blackguards. He will seek privacy amid the densest foliage, all in vain. Here are the very nooks where the unwashed most abound – here are the temples most desecrate. With sickness of the heart the wanderer will flee back to the polluted Paris as to a less odious because less incongruous sink of pollution. But if the vicinity of the city is so beset during the working days of the week, how much more so on the Sabbath! It is now especially that, released from the claims of labour, or deprived of the customary opportunities of crime, the town black-guard seeks the precincts of the town, not through love of the rural, which in his heart he despises, but by way of escape from the restraints and conventionalities of society. He desires less the fresh air and the green trees, than the utter *license* of the country. Here, at the roadside inn, or beneath the foliage of the woods, he indulges, unchecked by any eye except those of his boon companions, in all the mad excess of a counterfeit hilarity – the joint offspring of liberty and of rum. I say nothing more than what must be obvious to every dispassionate observer, when I repeat that the circumstance of the articles in question having remained undiscovered, for a longer period than from one Sunday to another, in *any* thicket in the immediate neighbourhood of Paris, is to be looked upon as little less than miraculous.

'But there are not wanting other grounds for the suspicion that the articles were placed in the thicket with the view of diverting attention from the real scene of the outrage. And, first, let me direct your notice to the *date* of the discovery of the articles. Collate this with the date of the fifth extract made by myself from the newspapers. You will find that the discovery followed, almost immediately, the urgent communications sent to the evening paper. These communications, although various, and apparently from various sources, tended all to the same point – viz., the directing of attention to *a gang* as the perpetrators of the outrage, and to the neighbourhood of the Barrière du Roule as its scene. Now here, of course, the suspicion is not that, in consequence of these communications, or of the public attention by them directed, the articles were found by the boys; but the suspicion might and may well have been, that the articles were not *before* found by the boys, for the reason that the articles had not before been in the thicket; having been deposited there only at so late a period as at the date, or shortly prior to the date of the communications, by the guilty authors of these communications themselves.

'This thicket was a singular – an exceedingly singular one. It was unusually dense. Within its naturally walled enclosure were three extraordinary stones, *forming a seat with a back and footstool*. And this thicket, so full of a natural art, was in the immediate vicinity, *within a few rods*, of the dwelling of Madame Deluc, whose boys were in the habit of closely examining the shrubberies about them in search of the bark of the sassafras.[8] Would it be a rash wager – a wager of one thousand to one – that *a day* never passed over the heads of these boys without finding at least one of them ensconced in the umbrageous hall, and enthroned upon its natural throne? Those who would hesitate at such a wager, have either never been boys themselves, or have forgotten the boyish nature. I repeat – it is exceedingly hard to comprehend how the articles could have remained in this thicket, undiscovered, for a longer period than one or two days; and that thus there is good ground for suspicion, in spite of the dogmatic ignorance of *Le Soleil*, that they were, at a comparatively late date, deposited where found.

'But there are still other and stronger reasons for believing them so deposited, than any which I have as yet urged. And now, let me beg your notice to the highly artificial arrangement of the articles. On the *upper* stone lay a white petticoat; on the *second* a silk scarf; scattered around, were a parasol, gloves, and a pocket-handkerchief bearing the name, "Marie Rogêt". Here is just such an arrangement as would *naturally* be made by a not over acute person wishing to dispose the articles *naturally*. But it is by no means a *really* natural arrangement. I should rather have looked to see the things *all* lying on the ground and trampled under foot. In the narrow limits of that bower, it would have been scarcely possible that the petticoat and scarf should have retained a position upon the stones, when subjected to the brushing to and fro of many struggling persons. "There was evidence," it is said, "of a struggle; and the earth was trampled, the bushes were broken" – but the petticoat and scarf are found deposited as if upon shelves. "The pieces of the frock torn out by the bushes were about three inches wide and six inches long. One part was the hem of the frock, and it had been mended. They *looked like strips torn off.*" Here, inadvertently, *Le Soleil* has employed an exceedingly suspicious phrase. The pieces, as described, do indeed "look like strips torn off"; but purposely and by hand. It is one of the rarest of accidents that a piece is "torn off", from any garment such as is now in question, by the agency *of a thorn*. From the very nature of such fabrics, a thorn or nail becoming entangled in them, tears them rectangularly – divides them into two longitudinal rents, at right angles with each other, and meeting at an apex where the thorn enters – but it is scarcely possible to conceive the piece "torn off". I never so knew it, nor did you. To tear a piece *off* from such fabric, two distinct forces, in different directions, will be, in almost every case, required. If there be two edges to the fabric – if, for example, it be a pocket-handkerchief, and it is desired to tear from it a slip, then, and then only will the one force serve the purpose. But in the present case the question is of a dress, presenting but one edge. To tear a piece from the interior, where no edge is presented, could only be effected by a miracle through the agency of thorns, and no *one* thorn could accomplish it. But, even where an edge is presented, two thorns will be necessary, operating, the one in two distinct directions, and the other in one. And this in the supposition that the edge is unhemmed. If hemmed, the matter is nearly out of the question. We thus see the numerous and great obstacles in the way of pieces being "torn off" through the simple agency of "thorns"; yet we are required to believe not only that one piece but that many have been so torn. "And one part," too, "*was the hem of the frock*"! Another piece was "*part of the skirt, not the hem*" – that is to say, was torn completely out through the agency of thorns, from the unedged interior of the dress! These, I say, are things which one may well be pardoned for disbelieving; yet, taken collectedly, they form, perhaps, less of reasonable ground for suspicion, than the one startling circumstance of the articles having been left in this thicket at all, by any *murderers* who had enough precaution to think of removing the corpse. You will not have apprehended me rightly, however, if you suppose it my design to *deny* this thicket as the scene of the outrage. There might have been a wrong *here*, or, more possibly, an accident at Madame Deluc's. But, in fact, this is a part of minor importance. We are not engaged in an attempt to discover the scene, but to produce the perpetrators of the murder. What I have adduced, notwithstanding the minuteness with which I have adduced it, has been with the view, first, to show the folly of the positive and headlong assertions of *Le Soleil*, but secondly and chiefly, to bring you, by the most natural route, to a further contemplation of the doubt whether this assassination has, or has not, been the work of *a gang*.

We will resume this question by mere allusion to the revolting details of the surgeon examined at the inquest. It is only necessary to say that his published *inferences*, in regard to the number of the ruffians, have been properly ridiculed as unjust and totally baseless, by all the reputable anatomists of Paris. Not that the matter *might not* have been as inferred, but that there was no ground for the inference – was there not much for another?

'Let us reflect now upon "the traces of a struggle"; and let me ask what these traces have been supposed to demonstrate. A gang. But do they not rather demonstrate the absence of a gang? What *struggle* could have taken place – what struggle so violent and so enduring as to have left its "traces" in all directions – between a weak and defenceless girl and the *gang* of ruffians imagined? The silent grasp of a few rough arms and all would have been over, the victim must have been absolutely passive at their will. You will here bear in mind that the arguments urged against the thicket as the scene, are applicable, in chief part, only against it as the scene of an outrage committed by *more than a single individual*. If we imagine but one violator, we can conceive, and thus only conceive, the struggle of so violent and so obstinate a nature as to have left the "traces" apparent.

'And again. I have already mentioned the suspicion to be excited by the fact that the articles in question were suffered to remain *at all* in the thicket where discovered. It seems almost impossible that these evidences of guilt should have been accidentally left where found. There was sufficient presence of mind (it is supposed) to remove the corpse; and yet a more positive evidence than the corpse itself (whose features might have been quickly obliterated by decay), is allowed to lie conspicuously in the scene of the outrage – I allude to the handkerchief with the *name* of the deceased. If this was accident, it was not the accident *of a gang*. We can imagine it only the accident of an individual. Let us see. An individual has committed the murder. He is alone with the ghost of the departed. He is appalled by what lies motionless before him. The fury of his passion is over, and there is abundant room in his heart for the natural awe of the deed. His is none of that confidence which the presence of numbers inevitably inspires. He is *alone* with the dead. He trembles and is bewildered. Yet there is a necessity for disposing of the corpse. He bears it to the river, but leaves behind him the other evidences of guilt; for it is difficult, if not impossible to carry all the burden at once, and it will be easy to return for what is left. But in his toilsome journey to the water his fears redouble within him. The sounds of life encompass his path. A dozen times he hears or fancies the step of an observer. Even the very lights from the city bewilder him. Yet, in time, and by long and frequent pauses of deep agony, he reaches the river's brink, and disposes of his ghastly charge – perhaps through the medium of a boat. But *now* what treasure does the world hold – what threat of vengeance could it hold out – which would have power to urge the return of that lonely murderer over that toilsome and perilous path, to the thicket and its blood-chilling recollections? He returns not, let the consequences be what they may. He *could* not return if he would. His sole thought is immediate escape. He turns his back *for ever* upon those dreadful shrubberies, and flees as from the wrath to come.

'But how with a gang? Their number would have inspired them with confidence; if, indeed, confidence is ever wanting in the breast of the arrant blackguard; and of arrant blackguards alone are the supposed *gangs* ever constituted. Their number, I say, would have prevented the bewildering and unreasoning terror which I have imagined to paralyse the single man. Could we suppose an oversight in one, or two, or three, this oversight would have been remedied by a fourth. They would have left nothing behind them; for their number would have enabled them to carry *all* at once. There would have been no need of *return*.

'Consider now the circumstance that, in the outer garment of the corpse when found, "a slip, about a foot wide, had been torn upward from the bottom hem to the waist, wound three times round the waist, and secured by a sort of hitch in the back." This was done with the obvious design of affording *a handle* by which to carry the body. But would any *number* of men have dreamed of resorting to such an expedient? To three or four, the limbs of the corpse would have afforded not only a sufficient, but the best possible hold. The device is that of a single individual; and this brings us to the fact that "between the thicket and the river, the rails of the fences were found taken down, and the ground bore evident traces of some heavy burden having been dragged along it"! But would a *number* of men have put themselves to the superfluous trouble of taking down a fence, for the purpose of dragging through it a corpse which they might have *lifted over* any fence in an instant? Would a *number* of men have so *dragged* a corpse at all as to have left evident *traces* of the dragging?

'And here we must refer to an observation of *Le Commerciel*; an observation upon which I have already, in some measure, commented. "A piece," says this journal, "of one of the unfortunate girl's petticoats was torn out and tied under her chin, and around the back of her head, probably to prevent screams. This was done by fellows who had no pocket-handkerchiefs."

'I have before suggested that a genuine blackguard is never *without* a pocket-handkerchief. But it is not to this fact that I now especially advert. That it was not through want of a handkerchief for the purpose imagined by *Le Commerciel*, that this bandage was employed, is rendered apparent by the handkerchief left in the thicket; and that the object was not "to prevent screams" appears, also, from the bandage having been employed in preference to what would so much better have answered the purpose. But the language of the evidence speaks of the strip in question as "found around the neck, fitting loosely, and secured with a hard knot." These words are sufficiently vague, but differ materially from those of *Le Commerciel*. The slip was eighteen inches wide, and therefore, although of muslin, would form a strong band when folded or rumpled longitudinally. And thus rumpled it was discovered. My inference is this. The solitary murderer, having borne the corpse, for some distance (whether from the thicket or elsewhere), by means of the bandage *hitched* around its middle, found the weight, in this mode of procedure, too much for his strength. He resolved to drag the burthen – the evidence goes to show that it was dragged. With this object in view, it became necessary to attach something like a rope to one of the extremities. It could be best attached about the neck, where the head would prevent it slipping off. And now the murderer bethought him, unquestionably, of the bandage about the loins. He would have used this, but for its volution about the corpse, the *hitch* which embarrassed it, and the reflection that it had not been "torn off" from the garment. It was easier to tear a new slip from the petticoat. He tore it, made it fast about the neck, and so *dragged* his victim to the brink of the river. That this "bandage", only attainable with trouble and delay, and but imperfectly answering its purpose – that this bandage was employed *at all*, demonstrates that the necessity for its employment sprang from circumstances arising at a period when the handkerchief was no longer attainable – that is to say, arising, as we have imagined, after quitting the thicket (if the thicket it was), and on the road between the thicket and the river.

'But the evidence, you will say, of Madame Deluc (!) points especially to the presence of *a gang*, in the vicinity of the thicket, at or about the epoch of the murder. This I grant. I doubt if there were not a *dozen* gangs, such as described by Madame Deluc, in and about the vicinity of the Barrière du Roule at *or about* the period of this tragedy. But the gang which has drawn upon itself the pointed animadversion, although the somewhat tardy and very suspicious evidence of Madame Deluc, is the *only* gang which is represented by that honest and scrupulous old lady as having eaten her cakes and swallowed her brandy, without putting themselves to the trouble of making her payment. *Et hinc illæ iræ*? [9]

'But what *is* the precise evidence of Madame Deluc? "A gang of miscreants made their appearance, behaved boisterously, ate and drank without making payment, followed in the route of the young man and girl, returned to the inn *about dusk*, and recrossed the river as if in great haste."

'Now this "great haste" very possibly seemed *greater* haste in the eyes of Madame Deluc, since she dwelt lingeringly and lamentingly upon her violated cakes and ale – cakes and ale for which she might still have entertained a faint hope of compensation. Why, otherwise, since it was *about dusk*, should she make a point of the *haste*? It is no cause for wonder, surely, that even a gang of blackguards should make *haste* to get home, when a wide river is to be crossed in small boats, when storm impends, and when night *approaches*.

'I say *approaches*; for the night had *not yet arrived*. It was only *about dusk* that the indecent haste of these "miscreants" offended the sober eyes of Madame Deluc. But we are told that it was upon this very evening that Madame Deluc, as well as her eldest son, "heard the screams of a female in the vicinity of the inn." And in what words does Madame Deluc designate the period of the evening at which these screams were heard? It was "*soon after dark*," she says. But "*soon after* dark," is at least *dark*; and "*about dusk*" is as certainly daylight. Thus it is abundantly clear that the gang quitted the Barrière du Roule *prior* to the screams overheard (?) by Madame Deluc. And although, in all the many reports of the evidence, the relative expressions in question are distinctly and invariably employed just as I have employed them in this conversation with yourself, no notice whatever of the gross discrepancy has, as yet, been taken by any of the public journals, or by any of the myrmidons of police.

'I shall add but one to the arguments against *a gang*; but this *one* has, to my own understanding at least, a weight altogether irresistible. Under the circumstances of large reward offered, and full pardon to any king's evidence, it is not to be imagined, for a moment, that some member of *a gang* of low ruffians, or of any body of men, would not long ago have betrayed his accomplices. Each one of a gang so placed is not so much greedy of reward, or anxious for escape, as *fearful of betrayal*. He betrays eagerly and early that *he may not himself be betrayed*. That the secret has not been divulged, is the very best of proof that it is, in fact, a secret. The horrors of this dark deed are known only to *one*, or two, living human beings, and to God.

'Let us sum up now the meagre yet certain fruits of our long analysis. We have attained the idea either of a fatal accident under the roof of Madame Deluc, or of a murder perpetrated, in the thicket at the Barrière du Roule, by a lover, or at least by an intimate and secret associate of the deceased. This associate is of swarthy complexion. This complexion, the "hitch" in the bandage, and the "sailor's knot" with which the bonnet-ribbon is tied, point to a seaman. His companionship with the deceased, a gay, but not an abject young girl, designates him as above the grade of the common sailor. Here the well-written and urgent communications to the journals are much in the way of corroboration. The circumstance of the first elopement, as mentioned by *Le Mercurie*, tends to blend the idea of this seaman with that of the "naval officer" who is first known to have led the unfortunate into crime.

'And here, most fitly, comes the consideration of the continued absence of him of the dark complexion. Let me pause to observe that the complexion of this man is dark and swarthy; it was no common swarthiness which constituted the *sole* point of remembrance, both as regards Valence and Madame Deluc. But why is this man absent? Was he murdered by the gang? If so, why are there only *traces* of the assassinated *girl*? The scene of the two outrages will naturally be supposed identical. And where is his corpse? The assassins would most probably have disposed of both in the same way. But it may be said that this man lives, and is deterred from making himself known, through dread of being charged with the murder. This consideration might be supposed to operate upon him now – at this late period – since it has been given in evidence that he was seen with Marie – but it would have had no force at the period of the deed. The first impulse of an innocent man would have been to announce the outrage, and to aid in identifying the ruffians. This, *policy* would have suggested. He had been seen with the girl. He had crossed the river with her in an open ferry-boat. The denouncing of the assassins would have appeared, even to an idiot, the surest and sole means of relieving himself from suspicion. We cannot suppose him, on the night of the fatal Sunday, both innocent himself and incognisant of an outrage committed. Yet only under such circumstances is it possible to imagine that he would have failed, if alive, in the denouncement of the assassins.

'And what means are ours of attaining the truth? We shall find these means multiplying and gathering distinctness as we proceed. Let us sift to the bottom this affair of the first elopement. Let us know the full history of "the officer", with his present circumstances, and his whereabouts at the precise period of the murder. Let us carefully compare with each other the various communications sent to the evening paper, in which the object was to inculpate a gang. This done, let us compare these communications, both as regards style and MS., with those sent to the morning paper, at a previous period, and insisting so vehemently upon the guilt of Mennais. And, all this done, let us again compare these various communications with the known MSS. of the officer. Let us endeavour to ascertain, by repeated questionings of Madame Deluc and her boys, as well as of the omnibus-driver, Valence, something more of the personal appearance and bearing of the "man of dark complexion." Queries, skilfully directed, will not fail to elicit, from some of these parties, information on this particular point (or upon others) – information which the parties themselves may not even be aware of possessing. And let us now trace *the boat* picked up by the bargeman on the morning of Monday the 23rd of June, and which was removed from the barge-office, without the cognisance of the officer in attendance, and *without the rudder*, at some period prior to the discovery of the corpse. With a proper caution and perseverance we shall infallibly trace this boat; for not only can the bargeman who picked it up identify it, but the *rudder is at hand*. The rudder *of a sail-boat* would not have been abandoned, without inquiry, by one altogether at ease in heart. And here let me pause to insinuate a question. There was no *advertisement* of the picking up of this boat. It was silently taken to the barge-office, and as silently removed. But its owner or employer – how *happened* he, at so early a period as Tuesday morning, to be informed, without the agency of advertisement, of the locality of the boat taken up on Monday, unless we imagine some connection with the navy – some personal permanent connection leading to cognisance of its minute interests – its petty local news?

'In speaking of the lonely assassin dragging his burden to the shore, I have already suggested the probability of his availing himself *of a boat*. Now we are to understand that Marie Rogêt *was* precipitated from a boat. This would naturally have been the case. The corpse could not have been trusted to the shallow waters of the shore. The peculiar marks on the back and shoulders of the victim tell of the bottom ribs of a boat. That the body was found without weight is also corroborative of the idea. If thrown from the shore a weight would have been attached. We can only account for its absence by supposing the murderer to have neglected the precaution of supplying himself with it before pushing off. In the act of consigning the corpse to the water, he would unquestionably have noticed his oversight; but then no remedy would have been at hand. Any risk would have been preferred to a return to that accursed shore. Having rid himself of his ghastly charge, the murderer would have hastened to the city. There, at some obscure wharf, he would have leaped on land. But the boat – would he have secured it? He would have been in too great haste for such things as securing a boat. Moreover, in fastening it to the wharf, he would have felt as if securing evidence against himself. His natural thought would have been to cast from him, as far as possible, all that had held connection with his crime. He would not only have fled from the wharf, but he would not have permitted *the boat* to remain. Assuredly he would have cast it adrift. Let us pursue our fancies. In the morning, the wretch is stricken with unutterable horror at finding that the boat has been picked up and detained at a locality which he is in the daily habit of frequenting – at a locality, perhaps, which his duty compels him to frequent. The next night, *without daring to ask for the rudder*, he removes it. Now *where* is that rudderless boat? Let it be one of our first purposes to discover. With the first glimpse we obtain of it, the dawn of our success shall begin. This boat shall guide us, with a rapidity which will surprise even ourselves, to him who employed it in the midnight of the fatal Sabbath. Corroboration will rise upon corroboration, and the murderer will be traced.'

[For reasons which we shall not specify, but which to many readers will appear obvious, we have taken the liberty of here omitting, from the MSS. placed in our hands, such portion as details the *following up* of the apparently slight clew obtained by Dupin. We feel it advisable only to state, in brief, that the result desired was brought to pass; and that the Prefect fulfilled punctually, although with reluctance, the terms of his compact with the Chevalier. Mr Poe's article concludes with the following words. – *Eds.**]

It will be understood that I speak of coincidence *and no more*. What I have said above upon this topic must suffice. In my own heart there dwells no faith in præter-nature. That Nature and its God are two, no man who thinks will deny. That the latter, creating the former, can, at will, control or modify it, is all unquestionable. I say 'at will'; for the question is of will, and not, as the insanity of logic has assumed, of power. It is not that the Deity *cannot* modify His laws, but that we insult Him in imagining a possible necessity for modification. In their origin these laws were fashioned to embrace *all* contingencies which *could* lie in the Future. With God all is *Now*.

I repeat, then, that I speak of these things only as of coincidences.

* Of the magazine in which the article was originally published

And further: in what I relate it will be seen that between the fate of the unhappy Marie Cecilia Rogers, so far as that fate is known, and the fate of one Marie Rogêt up to a certain epoch in her history, there has existed a parallel in the contemplation of whose wonderful exactitude the reason becomes embarrassed. I say all this will be seen. But let it not for a moment be supposed that, in proceeding with the sad narrative of Marie from the epoch just mentioned, and in tracing to its *dénouement* the mystery which enshrouded her, it is my covert design to hint at an extension of the parallel, or even to suggest that the measures adopted in Paris for the discovery of the assassin of a *grisette*, or measures founded in any similar ratiocination, would produce any similar result.

For, in respect to the latter branch of the supposition, it should be considered that the most trifling variation in the facts of the two cases might give rise to the most important miscalculations, by diverting thoroughly the two courses of events; very much as, in arithmetic, an error which, in its own individuality, may be inappreciable, produces, at length, by dint of multiplication at all points of the process, a result enormously at variance with truth. And, in regard to the former branch, we must not fail to hold in view that the very Calculus of Probabilities to which I have referred, forbids all idea of the extension of the parallel – forbids it with a positiveness strong and decided just in proportion as this parallel has already been long-drawn and exact. This is one of those anomalous propositions which, seemingly appealing to thought altogether apart from the mathematical, is yet one which only the mathematician can fully entertain. Nothing, for example, is more difficult than to convince the merely general reader that the fact of sixes having been thrown twice in succession by a player at dice, is sufficient cause for betting the largest odds that sixes will not be thrown in the third attempt. A suggestion to this effect is usually rejected by the intellect at once. It does not appear that the two throws which have been completed, and which lie now absolutely in the Past, can have influence upon the throw which exists only in the Future. The chance for throwing sixes seems to be precisely as it was at any ordinary time – that is to say, subject only to the influence of the various other throws which may be made by the dice. And this is a reflection which appears so exceedingly obvious that attempts to controvert it are received more frequently with a derisive smile than with anything like respectful attention. The error here involved – a gross error redolent of mischief – I cannot pretend to expose within the limits assigned me at present; and with the philosophical it needs no exposure. It may be sufficient here to say that it forms one of an infinite series of mistakes which arise in the path of Reason through her propensity for seeking truth *in detail*.

The Purloined Letter

Nil sapientiæ odiosius acumine nimio.[1]

SENECA

AT PARIS, just after dark one gusty evening in the autumn of 18—, I was enjoying the twofold luxury of meditation and a meerschaum, in company with my friend, C. Auguste Dupin, in his little back library or book-closet, *au troisième*, No. 33 Rue Dunôt, Faubourg St Germain. For one hour at least we had maintained a profound silence; while each, to any casual observer, might have seemed intently and exclusively occupied with the curling eddies of smoke that oppressed the atmosphere of the chamber. For myself, however, I was mentally discussing certain topics which had formed matter for conversation between us at an earlier period of the evening; I mean the affair of the Rue Morgue, and the mystery attending the murder of Marie Rogêt. I looked upon it, therefore, as something of a coincidence, when the door of our apartment was thrown open and admitted our old acquaintance, Monsieur G—, the Prefect of the Parisian police.

We gave him a hearty welcome; for there was nearly half as much of the entertaining as of the contemptible about the man, and we had not seen him for several years. We had been sitting in the dark, and Dupin now arose for the purpose of lighting a lamp, but sat down again, without doing so, upon G.'s saying that he had called to consult us, or rather to ask the opinion of my friend, about some official business which had occasioned a great deal of trouble.

'If it is any point requiring reflection,' observed Dupin, as he forbore to enkindle the wick, 'we shall examine it to better purpose in the dark.'

'That is another of your odd notions,' said the Prefect, who had a fashion of calling everything 'odd' that was beyond his comprehension, and thus lived amid an absolute legion of 'oddities.'

'Very true,' said Dupin, as he supplied his visitor with a pipe, and rolled towards him a comfortable chair.

'And what is the difficulty now?' I asked. 'Nothing more in the assassination way, I hope?'

'Oh, no; nothing of that nature. The fact is, the business is *very* simple indeed, and I make no doubt that we can manage it sufficiently well ourselves; but then I thought Dupin would like to hear the details of it, because it is so excessively *odd.*'

'Simple and odd,' said Dupin.

'Why, yes; and not exactly that, either. The fact is, we have all been a good deal puzzled because the affair *is* so simple, and yet baffles us altogether.'

'Perhaps it is the very simplicity of the thing which puts you at fault,' said my friend.

'What nonsense you *do* talk!' replied the Prefect, laughing heartily.

'Perhaps the mystery is a little *too* plain,' said Dupin.

'Oh, good heavens! who ever heard of such an idea?'

'A little *too* self-evident.'

'Ha! ha! ha! – ha! ha! ha! – ho! ho! ho!' roared our visitor, profoundly amused; 'O Dupin, you will be the death of me yet!'

'And what, after all, *is* the matter on hand?' I asked.

'Why, I will tell you,' replied the Prefect, as he gave a long, steady, and contemplative puff, and settled himself in his chair. 'I will tell you in a few words; but, before I begin, let me caution you that this is an affair demanding the greatest secrecy, and that I should most probably lose the position I now hold, were it known that I confided it to any one.'

'Proceed,' said I.

'Or not,' said Dupin.

'Well, then; I have received personal information, from a very high quarter, that a certain document of the last importance has been purloined from the royal apartments. The individual who purloined it is known; this beyond a doubt; he was seen to take it. It is known, also, that it still remains in his possession.'

'How is this known?' asked Dupin.

'It is clearly inferred,' replied the Prefect, 'from the nature of the document, and from the non-appearance of certain results which would at once arise from its passing *out* of the robber's possession – that is to say, from his employing it as he must design in the end to employ it.'

'Be a little more explicit,' I said.

'Well, I may venture so far as to say that the paper gives its holder a certain power in a certain quarter where such power is immensely valuable.' The Prefect was fond of the cant of diplomacy.

'Still I do not quite understand,' said Dupin.

'No? Well; the disclosure of the document to a third person, who shall be nameless, would bring in question the honour of a personage of most exalted station; and this fact gives the holder of the document an ascendency over the illustrious personage whose honour and peace are so jeopardised.'

'But this ascendency,' I interposed, 'would depend upon the robber's knowledge of the loser's knowledge of the robber. Who would dare – '

'The thief,' said G., 'is the Minister D—, who dares all things, those unbecoming as well as those becoming a man. The method of the theft was not less ingenious than bold. The document in question – a letter, to be frank – had been received by the personage robbed while alone in the royal *boudoir*. During its perusal she was suddenly interrupted by the entrance of the other exalted personage from whom especially it was her wish to conceal it. After a hurried and vain endeavour to thrust it in a drawer, she was forced to place it, open as it was, upon a table. The address, however, was uppermost, and, the contents thus unexposed, the letter escaped notice. At this juncture enters the Minister D—. His lynx eye immediately perceives the paper, recognises the handwriting of the address, observes the confusion of the personage addressed, and fathoms her secret. After some business transactions, hurried through in his ordinary manner, he produces a letter somewhat similar to the one in question, opens it, pretends to read it, and then places it in close juxtaposition to the other. Again he converses, for some fifteen minutes, upon the public affairs. At length, in taking leave, he takes also from the table the letter to which he had no claim. Its rightful owner saw, but, of course, dared not call attention to the act, in the presence of the third personage who stood at her elbow. The Minister decamped, leaving his own letter – one of no importance – upon the table.'

'Here, then,' said Dupin to me, 'you have precisely what you demand to make the ascendency complete – the robber's knowledge of the loser's knowledge of the robber.'

'Yes,' replied the Prefect; 'and the power thus attained has, for some months past, been wielded, for political purposes, to a very dangerous extent. The personage robbed is more thoroughly convinced, every day, of the necessity of reclaiming her letter. But this, of course, cannot be done openly. In fine, driven to despair, she has committed the matter to me.'

'Than whom,' said Dupin, amid a perfect whirlwind of smoke, 'no more sagacious agent could, I suppose, be desired, or even imagined.'

'You flatter me,' replied the Prefect; 'but it is possible that some such opinion may have been entertained.'

'It is clear,' said I, 'as you observe, that the letter is still in the possession of the Minister; since it is this possession, and not any employment of the letter, which bestows the power. With the employment the power departs.'

'True,' said G.; 'and upon this conviction I proceeded. My first care was to make thorough search of the Minister's hotel; and here my chief embarrassment lay in the necessity of searching without his knowledge. Beyond all things, I have been warned of the danger which would result from giving him reason to suspect our design.'

'But,' said I, 'you are quite *au fait* in these investigations. The Parisian police have done this thing often before.'

'Oh yes; and for this reason I did not despair. The habits of the Minister gave me, too, a great advantage. He is frequently absent from home all night. His servants are by no means numerous. They sleep at a distance from their master's apartment, and, being chiefly Neapolitans, are readily made drunk. I have keys, as you know, with which I can open any chamber or cabinet in Paris. For three months a night has not passed, during the greater part of which I have not been engaged, personally, in ransacking the D—Hôtel. My honour is interested, and, to mention a great secret, the reward is enormous. So I did not abandon the search until I had become fully satisfied that the thief is a more astute man than myself. I fancy that I have investigated every nook and corner of the premises in which it is possible that the paper can be concealed.'

'But is it not possible,' I suggested, 'that although the letter may be in possession of the Minister, as it unquestionably is, he may have concealed it elsewhere than upon his own premises?'

'This is barely possible,' said Dupin. 'The present peculiar condition of affairs at court, and especially of those intrigues in which D— is known to be involved, would render the instant availability of the document – its susceptibility of being produced at a moment's notice – a point of nearly equal importance with its possession.'

'Its susceptibility of being produced?' said I.

'That is to say, of being *destroyed*,' said Dupin.

'True,' I observed; 'the paper is clearly then upon the premises. As for its being upon the person of the Minister, we may consider that as out of the question.'

'Entirely,' said the Prefect. 'He has been twice waylaid, as if by footpads, and his person rigorously searched under my own inspection.'

'You might have spared yourself this trouble,' said Dupin. 'D—, I presume, is not altogether a fool, and, if not, must have anticipated these waylayings, as a matter of course.'

'Not *altogether* a fool,' said G.; 'but then he's a poet, which I take to be only one remove from a fool.'

'True,' said Dupin, after a long and thoughtful whiff from his meerschaum, 'although I have been guilty of certain doggerel myself.'

'Suppose you detail,' said I, 'the particulars of your search.'

'Why, the fact is we took our time, and we searched *everywhere*. I have had long experience in these affairs. I took the entire building, room by room; devoting the nights of a whole week to each. We examined, first, the furniture of each department. We opened every possible drawer; and I presume you know that, to a properly trained police agent, such a thing as a *secret* drawer is impossible. Any man is a dolt who permits a "secret" drawer to escape him in a search of this kind. The thing is *so* plain. There is a certain amount of bulk – of space – to be accounted for in every cabinet. Then we have accurate rules. The fiftieth part of a line could not escape us. After the cabinets we took the chairs. The cushions we probed with the fine long needles you have seen me employ. From the tables we removed the tops.'

'Why so?'

'Sometimes the top of a table, or other similarly arranged piece of furniture, is removed by the person wishing to conceal an article; then the leg is excavated, the article deposited within the cavity, and the top replaced. The bottoms and tops of bedposts are employed in the same way.'

'But could not the cavity be detected by sounding?' I asked.

'By no means, if, when the article is deposited, a sufficient wadding of cotton be placed around it. Besides, in our case, we were obliged to proceed without noise.'

'But you could not have removed – you could not have taken to pieces *all* articles of furniture in which it would have been possible to make a deposit in the manner you mention. A letter may be compressed into a thin spiral roll, not differing much in shape or bulk from a large knitting-needle, and in this form it might be inserted into the rung of a chair, for example. You did not take to pieces all the chairs?'

'Certainly not; but we did better – we examined the rungs of every chair in the hotel, and, indeed, the jointings of every description of furniture, by the aid of a most powerful microscope. Had there been any traces of recent disturbance we should not have failed to detect it instantly. A single grain of gimlet-dust, for example, would have been as obvious as an apple. Any disorder in the gluing – any unusual gaping in the joints – would have sufficed to ensure detection.'

'I presume you looked to the mirrors, between the boards and the plates, and you probed the beds and the bedclothes, as well as the curtains and carpets.'

'That of course; and when we had absolutely completed every article of the furniture in this way, then we examined the house itself. We divided its entire surface into compartments, which we numbered, so that none might be missed; then we scrutinised each individual square inch throughout the premises, including the two houses immediately adjoining, with the microscope, as before.'

'The two houses adjoining!' I exclaimed; 'you must have had a great deal of trouble.'

'We had; but the reward offered is prodigious.'

'You include the *grounds* about the houses?'

'All the grounds are paved with brick. They gave us comparatively little trouble. We examined the moss between the bricks, and found it undisturbed.'

'You looked among D—'s papers, of course, and into the books of the library?'

'Certainly; we opened every package and parcel; we not only opened every book, but we turned over every leaf in each volume, not contenting ourselves with a mere shake, according to the fashion of some of our police officers. We also measured the thickness of every book-*cover*, with the most accurate admeasurement, and applied to each the most jealous scrutiny of the microscope. Had any of the bindings been recently meddled with, it would have been utterly impossible that the fact should have escaped observation. Some five or six volumes, just from the hands of the binder, we carefully probed longitudinally, with the needles.'

'You explored the floors beneath the carpets?'

'Beyond doubt. We removed every carpet, and examined the boards with the microscope.'

'And the paper on the walls?'

'Yes.'

'You looked into the cellars?'

'We did.'

'Then,' I said, 'you have been making a miscalculation, and the letter is *not* upon the premises, as you suppose.'

'I fear you are right there,' said the Prefect. 'And now, Dupin, what would you advise me to do?'

'To make a thorough research of the premises.'

'That is absolutely needless,' replied G—. 'I am not more sure than I breathe than I am that the letter is not at the hotel.'

'I have no better advice to give you,' said Dupin. 'You have, of course, an accurate description of the letter?'

'Oh yes!' And here the Prefect, producing a memorandum-book, proceeded to read aloud a minute account of the internal, and especially of the external appearance of the missing document. Soon after finishing the perusal of this description, he took his departure more entirely depressed in spirits than I had ever known the good gentleman before.

In about a month afterwards he paid us another visit, and found us occupied very nearly as before. He took a pipe and a chair and entered into some ordinary conversation. At length I said –

'Well, but G—, what of the purloined letter? I presume you have at last made up your mind that there is no such thing as overreaching the Minister?'

'Confound him, say I – yes; I made the re-examination, however, as Dupin suggested – but it was all labour lost, as I knew it would be.'

'How much was the reward offered, did you say?' asked Dupin.

'Why, a very great deal – a *very* liberal reward – I don't like to say how much, precisely; but I *will* say, that I wouldn't mind giving my individual cheque for fifty thousand francs to any one who could obtain me that letter. The fact is, it is becoming of more and more importance every day; and the reward has been lately doubled. If it were trebled, however, I could do no more than I have done.'

'Why, yes,' said Dupin drawlingly, between the whiffs of his meerschaum, 'I really – think, G—, you have not exerted yourself – to the utmost – in this matter. You might – do a little more, I think, eh?'

'How? – in what way?'

'Why – puff, puff – you might – puff, puff – employ counsel in the matter, eh? – puff, puff, puff. Do you remember the story they tell of Abernethy?'[2]

'No; hang Abernethy!'

'To be sure! hang him and welcome. But once upon a time, a certain rich miser conceived the design of sponging upon this Abernethy for a medical opinion. Getting up, for this purpose, an ordinary conversation in a private company, he insinuated his case to the physician, as that of an imaginary individual.

' "We will suppose," said the miser, "that his symptoms are such and such; now, doctor, what would *you* have directed him to take?"

' "Take!" said Abernethy, "why, take *advice*, to be sure." '

'But,' said the Prefect, a little discomposed, 'I am *perfectly* willing to take advice, and to pay for it. I would *really* give fifty thousand francs to any one who would aid me in the matter.'

'In that case,' replied Dupin, opening a drawer, and producing a cheque-book, 'you may as well fill me up a cheque for the amount mentioned. When you have signed it, I will hand you the letter.'

I was astounded. The Prefect appeared absolutely thunderstricken. For some minutes he remained speechless and motionless, looking incredulously at my friend with open mouth, and eyes that seemed starting from their sockets; then, apparently recovering himself in some measure, he seized a pen, and after several pauses and vacant stares, finally filled up and signed a cheque for fifty thousand francs, and handed it across the table to Dupin. The latter examined it carefully and deposited it in his pocket-book; then, unlocking an *escritoire*, took thence a letter and gave it to the Prefect. This functionary grasped it in a perfect agony of joy, opened it with a trembling hand, cast a rapid glance at its contents, and then, scrambling and struggling to the door, rushed at length unceremoniously from the room and from the house, without having uttered a syllable since Dupin had requested him to fill up the cheque.

When he had gone, my friend entered into some explanations.

'The Parisian police,' he said, 'are exceedingly able in their way. They are persevering, ingenious, cunning, and thoroughly versed in the knowledge which their duties seem chiefly to demand. Thus, when G— detailed to us his mode of searching the premises at the Hôtel D—, I felt entire confidence in his having made a satisfactory investigation – so far as his labours extended.'

'So far as his labours extended?' said I.

'Yes,' said Dupin. 'The measures adopted were not only the best of their kind, but carried out to absolute perfection. Had the letter been deposited within the range of their search, these fellows would, beyond a question, have found it.'

I merely laughed – but he seemed quite serious in all that he said.

'The measures, then,' he continued, 'were good in their kind, and well executed; their defect lay in their being inapplicable to the case, and to the man. A certain set of highly ingenious resources are, with the Prefect, a sort of Procrustean bed, to which he forcibly adapts his designs. But he perpetually errs by being too deep or too shallow for the matter in hand; and many a schoolboy is a better reasoner than he. I knew one about eight years of age, whose success at guessing in the game of "even and odd" attracted universal admiration. This game is simple, and is played with marbles. One player holds in his hand a number of these toys, and demands of another whether that number is even or odd. If the guess is right, the guesser wins one; if wrong, he loses one. The boy to whom I allude won all the marbles of the school. Of course he had some principle of guessing; and this lay in mere observation and admeasurement of the astuteness of his opponents. For example, an arrant simpleton is his opponent, and, holding up his closed hand, asks, "Are they even or odd?" Our schoolboy replies "Odd", and loses; but upon the second trial he wins, for he then says to himself, "The simpleton had them even upon the first trial, and his amount of cunning is just sufficient to make him have them odd upon the second; I will therefore guess odd" – he guesses odd, and wins. Now, with a simpleton a degree above the first, he would have reasoned thus: "This fellow finds that in the first instance I guessed odd, and, in the second, he will propose to himself, upon the first impulse, a simple variation from even to odd, as did the first simpleton; but then a second thought will suggest that this is too simple a variation, and finally he will decide upon putting it even as before. I will therefore guess even" – he guesses even, and wins. Now this mode of reasoning in the schoolboy, whom his fellows termed "lucky" – what, in its last analysis, is it?'

'It is merely,' I said, 'an identification of the reasoner's intellect with that of his opponent.'

'It is,' said Dupin; 'and upon inquiring of the boy by what means, he effected the *thorough* identification in which his success, consisted, I received answer as follows: "When I wish to find out how wise, or how stupid, or how good, or how wicked is any one, or what are his thoughts at the moment, I fashion the expression of my face, as accurately as possible, in accordance with the expression of his, and then wait to see what thoughts or sentiments arise in my mind or heart, as if to match or correspond with the expression." This response of the schoolboy lies at the bottom of all the spurious profundity which has been attributed to Rochefoucauld,[3] to La Bougive,[4] to Machiavelli,[5] and to Campanella.'[6]

'And the identification,' I said, 'of the reasoner's, intellect with that of his opponent, depends, if I understand you aright, upon the accuracy with which the opponent's intellect is admeasured.'

'For its practical value it depends upon this,' replied Dupin; 'and the Prefect and his cohort fail so frequently, first, by default of his identification, and, secondly, by ill-admeasurement, or rather through non-admeasurement, of the intellect with which they are engaged. They consider only their *own* ideas of ingenuity; and, in searching for anything hidden, advert only to the modes in which *they* would have hidden it. They are right in this much – that their own ingenuity is a faithful representative of that of *the mass*; but when the cunning of the individual felon is diverse in character from their own, the felon foils them, of course. This always happens when it is above their own, and very usually when it is below. They have no variation of principle in their investigations; at best, when urged by some unusual emergency – by some extraordinary reward – they extend or exaggerate their old modes of *practice*, without touching their principles. What, for example, in this case of D—, has been done to vary the principle of action? What is all this boring, and probing, and sounding, and scrutinising with the microscope, and dividing the surface of the building into registered square inches – what is it all but an exaggeration *of the application* of the one principle or set of principles of search, which are based upon the one set of notions regarding human ingenuity, to which the Prefect, in the long routine of his duty, has been accustomed? Do you not see he has taken it for granted that *all* men proceed to conceal a letter – not exactly in a gimlet-hole bored in a chair-leg – but, at least, in *some* out-of-the-way hole or corner suggested by the same tenor of thought which would urge a man to secrete a letter in a gimlet-hole bored in a chair-leg? And do you not see also, that such *recherchés* nooks for concealment are adapted only for ordinary occasions, and would be adopted only by ordinary intellects; for, in all cases of concealment, a disposal of the article concealed – a disposal of it in this *recherché* manner – is, in the very first instance, presumable and presumed; and thus its discovery depends, not at all upon the acumen, but altogether upon the mere care, patience, and determination of the seekers; and where the case is of importance – or, what amounts to the same thing in the policial eyes, when the reward is of magnitude – the qualities in question have *never* been known to fail. You will now understand what I meant in suggesting that, had the purloined letter been hidden anywhere within the limits of the Prefect's examination – in other words, had the principle of its concealment been comprehended within the principles of the Prefect – its discovery would have been a matter altogether beyond question. This functionary, however, has been thoroughly mystified; and the remote source of his defeat lies in the supposition that the Minister is a fool, because he has acquired renown as a poet. All fools are poets – this the Prefect *feels*; and he is merely guilty of a *non distributio medii*[7] in thence inferring that all poets are fools.'

'But is this really the poet?' I asked. 'There are two brothers, I know; and both have attained reputation in letters. The Minister, I believe, has written learnedly on the Differential Calculus. He is a mathematician, and no poet.'

'You are mistaken; I know him well; he is both. As poet *and* mathematician, he would reason well; as mere mathematician, he could not have reasoned at all, and thus would have been at the mercy of the Prefect.'

'You surprise me,' I said, 'by these opinions, which have been contradicted by the voice of the world. You do not mean to set at naught the well-digested idea of centuries. The mathematical reason has long been regarded as *the* reason *par excellence*.'

' "*Il y a à parièr*," ' replied Dupin, quoting from Chamfort,[8] ' "*que toute idée publique, toute convention reçue, est une sottise, car elle a convenue au plus grand nombre*." The mathematicians, I grant you, have done their best to promulgate the popular error to which you allude, and which is none the less an error for its promulgation as truth. With an art worthy a better cause, for example, they have insinuated the term "analysis" into application to algebra. The French are the originators of this particular deception; but if a term is of any importance – if words derive any value from applicability – then "analysis" conveys "algebra" about as much as, in Latin, "*ambitus*" [9] implies "ambition", "*religio*" [10] "religion" or "*homines honesti*" [11] a set of *honourable* men.'

'You have a quarrel on hand, I see,' said I, 'with some of the algebraists of Paris; but proceed.'

'I dispute the availability, and thus the value, of that reason which is cultivated in any especial form other than the abstractly logical. I dispute, in particular, the reason educed by mathematical study. The mathematics are the science of form and quantity; mathematical reasoning is merely logic applied to observation upon form and quantity. The great error lies in supposing that even the truths of what is called *pure* algebra, are abstract or general truths. And this error is so egregious that I am confounded at the universality with which it has been received. Mathematical axioms are *not* axioms of general truth. What is true of *relation* – of form and quantity – is often grossly false in regard to morals, for example. In this latter science it is very usually *un*true that the aggregated parts are equal to the whole. In chemistry also the axiom fails. In the consideration of motive it fails; for two motives, each of a given value, have not, necessarily, a value when united, equal to the sum of their values apart. There are numerous other mathematical truths which are only truths within the limits of *relation*. But the mathematician argues, from his *finite truths*, through habit, as if they were of an absolutely general applicability – as the world indeed imagines them to be. Bryant,[12] in his very learned "Mythology," mentions an analogous source of error, when he says that "although the Pagan fables are not believed, yet we forget ourselves continually, and make inferences from them as existing realities." With the algebraists, however, who are Pagans themselves, the "Pagan fables" *are* believed, and the inferences are made, not so much through lapse of memory, as through an unaccountable addling of the brains. In short, I never yet encountered the mere mathematician who could be trusted out of equal roots, or one who did not clandestinely hold it as a point of his faith that x^2+px was absolutely and unconditionally equal to q. Say to one of these gentlemen, by way of experiment, if you please, that you believe occasions may occur where x^2+px is *not* altogether equal to q, and, having made him understand what you mean, get out of his reach as speedily as convenient, for, beyond doubt, he will endeavour to knock you down.

'I mean to say,' continued Dupin, while I merely laughed at his last observations, 'that if the Minister had been no more than a mathematician, the Prefect would have been under no necessity of giving me this cheque. I knew him, however, as both mathematician and poet, and my measures were adapted to his capacity, with reference to the circumstances by which he was surrounded. I knew him as a courtier, too, and as a bold *intriguant*.[13] Such a man, I considered, could not fail to be aware of the ordinary policial modes of action. He could not have failed to anticipate – and events have proved that he did not fail to anticipate – the waylayings to which he was subjected. He must have foreseen, I reflected, the secret investigations of his premises. His frequent absences from home at night, which were hailed by the Prefect as certain aids to his success, I regarded only as ruses, to afford opportunity for thorough search to the police, and thus the sooner to impress them with the conviction to which G—, in fact, did finally arrive – the conviction that the letter was not upon the premises. I felt, also, that the whole train of thought, which I was at some pains in detailing to you just now, concerning the invariable principle of policial action in searches for articles concealed – I felt that this whole train of thought would necessarily pass through the mind of the Minister. It would imperatively lead him to despise all the ordinary *nooks* of concealment. *He* could not, I reflected, be so weak as not to see that the most intricate and remote recess of his hotel would be as open as his commonest closets to the eyes, to the probes, to the gimlets,[14] and to the microscopes of the Prefect. I saw, in fine, that he would be driven, as a matter of course, to *simplicity*, if not deliberately induced to it as a matter of choice. You will remember, perhaps, how desperately the Prefect laughed when I suggested, upon our first interview, that it was just possible this mystery troubled him so much on account of its being so *very* self-evident.'

'Yes,' said I, 'I remember his merriment well. I really thought he would have fallen into convulsions.'

'The material world,' continued Dupin, 'abounds with very strict analogies to the immaterial; and thus some colour of truth has been given to the rhetorical dogma, that metaphor, or simile, may be made to strengthen an argument, as well as to embellish a description. The principle of the *vis inertiæ*,[15] for example, seems to be identical in physics and metaphysics. It is not more true in the former, that a large body is with more difficulty set in motion than a smaller one, and that its subsequent momentum is commensurate with this difficulty, than it is, in the latter, that intellects of the vaster capacity, while more forcible, more constant, and more eventful in their movements than those of inferior grade, are yet the less readily moved, and more embarrassed and full of hesitation in the first few steps of their progress. Again, have you ever noticed which of the street signs over the shop-doors are the most attractive of attention?'

'I have never given the matter a thought,' I said.

'There is a game of puzzles,' he resumed, 'which is played upon a map. One party playing requires another to find a given word – the name of town, river, state or empire – any word, in short, upon the motley and perplexed surface of the chart. A novice in the game generally seeks to embarrass his opponents by giving them the most minutely lettered names; but the adept selects such words as stretch, in large characters, from one end of the chart to the other. These, like the over-largely lettered signs and placards of the street, escape observation by dint of being excessively obvious; and here the physical oversight is precisely analogous with the moral inapprehension by which the intellect suffers to pass unnoticed those considerations which are too obtrusively and too palpably self-evident. But this is a point, it appears, somewhat above or beneath the understanding of the Prefect. He never once thought it probable, or possible, that the Minister had deposited the letter immediately beneath the nose of the whole world, by way of best preventing any portion of that world from perceiving it.

'But the more I reflected upon the daring, dashing, and discriminating ingenuity of D—; upon the fact that the document must always have been *at hand*, if he intended to use it to good purpose; and upon the decisive evidence, obtained by the Prefect, that it was not hidden within the limits of that dignitary's ordinary search – the more satisfied I became that, to conceal this letter, the Minister had resorted to the comprehensive and sagacious expedient of not attempting to conceal it at all.

'Full of these ideas, I prepared myself with a pair of green spectacles, and called one fine morning, quite by accident, at the Ministerial hotel. I found D— at home, yawning, lounging, and dawdling, as usual, and pretending to be in the last extremity of *ennui*. He is, perhaps, the most really energetic human being now alive – but that is only when nobody sees him.

'To be even with him, I complained of my weak eyes, and lamented the necessity of the spectacles, under cover of which I cautiously and thoroughly surveyed the whole apartment, while seemingly intent only upon the conversation of my host.

'I paid especial attention to a large writing-table near which he sat, and upon which lay confusedly some miscellaneous letters and other papers, with one or two musical instruments and a few books. Here, however, after a long and very deliberate scrutiny, I saw nothing to excite particular suspicion.

'At length my eyes, in going the circuit of the room, fell upon a trumpery filigree card-rack of paste-board, that hung dangling by a dirty blue ribbon, from a little brass knob just beneath the middle of the mantelpiece. In this rack, which had three or four compartments, were five or six visiting cards and a solitary letter. This last was much soiled and crumpled. It was torn nearly in two, across the middle – as if a design, in the first instance, to tear it entirely up as worthless, had been altered, or stayed, in the second. It had a large black seal, bearing the D— cipher *very* conspicuously, and was addressed, in a diminutive female hand, to D—, the Minister, himself. It was thrust carelessly, and even, as it seemed, contemptuously, into one of the uppermost divisions of the rack.

'No sooner had I glanced at this letter, than I concluded it to be that of which I was in search. To be sure, it was, to all appearance, radically different from the one of which the Prefect had read us so minute a description. Here the seal was large and black, with the D— cipher; there it was small and red, with the ducal arms of the S— family. Here, the address, to the Minister, was diminutive and feminine; there the superscription, to a certain royal personage, was markedly bold and decided; the size alone formed a point of correspondence. But then the *radicalness* of these differences, which was excessive; the dirt; the soiled and torn condition of the paper, so inconsistent with the *true* methodical habits of D—, and so suggestive of a design to delude the beholder into an idea of the worthlessness of the document; these things, together with the hyper-obtrusive situation of this document, full in the view of every visitor, and thus exactly in accordance with the conclusions to which I had previously arrived; these things, I say, were strongly corroborative of suspicion, in one who came with the intention to suspect.

'I protracted my visit as long as possible, and, while I maintained a most animated discussion with the Minister, upon a topic which I knew well had never failed to interest and excite him, I kept my attention really riveted upon the letter. In this examination, I committed to memory its external appearance and arrangement in the rack; and also fell, at length, upon a discovery, which set at rest whatever trivial doubt I might have entertained. In scrutinising the edges of the paper, I observed them to be more *chafed* than seemed necessary. They presented the *broken* appearance which is manifested when a stiff paper, having been once folded and pressed with a folder, is refolded in a reversed direction, in the same creases or edges which had formed the original fold. This discovery was sufficient. It was clear to me that the letter had been turned, as a glove, inside out, redirected and resealed. I bade the Minister good-morning, and took my departure at once, leaving a gold snuff-box upon the table.

'The next morning I called for the snuff-box, when we resumed, quite eagerly, the conversation of the preceding day. While thus engaged, however, a loud report, as if of a pistol, was heard immediately beneath the windows of the hotel, and was succeeded by a series of fearful screams, and the shoutings of a terrified mob. D— rushed to a casement, threw it open, and looked out. In the meantime, I stepped to the card-rack, took the letter, put it in my pocket, and replaced it by a fac-simile (so far as regards externals) which I had carefully prepared at my lodgings – imitating the D— cipher, very readily, by means of a seal formed of bread.

'The disturbance in the street had been occasioned by the frantic behaviour of a man with a musket. He had fired it among a crowd of women and children. It proved, however, to have been without ball, and the fellow was suffered to go his way as a lunatic or a drunkard. When he had gone, D— came from the window, whither I had followed him immediately upon securing the object in view. Soon afterwards I bade him farewell. The pretended lunatic was a man in my own pay.'

'But what purpose had you,' I asked, 'in replacing the letter by a fac-simile? Would it not have been better, at the first visit, to have seized it openly, and departed?'

'D—,' replied Dupin, 'is a desperate man, and a man of nerve. His hotel, too, is not without attendants devoted to his interests. Had I made the wild attempt you suggest, I might never have left the Ministerial presence alive. The good people of Paris might have heard of me no more. But I had an object apart from these considerations. You know my political prepossessions. In this matter, I act as a partisan of the lady concerned. For eighteen months the Minister has had her in his power. She has now him in hers – since, being unaware that the letter is not in his possession, he will proceed with his exactions as if it was. Thus will he inevitably commit himself, at once, to his political destruction. His downfall, too, will not be more precipitate than awkward. It is all very well to talk about the *facilis descensus Averni*; [16] but in all kinds of climbing, as Catalani [17] said of singing, it is far more easy to get up than to come down. In the present instance I have no sympathy – at least no pity – for him who descends. He is that *monstrum horrendum*, an unprincipled man of genius. I confess, however, that I should like very well to know the precise character of his thoughts, when, being defied by her whom the Prefect terms "a certain personage", he is reduced to opening the letter which I left for him in the card-rack.'

'How? did you put anything particular in it?'

'Why – it did not seem altogether right to leave the interior blank – that would have been insulting. D—, at Vienna once, did me an evil turn, which I told him, quite good-humouredly, that I should remember. So, as I knew he would feel some curiosity in regard to the identity of the person who had out-witted him, I thought it a pity not to give him a clew. He is well acquainted with my MS., and I just copied into the middle of the blank sheet the words:

> *Un dessein si funeste,*
> *S'il n'est digne d'Atrée, est digne de Thyeste.*

They are to be found in Crébillon's[18] "Atrée".'

The Fall of the House of Usher

Son cœur est un luth suspendu;
Sitôt qu'on le touche il résonne.[1]

DE BÉRANGER

DURING THE WHOLE of a dull, dark, and soundless day in the autumn of the year, when the clouds hung oppressively low in the heavens, I had been passing alone, on horseback, through a singularly dreary tract of country; and at length found myself, as the shades of evening drew on, within view of the melancholy House of Usher. I know not how it was – but, with the first glimpse of the building, a sense of insufferable gloom pervaded my spirit. I say insufferable; for the feeling was unrelieved by any of that half-pleasurable, because poetic, sentiment, with which the mind usually receives even the sternest natural images of the desolate or terrible. I looked upon the scene before me – upon the mere house, and the simple landscape features of the domain – upon the bleak walls – upon the vacant eyelike windows – upon a few rank sedges – and upon a few white trunks of decayed trees – with an utter depression of soul which I can compare to no earthly sensation more properly than to the after-dream of the reveller upon opium – the bitter lapse into every-day life – the hideous dropping off of the veil. There was an iciness, a sinking, a sickening of the heart – an unredeemed dreariness of thought which no goading of the imagination could torture into aught of the sublime. What was it – I paused to think – what was it that so unnerved me in the contemplation of the House of Usher? It was a mystery all insoluble; nor could I grapple with the shadowy fancies that crowded upon me as I pondered. I was forced to fall back upon the unsatisfactory conclusion, that while, beyond doubt, there *are* combinations of very simple natural objects which have the power of thus affecting us, still the analysis of this power lies among considerations beyond our depth. It was possible, I reflected, that a mere different arrangement of the particulars of the scene, of the details of the picture, would be sufficient to modify, or perhaps to annihilate its capacity for sorrowful impression; and, acting upon this idea, I reined my horse to the precipitous brink of a black and lurid tarn that lay in unruffled lustre by the dwelling, and gazed down – but with a shudder even more thrilling than before – upon the remodelled and inverted images of the grey sedge, and the ghastly tree-stems, and the vacant and eye-like windows.

Nevertheless, in this mansion of gloom I now proposed to myself a sojourn of some weeks. Its proprietor, Roderick Usher, had been one of my boon companions in boyhood; but many years had elapsed since our last meeting. A letter, however, had lately reached me in a distant part of the country – a letter from him – which, in its wildly importunate nature, had admitted of no other than the personal reply. The MS. gave evidence of nervous agitation. The writer spoke of acute bodily illness – of a mental disorder which oppressed him – and of an earnest desire to see me, as his best, and indeed his only personal friend, with a view of attempting, by the cheerfulness of my society, some alleviation of his malady. It was the manner in which all this, and much more, was said – it was the apparent *heart* that went with his request – which allowed me no room for hesitation; and I accordingly obeyed forthwith what I still considered a very singular summons.

Although, as boys, we had been even intimate associates, yet I really knew little of my friend. His reserve had been always excessive and habitual. I was aware, however, that his very ancient family had been noted, time out of mind, for a peculiar sensibility of temperament, displaying itself, through long ages, in many works of exalted art, and manifested, of late, in repeated deeds of munificent yet unobtrusive charity, as well as in a passionate devotion to the intricacies, perhaps even more than to the orthodox and easily recognisable beauties of musical science. I had learned, too, the very remarkable fact, that the stem of the Usher race, all time-honoured as it was, had put forth, at no period, any enduring branch; in other words, that the entire family lay in the direct line of descent, and had always, with very trifling and very temporary variation, so lain. It was this deficiency, I considered, while running over in thought the perfect keeping of the character of the premises with the accredited character of the people, and while speculating upon the possible influence which the one, in the long lapse of centuries, might have exercised upon the other – it was this deficiency, perhaps, of collateral issue, and the consequent undeviating transmission, from sire to son, of the patrimony with the name, which had, at length, so identified the two as to merge the original title of the estate in the quaint and equivocal appellation of the 'House of Usher' – an appellation which seemed to include, in the minds of the peasantry who wed it, both the family and the family mansion.

I have said that the sole effect of my somewhat childish experiment – that of looking down within the tarn – had been to deepen the first singular impression. There can be no doubt that the consciousness of the rapid increase of my superstition – for why should I not so term it? – served mainly to accelerate the increase itself. Such, I have long known, is the paradoxical law of all sentiments having terror as a basis. And it might have been for this reason only, that, when I again uplifted my eyes to the house itself, from its image in the pool, there grew in my mind a strange fancy – a fancy so ridiculous, indeed, that I but mention it to show the vivid force of the sensations which oppressed me. I had so worked upon my imagination as really to believe that about the whole mansion and domain there hung an atmosphere peculiar to themselves and their immediate vicinity – an atmosphere which had no affinity with the air of heaven, but which had reeked up from the decayed trees, and the grey wall, and the silent tarn – a pestilent and mystic vapour, dull, sluggish, faintly discernible, and leaden-hued.

Shaking off from my spirit what *must* have been a dream, I scanned more narrowly the real aspect of the building. Its principal feature seemed to be that of an excessive antiquity. The discoloration of ages had been great. Minute fungi overspread the whole exterior, hanging in a fine tangled webwork from the eaves. Yet all this was apart from any extraordinary dilapidation. No portion of the masonry had fallen; and there appeared to be a wild inconsistency between its still perfect adaptation of parts, and the crumbling condition of the individual stones. In this there was much that reminded me of the specious totality of old woodwork which has rotted for long years in some neglected vault, with no disturbance from the breath of the external air. Beyond this indication of extensive decay, however, the fabric gave little token of instability. Perhaps the eye of a scrutinising observer might have discovered a barely perceptible fissure, which, extending from the roof of the building in front, made its way down the wall in a zigzag direction, until it became lost in the sullen waters of the tarn.

Noticing these things, I rode over a short causeway to the house. A servant in waiting took my horse, and I entered the Gothic archway of the hall. A valet, of stealthy step, thence conducted me, in silence, through many dark and intricate passages in my progress to the studio of his master. Much that I encountered on the way contributed, I know not how, to heighten the vague sentiments of which I have already spoken. While the objects around me – while the carvings of the ceilings, the sombre tapestries of the walls, the ebon blackness of the floors, and the phantasmagoric armorial trophies which rattled as I strode, were but matters to which, or to such as which, I had been accustomed from my infancy – while I hesitated not to acknowledge how familiar was all this – I still wondered to find how unfamiliar were the fancies which ordinary images were stirring up. On one of the staircases I met the physician of the family. His countenance, I thought, wore a mingled expression of low cunning and perplexity. He accosted me with trepidation and passed on. The valet now threw open a door and ushered me into the presence of his master.

The room in which I found myself was very large and lofty. The windows were long, narrow, and pointed, and at so vast a distance from the black oaken floor as to be altogether inaccessible from within. Feeble gleams of encrimsoned light made their way through the trellised panes, and served to render sufficiently distinct the more prominent objects around; the eye, however, struggled in vain to reach the remoter angles of the chamber, or the recesses of the vaulted and fretted ceiling. Dark draperies hung upon the walls. The general furniture was profuse, comfortless, antique, and tattered. Many books and musical instruments lay scattered about, but failed to give any vitality to the scene. I felt that I breathed an atmosphere of sorrow. An air of stern, deep, and irredeemable gloom hung over and pervaded all.

Upon my entrance, Usher arose from a sofa on which he had been lying at full length, and greeted me with a vivacious warmth which had much in it, I at first thought, of an overdone cordiality – of the constrained effort of the *ennuyé* man of the world. A glance, however, at his countenance, convinced me of his perfect sincerity. We sat down; and for some moments, while he spoke not, I gazed upon him with a feeling half of pity, half of awe. Surely, man had never before so terribly altered, in so brief a period, as had Roderick Usher! It was with difficulty that I could bring myself to admit the identity of the wan being before me with the companion of my early boyhood. Yet the character of his face had been at all times remarkable. A cadaverousness of complexion; an eye large, liquid, and luminous beyond comparison; lips somewhat thin and very pallid, but of a surpassingly beautiful curve; a nose of a delicate Hebrew model, but with a breadth of nostril unusual in similar formations; a finely moulded chin, speaking, in its want of prominence, of a want of moral energy; hair of a more than weblike softness and tenuity; these features, with an inordinate expansion above the regions of the temple, made up altogether a countenance not easily to be forgotten. And now in the mere exaggeration of the prevailing character of these features, and of the expression they were wont to convey, lay so much of change that I doubted to whom I spoke. The now ghastly pallor of the skin, and the now miraculous lustre of the eye, above all things startled and even awed me. The silken hair, too, had been suffered to grow all unheeded, and as, in its wild gossamer texture, it floated rather than fell about the face, I could not, even with effort, connect its Arabesque expression with any idea of simple humanity.

In the manner of my friend I was at once struck with an incoherence –

an inconsistency; and I soon found this to arise from a series of feeble and futile struggles to overcome an habitual trepidancy – an excessive nervous agitation. For something of this nature I had indeed been prepared, no less by his letter, than by reminiscences of certain boyish traits, and by conclusions deduced from his peculiar physical conformation and temperament. His action was alternately vivacious and sullen. His voice varied rapidly from a tremulous indecision (when the animal spirits seemed utterly in abeyance) to that species of energetic concision – that abrupt, weighty, unhurried, and hollow-sounding enunciation – that leaden, self-balanced, and perfectly modulated guttural utterance, which may be observed in the lost drunkard, or the irreclaimable eater of opium, during the periods of his most intense excitement.

It was thus that he spoke of the object of my visit, of his earnest desire to see me, and of the solace he expected me to afford him. He entered, at some length, into what he conceived to be the nature of his malady. It was, he said, a constitutional and a family evil, and one for which he despaired to find a remedy – a mere nervous affection, he immediately added, which would undoubtedly soon pass off. It displayed itself in a host of unnatural sensations. Some of these, as he detailed them, interested and bewildered me; although, perhaps, the terms, and the general manner of the narration had their weight. He suffered much from a morbid acuteness of the senses; the most insipid food was alone endurable; he could wear only garments of certain texture; the odours of all flowers were oppressive; his eyes were tortured by even a faint light; and there were but peculiar sounds, and these from stringed instruments, which did not inspire him with horror.

To an anomalous species of terror I found him a bounden slave. 'I shall perish,' said he, 'I *must* perish in this deplorable folly. Thus, thus, and not otherwise, shall I be lost. I dread the events of the future, not in themselves, but in their results. I shudder at the thought of any, even the most trivial, incident, which may operate upon this intolerable agitation of soul. I have, indeed, no abhorrence of danger, except in its absolute effect – in terror. In this unnerved – in this pitiable condition – I feel that the period will sooner or later arrive when I must abandon life and reason together, in some struggle with the grim phantasm, FEAR.'

I learned, moreover, at intervals, and through broken and equivocal hints, another singular feature of his mental condition. He was enchained by certain superstitious impressions in regard to the dwelling which he tenanted, and whence, for many years, he had never ventured forth – in regard to an influence whose supposititious force was conveyed in terms too shadowy here to be restated – an influence which some peculiarities in the mere form and substance of his family mansion, had, by dint of long sufferance, he said, obtained over his spirit – an effect which the *physique* of the grey walls and turrets, and of the dim tarn into which they all looked down, had at length brought about upon the *morale* of his existence.

He admitted, however, although with hesitation, that much of the peculiar gloom which thus afflicted him could be traced to a more natural and far more palpable origin – to the severe and long-continued illness – indeed to the evidently approaching dissolution – of a tenderly beloved sister – his sole companion for long years – his last and only relative on earth. 'Her decease,' he said, with a bitterness which I can never forget, 'would leave him (him the hopeless and the frail) the last of the ancient race of the Ushers.' While he spoke, the Lady Madeline (for so was she called) passed slowly through a remote portion of the apartment, and, without having noticed my presence, disappeared. I regarded her with an utter astonishment not unmingled with dread – and yet I found it impossible to account for such feelings. A sensation of stupor oppressed me, as my eyes followed her retreating steps. When a door at length closed upon her, my glance sought instinctively and eagerly the countenance of the brother – but he had buried his face in his hands, and I could only perceive that a far more than ordinary wanness had overspread the emaciated fingers through which trickled many passionate tears.

The disease of the Lady Madeline had long baffled the skill of her physicians. A settled apathy, a gradual wasting away of the person, and frequent although transient affections of a partially cataleptical[2] character, were the unusual diagnosis. Hitherto she had steadily borne up against the pressure of her malady, and had not betaken herself finally to bed; but, on the closing in of the evening of my arrival at the house, she succumbed (as her brother told me at night with inexpressible agitation) to the prostrating power of the destroyer; and I learned that the glimpse I had obtained of her person would thus probably be the last I should obtain – that the lady, at least while living, would be seen by me no more.

For several days ensuing, her name was unmentioned by either Usher or myself; and during this period I was busied in earnest endeavours to alleviate the melancholy of my friend. We painted and read together; or I listened, as if in a dream, to the wild improvisations of his speaking guitar. And thus, as a closer and still closer intimacy admitted me more unreservedly into the recesses of his spirit, the more bitterly did I perceive the futility of all attempt at cheering a mind from which darkness, as if an inherent positive quality, poured forth upon all objects of the moral and physical universe, in one unceasing radiation of gloom.

I shall ever bear about me a memory of the many solemn hours I thus spent alone with the master of the House of Usher. Yet I should fail in any attempt to convey an idea of the exact character of the studies, or of the occupations, in which he involved me, or led me the way. An excited and highly distempered ideality threw a sulphureous lustre over all. His long improvised dirges will ring for ever in my ears. Among other things, I hold painfully in mind a certain singular perversion and amplification of the wild air of the last waltz of Von Weber.[3] From the paintings over which his elaborate fancy brooded, and which grew, touch by touch, into vaguenesses at which I shuddered the more thrillingly, because I shuddered knowing not why – from these paintings (vivid as their images now are before me) I would in vain endeavour to educe more than a small portion which should lie within the compass of merely written words. By the utter simplicity, by the nakedness of his designs, he arrested and overawed attention. If ever mortal painted an idea, that mortal was Roderick Usher. For me at least – in the circumstances then surrounding me – there arose out of the pure abstractions which the hypochondriac contrived to throw upon his canvas, an intensity of intolerable awe, no shadow of which felt I ever yet in the contemplation of the certainly glowing yet too concrete reveries of Fuseli.[4]

One of the phantasmagoric conceptions of my friend, partaking not so rigidly of the spirit of abstraction, may be shadowed forth, although feebly, in words. A small picture presented the interior of an immensely long and rectangular vault or tunnel, with low walls, smooth, white, and without interruption or device. Certain accessory points of the design served well to convey the idea that this excavation lay at an exceeding depth below the surface of the earth. No outlet was observed in any portion of its vast extent, and no torch, or other artificial source of light, was discernible; yet a flood of intense rays rolled throughout, and bathed the whole in a ghastly and inappropriate splendour.

I have just spoken of that morbid condition of the auditory nerve which rendered all music intolerable to the sufferer, with the exception of certain effects of stringed instruments. It was, perhaps, the narrow limits to which he thus confined himself upon the guitar, which gave birth, in great measure, to the fantastic character of his performances. But the fervid facility of his impromptus could not be so accounted for. They must have been, and were, in the notes, as well as in the words, of his wild fantasias (for he not unfrequently accompanied himself with rhymed verbal improvisations), the result of that intense mental collectedness and concentration to which I have previously alluded as observable only in particular moments of the highest artificial excitement. The words of one of these rhapsodies I have easily remembered. I was, perhaps, the more forcibly impressed with it, as he gave it, because, in the under or mystic current of its meaning, I fancied that I perceived, and for the first time, a full consciousness on the part of Usher, of the tottering of his lofty reason upon her throne. The verses, which were entitled 'The Haunted Palace,' ran very nearly, if not accurately, thus:

I

In the greenest of our valleys,
    By good angels tenanted,
Once a fair and stately palace –
    Radiant palace – reared its head.
In the monarch Thought's dominion –
    It stood there!
Never seraph spread a pinion
    Over fabric half so fair.

II

Banners yellow, glorious, golden,
    On its roof did float and flow
(This – all this – was in the olden
    Time long ago);
And every gentle air that dallied,
    In that sweet day,
Along the ramparts plumed and pallid,
    A winged odour went away.

III

Wanderers in that happy valley
    Through two luminous windows saw
Spirits moving musically
    To a lute's well-tunèd law,
Round about a throne, where sitting
    (Porphyrogene!)⁵
In state his glory well befitting,
    The ruler of the realm was seen.

IV

And all with pearl and ruby glowing
    Was the fair palace door,
Through which came flowing, flowing, flowing
    And sparkling evermore,
A troop of Echoes, whose sweet duty
    Was but to sing,
In voices of surpassing beauty,
    The wit and wisdom of their king.

V

But evil things, in robes of sorrow,
    Assailed the monarch's high estate.
(Ah, let us mourn, for never morrow
    Shall dawn upon him, desolate!)
And, round about his home, the glory
    That blushed and bloomed
Is but a dim-remembered story
    Of the old time entombed.

VI

And travellers now within that valley,
    Through the red-litten windows, see
Vast forms that move fantastically
    To a discordant melody;
While, like a rapid ghastly river,
    Through the pale door,
A hideous throng rush out for ever,
    And laugh – but smile no more.

I well remember that suggestions arising from this ballad led us into
a train of thought wherein there became manifest an opinion of
Usher's, which I mention not so much on account of its novelty (for
other men have thought thus), as on account of the pertinacity with
which he maintained it. This opinion, in its general form, was that of
the sentience of all vegetable things. But, in his disordered fancy, the
idea had assumed a more daring character, and trespassed, under
certain conditions, upon the kingdom of inorganisation. I lack words to
express the full extent, or the earnest *abandon* of his persuasion. The
belief, however, was connected (as I have previously hinted) with the
grey stones of the home of his forefathers. The conditions of the
sentience had been here, he imagined, fulfilled in the method of

collocation of these stones – in the order of their arrangement, as well as in that of the many fungi which overspread them, and of the decayed trees which stood around – above all, in the long undisturbed endurance of this arrangement, and in its reduplication in the still waters of the tarn. Its evidence – the evidence of the sentience – was to be seen, he said (and I here started as he spoke), in the gradual yet certain condensation of an atmosphere of their own about the waters and the walls. The result was discoverable, he added, in that silent, yet importunate and terrible influence which for centuries had moulded the destinies of his family, and which made *him* what I now saw him – what he was. Such opinions need no comment, and I will make none.

Our books[6] – the books which, for years, had formed no small portion of the mental existence of the invalid – were, as might be supposed, in strict keeping with this character of phantasm. We pored together over such works as the *Ververt et Chartreuse* of Gresset; the *Belphegor* of Machiavelli; the *Heaven and Hell* of Swedenborg; the *Subterranean Voyage of Nicholas Klimn*, by Holberg; the Chiromancy of Robert Flud, of Jean D'Indaginé, and of De la Chambre; the *Journey into the Blue Distance* of Tieck; and the *City of the Sun* of Campanella. One favourite volume was a small octavo edition of the *Directorium Inquisitorium*, by the Dominican Eymeric de Gironne; and there were passages in Pomponius Mela, about the old African Satyrs and Œgipans, over which Usher would sit dreaming for hours. His chief delight, however, was found in the perusal of an exceedingly rare and curious book in quarto Gothic – the manual of a forgotten church – the *Vigiliæ Mortuorum Secundum Chorum Ecclesiæ Maguntinæ*.

I could not help thinking of the wild ritual of this work, and of its probable influence upon the hypochondriac, when, one evening, having informed me abruptly that the Lady Madeline was no more, he stated his intention of preserving her corpse for a fortnight (previously to its final interment), in one of the numerous vaults within the main walls of the building. The worldly reason, however, assigned for this singular proceeding, was one which I did not feel at liberty to dispute. The brother had been led to his resolution (so he told me) by consideration of the unusual character of the malady of the deceased, of certain obtrusive and eager inquiries on the part of her medical men, and of the remote and exposed situation of the burial-ground of the family. I will not deny that when I called to mind the sinister countenance of the person whom I met upon the staircase, on the day of my arrival at the house, I had no desire to oppose what I regarded as at best but a harmless, and by no means an unnatural, precaution.

At the request of Usher, I personally aided him in the arrangements for the temporary entombment. The body having been encoffined, we two alone bore it to its rest. The vault in which we placed it (and which had been so long unopened that our torches, half smothered in its oppressive atmosphere, gave us little opportunity for investigation) was small, damp, and entirely without means of admission for light; lying, at great depth, immediately beneath that portion of the building in which was my own sleeping apartment. It had been used, apparently, in remote feudal times, for the worst purposes of a donjon-keep, and, in latter days, as a place of deposit for powder, or some other highly combustible substance, as a portion of its floor, and the whole interior of a long archway through which we reached it, were carefully sheathed with copper. The door, of massive iron, had been, also, similarly protected. Its immense weight caused an unusually sharp grating sound, as it moved upon its hinges.

Having deposited our mournful burden upon tressels within this region of horror, we partially turned aside the yet unscrewed lid of the coffin, and looked upon the face of the tenant. A striking similitude between the brother and sister now first arrested my attention; and Usher, divining, perhaps, my thoughts, murmured out some few words from which I learned that the deceased and himself had been twins, and that sympathies of a scarcely intelligible nature had always existed between them. Our glances, however, rested not long upon the dead – for we could not regard her unawed. The disease which had thus entombed the lady in the maturity of youth, had left, as usual in all maladies of a strictly cataleptical character, the mockery of a faint blush upon the bosom and the face, and that suspiciously lingering smile upon the lip which is so terrible in death. We replaced and screwed down the lid, and, having secured the door of iron, made our way, with toil, into the scarcely less gloomy apartments of the upper portion of the house.

And now, some days of bitter grief having elapsed, an observable change came over the features of the mental disorder of my friend. His ordinary manner had vanished. His ordinary occupations were neglected or forgotten. He roamed from chamber to chamber with hurried, unequal, and objectless step. The pallor of his countenance had assumed, if possible, a more ghastly hue – but the luminousness of his eye had utterly gone out. The more occasional huskiness of his tone was heard no more; and a tremulous quaver, as if of extreme terror, habitually characterised his utterance. There were times, indeed, when I thought his unceasingly agitated mind was labouring with some oppressive secret, to divulge which he struggled for the necessary courage. At times, again, I was obliged to resolve all into the mere inexplicable vagaries of madness, for I beheld him gazing upon vacancy for long hours, in an attitude of the profoundest attention, as if listening to some imaginary sound. It was no wonder that his condition terrified – that it infected me. I felt creeping upon me, by slow yet certain degrees, the wild influences of his own fantastic yet impressive superstitions.

It was, especially, upon retiring to bed late in the night of the seventh or eighth day after the placing of the Lady Madeline within the donjon, that I experienced the full power of such feelings. Sleep came not near my couch – while the hours waned and waned away. I struggled to reason off the nervousness which had dominion over me. I endeavoured to believe that much, if not all of what I felt, was due to the bewildering influence of the gloomy furniture of the room – of the dark and tattered draperies, which, tortured into motion by the breath of a rising tempest, swayed fitfully to and fro upon the walls, and rustled uneasily about the decorations of the bed. But my efforts were fruitless. An irrepressible tremor gradually pervaded my frame; and, at length, there sat upon my very heart an incubus of utterly causeless alarm. Shaking this off with a gasp and a struggle, I uplifted myself upon the pillows, and, peering earnestly within the intense darkness of the chamber, hearkened – I know not why, except that an instinctive spirit prompted me – to certain low and indefinite sounds which came, through the pauses of the storm, at long intervals, I knew not whence. Overpowered by an intense sentiment of horror, unaccountable yet unendurable, I threw on my clothes with haste (for I felt that I should sleep no more during the night), and endeavoured to arouse myself from the pitiable condition into which I had fallen, by pacing rapidly to and fro through the apartment.

I had taken but few turns in this manner, when a light step on an adjoining staircase arrested my attention. I presently recognised it as that of Usher. In an instant afterward he rapped with a gentle touch, at my door, and entered, bearing a lamp. His countenance was, as usual, cadaverously wan – but, moreover, there was a species of mad hilarity in his eyes – an evidently restrained hysteria in his whole demeanour. His air appalled me – but anything was preferable to the solitude which I had so long endured, and I even welcomed his presence as a relief.

'And you have not seen it?' he said abruptly, after having stared about him for some moments in silence – 'you have not then seen it? – but, stay! you shall.' Thus speaking, and having carefully shaded his lamp, he hurried to one of the casements, and threw it freely open to the storm.

The impetuous fury of the entering gust nearly lifted us from our feet. It was, indeed, a tempestuous yet sternly beautiful night, and one wildly singular in its terror and its beauty. A whirlwind had apparently collected its force in our vicinity; for there were frequent and violent alterations in the direction of the wind; and the exceeding density of the clouds (which hung so low as to press upon the turrets of the house) did not prevent our perceiving the life-like velocity with which they flew careering from all points against each other, without passing away into the distance. I say that even their exceeding density did not prevent our perceiving this – yet we had no glimpse of the moon or stars – nor was there any flashing forth of the lightning. But the under surfaces of the huge masses of agitated vapour, as well as all terrestrial objects immediately around us, were glowing in the unnatural light of a faintly luminous and distinctly visible gaseous exhalation which hung about and enshrouded the mansion.

'You must not – you shall not behold this!' said I, shudderingly, to Usher, as I led him, with a gentle violence, from the window to a seat. 'These appearances, which bewilder you, are merely electrical phenomena not uncommon – or it may be that they have their ghastly origin in the rank miasma of the tarn. Let us close this casement – the air is chilling and dangerous to your frame. Here is one of your favourite romances. I will read, and you shall listen – and so we will pass away this terrible night together.'

The antique volume which I had taken up was the 'Mad Trist'[7] of Sir Launcelot Canning; but I had called it a favourite of Usher's more in sad jest than in earnest; for, in truth, there is little in its uncouth and unimaginative prolixity which could have had interest for the lofty and spiritual ideality of my friend. It was, however, the only book immediately at hand; and I indulged a vague hope that the excitement which now agitated the hypochondriac, might find relief (for the history of mental disorder is full of similar anomalies) even in the extremeness of the folly which I should read. Could I have judged, indeed, by the wild overstrained air of vivacity with which he hearkened, or apparently hearkened, to the words of the tale, I might well have congratulated myself upon the success of my design.

I had arrived at that well-known portion of the story where Ethelred, the hero of the Trist, having sought in vain for peaceable admission into the dwelling of the hermit, proceeds to make good an entrance by force. Here, it will be remembered, the words of the narrative run thus:

'And Ethelred, who was by nature of a doughty heart, and who was now mighty withal, on account of the powerfulness of the wine which he had drunken, waited no longer to hold parley with the hermit, who, in sooth, was of an obstinate and maliceful turn, but, feeling the rain upon his shoulders, and fearing the rising of the tempest, uplifted his mace outright, and, with blows, made quickly room in the plankings of the door for his gauntleted hand; and now pulling therewith sturdily, he so cracked, and ripped, and tore all asunder, that the noise of the dry and hollow-sounding wood alarummed and reverberated throughout the forest.'

At the termination of this sentence I started, and for a moment paused; for it appeared to me (although I at once concluded that my excited fancy had deceived me) – it appeared to me that, from some very remote portion of the mansion, there came, indistinctly, to my ears, what might have been, in its exact similarity of character, the echo (but a stifled and dull one certainly) of the very cracking and ripping sound which Sir Launcelot had so particularly described. It was, beyond doubt, the coincidence alone which had arrested my attention; for, amid the rattling of the sashes of the casements, and the ordinary commingled noises of the still increasing storm, the sound, in itself, had nothing, surely, which should have interested or disturbed me. I continued the story:

'But the good champion Ethelred, now entering within the door, was sore enraged and amazed to perceive no signal of the maliceful hermit; but, in the stead thereof, a dragon of a scaly and prodigious demeanour, and of a fiery tongue, which sate in guard before a palace of gold, with a floor of silver; and upon the wall there hung a shield of shining brass with this legend enwritten:

> Who entereth herein, a conqueror hath bin;
> Who slayeth the dragon, the shield he shall win.

And Ethelred uplifted his mace, and struck upon the head of the dragon, which fell before him, and gave up his pesty breath, with a shriek so horrid and harsh, and withal so piercing, that Ethelred had fain to close his ears with his hands against the dreadful noise of it, the like whereof was never before heard.'

Here again I paused abruptly, and now with a feeling of wild amazement – for there could be no doubt whatever that, in this instance, I did actually hear (although from what direction it proceeded I found it impossible to say) a low and apparently distant, but harsh, protracted, and most unusual screaming or grating sound – the exact counterpart of what my fancy had already conjured up for the dragon's unnatural shriek as described by the romancer.

Oppressed as I certainly was, upon the occurrence of this second and most extraordinary coincidence, by a thousand conflicting sensations, in which wonder and extreme terror were predominant, I still retained sufficient presence of mind to avoid exciting, by any observation, the sensitive nervousness of my companion. I was by no means certain that he had noticed the sound in question; although, assuredly, a strange alteration had, during the last few minutes, taken place in his demeanour. From a position fronting my own, he had gradually brought round his chair, so as to sit with his face to the door of the chamber; and thus I could but partially perceive his features, although I saw that his lips trembled as if he were murmuring inaudibly. His head had dropped upon his breast – yet I knew that he was not asleep, from the wide and rigid opening of the eye as I caught a glance of it in profile. The motion of his body, too, was at variance with this idea – for he rocked from side to side with a gentle yet constant and uniform sway. Having rapidly taken notice of all this, I resumed the narrative of Sir Launcelot, which thus proceeded:

'And now, the champion, having escaped from the terrible fury of the dragon, bethinking himself of the brazen shield, and of the breaking up of the enchantment which was upon it, removed the carcass from out of the way before him, and approached valorously over the silver pavement of the castle to where the shield was upon the wall; which in sooth tarried not for his full coming, but fell down at his feet upon the silver floor, with a mighty great and terrible ringing sound.'

No sooner had these syllables passed my lips, than – as if a shield of brass had indeed, at the moment, fallen heavily upon a floor of silver – I became aware of a distinct, hollow, metallic, and clangorous, yet apparently muffled reverberation. Completely unnerved, I leaped to my feet; but the measured rocking movement of Usher was undisturbed. I rushed to the chair in which he sat. His eyes were bent fixedly before him, and throughout his whole countenance there reigned a stony rigidity. But, as I placed my hand upon his shoulder, there came a strong shudder over his whole person; a sickly smile quivered on his lips; and I saw that he spoke in a low, hurried, and gibbering murmur, as if unconscious of my presence. Bending closely over him, I at length drank in the hideous import of his words.

'Not hear it? – yes, I hear it, and *have* heard it. Long – long – long – many minutes, many hours, many days, have I heard it – yet I dared not – oh, pity me, miserable wretch that I am! – I dared not – I *dared* not speak! *We have put her living in the tomb*! Said I not that my senses were acute? I *now* tell you that I heard her first feeble movements in the hollow coffin. I heard them – many, many days ago – yet I dared not – *I dared not speak*! And now – tonight – Ethelred – ha! ha! – the breaking of the hermit's door, and the death-cry of the dragon, and the clangour of the shield! – say, rather, the rending of her coffin, and the grating of the iron hinges of her prison, and her struggles within the coppered archway of the vault! Oh, whither shall I fly? Will she not be here anon? Is she not hurrying to upbraid me for my haste? Have I not heard her footstep on the stair? Do I not distinguish that heavy and horrible beating of her heart? Madman!' – here he sprang furiously to his feet, and shrieked out his syllables, as if in the effort he were giving up his soul – '*Madman! I tell you that she now stands without the door*!'

As if in the superhuman energy of his utterance there had been found the potency of a spell – the huge antique panels to which the speaker pointed threw slowly back, upon the instant, their ponderous and ebony jaws. It was the work of the rushing gust – but then without those doors there *did* stand the lofty and enshrouded figure of the Lady Madeline of Usher. There was blood upon her white robes, and the evidence of some bitter struggle upon every portion of her emaciated frame. For a moment she remained trembling and reeling to and fro upon the threshold – then, with a low moaning cry, fell heavily inward upon the person of her brother, and in her violent and now final death-agonies, bore him to the floor a corpse, and a victim to the terrors he had anticipated.

From that chamber, and from that mansion, I fled aghast. The storm was still abroad in all its wrath as I found myself crossing the old causeway. Suddenly there shot along the path a wild light, and I turned to see whence a gleam so unusual could have issued; for the vast house and its shadows were alone behind me. The radiance was that of the full, setting, and blood-red moon, which now shone vividly through that once barely-discernible fissure, of which I have before spoken as extending from the roof of the building, in a zigzag direction, to the base. While I gazed, this fissure rapidly widened – there came a fierce breath of the whirlwind – the entire orb of the satellite burst at once upon my sight – my brain reeled as I saw the mighty walls rushing asunder – there was a long tumultuous shouting sound like a voice of a thousand waters – and the deep and dank tarn at my feet closed sullenly and silently over the fragments of the 'House of Usher.'

The Pit and the Pendulum

Impia tortorum longas hic turba furores
Sanguinis innocui, non satiata, aluit.
Sospite nunc patria, fracto nunc funeris antro,
Mors ubi dira fuit vita salusque patent.[1]

Quatrain composed for the gates of a market to be erected
upon the site of the Jacobin Club House at Paris

I WAS SICK – sick unto death with that long agony; and when they at length unbound me, and I was permitted to sit, I felt that my senses were leaving me. The sentence – the dread sentence of death – was the last of distinct accentuation which reached my ears. After that, the sound of the inquisitorial voices seemed merged in one dreamy indeterminate hum. It conveyed to my soul the idea of *revolution* – perhaps from its association in fancy with the burr of a mill-wheel. This only for a brief period; for presently I heard no more. Yet, for a while, I saw; but with how terrible an exaggeration! I saw the lips of the black-robed judges. They appeared to me white – whiter than the sheet upon which I trace these words and thin even to grotesqueness; thin with the intensity of their expression of firmness – of immovable resolution – of stern contempt of human torture. I saw that the decrees of what to me was Fate, were still issuing from those lips. I saw them writhe with a deadly locution. I saw them fashion the syllables of my name; and I shuddered because no sound succeeded. I saw, too, for a few moments of delirious horror, the soft and nearly imperceptible waving of the sable draperies which enwrapped the walls of the apartment. And then my vision fell upon the seven tall candles upon the table. At first they wore the aspect of charity, and seemed white slender angels who would save me; but then, all at once, there came a most deadly nausea over my spirit, and I felt every fibre in my frame thrill as if I had touched the wire of a galvanic battery, while the angel forms became meaningless spectres, with heads of flame, and I saw that from them there would be no help. And then there stole into my fancy, like a rich musical note, the thought of what sweet rest there must be in the grave. The thought came gently and stealthily, and it seemed long before it attained full appreciation; but just as my spirit came at length properly to feel and entertain it, the figures of the judges vanished, as if magically, from before me; the tall candles sank into nothingness; their flames went out utterly; the blackness of darkness supervened; all sensations appeared swallowed up in a mad rushing descent as of the soul into Hades. Then silence, and stillness, and night were the universe.

I had swooned; but still will not say that all of consciousness was lost. What of it there remained I will not attempt to define, or even to describe; yet all was not lost. In the deepest slumber – no! In delirium – no! In a swoon – no! In death – no! even in the grave all *is not* lost. Else there is no immortality for man. Arousing from the most profound of slumbers, we break the gossamer web of *some* dream. Yet in a second afterward (so frail may that web have been) we remember not that we have dreamed. In the return to life from the swoon there are two stages: first, that of the sense of mental or spiritual; secondly, that of the sense of physical existence. It seems probable that if, upon reaching the second stage, we could recall the impressions of the first, we should find these impressions eloquent in memories of the gulf beyond. And that gulf is – what? How at least shall we distinguish its shadows from those of the tomb? But if the impressions of what I have termed the first stage are not, at will, recalled, yet, after long interval, do they not come unbidden, while we marvel whence they come? He who has never swooned, is not he who finds strange palaces and wildly familiar faces in coals that glow; is not he who beholds floating in mid-air the sad visions that the many may not view; is not he who ponders over the perfume of some novel flower – is not he whose brain grows bewildered with the meaning of some musical cadence which has never before arrested his attention.

Amid frequent and thoughtful endeavours to remember; amid earnest struggles to regather some token of the state of seeming nothingness into which my soul had lapsed, there have been moments when I have dreamed of success; there have been brief, very brief periods when I have conjured up remembrances which the lucid reason of a later epoch assures me could have had reference only to that condition of seeming unconsciousness. These shadows of memory tell, indistinctly, of tall figures that lifted and bore me in silence down – down – still down – till a hideous dizziness oppressed me at the mere idea of the interminableness of the descent. They tell also of a vague horror at my heart, on account of that heart's unnatural stillness. Then comes a sense of sudden motionlessness throughout all things; as if those who bore me (a ghastly train!) had outrun, in their descent, the limits of the limitless, and paused from the wearisomeness of their toil. After this I call to mind flatness and dampness; and then all is *madness* – the madness of a memory which busies itself among forbidden things.

Very suddenly there came back to my soul motion and sound – the tumultuous motion of the heart, and, in my ears, the sound of its beating. Then a pause, in which all is blank. Then again sound, and motion, and touch – a tingling sensation pervading my frame. Then the mere consciousness of existence, without thought – a condition which lasted long. Then, very suddenly, *thought*, and shuddering terror, and earnest endeavour to comprehend my true state. Then a strong desire to lapse into insensibility. Then a rushing revival of soul and a successful effort to move. And now a full memory of the trial, of the judges, of the sable draperies, of the sentence, of the sickness, of the swoon. Then entire forgetfulness of all that followed; of all that a later day and much earnestness of endeavour have enabled me vaguely to recall.

So far, I had not opened my eyes. I felt that I lay upon my back, unbound. I reached out my hand, and it fell heavily upon something damp and hard. There I suffered it to remain for many minutes, while I strove to imagine where and *what* I could be. I longed, yet dared not to employ my vision. I dreaded the first glance at objects around me. It was not that I feared to look upon things horrible, but that I grew aghast lest there should be *nothing* to see. At length, with a wild desperation at heart, I quickly unclosed my eyes. My worst thoughts, then, were confirmed. The blackness of eternal night encompassed me. I struggled for breath. The intensity of the darkness seemed to oppress and stifle me. The atmosphere was intolerably close. I still lay quietly, and made effort to exercise my reason. I brought to mind the inquisitorial proceedings, and attempted from that point to deduce my real condition. The sentence had passed; and it appeared to me that a very long interval of time had since elapsed. Yet not for a moment did I suppose myself actually dead. Such a supposition, notwithstanding what we read in fiction, is altogether inconsistent with real existence – but where and in what state was I? The condemned to death, I knew, perished usually at the *autos da fé*,[2] and one of these had been held on the very night of the day of my trial. Had I been remanded to my dungeon, to await the next sacrifice, which would not take place for many months? This I at once saw could not be. Victims had been in immediate demand. Moreover, my dungeon, as well as all the condemned cells at Toledo,[3] had stone floors, and light was not altogether excluded.

A fearful idea now suddenly drove the blood in torrents upon my heart, and for a brief period I once more relapsed into insensibility. Upon recovering, I at once started to my feet, trembling convulsively in every fibre. I thrust my arms wildly above and around me in all directions. I felt nothing; yet dreaded to move a step, lest I should be impeded by the walls of a *tomb*. Perspiration burst from every pore, and stood in cold beads upon my forehead. The agony of suspense grew at length intolerable, and I cautiously moved forward, with my arms extended, and my eyes straining from their sockets, in the hope of catching some faint ray of light. I proceeded for many paces; but still all was blackness and vacancy. I breathed more freely. It seemed evident that mine was not, at least, the most hideous of fates.

And now, as I still continued to step cautiously onward, there came thronging upon my recollection a thousand vague rumours of the horrors of Toledo. Of the dungeons there had been strange things narrated – fables I had always deemed them – but yet strange, and too ghastly to repeat, save in a whisper. Was I left to perish of starvation in this subterranean world of darkness; or what fate, perhaps even more fearful, awaited me? That the result would be death, and a death of more than customary bitterness, I knew too well the character of my judges to doubt. The mode and the hour were all that occupied or distracted me.

My outstretched hands at length encountered some solid obstruction. It was a wall, seemingly of stone masonry – very smooth, slimy, and cold. I followed it up, stepping with all the careful distrust with which certain antique narratives had inspired me. This process, however, afforded me no means of ascertaining the dimensions of my dungeon, as I might make its circuit, and return to the point whence I set out, without being aware of the fact, so perfectly uniform seemed the wall. I therefore sought the knife which had been in my pocket, when led into the inquisitorial chamber, but it was gone; my clothes had been exchanged for a wrapper of coarse serge. I had thought of forcing the blade in some minute crevice of the masonry, so as to identify my point of departure. The difficulty, nevertheless, was but trivial; although, in the disorder of my fancy, it seemed at first insuperable. I tore a part of the hem from the robe and placed the fragment at full length, and at right angles to the wall. In groping my way around the prison, I could not fail to encounter this rag upon completing the circuit, So, at least, I thought; but I had not counted upon the extent of the dungeon, or upon my own weakness. The ground was moist and slippery. I staggered onward for some time, when I stumbled and fell. My excessive fatigue induced me to remain prostrate; and sleep soon overtook me as I lay.

Upon awaking, and stretching forth an arm, I found beside me a loaf and a pitcher with water. I was too much exhausted to reflect upon this circumstance, but ate and drank with avidity. Shortly afterward I resumed my tour around the prison, and, with much toil, came at last upon the fragment of the serge. Up to the period when I fell, I had counted fifty-two paces, and, upon resuming my walk, I had counted forty-eight more – when I arrived at the rag. There were in all, then, a hundred paces; and, admitting two paces to the yard, I presumed the dungeon to be fifty yards in circuit. I had met, however, with many angles in the wall, and thus I could form no guess at the shape of the vault; for vault I could not help supposing it to be.

I had little object – certainly no hope – in these researches; but a vague curiosity prompted me to continue them. Quitting the wall, I resolved to cross the area of the enclosure. At first, I proceeded with extreme caution, for the floor, although seemingly of solid material, was treacherous with slime. At length, however, I took courage, and did not hesitate to step firmly – endeavouring to cross in as direct a line as possible. I had advanced some ten or twelve paces in this manner, when the remnant of the torn hem of my robe became entangled between my legs. I stepped on it, and fell violently on my face.

In the confusion attending my fall, I did not immediately apprehend a somewhat startling circumstance, which yet, in a few seconds afterward, and while I still lay prostrate, arrested my attention. It was this: my chin rested upon the floor of the prison, but my lips, and the upper portion of my head, although seemingly at a less elevation than the chin, touched nothing. At the same time, my forehead seemed bathed in a clammy vapour, and the peculiar smell of decayed fungus arose to my nostrils. I put forward my arm, and shuddered to find that I had fallen at the very brink of a circular pit, whose extent, of course, I had no means of ascertaining at the moment. Groping about the masonry just below the margin, I succeeded in dislodging a small fragment, and let it fall into the abyss. For many seconds I hearkened to its reverberations as it dashed against the sides of the chasm in its descent. At length, there was a sullen plunge into water, succeeded by loud echoes. At the same moment, there came a sound resembling the quick opening, and as rapid closing of a door overhead, while a faint gleam of light flashed suddenly through the gloom, and as suddenly faded away.

I saw clearly the doom which had been prepared for me, and congratulated myself upon the timely accident by which I had escaped. Another step before my fall, and the world had seen me no more. And the death just avoided was of that very character which I had regarded as fabulous and frivolous in the tales respecting the Inquisition. To the victims of its tyranny, there was the choice of death with its direst physical agonies, or death with its most hideous moral horrors. I had been reserved for the latter. By long suffering my nerves had been unstrung, until I trembled at the sound of my own voice, and had become in every respect a fitting subject for the species of torture which awaited me.

Shaking in every limb, I groped my way back to the wall – resolving there to perish rather than risk the terrors of the wells, of which my imagination now pictured many in various positions about the dungeon. In other conditions of mind, I might have had courage to end my misery at once, by a plunge into one of these abysses; but now I was the veriest of cowards. Neither could I forget what I had read of these pits – that the *sudden* extinction of life formed no part of their most horrible plan.

Agitation of spirit kept me awake for many long hours; but at length I again slumbered. Upon arousing, I found by my side, as before, a loaf and a pitcher of water. A burning thirst consumed me, and I emptied the vessel at a draught. It must have been drugged – for scarcely had I drunk, before I became irresistibly drowsy. A deep sleep fell upon me – a sleep like that of death. How long it lasted, of course, I know not; but when, once again, I unclosed my eyes, the objects around me were visible. By a wild, sulphurous lustre, the origin of which I could not at first determine, I was enabled to see the extent and aspect of the prison.

In its size I had been greatly mistaken. The whole circuit of its walls did not exceed twenty-five yards. For some minutes this fact occasioned me a world of vain trouble; vain indeed – for what could be of less importance, under the terrible circumstances which environed me, than the mere dimensions of my dungeon? But my soul took a wild interest in trifles, and I busied myself in endeavours to account for the error I had committed in my measurement. The truth at length flashed upon me. In my first attempt at exploration I had counted fifty-two paces, up to the period when I fell; I must then have been within a pace or two of the fragment of serge; in fact, I had nearly performed the circuit of the vault. I then slept – and, upon awaking, I must have returned upon my steps – thus supposing the circuit nearly double what it actually was. My confusion of mind prevented me from observing that I began my tour with the wall to the left, and ended it with the wall to the right.

I had been deceived, too, in respect to the shape of the enclosure. In feeling my way, I had found many angles, and thus deduced an idea of great irregularity; so potent is the effect of total darkness upon one arousing from lethargy or sleep! The angles were simply those of a few slight depressions, or niches, at odd intervals. The general shape of the prison was square. What I had taken for masonry seemed now to be iron, or some other metal, in huge plates, whose sutures or joints occasioned the depression. The entire surface of this metallic enclosure was rudely daubed in all the hideous and repulsive devices to which the charnel superstition of the monks has given rise. The figures of fiends in aspects of menace, with skeleton forms, and other more really fearful images, overspread and disfigured the walls. I observed that the outlines of these monstrosities were sufficiently distinct, but that the colours seemed faded and blurred, as if from the effects of a damp atmosphere. I now noticed the floor, too, which was of stone. In the centre yawned the circular pit from whose jaws I had escaped; but it was the only one in the dungeon.

All this I saw indistinctly and by much effort – for my personal condition had been greatly changed during slumber. I now lay upon my back, and at full length, on a species of low framework of wood. To this I was securely bound by a long strap resembling a surcingle.[4] It passed in many convolutions about my limbs and body, leaving at liberty only my head and my left arm to such extent, that I could, by dint of much exertion, supply myself with food from an earthen dish which lay by my side on the floor. I saw, to my horror, that the pitcher had been removed. I say, to my horror – for I was consumed with intolerable thirst. This thirst it appeared to be the design of my persecutors to stimulate – for the food in the dish was meat pungently seasoned.

Looking upward, I surveyed the ceiling of my prison. It was some thirty or forty feet overhead, and constructed much as the side walls. In one of its panels a very singular figure riveted my whole attention. It was the painted figure of Time as he is commonly represented, save that, in lieu of a scythe, he held what, at a casual glance, I supposed to be the pictured image of a huge pendulum, such as we see on antique clocks. There was something, however, in the appearance of this machine which caused me to regard it more attentively. While I gazed directly upward at it (for its position was immediately over my own), I fancied that I saw it in motion. In an instant afterward the fancy was confirmed. Its sweep was brief, and, of course, slow. I watched it for some minutes, somewhat in fear, but more in wonder. Wearied at length with observing its dull movement, I turned my eyes upon the other objects in the cell.

A slight noise attracted my notice, and looking to the floor, I saw several enormous rats traversing it. They had issued from the well, which lay just within view to my right. Even then, while I gazed, they came up in troops, hurriedly, with ravenous eyes, allured by the scent of the meat. From this it required much effort and attention to scare them away.

It might have been half-an-hour, perhaps even an hour (for I could take but imperfect note of time) before I again cast my eyes upward. What I then saw, confounded and amazed me. The sweep of the pendulum had increased in extent by nearly a yard. As a natural consequence, its velocity was also much greater. But what mainly disturbed me, was the idea that it had perceptibly *descended*. I now observed – with what horror it is needless to say – that its nether extremity was formed of a crescent of glittering steel, about a foot in length from horn to horn; the horns upward, and the under edge evidently as keen as that of a razor. Like a razor also, it seemed massy and heavy, tapering from the edge into a solid and broad structure above. It was appended to a weighty rod of brass, and the whole *hissed* as it swung through the air.

I could no longer doubt the doom prepared for me by monkish ingenuity in torture. My cognisance of the pit had become known to the inquisitorial agents – *the pit*, whose horrors had been destined for so bold a recusant[5] as myself – *the pit*, typical of hell, and regarded by rumour as the Ultima Thule[6] of all their punishments. The plunge into this pit I had avoided by the merest of accidents, and I knew that surprise, or entrapment into torment, formed an important portion of all the grotesquerie of these dungeon deaths. Having failed to fall, it was no part of the demon plan to hurl me into the abyss; and thus (there being no alternative) a different and a milder destruction awaited me. Milder! I half smiled in my agony as I thought of such application of such a term.

What boots it to tell of the long, long hours of horror more than mortal, during which I counted the rushing oscillations of the steel! Inch by inch – line by line – with a descent only appreciable at intervals that seemed ages – down and still down it came! Days passed – it might have been that many days passed – ere it swept so closely over me as to fan me with its acrid breath. The odour of the sharp steel forced itself into my nostrils. I prayed – I wearied heaven with my prayer for its more speedy descent. I grew frantically mad, and struggled to force myself upward against the sweep of the fearful scimitar.[7] And then I fell suddenly calm, and lay smiling at the glittering death, as a child at some rare bauble.

There was another interval of utter insensibility; it was brief; for, upon again lapsing into life, there had been no perceptible descent in the pendulum. But it might have been long – for I knew there were demons who took note of my swoon, and who could have arrested the vibration at pleasure. Upon my recovery, too, I felt very – oh, inexpressibly – sick and weak, as if through long inanition. Even amid the agonies of that period the human nature craved food. With painful effort I outstretched my left arm as far as my bonds permitted, and took possession of the small remnant which had been spared me by the rats.

As I put a portion of it within my lips, there rushed to my mind a half-formed thought of joy – of hope. Yet what business had *I* with hope? It was, as I say, a half-formed thought – man has many such, which are never completed. I felt that it was of joy – of hope; but I felt also that it had perished in its formation. In vain I struggled to perfect – to regain it. Long suffering had nearly annihilated all my ordinary powers of mind. I was an imbecile – an idiot.

The vibration of the pendulum was at right angles to my length. I saw that the crescent was designed to cross the region of the heart. It would fray the serge of my robe – it would return and repeat its operations – again – and again. Notwithstanding its terrifically wide sweep (some thirty feet or more), and the hissing vigour of its descent, sufficient to sunder these very walls of iron, still the fraying of my robe would be all that, for several minutes, it would accomplish. And at this thought I paused. I dared not go farther than this reflection. I dwelt upon it with a pertinacity of attention – as if, in so dwelling, I could arrest *here* the descent of the steel. I forced myself to ponder upon the sound of the crescent as it should pass across the garment – upon the peculiar thrilling sensation which the friction of cloth produces on the nerves. I pondered upon all this frivolity until my teeth were on edge.

Down – steadily down it crept. I took a frenzied pleasure in contrasting its downward with its lateral velocity. To the right – to the left – far and wide – with the shriek of a damned spirit! to my heart, with the stealthy pace of the tiger! I alternately laughed and howled, as the one or the other idea grew predominant.

Down – certainly, relentlessly down! It vibrated within three inches of my bosom! I struggled violently – furiously – to free my left arm. This was free only from the elbow to the hand. I could reach the latter, from the platter beside me, to my mouth, with great effort, but no farther. Could I have broken the fastenings above the elbow, I would have seized and attempted to arrest the pendulum. I might as well have attempted to arrest an avalanche!

Down – still unceasingly – still inevitably down! I gasped and struggled at each vibration. I shrunk convulsively at its every sweep. My eyes followed its outward or upward whirls with the eagerness of the most unmeaning despair; they closed themselves spasmodically at the descent, although death would have been a relief, oh, how unspeakable! Still I quivered in every nerve to think how slight a sinking of the machinery would precipitate that keen, glistening axe upon my bosom. It was *hope* that prompted the nerve to quiver – the frame to shrink. It was *hope* – the hope that triumphs on the rack – that whispers to the death-condemned even in the dungeons of the Inquisition.[8]

I saw that some ten or twelve vibrations would bring the steel in actual contact with my robe – and with this observation there suddenly came over my spirit all the keen, collected calmness of despair. For the first time during many hours or perhaps days – I *thought*. It now occurred to me, that the bandage, or surcingle, which enveloped me, was *unique*. I was tied by no separate cord. The first stroke of the razor-like crescent athwart any portion of the band, would so detach it that it might be unwound from my person by means of my left hand. But how fearful, in that case, the proximity of the steel! The result of the slightest struggle, how deadly! Was it likely, moreover, that the minions of the torturer had not foreseen and provided for this possibility? Was it probable that the bandage crossed my bosom in the track of the pendulum? Dreading to find my faint, and, as it seemed, my last hope frustrated, I so far elevated my head as to obtain a distinct view of my breast. The surcingle enveloped my limbs and body close in all directions – *save in the path of the destroying crescent*.

Scarcely had I dropped my head back into its original position, when there flashed upon my mind what I cannot better describe than as the unformed half of that idea of deliverance to which I have previously alluded, and of which a moiety only floated indeterminately through my brain when I raised food to my burning lips. The whole thought was now present – feeble, scarcely sane, scarcely definite – but still entire. I proceeded at once, with the nervous energy of despair, to attempt its execution.

For many hours the immediate vicinity of the low framework upon which I lay, had been literally swarming with rats. They were wild, bold, ravenous – their red eyes glaring upon me as if they waited but for motionlessness on my part to make me their prey. 'To what food,' I thought, 'have they been accustomed in the well?'

They had devoured, in spite of all my efforts to prevent them, all but a small remnant of the contents of the dish. I had fallen into an habitual see-saw, or wave of the hand, about the platter; and at length the unconscious uniformity of the movement deprived it of effect. In their voracity, the vermin frequently fastened their sharp fangs in my fingers. With the particles of the oily and spicy viand which now remained, I thoroughly rubbed the bandage wherever I could reach it; then, raising my hand from the floor, I lay breathlessly still.

At first, the ravenous animals were startled and terrified at the change – at the cessation of movement. They shrank alarmedly back; many sought the well. But this was only for a moment. I had not counted in vain upon their voracity. Observing that I remained without motion, one or two of the boldest leaped upon the framework, and smelt at the surcingle. This seemed the signal for a general rush. Forth from the well they hurried in fresh troops. They clung to the wood – they overran it, and leaped in hundreds upon my person. The measured movement of the pendulum disturbed them not at all. Avoiding its strokes, they busied themselves with the anointed bandage. They pressed – they swarmed upon me in ever accumulating heaps. They writhed upon my throat; their cold lips sought my own; I was half stifled by their thronging pressure; disgust, for which the world has no name, swelled my bosom, and chilled, with a heavy clamminess, my heart. Yet one minute, and I felt that the struggle would be over. Plainly I perceived the loosening of the bandage. I knew that in more than one place it must be already severed. With a more than human resolution I lay still.

Nor had I erred in my calculations – nor had I endured in vain. I at length felt that I was *free*. The surcingle hung in ribands from my body. But the stroke of the pendulum already pressed upon my bosom. It had divided the serge of the robe. It had cut through the linen beneath. Twice again it swung, and a sharp sense of pain shot through every nerve. But the moment of escape had arrived. At a wave of my hand my deliverers hurried tumultuously away. With a steady movement – cautious, sidelong, shrinking, and slow – I slid from the embrace of the bandage and beyond the reach of the scimitar. For the moment, at least, *I was free*.

Free! – and in the grasp of the Inquisition! I had scarcely stepped from my wooden bed of horror upon the stone floor of the prison, when the motion of the hellish machine ceased, and I beheld it drawn up, by some invisible force, through the ceiling. This was a lesson which I took desperately to heart. My every motion was undoubtedly watched. Free! – I had but escaped death in one form of agony, to be delivered unto worse than death in some other. With that thought I rolled my eyes nervously around on the barriers of iron that hemmed me in. Something unusual – some change which, at first, I could not appreciate distinctly – it was obvious, had taken place in the apartment. For many minutes of a dreamy and trembling abstraction, I busied myself in vain, unconnected conjecture. During this period, I became aware, for the first time, of the origin of the sulphurous light which illumined the cell. It proceeded from a fissure, about half an inch in width, extending entirely around the prison at the base of the walls, which thus appeared, and were completely separated from the floor. I endeavoured, but of course in vain, to look through the aperture.

As I arose from the attempt, the mystery of the alteration in the chamber broke at once upon my understanding. I have observed that, although the outlines of the figures upon the walls were sufficiently distinct, yet the colours seemed blurred and indefinite. These colours had now assumed, and were momentarily assuming, a startling and most intense brilliancy, that gave to the spectral and fiendish portraitures an aspect that might have thrilled even firmer nerves than my own. Demon eyes, of a wild and ghastly vivacity, glared upon me in a thousand directions, where none had been visible before, and gleamed with the lurid lustre of a fire that I could not force my imagination to regard as unreal.

Unreal! Even while I breathed there came to my nostrils the breath of the vapour of heated iron! A suffocating odour pervaded the prison! A deeper glow settled each moment in the eyes that glared at my agonies! A richer tint of crimson diffused itself over the pictured horrors of blood. I panted! I gasped for breath! There could be no doubt of the design of my tormentors – oh! most unrelenting! oh! most demoniac of men! I shrank from the glowing metal to the centre of the cell. Amid the thought of the fiery destruction that impended, the idea of the coolness of the well came over my soul like balm. I rushed to its deadly brink. I threw my straining vision below. The glare from the enkindled roof illumined its inmost recesses. Yet, for a wild moment, did my spirit refuse to comprehend the meaning of what I saw. At length it forced – it wrestled its way into my soul – it burned itself in upon my shuddering reason. Oh! for a voice to speak! – oh! horror! – oh! any horror but this! With a shriek, I rushed from the margin, and buried my face in my hands – weeping bitterly.

The heat rapidly increased, and once again I looked up, shuddering as with a fit of the ague. There had been a second change in the cell – and now the change was obviously in the *form*. As before, it was in vain that I at first endeavoured to appreciate or understand what was taking place. But not long was I left in doubt. The inquisitorial vengeance had been hurried by my twofold escape, and there was to be no more dallying with the King of Terrors. The room had been square. I saw that two of its iron angles were now acute – two, consequently, obtuse. The fearful difference quickly increased with a low rumbling or moaning sound. In an instant the apartment had shifted its form into that of a lozenge. But the alteration stopped not here – I neither hoped nor desired it to stop. I could have clasped the red walls to my bosom as a garment of eternal peace. 'Death,' I said, 'any death but that of the pit!' Fool! might I not have known that *into the pit* it was the object of the burning iron to urge me? Could I resist its glow? or if even that, could I withstand its pressure? And now, flatter and flatter grew the lozenge, with a rapidity that left me no time for contemplation. Its centre, and of course, its greatest width, came just over the yawning gulf. I shrank back – but the closing walls pressed me resistlessly onward. At length for my seared and writhing body there was no longer an inch of foothold on the firm floor of the prison. I struggled no more, but the agony of my soul found vent in one loud, long, and final scream of despair. I felt that I tottered upon the brink – I averted my eyes –

There was a discordant hum of human voices! There was a loud blast as of many trumpets! There was a harsh grating as of a thousand thunders! The fiery walls rushed back! An outstretched arm caught my own as I fell, fainting, into the abyss. It was that of General Lasalle.[9] The French army had entered Toledo. The Inquisition was in the hands of its enemies.

The Premature Burial

THERE ARE CERTAIN themes of which the interest is all-absorbing, but which are too entirely horrible for the purposes of legitimate fiction. These the mere romanticist must eschew, if he does not wish to offend, or to disgust. They are with propriety handled only when the severity and majesty of truth sanctify and sustain them. We thrill, for example, with the most intense of 'pleasurable pain,' over the accounts of the Passage of the Beresina, of the Earthquake at Lisbon, of the Plague at London, of the Massacre of St Bartholomew, or of the stifling of the hundred and twenty-three prisoners in the Black Hole at Calcutta.[1] But, in these accounts, it is the fact – it is the reality – it is the history which excites. As inventions, we should regard them with simple abhorrence.

I have mentioned some few of the more prominent and august calamities on record; but in these it is the extent, not less than the character of the calamity, which so vividly impresses the fancy. I need not remind the reader that, from the long and weird catalogue of human miseries, I might have selected many individual instances more replete with essential suffering than any of these vast generalities of disaster. The true wretchedness, indeed – the ultimate woe – is particular, not diffuse. That the ghastly extremes of agony are endured by man the unit, and never by man the mass – for this let us thank a merciful God!

To be buried while alive is, beyond question, the most terrific of these extremes which has ever fallen to the lot of mere mortality. That it has frequently, very frequently, so fallen, will scarcely be denied by those who think. The boundaries which divide Life from Death are at best shadowy and vague. Who shall say where the one ends, and where the other begins? We know that there are diseases in which occur total cessations of all the apparent functions of vitality, and yet in which these cessations are merely suspensions, properly so called. They are only temporary pauses in the incomprehensible mechanism. A certain period elapses, and some unseen mysterious principle again sets in motion the magic pinions[2] and the wizard wheels. The silver cord was not for ever loosed, nor the golden bowl irreparably broken. But where, meantime, was the soul?

Apart, however, from the inevitable conclusion, *a priori*, that such causes must produce such effects – that the well-known occurrence of such cases of suspended animation must naturally give rise, now and then, to premature interments – apart from this consideration, we have the direct testimony of medical and ordinary experience, to prove that a vast number of such interments have actually taken place. I might refer at once, if necessary, to a hundred well-authenticated instances. One of very remarkable character, and of which the circumstances may be fresh in the memory of some of my readers, occurred, not very long ago, in the neighbouring city of Baltimore, where it occasioned a painful, intense, and widely extended excitement. The wife of one of the most respectable citizens – a lawyer of eminence and a member of Congress was seized with a sudden and unaccountable illness, which completely baffled the skill of her physicians. After much suffering, she died, or was supposed to die. No one suspected, indeed, or had reason to suspect, that she was not actually dead. She presented all the ordinary appearances of death. The face assumed the usual pinched and sunken outline. The lips were of the usual marble pallor. The eyes were lustreless. There was no warmth. Pulsation had ceased. For three days the body was preserved unburied, during which it had acquired a stony rigidity. The funeral, in short, was hastened, on account of the rapid advance of what was supposed to be decomposition.

The lady was deposited in her family vault, which, for three subsequent years, was undisturbed. At the expiration of this term, it was opened for the reception of a sarcophagus – but, alas! how fearful a shock awaited the husband, who, personally, threw open the door. As its portals swung outwardly back, some white-apparelled object fell rattling within his arms. It was the skeleton of his wife in her yet unmouldered shroud.

A careful investigation rendered it evident that she had revived within two days after her entombment – that her struggles within the coffin had caused it to fall from a ledge, or shelf, to the floor, where it was so broken as to permit her escape. A lamp which had been accidentally left, full of oil, within the tomb, was found empty; it might have been exhausted, however, by evaporation. On the uppermost of the steps which led down into the dread chamber, was a large fragment of the coffin, with which it seemed that she had endeavoured to arrest attention, by striking the iron door. While thus occupied, she probably swooned, or possibly died, through sheer terror; and, in falling, her shroud became entangled in some ironwork which projected interiorly. Thus she remained, and thus she rotted, erect.

In the year 1810, a case of living inhumation happened in France, attended with circumstances which go far to warrant the assertion that truth is, indeed, stranger than fiction. The heroine of the story was a Mademoiselle Victorine Lafourcade, a young girl of illustrious family, of wealth, and of great personal beauty. Among her numerous suitors was Julien Bossuet, a poor *litterateur*, or journalist, of Paris. His talents and general amiability had recommended him to the notice of the heiress, by whom he seems to have been truly beloved; but her pride of birth decided her, finally, to reject him, and to wed a Monsieur Renelle, a banker, and a diplomatist of some eminence. After marriage, however, this gentleman neglected, and, perhaps, even more positively ill-treated her. Having passed with him some wretched years, she died – at least her condition so closely resembled death as to deceive every one who saw her. She was buried – not in a vault – but in an ordinary grave in the village of her nativity. Filled with despair, and still inflamed by the memory of a profound attachment, the lover journeys from the capital to the remote province in which the village lies, with the romantic purpose of disinterring the corpse, and possessing himself of its luxuriant tresses. He reaches the grave. At midnight he unearths the coffin, opens it, and is in the act of detaching the hair, when he is arrested by the unclosing of the beloved eyes. In fact, the lady had been buried alive. Vitality had not altogether departed; and she was aroused, by the caresses of her lover, from the lethargy which had been mistaken for death. He bore her frantically to his lodgings in the village. He employed certain powerful restoratives suggested by no little medical learning. In fine, she revived. She recognised her preserver. She remained with him until, by slow degrees, she fully recovered her original health. Her woman's heart was not adamant, and this last lesson of love sufficed to soften it. She bestowed it upon Bossuet. She returned no more to her husband, but concealing from him her resurrection, fled with her lover to America. Twenty years afterwards, the two returned to France, in the persuasion that time had so greatly altered the lady's appearance, that her friends would be unable to recognise her. They were mistaken, however; for, at the first meeting, Monsieur Renelle did actually recognise and make claim to his wife. This claim she resisted; and a judicial tribunal sustained her in her resistance; deciding that the peculiar circumstances, with the long lapse of years, had extinguished, not only equitably, but legally, the authority of the husband.

The *Chirurgical Journal* of Leipsic – a periodical of high authority and merit, which some American bookseller would do well to translate and republish – records, in a late number, a very distressing event of the character in question.

An officer of artillery, a man of gigantic stature and of robust health, being thrown from an unmanageable horse, received a very severe contusion upon the head, which rendered him insensible at once; the skull was slightly fractured; but no immediate danger was apprehended. Trepanning was accomplished successfully. He was bled, and many other of the ordinary means of relief were adopted. Gradually, however, he fell into a more and more hopeless state of stupor; and, finally, it was thought that he died.

The weather was warm; and he was buried, with indecent haste, in one of the public cemeteries. His funeral took place on Thursday. On the Sunday following, the grounds of the cemetery were, as usual, much thronged with visitors; and about noon, an intense excitement was created by the declaration of a peasant, that, while sitting upon the grave of the officer, he had distinctly felt a commotion of the earth, as if occasioned by some one struggling beneath. At first, little attention was paid to the man's asseveration; but his evident terror, and the dogged obstinacy with which he persisted in his story, had at length their natural effect upon the crowd. Spades were hurriedly procured, and the grave, which was shamefully shallow, was, in a few minutes, so far thrown open that the head of its occupant appeared. He was then, seemingly, dead; but he sat nearly erect within his coffin, the lid of which, in his furious struggles, he had partially uplifted.

He was forthwith conveyed to the nearest hospital, and there pronounced to be still living, although in an asphytic condition.[3] After some hours he revived, recognised individuals of his acquaintance and, in broken sentences, spoke of his agonies in the grave.

From what he related, it was clear that he must have been conscious of life for more than an hour, while inhumed, before lapsing into insensibility. The grave was carelessly and loosely filled with an exceedingly porous soil; and thus some air was necessarily admitted. He heard the footsteps of the crowd over head, and endeavoured to make himself heard in turn. It was the tumult within the grounds of the cemetery, he said, which appeared to awaken him from a deep sleep – but no sooner was he awake than he became fully aware of the awful horrors of his position.

This patient, it is recorded, was doing well, and seemed to be in a fair way of ultimate recovery, but fell a victim to the quackeries of medical experiment. The galvanic battery[4] was applied, and he suddenly expired in one of those ecstatic paroxysms which, occasionally, it superinduces.

The mention of the galvanic battery, nevertheless, recalls to my memory a well-known and very extraordinary case in point, where its action proved the means of restoring to animation a young attorney of London, who had been interred for two days. This occurred in 1831, and created, at the time, a very profound sensation wherever it was made the subject of converse.

The patient, Mr Edward Stapleton, had died, apparently, of typhus fever, accompanied with some anomalous symptoms which had excited the curiosity of his medical attendants. Upon his seeming decease, his friends were requested to sanction a *post-mortem* examination, but declined to permit it. As often happens, when such refusals are made, the practitioners resolved to disinter the body and dissect it at leisure, in private. Arrangements were easily effected with some of the numerous corps of body-snatchers with which London abounds; and, upon the third night after the funeral, the supposed corpse was unearthed from a grave eight feet deep, and deposited in the operating chamber of one of the private hospitals.

An incision of some extent had been actually made in the abdomen, when the fresh and undecayed appearance of the subject suggested an application of the battery. One experiment succeeded another, and the customary effects supervened, with nothing to characterise them in any respect, except, upon one or two occasions, a more than ordinary degree of life-likeness in the convulsive action.

It grew late. The day was about to dawn; and it was thought expedient, at length, to proceed at once to the dissection. A student, however, was especially desirous of testing a theory of his own, and insisted upon applying the battery to one of the pectoral muscles. A rough gash was made, and a wire hastily brought in contact; when the patient, with a hurried, but quite unconvulsive movement, arose from the table, stepped into the middle of the floor, gazed about him uneasily for a few seconds, and then – spoke. What he said was unintelligible; but the words were uttered; the syllabification was distinct. Having spoken, he fell heavily to the floor.

For some moments all were paralysed with awe – but the urgency of the case soon restored them their presence of mind. It was seen that Mr Stapleton was alive, although in a swoon. Upon exhibition of ether he revived and was rapidly restored to health, and to the society of his friends – from whom, however, all knowledge of his resuscitation was withheld, until a relapse was no longer to be apprehended. Their wonder – their rapturous astonishment – may be conceived.

The most thrilling peculiarity of this incident, nevertheless, is involved in what Mr S. himself asserts. He declares that at no period was he altogether insensible – that, dully and confusedly, he was aware of everything which happened to him, from the moment in which he was pronounced *dead* by his physicians, to that in which he fell swooning to the floor of the hospital. 'I am alive,' were the uncomprehended words which, upon recognising the locality of the dissecting-room, he had endeavoured, in his extremity, to utter.

It were an easy matter to multiply such histories as these – but I forbear – for, indeed, we have no need of such to establish the fact that premature interments occur. When we reflect how very rarely, from the nature of the case, we have it in our power to detect them, we must admit that they may *frequently* occur without our cognisance. Scarcely, in truth, is a graveyard ever encroached upon, for any purpose, to any great extent, that skeletons are not found in postures which suggest the most fearful of suspicions.

Fearful indeed the suspicion – but more fearful the doom! It may be asserted, without hesitation, that *no* event is so terribly well adapted to inspire the supremeness of bodily and of mental distress, as is burial before death. The unendurable oppression of the lungs – the stifling fumes of the damp earth – the clinging to the death garments – the rigid embrace of the narrow house – the blackness of the absolute Night – the silence like a sea that overwhelms – the unseen but palpable presence of the Conqueror Worm[5] – these things, with thoughts of the air and grass above, with memory of dear friends who would fly to save us if but informed of our fate, and with consciousness that of this fate they can *never* be informed – that our hopeless portion is that of the really dead – these considerations, I say, carry into the heart, which still palpitates, a degree of appalling and intolerable horror from which the most daring imagination must recoil. We know of nothing so agonising upon Earth – we can dream of nothing half so hideous in the realms of the nethermost Hell. And thus all narratives upon this topic have an interest profound; an interest, nevertheless, which, through the sacred awe of the topic itself, very properly and very peculiarly depends upon our conviction of the *truth* of the matter narrated. What I have now to tell, is of my own actual knowledge – of my own positive and personal experience.

For several years I had been subject to attacks of the singular disorder which physicians have agreed to term catalepsy,[6] in default of a more definite title. Although both the immediate and the predisposing causes, and even the actual diagnosis of this disease, are still mysteries, its obvious and apparent character is sufficiently well understood. Its variations seem to be chiefly of degree. Sometimes the patient lies, for a day only, or even for a shorter period, in a species of exaggerated lethargy. He is senseless and externally motionless; but the pulsation of the heart is still faintly perceptible; some traces of warmth remain; a slight colour lingers within the centre of the cheek; and, upon application of a mirror to the lips, we can detect a torpid, unequal, and vacillating action of the lungs. Then, again, the duration of the trance is for weeks – even for months; while the closest scrutiny, and the most rigorous medical tests, fail to establish any material distinction between the state of the sufferer and what we conceive of absolute death. Very usually, he is saved from premature interment solely by the knowledge of his friends that he has been previously subject to catalepsy, by the consequent suspicion excited, and, above all, by the non-appearance of decay. The advances of the malady are, luckily, gradual. The first manifestations, although marked, are unequivocal. The fits grow successively more and more distinctive, and endure each for a longer term than the preceding. In this lies the principal security from inhumation. The unfortunate whose *first* attack should be of the extreme character which is occasionally seen, would almost inevitably be consigned alive to the tomb.

My own case differed in no important particular from those mentioned in medical books. Sometimes, without any apparent cause, I sank, little by little, into a condition of semi-syncope,[7] or half swoon; and, in this condition, without pain, without ability to stir, or strictly speaking, to think, but with a dull lethargic consciousness of life and of the presence of those who surrounded my bed, I remained, until the crisis of the disease restored me, suddenly, to perfect sensation. At other times I was quickly and impetuously smitten. I grew sick, and numb, and chilly, and dizzy, and so fell prostrate at once. Then, for weeks, all was void, and black, and silent, and Nothing became the universe. Total annihilation could be no more. From these latter attacks I awoke, however, with a gradation slow in proportion to the suddenness of the seizure. Just as the day dawns to the friendless and houseless beggar who roams the streets throughout the long desolate winter night – just so tardily – just so wearily – just so cheerily came back the light of the Soul to me.

Apart from the tendency to trance, however, my general health appeared to be good; nor could I perceive that it was at all affected by the one prevalent malady – unless, indeed, an idiosyncrasy in an ordinary *sleep* may be looked upon as superinduced. Upon awaking from slumber, I could never gain, at once, thorough possession of my senses, and always remained, for many minutes, in much bewilderment and perplexity – the mental faculties in general, but the memory in especial, being in a condition of absolute abeyance.

In all that I endured there was no physical suffering, but of moral distress an infinitude. My fancy grew charnel. I talked 'of worms, of tombs and epitaphs.'[8] I was lost in reveries of death, and the idea of premature burial held continual possession of my brain. The ghastly danger to which I was subjected haunted me day and night. In the former, the torture of meditation was excessive – in the latter, supreme.

When the grim darkness overspread the earth, then, with very horror of thought, I shook – shook as the quivering plumes upon the hearse. When nature could endure wakefulness no longer, it was with a struggle that I consented to sleep – for I shuddered to reflect that, upon awaking, I might find myself the tenant of a grave. And when, finally, I sank into slumber, it was only to rush at once into a world of phantasms, above which, with vast, sable, overshadowing wings, hovered, predominant, the one sepulchral Idea.

From the innumerable images of gloom which thus oppressed me in dreams, I select for record but a solitary vision. Methought I was immersed in a cataleptic trance of more than usual duration and profundity. Suddenly there came an icy hand upon my forehead, and an impatient, gibbering voice whispered the word 'Arise!' within my ear.

I sat erect. The darkness was total. I could not see the figure of him who had aroused me. I could call to mind neither the period at which I had fallen into the trance, nor the locality in which I then lay. While I remained motionless, and busied in endeavours to collect my thoughts, the cold hand grasped me fiercely by the wrist, shaking it petulantly, while the gibbering voice said again –

'Arise! did I not bid thee arise?'

'And who,' I demanded, 'art thou?'

'I have no name in the regions which I inhabit,' replied the voice mournfully; 'I was mortal, but am fiend. I was merciless, but am pitiful. Thou dost feel that I shudder. My teeth chatter as I speak, yet it is not with the chilliness of the night – of the night without end. But this hideousness is insufferable. How canst *thou* tranquilly sleep? I cannot rest for the cry of these great agonies. These sights are more than I can bear. Get thee up! Come with me into the outer Night, and let me unfold to thee the graves. Is not this a spectacle of woe? Behold!'

I looked; and the unseen figure, which still grasped me by the wrist, had caused to be thrown open the graves of all mankind; and from each issued the faint phosphoric radiance of decay, so that I could see into the innermost recesses, and there view the shrouded bodies in their sad and solemn slumbers with the worm. But, alas! the real sleepers were fewer, by many millions, than those who slumbered not at all; and there was a feeble struggling; and there was a general sad unrest; and from out the depths of the countless pits there came a melancholy rustling from the garments of the buried. And, of those who seemed tranquilly to repose, I saw that a vast number had changed, in a greater or less degree, the rigid and uneasy position in which they had originally been entombed. And the voice again said to me, as I gazed –

'Is it not – oh, is it *not* a pitiful sight?' But, before I could find words to reply, the figure had ceased to grasp my wrist, the phosphoric lights expired, and the graves were closed with a sudden violence, while from out them arose a tumult of despairing cries, saying again, 'Is it not – O God! is it *not* a very pitiful sight?'

Phantasies such as these, presenting themselves at night, extended their terrific influence far into my waking hours. My nerves became thoroughly unstrung, and I fell a prey to perpetual horror. I hesitated to ride, or to walk, or to indulge in any exercise that would carry me from home. In fact, I no longer dared trust myself out of the immediate presence of those who were aware of my proneness to catalepsy, lest, falling into one of my usual fits, I should be buried before my real condition could be ascertained. I doubted the care, the fidelity of my dearest friends. I dreaded that, in some trance of more than customary duration, they might be prevailed upon to regard me as irrecoverable. I even went so far as to fear that, as I occasioned much trouble, they might be glad to consider any very protracted attack as sufficient excuse for getting rid of me altogether. It was in vain they endeavoured to reassure me by the most solemn promises. I exacted the most sacred oaths, that under no circumstances they would bury me until decomposition had so materially advanced as to render further preservation impossible. And, even then, my mortal terrors would listen to no reason – would accept no consolation. I entered into a series of elaborate precautions. Among other things, I had the family vault so remodelled as to admit of being readily opened from within. The slightest pressure upon a long lever that extended far into the tomb would cause the iron portals to fly back. There were arrangements also for the free admission of air and light, and convenient receptacles for food and water, within immediate reach of the coffin intended for my reception. This coffin was warmly and softly padded, and was provided with a lid, fashioned upon the principle of the vault-door, with the addition of springs so contrived that the feeblest movement of the body would be sufficient to set it at liberty. Besides all this, there was suspended from the roof of the tomb a large bell, the rope of which, it was designed, should extend through a hole in the coffin, and so be fastened to one of the hands of the corpse. But, alas! what avails the vigilance against the Destiny of man? Not even these well-contrived securities sufficed to save from the uttermost agonies of living inhumation a wretch to these agonies foredoomed!

There arrived an epoch – as often before there had arrived – in which I found myself emerging from total unconsciousness into the first feeble and indefinite sense of existence. Slowly – with a tortoise gradation – approached the faint grey dawn of the psychal day. A torpid uneasiness. An apathetic endurance of dull pain. No care – no hope – no effort. Then, after long interval, a ringing in the ears; then, after a lapse still longer, a prickling or tingling sensation in the extremities; then a seemingly eternal period of pleasurable quiescence, during which the awakening feelings are struggling into thought; then a brief resinking into nonentity; then a sudden recovery. At length the slight quivering of an eyelid, and immediately thereupon an electric shock of a terror, deadly and indefinite, which sends the blood in torrents from the temples to the heart. And now the first positive effort to think. And now the first endeavour to remember. And now a partial and evanescent success. And now the memory has so far regained its dominion, that, in some measure, I am cognisant of my state. I feel that I am not awaking from ordinary sleep. I recollect that I have been subject to catalepsy. And now, at last, as if by the rush of an ocean, my shuddering spirit is overwhelmed by the one grim Danger – by the one spectral and ever-prevalent Idea.

For some minutes after this fancy possessed me, I remained without motion. And why? I could not summon courage to move. I dared not make the effort which was to satisfy me of my fate – and yet there was something at my heart which whispered me *it was sure*. Despair – such as no other species of wretchedness ever calls into being – despair alone urged me, after long irresolution, to uplift the heavy lids of my eyes. I uplifted them. It was dark – all dark. I knew that the fit was over. I knew that the crisis of my disorder had long passed. I knew that I had now fully recovered the use of my visual faculties – and yet it was dark – all dark – the intense and utter raylessness of the Night that endureth for evermore.

I endeavoured to shriek; and my lips and my parched tongue moved convulsively together in the attempt – but no voice issued from the cavernous lungs, which, oppressed as if by the weight of some incumbent mountain, gasped and palpitated, with the heart, at every elaborate and struggling inspiration.

The movement of the jaws, in this effort to cry aloud, showed me that they were bound up, as is usual with the dead. I felt, too, that I lay upon some hard substance; and by something similar my sides were, also, closely compressed. So far, I had not ventured to stir any of my limbs – but now I violently threw up my arms, which had been lying at length, with the wrists crossed. They struck a solid wooden substance, which extended above my person at an elevation of not more than six inches from my face. I could no longer doubt that I reposed within a coffin at last.

And now, amid all my infinite miseries, came sweetly the cherub

Hope – for I thought of my precautions. I writhed, and made spasmodic exertions to force open the lid; it would not move. I felt my wrists for the bell-rope; it was not to be found. And now the Comforter fled for ever, and a still sterner Despair reigned triumphant; for I could not help perceiving the absence of the paddings which I had so carefully prepared – and then, too, there came suddenly to my nostrils the strong peculiar odour of moist earth. The conclusion was irresistible. I was *not* within the vault. I had fallen into a trance while absent from home – while among strangers – when, or how, I could not remember – and it was they who had buried me as a dog – nailed up in some common coffin – and thrust, deep, deep, and for ever, into some ordinary and nameless *grave*.

As this awful conviction forced itself, thus, into the innermost chambers of my soul, I once again struggled to cry aloud. And in this second endeavour I succeeded. A long, wild, and continuous shriek, or yell, of agony, resounded through the realms of the subterrene Night.

'Hillo! hillo, there!' said a gruff voice, in reply.

'What the devil's the matter now?' said a second.

'Get out o' that!' said a third.

'What do you mean by yowling in that ere kind of style, like a cattymount?' said a fourth; and hereupon I was seized and shaken without ceremony, for several minutes, by a junto of very rough-looking individuals. They did not arouse me from my slumber – for I was wide awake when I screamed – but they restored me to full possession of my memory.

This adventure occurred near Richmond, in Virginia. Accompanied by a friend, I had proceeded, upon a gunning expedition, some miles down the banks of James River. Night approached, and we were overtaken by a storm. The cabin of a small sloop lying at anchor in the stream, and laden with garden mould, afforded us the only available shelter. We made the best of it, and passed the night on board. I slept in one of the only two berths in the vessel – and the berths of a sloop of sixty or seventy tons need scarcely be described. That which I occupied had no bedding of any kind. Its extreme width was eighteen inches. The distance of its bottom from the deck overhead was precisely the same. I found it a matter of exceeding difficulty to squeeze myself in. Nevertheless, I slept soundly; and the whole of my vision – for it was no dream, and no nightmare – arose naturally from the circumstances of my position – from my ordinary bias of thought – and from the difficulty, to which I have alluded, of collecting my senses, and especially of regaining my memory, for a long time after awaking from slumber. The men who shook me were the crew of the sloop, and some labourers engaged to unload it. From the load itself came the earthy smell. The bandage about the jaws was a silk handkerchief in which I bound up my head, in default of my customary nightcap.

The tortures endured, however, were indubitably quite equal, for the time, to those of actual sepulture. They were fearfully – they were inconceivably hideous; but out of evil proceeded good; for their very excess wrought in my spirit an inevitable revulsion. My soul acquired tone – acquired temper. I went abroad. I took vigorous exercise. I breathed the free air of heaven. I thought upon other subjects than death. I discarded my medical books. 'Buchan'⁹ I burned. I read no 'Night Thoughts'¹⁰ – no fustian about churchyards – no bugaboo tales – *such as this*. In short I became a new man, and lived a man's life. From that memorable night I dismissed for ever my charnel apprehensions, and with them vanished the cataleptic disorder, of which, perhaps, they had been less the consequence than the cause.

There are moments when, even to the sober eye of Reason, the world of our sad Humanity may assume the semblance of a Hell – but the imagination of man is no Carathis,¹¹ to explore with impunity its every cavern. Alas! the grim legion of sepulchral terrors cannot be regarded as altogether fanciful – but, like the Demons in whose company Afrasiab¹² made his voyage down the Oxus,¹³ they must sleep, or they will devour us – they must be suffered to slumber, or we perish.

The Black Cat

FOR THE MOST wild, yet most homely narrative which I am about to pen, I neither expect nor solicit belief. Mad indeed would I be to expect it, in a case where my very senses reject their own evidence. Yet, mad am I not – and very surely do I not dream. But tomorrow I die, and today I would unburden my soul. My immediate purpose is to place before the world, plainly, succinctly, and without comment, a series of mere household events. In their consequences, these events have terrified – have tortured – have destroyed me. Yet I will not attempt to expound them. To me, they have presented little but horror – to many they will seem less terrible than *baroques*.[1] Hereafter, perhaps, some intellect may be found which will reduce my phantasm to the commonplace – some intellect more calm, more logical, and far less excitable than my own, which will perceive, in the circumstances I detail with awe, nothing more than an ordinary succession of very natural causes and effects.

From my infancy I was noted for the docility and humanity of my disposition. My tenderness of heart was even so conspicuous as to make me the jest of my companions. I was especially fond of animals, and was indulged by my parents with a great variety of pets. With these I spent most of my time, and never was so happy as when feeding and caressing them. This peculiarity of character grew with my growth, and, in my manhood, I derived from it one of my principal sources of pleasure. To those who have cherished an affection for a faithful and sagacious dog, I need hardly be at the trouble of explaining the nature or the intensity of the gratification thus derivable. There is something in the unselfish and self-sacrificing love of a brute, which goes directly to the heart of him who has had frequent occasion to test the paltry friendship and gossamer fidelity of mere *Man*.

I married early, and was happy to find in my wife a disposition not uncongenial with my own. Observing my partiality for domestic pets, she lost no opportunity of procuring those of the most agreeable kind. We had birds, gold-fish, a fine dog, rabbits, a small monkey, and *a cat*.

This latter was a remarkably large and beautiful animal, entirely black, and sagacious to an astonishing degree. In speaking of his intelligence, my wife, who at heart was not a little tinctured with superstition, made frequent allusion to the ancient popular notion, which regarded all black cats as witches in disguise. Not that she was ever *serious* upon this point – and I mention the matter at all for no better reason than that it happens, just now, to be remembered.

Pluto [2] – this was the cat's name – was my favourite pet and playmate. I alone fed him, and he attended me wherever I went about the house. It was even with difficulty that I could prevent him from following me through the streets.

Our friendship lasted, in this manner, for several years, during which my general temperament and character – through the instrumentality of the fiend Intemperance – had (I blush to confess it) experienced a radical alteration for the worse. I grew, day by day, more moody, more irritable, more regardless of the feelings of others. I suffered myself to use intemperate language to my wife. At length, I even offered her personal violence. My pets, of course, were made to feel the change in my disposition. I not only neglected, but ill-used them. For Pluto, however, I still retained sufficient regard to restrain me from maltreating him, as I made no scruple of maltreating the rabbits, the monkey, or even the dog, when by accident, or through affection, they came in my way. But my disease grew upon me – for what disease is like alcohol? – and at length even Pluto, who was now becoming old, and consequently somewhat peevish – even Pluto began to experience the effects of my ill temper.

One night, returning home, much intoxicated, from one of my haunts about town, I fancied that the cat avoided my presence. I seized him; when, in his fright at my violence, he inflicted a slight wound upon my hand with his teeth. The fury of a demon instantly possessed me. I knew myself no longer. My original soul seemed, at once, to take its flight from my body; and a more than fiendish malevolence, gin-nurtured, thrilled every fibre of my frame. I took from my waistcoat pocket a pen-knife, opened it, grasped the poor beast by the throat, and deliberately cut one of its eyes from the socket! I blush, I burn, I shudder, while I pen the damnable atrocity.

When reason returned with the morning – when I had slept off the fumes of the night's debauch – I experienced a sentiment half of horror, half of remorse, for the crime of which I had been guilty; but it was, at best, a feeble and equivocal feeling, and the soul remained untouched. I again plunged into excess, and soon drowned in wine all memory of the deed.

In the meantime the cat slowly recovered. The socket of the lost eye presented, it is true, a frightful appearance, but he no longer appeared to suffer any pain. He went about the house as usual, but, as might be expected, fled in extreme terror at my approach. I had so much of my old heart left, as to be at first grieved by this evident dislike on the part of a creature which had once so loved me. But this feeling soon gave place to irritation. And then came, as if to my final and irrevocable overthrow, the spirit of PERVERSENESS. Of this spirit philosophy takes no account. Yet I am not more sure that my soul lives, than I am that perverseness is one of the primitive impulses of the human heart – one of the indivisible primary faculties, or sentiments, which give direction to the character of man. Who has not, a hundred times, found himself committing a vile or a silly action, for no other reason than because he knows he should *not*? Have we not a perpetual inclination, in the teeth of our best judgment, to violate that which is *Law*, merely because we understand it to be such? This spirit of perverseness, I say, came to my final overthrow. It was this unfathomable longing of the soul *to vex itself* – to offer violence to its own nature – to do wrong for the wrong's sake only – that urged me to continue and finally to consummate the injury I had inflicted upon the unoffending brute. One morning, in cool blood, I slipped a noose about its neck and hung it to the limb of a tree – hung it with the tears streaming from my eyes, and with the bitterest remorse at my heart – hung it *because* I knew that it had loved me, and *because* I felt it had given me no reason of offence – hung it *because* I knew that in so doing I was committing a sin – a deadly sin that would so jeopardise my immortal soul as to place it – if such a thing were possible – even beyond the reach of the infinite mercy of the Most Merciful and Most Terrible God.

On the night of the day on which this cruel deed was done, I was aroused from sleep by the cry of 'Fire!' The curtains of my bed were in flames. The whole house was blazing. It was with great difficulty that my wife, a servant, and myself, made our escape from the conflagration. The destruction was complete. My entire worldly wealth was swallowed up, and I resigned myself thenceforward to despair.

I am above the weakness of seeking to establish a sequence of cause and effect between the disaster and the atrocity. But I am detailing a chain of facts, and wish not to leave even a possible link imperfect. On the day succeeding the fire, I visited the ruins. The walls, with one exception, had fallen in. This exception was found in a compartment wall, not very thick, which stood about the middle of the house, and against which had rested the head of my bed. The plastering had here, in great measure, resisted the action of the fire – a fact which I attributed to its having been recently spread. About this wall a dense crowd were collected, and many persons seemed to be examining a particular portion of it with very minute and eager attention. The words 'strange!' 'singular!' and other similar expressions, excited my curiosity. I approached and saw, as if graven in bas-relief upon the white surface, the figure of a gigantic *cat*. The impression was given with an accuracy truly marvellous. There was a rope about the animal's neck.

When I first beheld this apparition – for I could scarcely regard it as less – my wonder and my terror were extreme. But at length reflection came to my aid. The cat, I remembered, had been hung in a garden adjacent to the house. Upon the alarm of fire, this garden had been immediately filled by the crowd – by some one of whom the animal must have been cut from the tree and thrown, through an open window, into my chamber. This had probably been done with the view of arousing me from sleep. The falling of other walls had compressed the victim of my cruelty into the substance of the freshly-spread plaster; the lime of which, with the flames and the *ammonia* from the carcass, had then accomplished the portraiture as I saw it.

Although I thus readily accounted to my reason, if not altogether to my conscience, for the startling fact just detailed, it did not the less fail to make a deep impression upon my fancy. For months I could not rid myself of the phantasm of the cat; and, during this period, there came back into my spirit a half-sentiment that seemed, but was not, remorse. I went so far as to regret the loss of the animal, and to look about me, among the vile haunts which I now habitually frequented, for another pet of the same species, and of somewhat similar appearance, with which to supply its place.

One night as I sat, half stupefied, in a den of more than infamy, my attention was suddenly drawn to some black object, reposing upon the head of one of the immense hogsheads of gin, or of rum, which constituted the chief furniture of the apartment. I had been looking steadily at the top of this hogshead for some minutes, and what now caused me surprise was the fact that I had not sooner perceived the object thereupon. I approached it, and touched it with my hand. It was a black cat – a very large one – fully as large as Pluto, and closely resembling him in every respect but one. Pluto had not a white hair upon any portion of his body; but this cat had a large, although indefinite, splotch of white, covering nearly the whole region of the breast.

Upon my touching him, he immediately arose, purred loudly, rubbed against my hand, and appeared delighted with my notice. This, then, was the very creature of which I was in search. I at once offered to purchase it of the landlord; but this person made no claim to it – knew nothing of it – had never seen it before.

I continued my caresses, and when I prepared to go home, the animal evinced a disposition to accompany me. I permitted it to do so; occasionally stooping and patting it as I proceeded. When it reached the house it domesticated itself at once, and became immediately a great favourite with my wife.

For my own part, I soon found a dislike to it arising within me. This was just the reverse of what I had anticipated; but – I know not how or why it was – its evident fondness for myself rather disgusted and annoyed me. By slow degrees, these feelings of disgust and annoyance rose into the bitterness of hatred. I avoided the creature; a certain sense of shame, and the remembrance of my former deed of cruelty, preventing me from physically abusing it. I did not, for some weeks, strike, or otherwise violently ill-use it; but gradually – very gradually – I came to look upon it with unutterable loathing, and to flee silently from its odious presence, as from the breath of a pestilence.

What added, no doubt, to my hatred of the beast, was the discovery, on the morning after I brought it home, that, like Pluto, it also had been deprived of one of its eyes. This circumstance, however, only endeared it to my wife, who, as I have already said, possessed, in a high degree, that humanity of feeling which had once been my distinguishing trait, and the source of many of my simplest and purest pleasures.

With my aversion to this cat, however, its partiality for myself seemed to increase. It followed my footsteps with a pertinacity which it would be difficult to make the reader comprehend. Whenever I sat, it would crouch beneath my chair, or spring upon my knees, covering me with its loathsome caresses. If I arose to walk, it would get between my feet, and thus nearly throw me down, or, fastening its long and sharp claws in my dress, clamber, in this manner, to my breast. At such times, although I longed to destroy it with a blow, I was yet withheld from so doing, partly by a memory of my former crime, but chiefly – let me confess it at once – by absolute *dread* of the beast.

This dread was not exactly a dread of physical evil – and yet I should be at a loss how otherwise to define it. I am almost ashamed to own – yes, even in this felon's cell, I am almost ashamed to own – that the terror and horror with which the animal inspired me, had been heightened by one of the merest chimeras it would be possible to conceive. My wife had called my attention, more than once, to the character of the mark of white hair, of which I have spoken, and which constituted the sole visible difference between the strange beast and the one I had destroyed. The reader will remember that this mark, although large, had been originally very indefinite; but, by slow degrees – degrees nearly imperceptible, and which for a long time my reason struggled to reject as fanciful – it had, at length, assumed a rigorous distinctness of outline. It was now the representation of an object that I shudder to name – and for this, above all, I loathed, and dreaded, and would have rid myself of the monster *had I dared* – it was now, I say, the image of a hideous – of a ghastly thing – of the GALLOWS! – oh, mournful and terrible engine of horror and of crime – of agony and of death!

And now was I indeed wretched beyond the wretchedness of mere humanity. And a *brute beast* – whose fellow I had contemptuously destroyed – *a brute beast* to work out for *me* – for me, a man, fashioned in the image of the High God – so much of insufferable woe! Alas! neither by day nor by night knew I the blessing of rest any more! During the former the creature left me no moment alone; and, in the latter, I started, hourly, from dreams of unutterable fear, to find the hot breath of *the thing* upon my face, and its vast weight – an incarnate nightmare that I had no power to shake off – incumbent eternally upon my *heart*!

Beneath the pressure of torments such as these, the feeble remnant of the good within me succumbed. Evil thoughts became my sole intimates – the darkest and most evil of thoughts. The moodiness of my usual temper increased to hatred of all things and of all mankind; while, from the sudden, frequent, and ungovernable outbursts of a fury to which I now blindly abandoned myself, my uncomplaining wife, alas! was the most usual and the most patient of sufferers.

One day she accompanied me, upon some household errand, into the cellar of the old building which our poverty compelled us to inhabit. The cat followed me down the steep stairs, and, nearly throwing me headlong, exasperated me to madness. Uplifting an axe, and forgetting, in my wrath, the childish dread which had hitherto stayed my hand, I aimed a blow at the animal which, of course, would have proved instantly fatal had it descended as I wished. But this blow was arrested by the hand of my wife. Goaded, by the interference, into a rage more than demoniacal, I withdrew my arm from her grasp, and buried the axe in her brain. She fell dead upon the spot, without a groan.

This hideous murder accomplished, I set myself forthwith, and with entire deliberation, to the task of concealing the body. I knew that I could not remove it from the house, either by day or by night, without the risk of being observed by the neighbours. Many projects entered my mind. At one period I thought of cutting the corpse into minute fragments, and destroying them by fire. At another, I resolved to dig a grave for it in the floor of the cellar. Again, I deliberated about casting it into the well in the yard – about packing it in a box, as if merchandise, with the usual arrangements, and so getting a porter to take it from the house. Finally I hit upon what I considered a far better expedient than either of these. I determined to wall it up in the cellar – as the monks of the Middle Ages are recorded to have walled up their victims.

For a purpose such as this the cellar was well adapted. Its walls were loosely constructed, and had lately been plastered throughout with a rough plaster, which the dampness of the atmosphere had prevented from hardening. Moreover, in one of the walls was a projection, caused by a false chimney, or fireplace, that had been filled up, and made to resemble the rest of the cellar. I made no doubt that I could readily displace the bricks at this point, insert the corpse, and wall the whole up as before, so that no eye could detect anything suspicious.

And in this calculation I was not deceived. By means of a crowbar I easily dislodged the bricks, and, having carefully deposited the body against the inner wall, I propped it in that position, while, with little trouble, I relaid the whole structure as it originally stood. Having procured mortar, sand, and hair, with every possible precaution, I prepared a plaster which could not be distinguished from the old, and with this I very carefully went over the new brickwork. When I had finished, I felt satisfied that all was right. The wall did not present the slightest appearance of having been disturbed. The rubbish on the floor was picked up with the minutest care. I looked around triumphantly, and said to myself, 'Here at least, then, my labour has not been in vain.'

My next step was to look for the beast which had been the cause of so much wretchedness; for I had, at length, firmly resolved to put it to death. Had I been able to meet with it, at the moment, there could have been no doubt of its fate; but it appeared that the crafty animal had been alarmed at the violence of my previous anger, and forebore to present itself in my present mood. It is impossible to describe, or to imagine, the deep, the blissful sense of relief which the absence of the detested creature occasioned in my bosom. It did not make its appearance during the night – and thus for one night at least, since its introduction into the house, I soundly and tranquilly slept; aye, *slept* even with the burden of murder upon my soul!

The second and the third day passed, and still my tormentor came not. Once again I breathed as a free man. The monster, in terror, had fled the premises for ever! I should behold it no more! My happiness was supreme! The guilt of my dark deed disturbed me but little. Some few inquiries had been made, but these had been readily answered. Even a search had been instituted – but of course nothing was to be discovered. I looked upon my future felicity as secured.

Upon the fourth day of the assassination, a party of the police came, very unexpectedly, into the house, and proceeded again to make rigorous investigation of the premises. Secure, however, in the inscrutability of my place of concealment, I felt no embarrassment whatever. The officers bade me accompany them in their search. They left no nook or corner unexplored. At length, for the third or fourth time, they descended into the cellar. I quivered not in a muscle. My heart beat calmly as that of one who slumbers in innocence. I walked the cellar from end to end. I folded my arms upon my bosom, and roamed easily to and fro. The police were thoroughly satisfied, and prepared to depart. The glee at my heart was too strong to be restrained. I burned to say if but one word, by way of triumph, and to render doubly sure their assurance of my guiltlessness.

'Gentlemen,' I said at last, as the party ascended the steps, 'I delight to have allayed your suspicions. I wish you all health, and a little more courtesy. By-the-bye, gentlemen, this – this is a very well-constructed house.' (In the rabid desire to say something easily, I scarcely knew what I uttered at all.) 'I may say an *excellently* well-constructed house. These walls – are you going, gentlemen? – these walls are solidly put together;' and here, through the mere frenzy of bravado, I rapped heavily, with a cane which I held in my hand, upon that very portion of the brickwork behind which stood the corpse of the wife of my bosom.

But may God shield and deliver me from the fangs of the Arch-Fiend! No sooner had the reverberation of my blows sunk into silence, than I was answered by a voice from within the tomb! – by a cry, at first muffled and broken, like the sobbing of a child, and then quickly swelling into one long, loud, and continuous scream, utterly anomalous and inhuman – a howl – a wailing shriek, half of horror and half of triumph, such as might have arisen only out of hell, conjointly from the throats of the damned in their agony and of the demons that exult in the damnation.

Of my own thoughts it is folly to speak. Swooning, I staggered to the opposite wall. For one instant the party upon the stairs remained motionless, through extremity of terror and of awe. In the next, a dozen stout arms were toiling at the wall. It fell bodily. The corpse, already greatly decayed and clotted with gore, stood erect before the eyes of the spectators. Upon its head, with red extended mouth and solitary eye of fire, sat the hideous beast whose craft had seduced me into murder, and whose informing voice had consigned me to the hangman. I had walled the monster up within the tomb!

The Masque of the Red Death

THE 'RED DEATH' had long devastated the country. No pestilence had ever been so fatal, or so hideous. Blood was its Avatar[1] and its seal – the redness and the horror of blood. There were sharp pains, and sudden dizziness, and then profuse bleeding at the pores, with dissolution. The scarlet stains upon the body and especially upon the face of the victim, were the pest ban which shut him out from the aid and from the sympathy of his fellow-men. And the whole seizure, progress, and termination of the disease, were the incidents of half-an-hour.

But the Prince Prospero[2] was happy and dauntless and sagacious. When his dominions were half depopulated, he summoned to his presence a thousand hale and light-hearted friends from among the knights and dames of his court, and with these retired to the deep seclusion of one of his castellated abbeys. This was an extensive and magnificent structure, the creation of the prince's own eccentric yet august taste. A strong and lofty wall girdled it in. This wall had gates of iron. The courtiers, having entered, brought furnaces and massy hammers and welded the bolts. They resolved to leave means neither of ingress or egress to the sudden impulses of despair or of frenzy from within. The abbey was amply provisioned. With such precautions the courtiers might bid defiance to contagion. The external world could take care of itself. In the meantime it was folly to grieve, or to think. The prince had provided all the appliances of pleasure. There were buffoons, there were improvisatori,[3] there were ballet-dancers, there were musicians, there was beauty, there was wine. All these and security were within. Without was the 'Red Death'.

It was toward the close of the fifth or sixth month of his seclusion, and while the pestilence raged most furiously abroad, that the Prince Prospero entertained his thousand friends at a masked ball of the most unusual magnificence.

It was a voluptuous scene, that masquerade. But first let me tell of the rooms in which it was held. There were seven – an imperial suite. In many palaces, however, such suites form a long and straight vista, while the folding doors slide back nearly to the walls on either hand, so that the view of the whole extent is scarcely impeded. Here the case was very different, as might have been expected from the duke's love of the bizarre. The apartments were so irregularly disposed that the vision embraced but little more than one at a time. There was a sharp turn at every twenty or thirty yards, and at each turn a novel effect. To the right and left, in the middle of each wall, a tall and narrow Gothic window looked out upon a closed corridor which pursued the windings of the suite. These windows were of stained glass, whose colour varied in accordance with the prevailing hue of the decorations of the chamber into which it opened. That at the eastern extremity was hung, for example, in blue – and vividly blue were its windows. The second chamber was purple in its ornaments and tapestries, and here the panes were purple. The third was green throughout, and so were the casements. The fourth was furnished and lighted with orange – the fifth with white – the sixth with violet. The seventh apartment was closely shrouded in black velvet tapestries that hung all over the ceiling and down the walls, falling in heavy folds upon a carpet of the same material and hue. But in this chamber only the colour of the windows failed to correspond with the decorations. The panes here were scarlet – a deep blood colour. Now in no one of the seven apartments was there any lamp or candelabrum, amid the profusion of golden ornaments that lay scattered to and fro, or depended from the roof. There was no light of any kind emanating from lamp or candle within the suite of chambers. But in the corridors that followed the suite, there stood, opposite to each window, a heavy tripod, bearing a brazier of fire, that projected its rays through the tinted glass, and so glaringly illumined the room. And thus were produced a multitude of gaudy and fantastic appearances. But in the western or black chamber the effect of the firelight that streamed upon the dark hangings through the blood-tinted panes, was ghastly in the extreme, and produced so wild a look upon the countenances of those who entered, that there were few of the company bold enough to set foot within its precincts at all.

It was in this apartment, also, that there stood against the western wall a gigantic clock of ebony. Its pendulum swung to and fro with a dull, heavy, monotonous clang; and when the minute-hand made the circuit of the face, and the hour was to be stricken, there came from the brazen lungs of the clock a sound which was clear and loud and deep and exceedingly musical; but of so peculiar a note and emphasis that, at each lapse of an hour, the musicians of the orchestra were constrained to pause, momentarily, in their performance, to hearken to the sound; and thus the waltzers perforce ceased their evolutions; and there was a brief disconcert of the whole gay company; and, while the chimes of the clock yet rang, it was observed that the giddiest grew pale, and the more aged and sedate passed their hands over their brows as if in confused reverie or meditation. But when the echoes had fully ceased, a light laughter at once pervaded the assembly; the musicians looked at each other and smiled as if at their own nervousness and folly, and made whispering vows, each to the other, that the next chiming of the clock should produce in them no similar emotion; and then, after the lapse of sixty minutes (which embrace three thousand and six hundred seconds of the Time that flies), there came yet another chiming of the clock, and then were the same disconcert and tremulousness and meditation as before.

But, in spite of these things, it was a gay and magnificent revel. The tastes of the duke were peculiar. He had a fine eye for colours and effects. He disregarded the *decora*[4] of mere fashion. His plans were bold and fiery, and his conceptions glowed with barbaric lustre. There are some who would have thought him mad. His followers felt that he was not. It was necessary to hear and see and touch him to be *sure* that he was not.

He had directed, in great part, the movable embellishments of the seven chambers, upon occasion of this great *fête*; and it was his own guiding taste which had given character to the masqueraders. Be sure they were grotesque. There were much glare and glitter and piquancy and phantasm – much of what has been since seen in 'Hernani'.[5] There were arabesque figures with unsuited limbs and appointments. There were delirious fancies as the madman fashions.

There were much of the beautiful, much of the wanton, much of the bizarre, something of the terrible, and not a little of that which might have excited disgust. To and fro in the seven chambers there stalked, in fact, a multitude of dreams. And these – the dreams – writhed in and about, taking hue from the rooms, and causing the wild music of the orchestra to seem as the echo of their steps. And, anon, there strikes the ebony clock which stands in the hall of the velvet. And then, for a moment, all is still, and all is silent save the voice of the clock. The dreams are stiff-frozen as they stand. But the echoes of the chime die away – they have endured but an instant – and a light, half-subdued laughter floats after them as they depart. And now again the music swells, and the dreams live, and writhe to and fro more merrily than ever, taking hue from the many tinted windows through which stream the rays from the tripods. But to the chamber which lies most westwardly of the seven, there are now none of the maskers who venture; for the night is waning away; and there flows a ruddier light through the blood-coloured panes; and the blackness of the sable drapery appals; and to him whose foot falls upon the sable carpet, there comes from the near clock of ebony a muffled peal more solemnly emphatic than any which reaches *their* ears who indulge in the more remote gaieties of the other apartments.

But these other apartments were densely crowded, and in them beat feverishly the heart of life. And the revel went whirlingly on, until at length there commenced the sounding of midnight upon the clock. And then the music ceased, as I have told; and the evolutions of the waltzers were quieted; and there was an uneasy cessation of all things as before. But now there were twelve strokes to be sounded by the bell of the clock; and thus it happened, perhaps, that more of thought crept, with more of time, into the meditations of the thoughtful among those who revelled. And thus, too, it happened, perhaps, that before the last echoes of the last chime had utterly sunk into silence, there were many individuals in the crowd who had found leisure to become aware of the presence of a masked figure which had arrested the attention of no single individual before. And the rumour of this new presence having spread itself whisperingly around, there arose at length from the whole company a buzz, or murmur, expressive of disapprobation and surprise – then, finally, of terror, of horror, and of disgust.

In an assembly of phantasms, such as I have painted, it may well be supposed that no ordinary appearance could have excited such sensation. In truth the masquerade license of the night was nearly unlimited; but the figure in question had out-Heroded Herod, and gone beyond the bounds of even the prince's indefinite decorum. There are chords in the hearts of the most reckless which cannot be touched without emotion. Even with the utterly lost, to whom life and death are equally jests, there are matters of which no jests can be made. The whole company, indeed, seemed now deeply to feel that in the costume and bearing of the stranger neither wit nor propriety existed. The figure was tall and gaunt, and shrouded from head to foot in the habiliments of the grave. The mask which concealed the visage was made so nearly to resemble the countenance of a stiffened corpse that the closest scrutiny must have had difficulty in detecting the cheat. And yet all this might have been endured, if not approved, by the mad revellers around. But the mummer had gone so far as to assume the type of the Red Death. His vesture was dabbled in *blood* – and his broad brow, with all the features of the face, was besprinkled with the scarlet horror.

When the eyes of Prince Prospero fell upon this spectral image (which with a slow and solemn movement, as if more fully to sustain its *rôle*, stalked to and fro among the waltzers), he was seen to be convulsed, in the first moment, with a strong shudder either of terror or distaste; but, in the next, his brow reddened with rage.

'Who dares?' he demanded hoarsely of the courtiers who stood near him – 'who dares insult us with this blasphemous mockery? Seize him and unmask him – that we may know whom we have to hang at sunrise from the battlements!'

It was in the eastern or blue chamber in which stood the Prince Prospero as he uttered these words. They rang throughout the seven rooms loudly and clearly – for the prince was a bold and robust man, and the music had become hushed at the waving of his hand.

It was in the blue room where stood the prince with a group of pale courtiers by his side. At first, as he spoke, there was a slight rushing movement of this group in the direction of the intruder, who, at the moment, was also near at hand, and now, with deliberate and stately step, made closer approach to the speaker. But from a certain nameless awe with which the mad assumptions of the mummer had inspired the whole party, there were found none who put forth hand to seize him; so that, unimpeded, he passed within a yard of the prince's person; and, while the vast assembly, as if with one impulse, shrank from the centres of the rooms to the walls, he made his way uninterruptedly, but with the same solemn and measured step which had distinguished him from the first, through the blue chamber to the purple – through the purple to the green – through the green to the orange – through this again to the white – and even thence to the violet, ere a decided movement had been made to arrest him. It was then, however, that the Prince Prospero, maddened with rage and the shame of his own momentary cowardice, rushed hurriedly through the six chambers, while none followed him on account of a deadly terror that had seized upon all. He bore aloft a drawn dagger, and had approached, in rapid impetuosity, to within three or four feet of the retreating figure, when the latter, having attained the extremity of the velvet apartment, turned suddenly and confronted his pursuer. There was a sharp cry – and the dagger dropped gleaming upon the sable carpet, upon which, instantly afterwards, fell prostrate in death the Prince Prospero. Then, summoning the wild courage of despair, a throng of the revellers at once threw themselves into the black apartment, and, seizing the mummer, whose tall figure stood erect and motionless within the shadow of the ebony clock, gasped in unutterable horror at finding the grave cerements and corpse-like mask which they handled with so violent a rudeness, untenanted by any tangible form.

And now was acknowledged the presence of the Red Death. He had come like a thief in the night. And one by one dropped the revellers in the blood-bedewed halls of their revel, and died each in the despairing posture of his fall. And the life of the ebony clock went out with that of the last of the gay. And the flames of the tripods expired. And Darkness and Decay and the Red Death held illimitable dominion over all.

The Cask of Amontillado

THE THOUSAND INJURIES of Fortunato I had borne as I best could; but when he ventured upon insult, I vowed revenge. You, who so well know the nature of my soul, will not suppose, however, that I gave utterance to a threat. *At length* I would be avenged; this was a point definitely settled – but the very definitiveness with which it was resolved, precluded the idea of risk. I must not only punish, but punish with impunity. A wrong is unredressed when retribution overtakes its redresser. It is equally unredressed when the avenger fails to make himself felt as such to him who has done the wrong.

It must be understood, that neither by word nor deed had I given Fortunato cause to doubt my goodwill. I continued, as was my wont, to smile in his face, and he did not perceive that my smile *now* was at the thought of his immolation.

He had a weak point – this Fortunato – although in other regards he was a man to be respected and even feared. He prided himself on his connoisseurship in wine. Few Italians have the true virtuoso spirit. For the most part their enthusiasm is adapted to suit the time and opportunity – to practise imposture upon the British and Austrian millionaires. In painting and gemmary[1] Fortunato, like his countrymen, was a quack – but in the matter of old wines he was sincere. In this respect I did not differ from him materially: I was skilful in the Italian vintages myself, and bought largely whenever I could.

It was about dusk, one evening during the supreme madness of the Carnival season, that I encountered my friend. He accosted me with excessive warmth, for he had been drinking much. The man wore motley. He had on a tight-fitting parti-striped dress, and his head was surmounted by the conical cap and bells. I was so pleased to see him, that I thought I should never have done wringing his hand.

I said to him, 'My dear Fortunato, you are luckily met. How remarkably well you are looking today! But I have received a pipe of what passes for Amontillado,[2] and I have my doubts.'

'How?' said he; 'Amontillado? A pipe? Impossible! And in the middle of the Carnival!'

'I have my doubts,' I replied; 'and I was silly enough to pay the full Amontillado price without consulting you in the matter. You were not to be found, and I was fearful of losing a bargain.'

'Amontillado!'

'I have my doubts.'

'Amontillado!'

'And I must satisfy them.'

'Amontillado!'

'As you are engaged, I am on my way to Luchesi. If any one has a critical turn, it is he. He will tell me – '

'Luchesi cannot tell Amontillado from Sherry.'

'And yet some fools will have it that his taste is a match for your own.'

'Come, let us go.'

'Whither?'

'To your vaults.'

'My friend, no; I will not impose upon your good-nature. I perceive you have an engagement. Luchesi – '

'I have no engagement; come.'

'My friend, no. It is not the engagement, but the severe cold with which I perceive you are afflicted. The vaults are insufferably damp. They are encrusted with nitre.'

'Let us go nevertheless. The cold is merely nothing. Amontillado! You have been imposed upon. And as for Luchesi he cannot distinguish Sherry from Amontillado.'

Thus speaking, Fortunato possessed himself of my arm. Putting on a mask of black silk, and drawing a *roquelaire*[3] closely about my person, I suffered him to hurry me to my palazzo.

There were no attendants at home; they had absconded to make merry in honour of the time. I had told them that I should not return until the morning, and had given them explicit orders not to stir from the house. These orders were sufficient, I well knew, to ensure their immediate disappearance, one and all, as soon as my back was turned.

I took from their sconces two flambeaux,[4] and giving one to Fortunato, bowed him through several suites of rooms to the archway that led into the vaults. I passed down a long and winding staircase, requesting him to be cautious as he followed. We came at length to the foot of the descent, and stood together on the damp ground of the catacombs of the Montresors.

The gait of my friend was unsteady, and the bells upon his cap jingled as he strode.

'The pipe,' said he.

'It is farther on,' said I; 'but observe the white webwork which gleams from these cavern walls.'

He turned towards me, and looked into my eyes with two filmy orbs that distilled the rheum of intoxication.

'Nitre?' he asked, at length.

'Nitre,' I replied. 'How long have you had that cough?'

'Ugh! ugh! ugh! – ugh! ugh! ugh! – ugh! ugh! ugh! – ugh! ugh! ugh! – ugh! ugh! ugh!'

My poor friend found it impossible to reply for many minutes.

'It is nothing,' he said, at last.

'Come,' I said, with decision, 'we will go back; your health is precious. You are rich, respected, admired, beloved; you are happy, as once I was. You are a man to be missed. For me it is no matter. We will go back; you will be ill, and I cannot be responsible. Besides, there is Luchesi – '

'Enough,' he said, 'the cough is a mere nothing; it will not kill me. I shall not die of a cough.'

'True – true,' I replied; 'and, indeed, I had no intention of alarming you unnecessarily – but you should use all proper caution. A draught of this Medoc[5] will defend us from the damps.'

Here I knocked off the neck of a bottle which I drew from a long row of its fellows that lay upon the mould.

'Drink,' I said, presenting him the wine.

He raised it to his lips with a leer. He paused and nodded to me familiarly, while his bells jingled.

'I drink,' he said, 'to the buried that repose around us.'

'And I to your long life.'

He again took my arm, and we proceeded.

'These vaults,' he said, 'are extensive.'

'The Montresors,' I replied, 'were a great and numerous family.'

'I forget your arms.'

'A huge human foot d'or, in a field azure; the foot crushes a serpent rampant whose fangs are embedded in the heel.'

'And the motto?'

'*Nemo me impune lacessit.*'[6]

'Good!' he said.

The wine sparkled in his eyes and the bells jingled. My own fancy grew warm with the Medoc. We had passed through walls of piled bones, with casks and puncheons[7] intermingling, into the inmost recesses of the catacombs. I paused again, and this time I made bold to seize Fortunato by an arm above the elbow.

'The nitre!' I said; 'see, it increases. It hangs like moss upon the vaults. We are below the river's bed. The drops of moisture trickle among the bones. Come, we will go back ere it is too late. Your cough – '

'It is nothing,' he said; 'let us go on. But first, another draught of the Medoc.'

I broke and reached him a flagon of De Grâve.[8] He emptied it at a breath. His eyes flashed with a fierce light. He laughed and threw the bottle upwards with a gesticulation I did not understand.

I looked at him in surprise. He repeated the movement – a grotesque one.

'You do not comprehend?' he said.

'Not I,' I replied.

'Then you are not of the brotherhood.'

'How?'

'You are not of the masons.'

'Yes, yes,' I said; 'yes, yes.'

'You? Impossible! A mason?'

'A mason,' I replied.

'A sign,' he said.

'It is this,' I answered, producing a trowel from beneath the folds of my *roquelaire*.

'You jest,' he exclaimed, recoiling a few paces. 'But let us proceed to the Amontillado.'

'Be it so,' I said, replacing the tool beneath the cloak, and again offering him my arm. He leaned upon it heavily. We continued our route in search of the Amontillado. We passed through a range of low arches, descended, passed on, and descending again, arrived at a deep crypt, in which the foulness of the air caused our flambeaux rather to glow than flame.

At the most remote end of the crypt there appeared another less spacious. Its walls had been lined with human remains, piled to the vault overhead, in the fashion of the great catacombs of Paris. Three sides of this interior crypt were still ornamented in this manner. From the fourth the bones had been thrown down, and lay promiscuously upon the earth, forming at one point a mound of some size. Within the wall thus exposed by the displacing of the bones, we perceived a still interior recess, in depth about four feet, in width three, in height six or seven. It seemed to have been constructed for no especial use within itself, but formed merely the interval between two of the colossal supports of the roof of the catacombs, and was backed by one of their circumscribing walls of solid granite.

It was in vain that Fortunato, uplifting his dull torch, endeavoured to pry into the depth of the recess. Its termination the feeble light did not enable us to see.

'Proceed,' I said; 'herein is the Amontillado. As for Luchesi – '

'He is an ignoramus,' interrupted my friend, as he stepped unsteadily forward, while I followed immediately at his heels. In an instant he had reached the extremity of the niche, and finding his progress arrested by the rock, stood stupidly bewildered. A moment more and I had fettered him to the granite. In its surface were two iron staples, distant from each other about two feet, horizontally. From one of these depended a short chain, from the other a padlock. Throwing the links about his waist, it was but the work of a few seconds to secure it. He was too much astounded to resist. Withdrawing the key, I stepped back from the recess.

'Pass your hand,' I said, 'over the wall; you cannot help feeling the nitre. Indeed it is *very* damp. Once more let me *implore you* to return. No? Then I must positively leave you. But I must first render you all the little attentions in my power.'

'The Amontillado!' ejaculated my friend, not yet recovered from his astonishment.

'True,' I replied, 'the Amontillado.'

As I said these words I busied myself among the pile of bones of which I have before spoken. Throwing them aside, I soon uncovered a quantity of building stone and mortar. With these materials, and with the aid of my trowel, I began vigorously to wall up the entrance of the niche.

I had scarcely laid the first tier of the masonry when I discovered that the intoxication of Fortunato had in a great measure worn off. The earliest indication I had of this was a low moaning cry from the depth of the recess. It was *not* the cry of a drunken man. There was then a long and obstinate silence. I laid the second tier, and the third, and the fourth; and then I heard the furious vibrations of the chain. The noise lasted for several minutes, during which, that I might hearken to it with the more satisfaction, I ceased my labours and sat down upon the bones. When at last the clanking subsided, I resumed the trowel, and finished without interruption the fifth, the sixth, and the seventh tier. The wall was now nearly upon a level with my breast. I again paused, and holding the flambeaux over the mason-work, threw a few feeble rays upon the figure within.

A succession of loud and shrill screams, bursting suddenly from the throat of the chained form, seemed to thrust me violently back. For a brief moment I hesitated – I trembled. Unsheathing my rapier, I began to grope with it about the recess; but the thought of an instant reassured me. I placed my hand upon the solid fabric of the catacombs, and felt satisfied. I reapproached the wall. I replied to the yells of him who clamoured. I re-echoed – I aided – I surpassed them in volume and in strength. I did this, and the clamourer grew still.

It was now midnight, and my task was drawing to a close. I had completed the eighth, the ninth, and the tenth tier. I had finished a portion of the last and the eleventh; there remained but a single stone to be fitted and plastered in. I struggled with its weight; I placed it partially in its destined position. But now there came from out the niche a low laugh that erected the hairs upon my head. It was succeeded by a sad voice, which I had difficulty in recognising as that of the noble Fortunato. The voice said –

'Ha! ha! ha! – he! he! very good joke indeed – an excellent jest. We will have many a rich laugh about it at the palazzo – he! he! he! – over our wine – he! he! he!'

'The Amontillado!' I said.

'He! he! he! – he! he! he! – yes, the Amontillado. But is it not getting late? Will not they be awaiting us at the palazzo, the Lady Fortunato and the rest? Let us be gone.'

'Yes,' I said, 'let us be gone.'

'*For the love of God, Montresor!*'

'Yes,' I said, 'for the love of God!'

But to these words I hearkened in vain for a reply. I grew impatient. I called aloud –

'Fortunato!'

No answer. I called again –

'Fortunato!'

No answer still. I thrust a torch through the remaining aperture and let it fall within. There came forth in return only a jingling of the bells. My heart grew sick – on account of the dampness of the catacombs. I hastened to make an end of my labour. I forced the last stone into its position; I plastered it up. Against the new masonry I re-erected the old rampart of bones. For the half of a century no mortal has disturbed them. *In pace requiescat!*[9]

The Oval Portrait

THE CHÂTEAU into which my valet had ventured to make forcible entrance, rather than permit me, in my desperately wounded condition, to pass a night in the open air, was one of those piles of commingled gloom and grandeur which have so long frowned among the Appenines, not less in fact than in the fancy of Mrs Radcliffe.[1] To all appearance it had been temporarily and very lately abandoned. We established ourselves in one of the smallest and least sumptuously furnished apartments. It lay in a remote turret of the building. Its decorations were rich, yet tattered and antique. Its walls were hung with tapestry and bedecked with manifold and multiform armorial trophies, together with an unusually great number of very spirited modern paintings in frames of rich golden arabesque. In these paintings, which depended from the walls not only in their main surfaces, but in very many nooks which the bizarre architecture of the château rendered necessary – in these paintings my incipient delirium, perhaps, had caused me to take deep interest; so that I bade Pedro to close the heavy shutters of the room – since it was already night – to light the tongues of a tall candelabrum which stood by the head of my bed – and to throw open far and wide the fringed curtains of black velvet which enveloped the bed itself. I wished all this done that I might resign myself, if not to sleep, at least alternately to the contemplation of these pictures, and the perusal of a small volume which had been found upon the pillow, and which purported to criticise and describe them.

Long, long I read – and devoutly, devotedly I gazed. Rapidly and gloriously the hours flew by, and the deep midnight came. The position of the candelabrum displeased me, and outreaching my hand with difficulty, rather than disturb my slumbering valet, I placed it so as to throw its rays more fully upon the book.

But the action produced an effect altogether unanticipated. The rays of the numerous candles (for there were many) now fell within a niche of the room which had hitherto been thrown into deep shade by one of the bedposts. I thus saw in vivid light a picture all unnoticed before. It was the portrait of a young girl just ripening into womanhood. I glanced at the painting hurriedly, and then closed my eyes. Why I did this was not at first apparent even to my own perception. But while my lids remained thus shut, I ran over in mind my reason for so shutting them. It was an impulsive movement to gain time for thought – to make sure that my vision had not deceived me – to calm and subdue my fancy for a more sober and more certain gaze. In a very few moments I again looked fixedly at the painting.

That I now saw aright I could not and would not doubt; for the first flashing of the candles upon that canvas had seemed to dissipate the dreamy stupor which was stealing over my senses, and to startle me at once into waking life.

The portrait, I have already said, was that of a young girl. It was a mere head and shoulders, done in what is technically termed a *vignette*[2] manner – much in the style of the favourite heads of Sully.[3] The arms, the bosom, and even the ends of the radiant hair, melted imperceptibly into the vague yet deep shadow which formed the background of the whole. The frame was oval, richly gilded and filigreed in Moresque.[4] As a thing of art nothing could be more admirable than the painting itself. But it could have been neither the execution of the work, nor the immortal beauty of the countenance, which had so suddenly and so vehemently moved me. Least of all could it have been that my fancy, shaken from its half slumber, had mistaken the head for that of a living person. I saw at once that the peculiarities of the design, of the vignetting, and of the frame, must have instantly dispelled such idea – must have prevented even its momentary entertainment. Thinking earnestly upon these points, I remained for an hour, perhaps, half sitting, half reclining, with my vision riveted upon the portrait. At length, satisfied with the true secret of its effect, I fell back within the bed. I had found the spell of the picture in an absolute *life-likeness* of expression, which, at first startling, finally confounded, subdued, and appalled me. With deep and reverent awe I replaced the candelabrum in its former position. The cause of my deep agitation being thus shut from view, I sought eagerly the volume which discussed the paintings and their histories. Turning to the number which designated the oval portrait, I there read the vague and quaint words which follow:

'She was a maiden of rarest beauty, and not more lovely than full of glee. And evil was the hour when she saw, and loved, and wedded the painter. He, passionate, studious, austere, and having already a bride in his Art. She, a maiden of rarest beauty, and not more lovely than full of glee – all light and smiles, and frolicsome as the young fawn; loving and cherishing all things; hating only the Art which was her rival; dreading only the palette and brushes and other untoward instruments which deprived her of the countenance of her lover. It was thus a terrible thing for this lady to hear the painter speak of his desire to portray even his young bride. But she was humble and obedient, and sat meekly for many weeks in the dark high turret-chamber where the light dripped upon the pale canvas only from overhead. But he, the painter, took glory in his work, which went on from hour to hour, and from day to day. And he was a passionate, and wild, and moody man, who became lost in reveries; so that he *would* not see that the light which fell so ghastlily in that lone turret withered the health and the spirits of his bride, who pined visibly to all but him. Yet she smiled on and still on, uncomplainingly, because she saw that the painter (who had high renown), took a fervid and burning pleasure in his task, and wrought day and night to depict her who so loved him, yet who grew daily more dispirited and weak. And in sooth some who beheld the portrait spoke of its resemblance in low words, as of a mighty marvel, and a proof not less of the power of the painter than of his deep love for her whom he depicted so surpassingly well. But at length, as the labour drew nearer to its conclusion, there were admitted none into the turret; for the painter had grown wild with the ardour of his work, and turned his eyes from the canvas rarely, even to regard the countenance of his wife. And he *would* not see that the tints which he spread upon the canvas were drawn from the cheeks of her who sat beside him. And when many weeks had passed, and but little remained to do, save one brush upon the mouth and one tint upon the eye, the spirit of the lady again flickered up as the flame within the socket of the lamp. And then the brush was given, and then the tint was placed; and, for one moment, the painter stood entranced before the work which he had wrought; but in the next, while he yet gazed, he grew tremulous and very pallid, and aghast, and crying with a loud voice, "This is indeed *Life* itself!" turned suddenly to regard his beloved – *she was dead!*'

The Oblong Box

SOME YEARS AGO, I engaged passage from Charleston, S. C., to the city of New York, in the fine packet-ship *Independence*, Captain Hardy. We were to sail on the fifteenth of the month (June), weather permitting; and on the fourteenth, I went on board to arrange some matters in my state-room.

I found that we were to have a great many passengers, including a more than usual number of ladies. On the list were several of my acquaintances; and among other names, I was rejoiced to see that of Mr Cornelius Wyatt, a young artist, for whom I entertained feelings of warm friendship. He had been with me a fellow-student at C— University, where we were very much together. He had the ordinary temperament of genius, and was a compound of misanthropy, sensibility, and enthusiasm. To these qualities he united the warmest and truest heart which ever beat in a human bosom.

I observed that his name was carded upon *three* state-rooms; and, upon again referring to the list of passengers, I found that he had engaged passage for himself, wife, and two sisters – his own. The staterooms were sufficiently roomy, and each had two berths, one above the other. These berths, to be sure, were so exceedingly narrow as to be insufficient for more than one person; still, I could not comprehend why there were *three* state-rooms for these four persons. I was, just at that epoch, in one of those moody frames of mind which make a man abnormally inquisitive about trifles; and I confess, with shame, that I busied myself in a variety of ill-bred and preposterous conjectures about this matter of the supernumerary state-room. It was no business of mine, to be sure; but with none the less pertinacity did I occupy myself in attempts to resolve the enigma. At last I reached a conclusion which wrought in me great wonder why I had not arrived at it before. 'It is a servant, of course,' I said; 'what a fool I am not sooner to have thought of so obvious a solution!' And then I again repaired to the list – but here I saw distinctly that *no* servant was to come with the party; although, in fact, it had been the original design to bring one – for the words 'and servant' had been first written and then over-scored. 'Oh, extra baggage, to be sure,' I now said to myself – 'something he wishes not to be put in the hold – something to be kept under his own eye – ah, I have it – a painting or so – and this is what he has been bargaining about with Nicolino, the Italian Jew.' This idea satisfied me, and I dismissed my curiosity for the nonce.

Wyatt's two sisters I knew very well, and most amiable and clever girls they were. His wife he had newly married, and I had never yet seen her. He had often talked about her in my presence, however, and in his usual style of enthusiasm. He described her as of surpassing beauty, wit, and accomplishment. I was, therefore, quite anxious to make her acquaintance.

On the day in which I visited the ship (the fourteenth), Wyatt and party were also to visit it – so the captain informed me – and I waited on board an hour longer than I had designed, in hope of being presented to the bride; but then an apology came. 'Mrs W. was a little indisposed, and would decline coming on board until tomorrow, at the hour of sailing.'

The morrow having arrived, I was going from my hotel to the wharf, when Captain Hardy met me and said that, 'owing to circumstances' (a stupid but convenient phrase), 'he rather thought the *Independence* would not sail for a day or two, and that when all was ready, he would send up and let me know.' This I thought strange, for there was a stiff southerly breeze; but as 'the circumstances' were not forthcoming, although I pumped for them with much perseverance, I had nothing to do but to return home and digest my impatience at leisure.

I did not receive the expected message from the captain for nearly a week. It came at length, however, and I immediately went on board. The ship was crowded with passengers, and everything was in the bustle attendant upon making sail. Wyatt's party arrived in about ten minutes after myself. There were the two sisters, the bride, and the artist – the latter in one of his customary fits of moody misanthropy. I was too well used to these, however, to pay them any special attention. He did not even introduce me to his wife; this courtesy devolving, perforce, upon his sister Marian – a very sweet and intelligent girl, who, in a few hurried words, made us acquainted.

Mrs Wyatt had been closely veiled; and when she raised her veil, in acknowledging my bow, I confess that I was very profoundly astonished. I should have been much more so, however, had not long experience advised me not to trust, with too implicit a reliance, the enthusiastic description of my friend, the artist, when indulging in comments upon the loveliness of woman. When beauty was the theme, I well knew with what facility he soared into the regions of the purely ideal.

The truth is, I could not help regarding Mrs Wyatt as a decidedly plain-looking woman. If not positively ugly, she was not, I think, very far from it. She was dressed, however, in exquisite taste – and then I had no doubt that she had captivated my friend's heart by the more

enduring graces of the intellect and soul. She said very few words, and
passed at once into her state-room with Mr W.

My old inquisitiveness now returned. There was *no* servant – *that* was
a settled point. I looked, therefore, for the extra baggage. After some
delay, a cart arrived at the wharf with an oblong pine box, which was
everything that seemed to be expected. Immediately upon its arrival we
made sail, and in a short time were safely over the bar and standing out
at sea.

The box in question was, as I say, oblong. It was about six feet in
length by two and a half in breadth; I observed it attentively, and like to
be precise. Now this shape was *peculiar*; and no sooner had I seen it,
than I took credit to myself for the accuracy of my guessing. I had
reached the conclusion, it will be remembered, that the extra baggage of
my friend, the artist, would prove to be pictures, or at least a picture –
for I knew he had been for several weeks in conference with Nicolino;
and now here was a box which, from its shape, *could* possibly contain
nothing in the world but a copy of Leonardo's 'Last Supper'; and a copy
of this very 'Last Supper', done by Rubini[1] the younger, at Florence, I
had known, for some time, to be in the possession of Nicolino. This
point, therefore, I considered as sufficiently settled. I chuckled excessively when I thought of my acumen. It was the first time I had ever
known Wyatt to keep from me any of his artistical secrets; but here he
evidently intended to steal a march upon me, and smuggle a fine picture
to New York, under my very nose; expecting me to know nothing of the
matter. I resolved to quiz him well, now and hereafter.

One thing, however, annoyed me not a little. The box did *not* go into
the extra state-room. It was deposited in Wyatt's own; and there, too, it
remained, occupying very nearly the whole of the floor – no doubt to
the exceeding discomfort of the artist and his wife; this the more
especially as the tar or paint with which it was lettered in sprawling
capitals emitted a strong, disagreeable, and, to my fancy, a peculiarly
disgusting odour. On the lid were painted the words – '*Mrs Adelaide
Curtis, Albany, New York. Charge of Cornelius Wyatt, Esq. This side up. To
be handled with care.*'

Now, I was aware that Mrs Adelaide Curtis, of Albany, was the
artist's wife's mother; but then I looked upon the whole address as a
mystification, intended especially for myself. I made up my mind, of
course, that the box and contents would never get farther north than
the studio of my misanthropic friend in Chambers Street, New York.

For the first three or four days we had fine weather, although the
wind was dead ahead; having chopped round to the northward,
immediately upon our losing sight of the coast. The passengers were,

consequently, in high spirits, and disposed to be social. I must except, however, Wyatt and his sisters, who behaved stiffly, and I could not help thinking, uncourteously to the rest of the party. *Wyatt's* conduct, I did not so much regard. He was gloomy, even beyond his usual habit – in fact he was *morose* – but in him I was prepared for eccentricity. For the sisters, however, I could make no excuse. They secluded themselves in their state-rooms during the greater part of the passage, and absolutely refused, although I repeatedly urged them, to hold communication with any person on board.

Mrs Wyatt herself was far more agreeable. That is to say, she was *chatty*; and to be chatty is no slight recommendation at sea. She became *excessively* intimate with most of the ladies; and, to my profound astonishment, evinced no equivocal disposition to coquet with the men. She amused us all very much. I say '*amused*' – and scarcely know how to explain myself. The truth is, I soon found that Mrs W. was far oftener laughed *at* than *with*. The gentlemen said little about her; but the ladies, in a little while, pronounced her 'a good-hearted thing, rather indifferent-looking, totally uneducated, and decidedly vulgar.' The great wonder was how Wyatt had been entrapped into such a match. Wealth was the general solution – but this I knew to be no solution at all; for Wyatt had told me she neither brought him a dollar nor had any expectations from any source whatever. 'He had married,' he said, 'for love, and for love only; and his bride was far more than worthy of his love.' When I thought of these expressions, on the part of my friend, I confess that I felt indescribably puzzled. Could it be possible that he was taking leave of his senses? What else could I think? *He*, so refined, so intellectual, so fastidious, with so exquisite a perception of the faulty, and so keen an appreciation of the beautiful! To be sure, the lady seemed especially fond of *him* – particularly so in his absence – when she made herself ridiculous by frequent quotations of what had been said by her 'beloved husband, Mr Wyatt.' The word 'husband' seemed for ever – to use one of her own delicate expressions – for ever 'on the tip of her tongue.' In the meantime, it was observed by all on board, that he avoided *her* in the most pointed manner, and, for the most part, shut himself up alone in his state-room, where, in fact, he might have been said to live altogether, leaving his wife at full liberty to amuse herself as she thought best, in the public society of the main cabin.

My conclusion, from what I saw and heard, was, that the artist, by some unaccountable freak of fate, or perhaps in some fit of enthusiastic and fanciful passion, had been induced to unite himself with a person altogether beneath him, and that the natural result, entire and speedy disgust, had ensued. I pitied him from the bottom of my heart – but could not, for that reason, quite forgive his incommunicativeness in the matter of the 'Last Supper.' For this I resolved to have my revenge.

One day he came upon deck, and, taking his arm as had been my wont, I sauntered with him backwards and forwards. His gloom, however (which I considered quite natural under the circumstances), seemed entirely unabated. He said little, and that moodily, and with evident effort. I ventured a jest or two, and he made a sickening attempt at a smile. Poor fellow! – as I thought of *his wife*, I wondered that he could have heart to put on even the semblance of mirth. At last I ventured a home thrust. I determined to commence a series of covert insinuations, or innuendoes, about the oblong box – just to let him perceive, gradually, that I was *not* altogether the butt, or victim, of his little bit of pleasant mystification. My first observation was by way of opening a masked battery. I said something about the 'peculiar shape of *that* box'; and, as I spoke the words, I smiled knowingly, winked, and touched him gently with my forefinger in the ribs.

The manner in which Wyatt received this harmless pleasantry convinced me at once that he was mad. At first he stared at me as if he found it impossible to comprehend the witticism of my remark; but as its point seemed slowly to make its way into his brain, his eyes in the same proportion seemed protruding from their sockets. Then he grew very red – then hideously pale – then, as if highly amused with what I had insinuated, he began a loud and boisterous laugh, which, to my astonishment, he kept up with gradually increasing vigour, for ten minutes or more. In conclusion, he fell flat and heavily upon the deck. When I ran to uplift him, to all appearance he was *dead*.

I called assistance, and, with much difficulty, we brought him to himself. Upon reviving, he spoke incoherently for some time. At length we bled him and put him to bed. The next morning he was quite recovered, so far as regarded his mere bodily health. Of his mind I say nothing, of course. I avoided him during the rest of the passage, by advice of the captain, who seemed to coincide with me altogether in my views of his insanity, but cautioned me to say nothing on this head to any person on board.

Several circumstances occurred immediately after this fit of Wyatt's, which contributed to heighten the curiosity with which I was already possessed. Among other things, this: I had been nervous – drank too much strong green tea, and slept ill at night – in fact, for two nights I could not be properly said to sleep at all. Now, my state-room opened into the main cabin, or dining-room, as did those of all the single men on board. Wyatt's three rooms were in the after-cabin, which was separated from the main one by a slight sliding door, never locked even at night. As we were almost constantly on a wind, and the breeze was not a little stiff, the ship heeled to leeward very considerably; and whenever her starboard side was to leeward, the sliding door between the cabins slid open, and so remained, nobody taking the trouble to get up and shut it. But my berth was in such a position, that when my own state-room door was open, as well as the sliding door in question (and my own door was *always* open on account of the heat), I could see into the after-cabin quite distinctly, and just at that portion of it, too, where were situated the state-rooms of Mr Wyatt. Well, during two nights (*not* consecutive) while I lay awake, I clearly saw Mrs W., about eleven o'clock upon each night, steal cautiously from the state-room of Mr W., and enter the extra room, where she remained until daybreak, when she was called by her husband and went back. That they were virtually separated was clear. They had separate apartments – no doubt in contemplation of a more permanent divorce; and here after all, I thought, was the mystery of the extra state-room.

There was another circumstance, too, which interested me much. During the two wakeful nights in question, and immediately after the disappearance of Mrs Wyatt into the extra state-room, I was attracted by certain singular, cautious, subdued noises in that of her husband. After listening to them for some time, with thoughtful attention, I at length succeeded perfectly in translating their import. They were sounds occasioned by the artist in prising open the oblong box by means of a chisel and mallet – the latter being apparently muffled or deadened by some soft woollen or cotton substance in which its head was enveloped.

In this manner I fancied I could distinguish the precise moment when he fairly disengaged the lid – also, that I could determine when he removed it altogether, and when he deposited it upon the lower berth in his room; this latter point I knew, for example, by certain slight taps which the lid made in striking against the wooden edges of the berth, as he endeavoured to lay it down very gently – there being no room for it on the floor. After this there was a dead stillness, and I heard nothing more, upon either occasion, until nearly daybreak; unless, perhaps, I may mention a low sobbing or murmuring sound, so very much suppressed as to be nearly inaudible – if, indeed, the whole of this latter noise were not rather produced by my own imagination. I say it seemed to *resemble* sobbing or sighing – but, of course, it could not have been either. I rather think it was a ringing in my own ears. Mr Wyatt, no doubt, according to custom, was merely giving the rein to one of his hobbies – indulging in one of his fits of artistic enthusiasm. He had opened his oblong box in order to feast his eyes on the pictorial treasure within. There was nothing in this, however, to make him *sob*. I repeat, therefore, that it must have been simply a freak of my own fancy, distempered by good Captain Hardy's green tea. Just before dawn, on each of the two nights of which I speak, I distinctly heard Mr Wyatt replace the lid upon the oblong box, and force the nails into their old places, by means of the muffled mallet. Having done this, he issued from his state-room, fully dressed, and proceeded to call Mrs W. from hers.

We had been at sea seven days, and were now off Cape Hatteras, when there came a tremendously heavy blow from the south-west. We were, in a measure, prepared for it, however, as the weather had been holding out threats for some time. Everything was made snug, alow and aloft; and as the wind steadily freshened, we lay to, at length, under spanker[2] and foretopsail,[3] both double-reefed.[4]

In this trim we rode safely enough for forty-eight hours – the ship proving herself an excellent sea-boat, in many respects, and shipping no water of any consequence. At the end of this period, however, the gale had freshened into a hurricane, and our after-sail split into ribbons, bringing us so much in the trough of the water that we shipped several prodigious seas, one immediately after the other. By this accident we lost three men overboard with the caboose,[5] and nearly the whole of the larboard bulwarks.[6] Scarcely had we recovered our senses before the foretopsail went into shreds, when we got up a storm stay-sail,[7] and with this did pretty well for some hours, the ship heading the sea much more steadily than before.

The gale still held on, however, and we saw no signs of its abating. The rigging was found to be ill-fitted and greatly strained; and on the third day of the blow, about five in the afternoon, our mizzen-mast, in a heavy lurch to windward, went by the board. For an hour or more we tried in vain to get rid of it on account of the prodigious rolling of the ship; and, before we had succeeded, the carpenter came aft and announced four feet of water in the hold. To add to our dilemma, we found the pumps choked and nearly useless.

All was now confusion and despair – but an effort was made to lighten the ship by throwing overboard as much of her cargo as could be reached, and by cutting away the two masts that remained. This we at last accomplished – but we were still unable to do anything at the pumps; and, in the meantime, the leak gained on us fast.

At sundown, the gale had sensibly diminished in violence, and, as the sea went down with it, we still entertained faint hopes of saving ourselves in the boats. At eight P.M. the clouds broke away to windward, and we had the advantage of a full moon – a piece of good fortune which served wonderfully to cheer our drooping spirits.

After incredible labour we succeeded, at length, in getting the long-boat over the side without material accident, and into this we crowded the whole of the crew and most of the passengers. This party made off immediately, and, after undergoing much suffering, finally arrived, in safety, at Ocracoke Inlet,[8] on the third day after the wreck.

Fourteen passengers, with the captain, remained on board, resolving to trust their fortunes to the jolly-boat at the stern. We lowered it without difficulty, although it was only by a miracle that we prevented it from swamping as it touched the water. It contained, when afloat, the captain and his wife, Mr Wyatt and party, a Mexican officer, wife, four children, and myself, with a negro valet.

We had no room, of course, for anything except a few positively necessary instruments, some provisions, and the clothes upon our backs. No one had thought of even attempting to save anything more. What must have been the astonishment of all then, when, having proceeded a few fathoms from the ship, Mr Wyatt stood up in the stern-sheets, and coolly demanded of Captain Hardy that the boat should be put back for the purpose of taking in his oblong box!

'Sit down, Mr Wyatt,' replied the captain, somewhat sternly, 'you will capsize us if you do not sit quite still. Our gunwale is almost in the water now.'

'The box!' vociferated Mr Wyatt, still standing – 'the box, I say! Captain Hardy, you cannot, you *will* not refuse me. Its weight will be but a trifle – it is nothing – mere nothing. By the mother who bore you – for the love of Heaven – by your hope of salvation, I *implore* you to put back for the box!'

The captain, for a moment, seemed touched by the earnest appeal of the artist; but he regained his stern composure, and merely said –

'Mr Wyatt, you are mad. I cannot listen to you. Sit down, I say, or you will swamp the boat. Stay – hold him – seize him! – he is about to spring overboard! There – I knew it – he is over!'

As the captain said this, Mr Wyatt, in fact, sprang from the boat, and, as we were yet in the lee[9] of the wreck, succeeded, by almost superhuman exertion, in getting hold of a rope which hung from the fore-chains. In another moment he was on board, and rushing frantically down into the cabin.

In the meantime, we had been swept astern of the ship, and being quite out of her lee, were at the mercy of the tremendous sea which was still running. We made a determined effort to put back, but our little boat was like a feather in the breath of the tempest. We saw at a glance that the doom of the unfortunate artist was sealed.

As our distance from the wreck rapidly increased, the madman (for as such only could we regard him) was seen to emerge from the companion-way, up which, by dint of a strength that appeared gigantic, he dragged, bodily, the oblong box. While we gazed in the extremity of astonishment, he passed, rapidly, several turns of a three-inch rope, first around the box and then around his body. In another instant both body and box were in the sea – disappearing suddenly, at once and for ever.

We lingered awhile sadly upon our oars, with our eyes riveted upon the spot. At length we pulled away. The silence remained unbroken for an hour. Finally, I hazarded a remark.

'Did you observe, captain, how suddenly they sank? Was not that an exceedingly singular thing? I confess that I entertained some feeble hope of his final deliverance, when I saw him lash himself to the box, and commit himself to the sea.'

'They sank as a matter of course,' replied the captain, 'and that like a shot. They will soon rise again, however – *but not till the salt melts.*'

'The salt!' I ejaculated.

'Hush!' said the captain, pointing to the wife and sisters of the deceased. 'We must talk of these things at some more appropriate time.'

We suffered much, and made a narrow escape; but fortune befriended *us*, as well as our mates in the long-boat. We landed, in fine, more dead than alive, after four days of intense distress, upon the beach opposite Roanoke Island.[10] We remained here a week, were not ill-treated by the wreckers, and at length obtained a passage to New York.

About a month after the loss of the *Independence*, I happened to meet Captain Hardy in Broadway. Our conversation turned, naturally, upon the disaster, and especially upon the sad fate of poor Wyatt. I thus learned the following particulars.

The artist had engaged passage for himself, wife, two sisters, and a servant. His wife was, indeed, as she had been represented, a most lovely and most accomplished woman. On the morning of the fourteenth of June (the day in which I first visited the ship), the lady suddenly sickened and died. The young husband was frantic with grief – but circumstances imperatively forbade the deferring his voyage to New York. It was necessary to take to her mother the corpse of his adored wife, and on the other hand, the universal prejudice which would prevent his doing so openly was well known. Nine-tenths of the passengers would have abandoned the ship rather than take passage with a dead body.

In this dilemma, Captain Hardy arranged that the corpse, being first partially embalmed, and packed, with a large quantity of salt, in a box of suitable dimensions, should be conveyed on board as merchandise. Nothing was to be said of the lady's decease; and, as it was well understood that Mr Wyatt had engaged passage for his wife, it became necessary that some person should personate her during the voyage. This the deceased's lady's-maid was easily prevailed on to do. The extra state-room, originally engaged for this girl, during her mistress' life, was now merely retained. In this state-room the pseudo wife slept, of course, every night. In the day-time she performed, to the best of her ability, the part of her mistress – whose person, it had been carefully ascertained, was unknown to any of the passengers on board.

My own mistakes arose, naturally enough, through too careless, too inquisitive, and too impulsive a temperament. But of late, it is a rare thing that I sleep soundly at night. There is a countenance which haunts me, turn as I will. There is an hysterical laugh which will for ever ring within my ears.

The Tell-Tale Heart

TRUE! – nervous – very, very dreadfully nervous I had been and am; but why will you say that I am mad? The disease had sharpened my senses – not destroyed – not dulled them. Above all was the sense of hearing acute. I heard all things in the heaven and in the earth. I heard many things in hell. How, then, am I mad? Hearken! and observe how healthily – how calmly I can tell you the whole story.

It is impossible to say how first the idea entered my brain; but once conceived, it haunted me day and night. Object there was none. Passion there was none. I loved the old man. He had never wronged me. He had never given me insult. For his gold I had no desire. I think it was his eye! yes, it was this! One of his eyes resembled that of a vulture[1] – a pale blue eye, with a film over it. Whenever it fell upon me, my blood ran cold; and so by degrees – very gradually – I made up my mind to take the life of the old man, and thus rid myself of the eye for ever.

Now this is the point. You fancy me mad. Madmen know nothing. But you should have seen me. You should have seen how wisely I proceeded – with what caution – with what foresight – with what dissimulation I went to work! I was never kinder to the old man than during the whole week before I killed him. And every night, about midnight, I turned the latch of his door and opened it – oh, so gently! And then, when I had made an opening sufficient for my head, I put in a dark lantern, all closed, closed, so that no light shone out, and then I thrust in my head. Oh, you would have laughed to see how cunningly I thrust it in! I moved it slowly – very, very slowly, so that I might not disturb the old man's sleep. It took me an hour to place my whole head within the opening so far that I could see him as he lay upon his bed. Ha! – would a madman have been so wise as this? And then, when my head was well in the room, I undid the lantern, cautiously – oh, so cautiously – cautiously (for the hinges creaked) I undid it just so much that a single thin ray fell upon the vulture eye. And this I did for seven long nights – every night just at midnight – but I found the eye always closed; and so it was impossible to do the work; for it was not the old man who vexed me, but his Evil Eye. And every morning, when the day broke, I went boldly into the chamber, and spoke courageously to him, calling him by name in a hearty tone, and inquiring how he had passed the night. So you see he would have been a very profound old man, indeed, to suspect that every night, just at twelve, I looked in upon him while he slept.

Upon the eighth night I was more than usually cautious in opening the door. A watch's minute hand moves more quickly than did mine. Never before that night had I *felt* the extent of my own powers – of my sagacity. I could scarcely contain my feelings of triumph. To think that there I was, opening the door, little by little, and he not even to dream of my secret deeds or thoughts. I fairly chuckled at the idea; and perhaps he heard me – for he moved on the bed suddenly, as if startled. Now you may think that I drew back – but no. His room was as black as pitch with the thick darkness (for the shutters were close-fastened, through fear of robbers), and so I knew that he could not see the opening of the door, and I kept pushing it on steadily, steadily.

I had my head in, and was about to open the lantern, when my thumb slipped upon the tin fastening, and the old man sprang up in the bed, crying out, 'Who's there?'

I kept quite still and said nothing. For a whole hour I did not move a muscle, and in the meantime I did not hear him lie down. He was still sitting up in the bed, listening – just as I have done, night after night, hearkening to the death-watches in the wall.

Presently I heard a groan, and I knew it was the groan of mortal terror. It was not a groan of pain or of grief – oh, no! – it was the low stifled sound that arises from the bottom of the soul when overcharged with awe. I knew the sound well. Many a night, just at midnight, when all the world slept, it has welled up from my own bosom, deepening, with its dreadful echo, the terrors that distracted me. I say I knew it well. I knew what the old man felt, and pitied him, although I chuckled at heart. I knew that he had been lying awake ever since the first slight noise, when he had turned in the bed. His fears had been ever since growing upon him. He had been trying to fancy them causeless, but could not. He had been saying to himself, 'It is nothing but the wind in the chimney – it is only a mouse crossing the floor,' or, 'It is merely a cricket which has made a single chirp.' Yes, he had been trying to comfort himself with these suppositions; but he had found all in vain. *All in vain;* because Death, in approaching him, had stalked with his black shadow before him, and enveloped the victim. And it was the mournful influence of the unperceived shadow that caused him to feel – although he neither saw nor heard – to *feel* the presence of my head within the room.

When I had waited a long time, very patiently, without hearing him lie down, I resolved to open a little – a very, very little crevice in the lantern. So I opened it – you cannot imagine how stealthily, stealthily – until, at length, a single dim ray, like the thread of the spider, shot from out the crevice and fell upon the vulture eye.

It was open – wide, wide open – and I grew furious as I gazed upon it. I saw it with perfect distinctness – all a dull blue, with a hideous veil over it that chilled the very marrow in my bones; but I could see nothing else of the old man's face or person, for I had directed the ray, as if by instinct, precisely upon the damned spot.

And now have I not told you that what you mistake for madness is but over-acuteness of the senses? – now, I say, there came to my ears a low, dull, quick sound, such as a watch makes when enveloped in cotton. I knew *that* sound well, too. It was the beating of the old man's heart. It increased my fury, as the beating of a drum stimulates the soldier into courage.

But even yet I refrained and kept still. I scarcely breathed. I held the lantern motionless. I tried how steadily I could maintain the ray upon the eye. Meantime the hellish tattoo of the heart increased. It grew quicker and quicker, and louder and louder every instant. The old man's terror *must* have been extreme! It grew louder, I say, louder every moment! – do you mark me well? I have told you that I am nervous: so I am. And now, at the dead hour of the night, amid the dreadful silence of that old house, so strange a noise as this excited me to uncontrollable terror. Yet, for some minutes longer, I refrained and stood still. But the beating grew louder, louder! I thought the heart must burst. And now a new anxiety seized me – the sound would be heard by a neighbour! The old man's hour had come! With a loud yell I threw open the lantern and leaped into the room. He shrieked once – once only. In an instant I dragged him to the floor, and pulled the heavy bed over him. I then smiled gaily, to find the deed so far done. But, for many minutes, the heart beat on with a muffled sound. This, however, did not vex me; it would not be heard through the wall. At length it ceased. The old man was dead. I removed the bed and examined the corpse. Yes, he was stone, stone dead. I placed my hand upon the heart and held it there many minutes. There was no pulsation. He was stone dead. His eye would trouble me no more.

If still you think me mad, you will think so no longer when I describe the wise precautions I took for the concealment of the body. The night waned, and I worked hastily, but in silence. First of all I dismembered the corpse. I cut off the head and the arms and the legs.

I then took up three planks from the flooring of the chamber and deposited all between the scantlings. I then replaced the boards so cleverly, so cunningly, that no human eye – not even *his* – could have detected anything wrong. There was nothing to wash out – no stain of any kind – no blood-spot whatever. I had been too wary for that. A tub had caught all – ha! ha!

When I had made an end of these labours, it was four o'clock – still dark as midnight. As the bell sounded the hour, there came a knocking at the street door. I went down to open it with a light heart – for what had I *now* to fear? There entered three men, who introduced themselves, with perfect suavity, as officers of the police. A shriek had been heard by a neighbour during the night; suspicion of foul play had been aroused; information had been lodged at the police office, and they (the officers) had been deputed to search the premises.

I smiled – for *what* had I to fear? I bade the gentlemen welcome. The shriek, I said, was my own in a dream. The old man, I mentioned, was absent in the country. I took my visitors all over the house. I bade them search – search *well*. I led them, at length, to *his* chamber. I showed them his treasures, secure, undisturbed. In the enthusiasm of my confidence, I brought chairs into the room, and desired them *here* to rest from their fatigues, while I myself, in the wild audacity of my perfect triumph, placed my own seat upon the very spot beneath which reposed the corpse of the victim.

The officers were satisfied. My manner had convinced them. I was singularly at ease. They sat, and while I answered cheerily, they chatted of familiar things. But, ere long, I felt myself getting pale and wished them gone. My head ached, and I fancied a ringing in my ears; but still they sat and still chatted. The ringing became more distinct – it continued and became more distinct. I talked more freely to get rid of the feeling; but it continued and gained definitiveness – until, at length, I found that the noise was *not* within my ears.

No doubt I now grew very pale; but I talked more fluently, and with a heightened voice. Yet the sound increased – and what could I do? It was *a low, dull, quick sound – much such a sound as a watch makes when enveloped in cotton*. I gasped for breath – and yet the officers heard it not. I talked more quickly – more vehemently; but the noise steadily increased. I arose and argued about trifles, in a high key and with violent gesticulations; but the noise steadily increased. Why *would* they not be gone? I paced the floor to and fro with heavy strides, as if excited to fury by the observations of the men – but the noise steadily increased. O God! what *could* I do? I foamed – I raved – I swore! I swung the chair upon which I had been sitting, and grated it upon the boards, but the noise arose over all and continually increased. It grew louder – louder – *louder*! And still the men chatted pleasantly, and smiled. Was it possible they heard not? Almighty God! – no, no! They heard! – they suspected! – they *knew*! – they were making a mockery of my horror! – this I thought, and this I think. But anything was better than this agony! Anything was more tolerable than this derision! I could bear those hypocritical smiles no longer! I felt that I must scream or die! – and now – again! hark! louder! louder! louder! *louder*! –

'Villains!' I shrieked, 'dissemble no more! I admit the deed! – tear up the planks! – here, here! – it is the beating of his hideous heart!'

Ligeia

I CANNOT for my soul, remember how, when, or even precisely where, I first became acquainted with the Lady Ligeia. Long years have since elapsed, and my memory is feeble through much suffering. Or, perhaps, I cannot *now* bring these points to mind, because, in truth, the character of my beloved, her rare learning, her singular yet placid cast of beauty, and the thrilling and enthralling eloquence of her low musical language, made their way into my heart by paces so steadily and stealthily progressive, that they have been unnoticed and unknown. Yet I believe that I met her first and most frequently in some large, old, decaying city near the Rhine. Of her family – I have surely heard her speak. That it is of a remotely ancient date cannot be doubted. Ligeia! Ligeia! Buried in studies of a nature more than all else adapted to deaden impressions of the outward world, it is by that sweet word alone – by Ligeia – that I bring before mine eyes in fancy the image of her who is no more. And now, while I write, a recollection flashes upon me that I have *never known* the paternal name of her who was my friend and my betrothed, and who became the partner of my studies, and finally the wife of my bosom. Was it a playful charge on the part of my Ligeia? or was it a test of my strength of affection, that I should institute no inquiries upon this point? or was it rather a caprice of my own – a wildly romantic offering on the shrine of the most passionate devotion? I but indistinctly recall the fact itself – what wonder that I have utterly forgotten the circumstances which originated or attended it? And, indeed, if ever that spirit which is entitled *Romance* – if ever she, the wan and the misty-winged *Ashtophet*[2] of idolatrous Egypt, presided, as they tell, over marriages ill-omened, then most surely she presided over mine.

There is one dear topic, however, on which my memory fails me not. It is the *person* of Ligeia. In stature she was tall, somewhat slender, and, in her latter days, even emaciated. I would in vain attempt to portray the majesty, the quiet ease, of her demeanour, or the incomprehensible lightness and elasticity of her footfall. She came and departed as a shadow. I was never made aware of her entrance into my closed study, save by the dear music of her low sweet voice, as she placed her marble hand upon my shoulder. In beauty of face no maiden ever equalled her. It was the radiance of an opium-dream – an airy and spirit-lifting vision more wildly divine than the fantasies which hovered about the slumbering souls of the daughters of Delos.[3] Yet her features were not of that regular mould which we have been falsely taught to worship in the classical labours of the heathen. 'There is no exquisite beauty,' says Bacon,[4] Lord Verulam, speaking truly of all the forms and genera of beauty, 'without some *strangeness* in the proportion.' Yet, although I saw that the features of Ligeia were not of a classic regularity – although I perceived that her loveliness was indeed 'exquisite,' and felt that there was much of 'strangeness' pervading it, yet I have tried in vain to detect the irregularity and to trace home my own perception of 'the strange.' I examined the contour of the lofty and pale forehead – it was faultless – how cold indeed that word when applied to a majesty so divine! – the skin rivalling the purest ivory, the commanding extent and repose, the gentle prominence of the regions above the temples; and then the raven-black, the glossy, the luxuriant and naturally-curling tresses, setting forth the full force of the Homeric epithet, 'hyacinthine!'[5] I looked at the delicate outlines of the nose – and nowhere but in the graceful medallions of the Hebrews had I beheld a similar perfection. There were the same luxurious smoothness of surface, the same scarcely perceptible tendency to the aquiline, the same harmoniously curved nostrils speaking the free spirit. I regarded the sweet mouth. Here was indeed the triumph of all things heavenly – the magnificent turn of the short upper lip – the soft, voluptuous slumber of the under – the dimples which sported, and the colour which spoke – the teeth glancing back, with a brilliancy almost startling, every ray of the holy light which fell upon them in her serene and placid, yet most exultingly radiant of all smiles. I scrutinised the formation of the chin – and here, too, I found the gentleness of breadth, the softness and the majesty, the fulness and the spirituality, of the Greek – the contour which the god Apollo revealed but in a dream, to Cleomenes,[6] the son of the Athenian. And then I peered into the large eyes of Ligeia.

For eyes we have no models in the remotely antique. It might have been, too, that in these eyes of my beloved lay the secret to which Lord Verulam alludes. They were, I must believe, far larger than the ordinary eyes of our own race. They were even fuller than the fullest of the gazelle eyes of the tribe of the valley of Nourjahad.[7] Yet it was only at intervals – in moments of intense excitement – that this peculiarity became more than slightly noticeable in Ligeia. And at such moments was her beauty – in my heated fancy thus it appeared, perhaps – the beauty of beings either above or apart from the earth – the beauty of the fabulous Houri[8] of the Turk. The hue of the orbs was the most brilliant of black, and, far over them, hung jetty lashes of great length. The brows, slightly irregular in outline, had the same tint. The 'strangeness,' however, which I found in the eyes, was of a nature distinct from the formation, or the colour, or the brilliancy of the features, and must, after all, be referred to the *expression*. Ah, word of no meaning! behind whose vast latitude of mere sound we intrench our ignorance of so much of the spiritual. The expression of the eyes of Ligeia – how for long hours have I pondered upon it! How have I, through the whole of a midsummer night, struggled to fathom it! What was it – that something more profound than the well of Democritus[9] – which lay far within the pupils of my beloved? what *was* it? I was possessed with a passion to discover. Those eyes, those large, those shining, those divine orbs? they became to me twin stars of Leda, [10]and I to them devoutest of astrologers.

There is no point, among the many incomprehensible anomalies of the science of mind, more thrillingly exciting than the fact – never, I believe, noticed in the schools – that in our endeavours to recall to memory something long forgotten, we often find ourselves *upon the very verge* of remembrance, without being able, in the end, to remember. And thus how frequently, in my intense scrutiny of Ligeia's eyes, have I felt approaching the full knowledge of their expression – felt it approaching – yet not quite be mine – and so at length entirely depart! And (strange – oh, strangest mystery of all!) I found in the commonest objects of the universe, a circle of analogies to that expression. I mean to say that, subsequently to the period when Ligeia's beauty passed into my spirit, there dwelling as in a shrine, I derived, from many existences in the material world, a sentiment such as I felt always around, within me, by her large and luminous orbs. Yet not the more could I define that sentiment, or analyse, or even steadily view it. I recognised it, let me repeat, sometimes in the survey of a rapidly growing vine – in the contemplation of a moth, a butterfly, a chrysalis, a stream of running water. I have felt it in the ocean; in the falling of a meteor. I have felt it in the glances of unusually aged people. And there are one or two stars in heaven (one especially, a star of the sixth magnitude, double and changeable, to be found near the large star in Lyra),[11] in a telescopic scrutiny of which I have been made aware of the feeling. I have been filled with it by certain sounds from stringed instruments, and not unfrequently by passages from books. Among innumerable other instances, I well remember something in a volume of Joseph Glanvill, which (perhaps merely from its quaintness – who shall say?) never failed to inspire me with the sentiment: 'And the will therein lieth, which dieth not. Who knoweth the mysteries of the will, with its vigour? For God is but a great will pervading all things by nature of its intentness. Man doth not yield him to the angels, nor unto death utterly, save only through the weakness of his feeble will.'

Length of years and subsequent reflection have enabled me to trace, indeed, some remote connection between this passage in the English moralist and a portion of the character of Ligeia. An *intensity* in thought, action, or speech, was possibly, in her, a result, or at least an index, of that gigantic volition which, during our long intercourse, failed to give other and more immediate evidence of its existence. Of all the women whom I have ever known, she, the outwardly calm, the ever-placid Ligeia, was the most violently a prey to the tumultuous vultures of stern passion. And of such passion I could form no estimate, save by the miraculous expansion of those eyes which at once so delighted and appalled me – by the almost magical melody, modulation, distinctness, and placidity of her very low voice – and by the fierce energy (rendered doubly effective by contrast with her manner of utterance) of the wild words which she habitually uttered.

I have spoken of the learning of Ligeia: it was immense – such as I have never known in woman. In the classical tongues was she deeply proficient, and, as far as my own acquaintance extended in regard to the modern dialects of Europe, I have never known her at fault. Indeed upon any theme of the most admired, because simply the most abstruse of the boasted erudition of the academy, have I *ever* found Ligeia at fault? How singularly – how thrillingly, this one point in the nature of my wife has forced itself, at this late period only, upon my attention! I said her knowledge was such as I have never known in woman – but where breathes the man who has traversed, and successfully, *all* the wide areas of moral, physical, and mathematical science? I saw not then what I now clearly perceive, that the acquisitions of Ligeia were gigantic, were astounding; yet I was sufficiently aware of her infinite supremacy to resign myself, with a childlike confidence, to her guidance through the chaotic world of metaphysical investigation at which I was most busily occupied during the earlier years of our marriage. With how vast a triumph – with how vivid a delight – with how much of all that is ethereal in hope – did I *feel*, as she bent over me in studies but little sought – but less known – that delicious vista by slow degrees expanding before me, down whose long, gorgeous, and all untrodden path, I might at length pass onward to the goal of a wisdom too divinely precious not to be forbidden!

How poignant, then, must have been the grief with which, after some years, I beheld my well-grounded expectations take wings to themselves and fly away! Without Ligeia I was but as a child groping benighted. Her presence, her readings alone, rendered vividly luminous the many mysteries of the transcendentalism in which we were immersed. Wanting the radiant lustre of her eyes, letters, lambent and golden, grew duller than Saturnian lead.[12] And now those eyes shone less and less frequently upon the pages over which I pored. Ligeia grew ill. The wild eyes blazed with a too – too glorious effulgence; the pale fingers became of the transparent waxen hue of the grave; and the blue veins upon the lofty forehead swelled and sank impetuously with the tides of the most gentle emotion. I saw that she must die – and I struggled desperately in spirit with the grim Azrael.[13] And the struggles of the passionate wife were, to my astonishment, even more energetic than my own. There had been much in her stern nature to impress me with the belief that, to her, death would have come without its terrors; but not so. Words are impotent to convey any just idea of the fierceness of resistance with which she wrestled with the Shadow. I groaned in anguish at the pitiable spectacle. I would have soothed – I would have reasoned; but, in the intensity of her wild desire for life – for life – *but* for life – solace and reason were alike the uttermost of folly. Yet not until the last instance, amid the most convulsive writhings of her fierce spirit, was shaken the external placidity of her demeanour. Her voice grew more gentle – grew more low – yet I would not wish to dwell upon the wild meaning of the quietly uttered words. My brain reeled as I hearkened, entranced, to a melody more than mortal – to assumptions and aspirations which mortality had never before known.

That she loved me I should not have doubted; and I might have been easily aware that, in a bosom such as hers, love would have reigned no ordinary passion. But in death only was I fully impressed with the strength of her affection. For long hours, detaining my hand, would she pour out before me the overflowing of a heart whose more than passionate devotion amounted to idolatry. How had I deserved to be so blessed by such confessions? – how had I deserved to be so cursed with the removal of my beloved in the hour of her making them? But upon this subject I cannot bear to dilate. Let me say only, that in Ligeia's more than womanly abandonment to a love, alas! all unmerited, all unworthily bestowed, I at length recognised the principle of her longing, with so wildly earnest a desire, for the life which was now fleeing so rapidly away. It is this wild longing – it is this eager vehemence of desire for life – *but* for life – that I have no power to portray – no utterance capable of expressing.

At high noon of the day in which she departed, beckoning me, peremptorily, to her side, she bade me repeat certain verses composed by herself not many days before. I obeyed her. They were these:

> Lo! 'tis a gala night
> Within the lonesome latter years!
> An angel throng, bewinged, bedight
> In veils, and drowned in tears,
> Sit in a theatre, to see
> A play of hopes and fears,
> While the orchestra breathes fitfully
> The music of the spheres.
>
> Mimes, in the form of God on high,
> Mutter and mumble low,
> And hither and thither fly;
> Mere puppets they, who come and go
> At bidding of vast formless things
> That shift the scenery to and fro,
> Flapping from out their condor wings
> Invisible Woe!
>
> That motley drama! – oh, be sure
> It shall not be forgot!
> With its Phantom chased for evermore,
> By a crowd that seize it not,
> Through a circle that ever returneth in
> To the self-same spot;
> And much of Madness, and more of Sin,
> And Horror, the soul of the plot!
>
> But see, amid the mimic rout
> A crawling shape intrude!
> A blood-red thing that writhes from out
> The scenic solitude!
> It writhes! – it writhes! – with mortal pangs
> The mimes become its food,
> And the seraphs sob at vermin fangs
> In human gore imbued.
>
> Out – out are the lights – out all!
> And over each quivering form,

> The curtain, a funeral pall,
>> Comes down with the rush of a storm –
> And the angels, all pallid and wan,
>> Uprising, unveiling, affirm
> That the play is the tragedy, 'Man,'
>> And its hero, the Conqueror Worm.

'O God!' half-shrieked Ligeia, leaping to her feet and extending her arms aloft with a spasmodic movement, as I made an end of these lines – 'O God! O Divine Father! – shall these things be undeviatingly so? – shall this conqueror be not once conquered? Are we not part and parcel in Thee? Who – who knoweth the mysteries of the will, with its vigour? Man doth not yield him to the angels, *nor unto death utterly*, save only through the weakness of his feeble will.'

And now, as if exhausted with emotion, she suffered her white arms to fall, and returned solemnly to her bed of death. And as she breathed her last sighs, there came mingled with them a low murmur from her lips. I bent to them my ear, and distinguished again the concluding words of the passage in Glanvill: *'Man doth not yield him to the angels, nor unto death utterly, save only through the weakness of his feeble will.'*

She died; and I, crushed into the very dust with sorrow, could no longer endure the lonely desolation of my dwelling in the dim and decaying city by the Rhine. I had no lack of what the world calls wealth. Ligeia had brought me far more, very far more than ordinarily falls to the lot of mortals. After a few months, therefore, of weary and aimless wandering, I purchased, and put in some repair, an abbey, which I shall not name, in one of the wildest and least frequented portions of fair England. The gloomy and dreary grandeur of the building, the almost savage aspect of the domain, the many melancholy and time-honoured memories connected with both, had much in unison with the feelings of utter abandonment which had driven me into that remote and unsocial region of the country. Yet although the external abbey, with its verdant decay hanging about it, suffered but little alteration, I gave way, with a childlike perversity, and perchance with a faint hope of alleviating my sorrows, to a display of more than regal magnificence within. For such follies, even in childhood, I had imbibed a taste, and now they came back to me as if in the dotage of grief. Alas, I feel how much even of incipient madness might have been discovered in the gorgeous and fantastic draperies, in the solemn carvings of Egypt, in the wild cornices and furniture, in the Bedlam[14] patterns of the carpets of tufted gold? I had become a bounden slave in the trammels of opium, and my labours and my orders had taken a colouring from my dreams. But these absurdities I must not pause to detail. Let me speak only of that one chamber, ever accursed, whither in a moment of mental alienation, I led from the altar as my bride – as the successor of the unforgotten Ligeia – the fair-haired and blue-eyed Lady Rowena Trevanion, of Tremaine.

There is no individual portion of the architecture and decoration of that bridal chamber which is not now visibly before me. Where were the souls of the haughty family of the bride, when, through thirst of gold, they permitted to pass the threshold of an apartment *so* bedecked, a maiden and a daughter so beloved? I have said that I minutely remember the details of the chamber – yet I am sadly forgetful on topics of deep moment – and here there was on system, no keeping, in the fantastic display, to take hold upon the memory. The room lay in a high turret of the castellated abbey, was pentagonal[15] in shape, and of capacious size. Occupying the whole southern face of the pentagon was the sole window – an immense sheet of unbroken glass from Venice – a single pane, and tinted of a leaden hue, so that the rays of either the sun or moon passing through it, fell with a ghastly lustre on the objects within. Over the upper portion of this huge window extended the trellis-work of an aged vine, which clambered up the massy walls of the turret. The ceiling, of gloomy-looking oak, was excessively lofty, vaulted, and elaborately fretted with the wildest and most grotesque specimens of a semi-Gothic,[16] semi-Druidical[17] device. From out the most central recess of this melancholy vaulting, depended, by a single chain of gold with long links, a huge censer of the same metal, Saracenic[18] in pattern, and with many perforations so contrived that there writhed in and out of them, as if endued with a serpent vitality, a continual succession of parti-coloured fires.

Some few ottomans and golden candelabra, of Eastern figure, were in various stations about; and there was the couch, too – the bridal couch – of an Indian model, and low, and sculptured of solid ebony, with a pall-like canopy above. In each of the angles of the chamber stood on end a gigantic sarcophagus of black granite, from the tombs of the kings over against Luxor,[19] with their aged lids full of immemorial sculpture. But in the draping of the apartment lay, alas! the chief fantasy of all. The lofty walls, gigantic in height – even unproportionably so – were hung from summit to foot, in vast folds, with a heavy and massive-looking tapestry – tapestry of a material which was found alike as a carpet on the floor, as a covering for the ottomans and the ebony bed, as a canopy for the bed, and as the gorgeous volutes[20] of the curtains which partially shaded the window. The material was the richest cloth of gold. It was spotted all over, at irregular intervals, with arabesque figures, about a foot in diameter, and wrought upon the cloth in patterns of the most jetty black. But these figures partook of the true character of the arabesque only when regarded from a single point of view. By a contrivance now common, and indeed traceable to a very remote period of antiquity, they were made changeable in aspect. To one entering the room, they bore the appearance of simple monstrosities; but upon a farther advance, this appearance gradually departed; and, step by step, as the visitor moved his station in the chamber, he saw himself surrounded by an endless succession of the ghastly forms which belong to the superstition of the Norman, or arise in the guilty slumbers of the monk. The phantasmagoric effect was vastly heightened by the artificial introduction of a strong continual current of wind behind the draperies – giving a hideous and uneasy animation to the whole.

In halls such as these – in a bridal chamber such as this – I passed, with the Lady of Tremaine, the unhallowed hours of the first month of our marriage – passed them with but little disquietude. That my wife dreaded the fierce moodiness of my temper – that she shunned me, and loved me but little – I could not help perceiving; but it gave me rather pleasure than otherwise. I loathed her with a hatred belonging more to demon than to man. My memory flew back (oh, with what intensity of regret!) to Ligeia, the beloved, the august, the beautiful, the entombed. I revelled in recollections of her purity; of her wisdom; of her lofty, her ethereal nature; of her passionate, her idolatrous love. Now, then, did my spirit fully and freely burn with more than all the fires of her own. In the excitement of my opium dreams (for I was habitually fettered in the shackles of the drug) I would call aloud upon her name, during the silence of the night, or among the sheltered recesses of the glens by day, as if, through the wild eagerness, the solemn passion, the consuming ardour of my longing for the departed, I could restore her to the pathway she had abandoned – ah, *could* it be for ever? – upon the earth.

About the commencement of the second month of the marriage, the Lady Rowena was attacked with sudden illness, from which her recovery was slow. The fever which consumed her rendered her nights uneasy; and in her perturbed state of half-slumber, she spoke of sounds, and of motions, in and about the chamber of the turret, which I concluded had no origin save in the distemper of her fancy, or perhaps in the phantasmagoric influences of the chamber itself. She became at length convalescent – finally, well. Yet but a brief period elapsed ere a second more violent disorder again threw her upon a bed of suffering; and from this attack her frame, at all times feeble, never altogether recovered. Her illnesses were, after this epoch, of alarming character, and of more alarming recurrence, defying alike the knowledge and the great exertions of her physicians. With the increase of the chronic disease, which had thus, apparently, taken too sure hold upon her constitution to be eradicated by human means, I could not fail to observe a similar increase in the nervous irritation of her temperament, and in her excitability by trivial causes of fear. She spoke again, and now more frequently and pertinaciously, of the sounds – of the slight sounds – and of the unusual motions among the tapestries, to which she had formerly alluded.

One night, near the closing in of September, she pressed this distressing subject with more than usual emphasis upon my attention. She had just awakened from an unquiet slumber, and I had been watching, with feelings half of anxiety, half of vague terror, the workings of her emaciated countenance. I sat by the side of her ebony bed, upon one of the ottomans of India. She partly arose, and spoke, in an earnest low whisper, of sounds which she *then* heard, but which I could not hear – of motions which she *then* saw, but which I could not perceive. The wind was rushing hurriedly behind the tapestries, and I wished to show her (what, let me confess it, I could not *all* believe) that those almost inarticulate breathings, and those very gentle variations of the figures upon the wall, were but the natural effects of that customary rushing of the wind. But a deadly pallor, overspreading her face, had proved to me that my exertions to reassure her would be fruitless. She appeared to be fainting, and no attendants were within call. I remembered where was deposited a decanter of light wine which had been ordered by her physicians, and hastened across the chamber to procure it. But, as I stepped beneath the light of the censer, two circumstances of a startling nature attracted my attention. I had felt that some palpable although invisible object had passed lightly by my person; and I saw that there lay upon the golden carpet, in the very middle of the rich lustre thrown from the censer, a shadow – a faint, indefinite shadow of angelic aspect – such as might be fancied for the shadow of a shade. But I was wild with the excitement of an immoderate dose of opium, and heeded these things but little, nor spoke of them to Rowena. Having found the wine, I recrossed the chamber, and poured out a gobletful, which I held to the lips of the fainting lady. She had now partially recovered, however, and took the vessel herself, while I sank upon an ottoman near me, with my eyes fastened upon her person. It was then that I became distinctly aware of a gentle footfall upon the carpet, and near the couch; and in a second thereafter, as Rowena was in the act of raising the wine to her lips, I saw, or may have dreamed that I saw, fall within the goblet, as if from some invisible spring in the atmosphere of the room, three or four large drops of a brilliant and ruby-coloured fluid. If this I saw – not so Rowena. She swallowed the wine unhesitatingly, and I forbore to speak to her of a circumstance which must, after all, I considered, have been but the suggestion of a vivid imagination, rendered morbidly active by the terror of the lady, by the opium, and by the hour.

Yet I cannot conceal it from my own perception that, immediately subsequent to the fall of the ruby drops, a rapid change for the worse took place in the disorder of my wife; so that, on the third subsequent night, the hands of her menials prepared her for the tomb, and on the fourth, I sat alone, with her shrouded body, in that fantastic chamber which had received her as my bride. Wild visions, opium-engendered, flitted, shadow-like, before me. I gazed with unquiet eye upon the sarcophagi in the angles of the room, upon the varying figures of the drapery, and upon the writhing of the parti-coloured fires in the censer overhead. My eyes then fell, as I called to mind the circumstances of a former night, to the spot beneath the glare of the censer where I had seen the faint traces of the shadow. It was there, however, no longer; and breathing with greater freedom, I turned my glances to the pallid and rigid figure upon the bed. Then rushed upon me a thousand memories of Ligeia – and then came back upon my heart, with the turbulent violence of a flood, the whole of that unutterable woe with which I had regarded *her* thus enshrouded. The night waned; and still, with a bosom full of bitter thoughts of the one only and supremely beloved, I remained gazing upon the body of Rowena.

It might have been midnight, or perhaps earlier, or later, for I had taken no note of time, when a sob, low, gentle, but very distinct, startled me from my reverie. I *felt* that it came from the bed of ebony – the bed of death. I listened in an agony of superstitious terror – but there was no repetition of the sound. I strained my vision to detect any motion in the corpse – but there was not the slightest perceptible. Yet I could not have been deceived. I *had* heard the noise, however faint, and my soul was awakened within me. I resolutely and perseveringly kept my attention riveted upon the body. Many minutes elapsed before any circumstance occurred tending to throw light upon the mystery. At length it became evident that a slight, a very feeble, and barely noticeable tinge of colour had flushed up within the cheeks, and along the sunken small veins of the eyelids. Through a species of unutterable horror and awe, for which the language of mortality has no sufficiently energetic expression, I felt my heart cease to beat, my limbs grow rigid where I sat. Yet a sense of duty finally operated to restore my self-possession. I could no longer doubt that we had been precipitate in our preparations – that Rowena still lived. It was necessary that some immediate exertion be made; yet the turret was altogether apart from the portion of the abbey tenanted by the servants – there were none within call – I had no means of summoning them to my aid without leaving the room for many minutes and this I could not venture to do. I therefore struggled alone in my endeavours to call back the spirit still hovering. In a short period it was certain, however, that a relapse had taken place; the colour disappeared from both eyelid and cheek, leaving a wanness even more than that of marble; the lips became doubly shrivelled and pinched up in the ghastly expression of death; a repulsive clamminess and coldness overspread rapidly the surface of the body; and all the usual rigorous stiffness immediately supervened. I fell back with a shudder upon the couch from which I had been so startlingly aroused, and again gave myself up to passionate waking visions of Ligeia.

An hour thus elapsed, when (could it be possible?) I was a second time aware of some vague sound issuing from the region of the bed. I listened – in extremity of horror. The sound came again – it was a sigh. Rushing to the corpse, I saw – distinctly saw – a tremor upon the lips. In a minute afterwards they relaxed, disclosing a bright line of the pearly teeth. Amazement now struggled in my bosom with the profound awe which had hitherto reigned there alone. I felt that my vision grew dim, that my reason wandered; and it was only by a violent effort that I at length succeeded in nerving myself to the task which duty thus once more had pointed out. There was now a partial glow upon the forehead and upon the cheek and throat; a perceptible warmth pervaded the whole frame; there was even a slight pulsation at the heart. The lady *lived*; and with redoubled ardour I betook myself to the task of restoration. I chafed and bathed the temples and the hands, and used every exertion which experience, and no little medical reading, could suggest. But in vain. Suddenly, the colour fled, the pulsation ceased, the lips resumed the expression of the dead, and, in an instant afterward, the whole body took upon itself the icy chilliness, the livid hue, the intense rigidity, the sunken outline, and all the loathsome peculiarities of that which has been, for many days, a tenant of the tomb.

And again I sunk into visions of Ligeia – and again (what marvel that I shudder while I write?) *again* there reached my ears a low sob from the region of the ebony bed. But why shall I minutely detail the unspeakable horrors of that night? Why shall I pause to relate how, time after time, until near the period of the grey dawn, this hideous drama of revivification was repeated; how each terrific relapse was only into a sterner and apparently more irredeemable death; how each agony wore the aspect of a struggle with some invisible foe; and how each struggle was succeeded by I know not what of wild change in the personal appearance of the corpse? Let me hurry to a conclusion.

The greater part of the fearful night had worn away, and she who had been dead, once again stirred – and now more vigorously than hitherto, although arousing from a dissolution more appalling in its utter hopelessness than any. I had long ceased to struggle or to move, and remained sitting rigidly upon the ottoman, a helpless prey to a whirl of violent emotions, of which extreme awe was perhaps the least terrible, the least consuming. The corpse, I repeat, stirred, and now more vigorously than before. The hues of life flushed up with unwonted energy into the countenance – the limbs relaxed – and, save that the eyelids were yet pressed heavily together and that the bandages and draperies of the grave still imparted their charnel character to the figure, I might have dreamed that Rowena had indeed shaken off, utterly, the fetters of death. But if this idea was not, even then, altogether adopted, I could at least doubt no longer, when arising from the bed, tottering, with feeble steps, with closed eyes, and with the manner of one bewildered in a dream, the thing that was enshrouded advanced boldly and palpably into the middle of the apartment.

I trembled not – I stirred not – for a crowd of unutterable fancies connected with the air, the stature, the demeanour of the figure, rushing hurriedly through my brain, had paralysed – had chilled me into stone. I stirred not – but gazed upon the apparition. There was a mad disorder in my thoughts – a tumult unappeasable. Could it, indeed, be the *living* Rowena who confronted me? Could it indeed be Rowena *at all* – the fair-haired, the blue-eyed Lady Rowena Trevanion of Tremaine? Why, *why* should I doubt it? The bandage lay heavily about the mouth – but then might it not be the mouth of the breathing Lady of Tremaine? And the cheeks – there were the roses as in her noon of life – yes, these might indeed be the fair cheeks of the living Lady of Tremaine. And the chin, with its dimples, as in health, might it not be hers? – but *had she then grown taller since her malady*? What inexpressible madness seized me with that thought? One bound, and I had reached her feet! Shrinking from my touch, she let fall from her head, unloosened, the ghastly cerements which had confined it, and there streamed forth, into the rushing atmosphere of the chamber, huge masses of long and dishevelled hair; *it was blacker than the raven wings of midnight*! And now slowly opened *the eyes* of the figure which stood before me. 'Here then, at least,' I shrieked aloud, 'can I never – can I never be mistaken – these are the full, and the black, and the wild eyes – of my lost love – of the Lady – of the LADY LIGEIA.'

Loss of Breath

A TALE NEITHER IN NOR OUT OF 'BLACKWOOD.'[1]

'Oh, breathe not,' &c.[2]

MOORE'S *Melodies*

THE MOST NOTORIOUS ill-fortune must in the end yield to the untiring courage of philosophy – as the most stubborn city to the ceaseless vigilance of an enemy. Shalmaneser,[3] as we have it in the holy writings, lay three years before Samaria; yet it fell. Sardanapalus – see Diodorus – maintained himself seven in Nineveh; but to no purpose. Troy expired at the close of the second lustrum; and Azoth, as Aristæus declares upon his honour as a gentleman, opened at last her gates to Psammetichus, after having barred them for the fifth part of a century.

'Thou wretch! – thou vixen – thou shrew!' said I to my wife on the morning after our wedding, 'thou witch! – thou hag! – thou whipper-snapper! – thou sink of iniquity! – thou fiery-faced quintessence of all that is abominable! – thou – thou – ' here standing upon tiptoe, seizing her by the throat, and placing my mouth close to her ear, I was preparing to launch forth a new and more decided epithet of oppro-brium, which should not fail, if ejaculated, to convince her of her insignificance, when, to my extreme horror and astonishment, I discovered that *I had lost my breath*.

The phrases 'I am out of breath,' 'I have lost my breath,' &c., are often enough repeated in common conversation; but it had never occurred to me that the terrible accident of which I speak could *bona fide* and actually happen! Imagine – that is, if you have a fanciful turn – imagine, I say, my wonder – my consternation – my despair!

There is a good genius, however, which has never entirely deserted me. In my most ungovernable moods I still retain a sense of propriety, *et le chemin des passions me conduit*[4] – as Lord Edouard in the 'Julie' says it did him – *à la philosophie veritable*.

Although I could not at first precisely ascertain to what degree the occurrence had affected me, I determined, at all events, to conceal the matter from my wife until further experience should discover to me the extent of this my unheard-of calamity. Altering my countenance, therefore, in a moment, from its bepuffed and distorted appearance, to an expression of arch and coquettish benignity, I gave my lady a pat on the one cheek, and a kiss on the other, and without saying one syllable

(Furies! I could not), left her astonished at my drollery, as I pirouetted out of the room in a *Pas de Zephyr*.[5]

Behold me, then, safely ensconced in my private boudoir, a fearful instance of the ill consequences attending upon irascibility – alive, with the qualifications of the dead – dead, with the propensities of the living – an anomaly on the face of the earth – being very calm, yet breathless.

Yes! breathless. I am serious in asserting that my breath was entirely gone. I could not have stirred with it a feather if my life had been at issue, or sullied even the delicacy of a mirror. Hard fate! – yet there was some alleviation to the first overwhelming paroxysm of my sorrow. I found, upon trial, that the powers of utterance which, upon my inability to proceed in the conversation with my wife, I then concluded to be totally destroyed, were in fact only partially impeded, and I discovered that had I at that interesting crisis dropped my voice to a singularly deep guttural, I might still have continued to her the communication of my sentiments; this pitch of voice (the guttural) depending, I find, not upon the current of the breath, but upon a certain spasmodic action of the muscles of the throat.

Throwing myself upon a chair, I remained for some time absorbed in meditation. My reflections, be sure, were of no consolatory kind. A thousand vague and lachrymatory fancies took possession of my soul – and even the idea of suicide flitted across my brain; but it is a trait in the perversity of human nature to reject the obvious and the ready, for the far-distant and equivocal. Thus I shuddered at self-murder as the most decided of atrocities, while the tabby cat purred strenuously upon the rug, and the very water-dog wheezed assiduously under the table; each taking to itself much merit for the strength of its lungs, and all obviously done in derision of my own pulmonary incapacity.

Oppressed with a tumult of vague hopes and fears, I at length heard the footsteps of my wife descending the staircase. Being now assured of her absence, I returned with a palpitating heart to the scene of my disaster.

Carefully locking the door in the inside, I commenced a vigorous search. It was possible, I thought, that concealed in some obscure corner, or lurking in some closet or drawer, might be found the lost object of my inquiry. It might have a vapoury – it might even have a tangible form. Most philosophers, upon many points of philosophy, are still very unphilosophical. William Godwin,[6] however, says in his 'Mandeville,' that 'invisible things are the only realities,' and this, all will allow, is a case in point. I would have the judicious reader pause before accusing such asseverations of an undue quantum of absurdity. Anaxagoras,[7] it will be remembered, maintained that snow is black, and

this I have since found to be the case.

Long and earnestly did I continue the investigation; but the contempt-ible reward of my industry and perseverance proved to be only a set of false teeth, two pair of hips, an eye, and a bundle of *billets-doux* from Mr Windenough to my wife. I might as well here observe that this confirma-tion of my lady's partiality for Mr W. occasioned me little uneasiness. That Mrs Lackobreath should admire anything so dissimilar to myself was a natural and necessary evil. I am, it is well known, of a robust and corpulent appearance, and at the same time somewhat diminutive in stature. What wonder, then, that the lathlike tenuity of my acquaintance, and his altitude, which has grown into a proverb, should have met with all due estimation in the eyes of Mrs Lackobreath. But to return.

My exertions, as I have before said, proved fruitless. Closet after closet – drawer after drawer – corner after corner – were scrutinised to no purpose. At one time, however, I thought myself sure of my prize, having, in rummaging a dressing-case, accidentally demolished a bottle of Grandjean's Oil of Archangels – which, as an agreeable perfume, I here take the liberty of recommending.

With a heavy heart I returned to my boudoir – there to ponder upon some method of eluding my wife's penetration, until I could make arrangements prior to my leaving the country, for to this I had already made up my mind. In a foreign climate, being unknown, I might, with some probability of success, endeavour to conceal my unhappy calam-ity – a calamity calculated, even more than beggary, to estrange the affections of the multitude, and to draw down upon the wretch the well-merited indignation of the virtuous and the happy. I was not long in hesitation. Being naturally quick, I committed to memory the entire tragedy of 'Metamora.'[8] I had the good fortune to recollect that in the accentuation of this drama, or at least of such portion of it as is allotted to the hero, the tones of voice in which I found myself deficient were altogether unnecessary, and that the deep guttural was expected to reign monotonously throughout.

I practised for some time by the borders of a well-frequented marsh – herein, however, having no reference to a similar proceeding of Demosthenes,[9] but from a design peculiarly and conscientiously my own. Thus armed at all points, I determined to make my wife believe that I was suddenly smitten with a passion for the stage. In this I succeeded to a miracle; and to every question or suggestion found myself at liberty to reply in my most frog-like and sepulchral tones with some passage from the tragedy – any portion of which, as I soon took great pleasure in observing, would apply equally well to any particular subject. It is not to be supposed, however, that in the delivery of such

passages I was found at all deficient in the looking asquint – the showing my teeth – the working my knees – the shuffling my feet – or in any of those unmentionable graces which are now justly considered the characteristics of a popular performer. To be sure they spoke of confining me in a straitjacket – but, good God! they never suspected me of having lost my breath.

Having at length put my affairs in order, I took my seat very early one morning in the mail stage for —, giving it to be understood, among my acquaintances, that business of the last importance required my immediate personal attendance in that city.

The coach was crammed to repletion; but, in the uncertain twilight, the features of my companions could not be distinguished. Without making any effectual resistance, I suffered myself to be placed between two gentlemen of colossal dimensions; while a third, of a size larger, requesting pardon for the liberty he was about to take, threw himself upon my body at full length, and falling asleep in an instant, drowned all my guttural ejaculations for relief, in a snore which would have put to blush the roarings of the bull of Phalaris.[10] Happily the state of my respiratory faculties rendered suffocation an accident entirely out of the question.

As, however, the day broke more distinctly in our approach to the outskirts of the city, my tormentor arose, and adjusting his shirt-collar, thanked me in a very friendly manner for my civility. Seeing that I remained motionless (all my limbs were dislocated and my head twisted on one side), his apprehensions began to be excited; and arousing the rest of the passengers, he communicated, in a very decided manner, his opinion that a dead man had been palmed upon them during the night for a living and responsible fellow-traveller; here giving me a thump on the right eye, by way of demonstrating the truth of his suggestion.

Hereupon all, one after another (there were nine in company), believed it their duty to pull me by the ear. A young practising physician, too, having applied a pocket-mirror to my mouth, and found me without breath, the assertion of my persecutor was pronounced a true bill; and the whole party expressed a determination to endure tamely no such impositions for the future, and to proceed no farther with any such carcasses for the present.

I was here, accordingly, thrown out at the sign of the 'Crow' (by which tavern the coach happened to be passing), without meeting with any further accident than the breaking of both my arms, under the left hind wheel of the vehicle. I must, besides, do the driver the justice to state that he did not forget to throw after me the largest of my trunks, which, unfortunately falling on my head, fractured my skull in a

manner at once interesting and extraordinary.

The landlord of the 'Crow,' who is a hospitable man, finding that my trunk contained sufficient to indemnify him for any little trouble he might take in my behalf, sent forthwith for a surgeon of his acquaintance, and delivered me to his care with a bill and receipt for ten dollars.

The purchaser took me to his apartments and commenced operations immediately. Having cut off my ears, however, he discovered signs of animation. He now rang the bell, and sent for a neighbouring apothecary with whom to consult in the emergency. In case of his suspicions with regard to my existence proving ultimately correct, he, in the meantime, made an incision in my stomach, and removed several of my viscera for private dissection.

The apothecary had an idea that I was actually dead. This idea I endeavoured to confute, kicking and plunging with all my might, and making the most furious contortions – for the operations of the surgeon had, in a measure, restored me to the possession of my faculties. All, however, was attributed to the effects of a new galvanic battery, wherewith the apothecary, who was really a man of information, performed several curious experiments, in which, from my personal share in their fulfilment, I could not help feeling deeply interested. It was a source of mortification to me, nevertheless, that, although I made several attempts at conversation, my powers of speech were so entirely in abeyance that I could not even open my mouth; much less then make reply to some ingenious but fanciful theories of which, under other circumstances, my minute acquaintance with the Hippocratian [11] pathology would have afforded me a ready confutation.

Not being able to arrive at a conclusion, the practitioners remanded me for further examination. I was taken up into a garret; and the surgeon's lady having accommodated me with drawers and stockings, the surgeon himself fastened my hands, and tied up my jaws with a pocket handkerchief – then bolted the door on the outside as he hurried to his dinner, leaving me to silence and to meditation.

I now discovered, to my extreme delight, that I could have spoken had not my mouth been tied up by the pocket handkerchief. Consoling myself with this reflection, I was mentally repeating some passages of the 'Omnipresence of the Deity,' [12] as is my custom before resigning myself to sleep, when two cats, of a greedy and vituperative turn, entering at a hole in the wall, leaped up with a flourish *à la Catalani*,[13] and alighting opposite one another on my visage, betook themselves to indecorous contention for the paltry consideration of my nose.

But, as the loss of his ears proved the means of elevating to the throne of Cyrus [14] the Magian or Mige-Gush of Persia, and as the cutting off his nose gave Zopyrus [15] possession of Babylon, so the loss of a few ounces of my countenance proved the salvation of my body. Aroused by the pain, and burning with indignation, I burst, at a single effort, the fastenings and the bandage. Stalking across the room I cast a glance of contempt at the belligerents, and throwing open the sash, to their extreme horror and disappointment, precipitated myself very dexterously from the window.

The mail-robber W—, to whom I bore a singular resemblance, was at this moment passing from the city jail to the scaffold erected for his execution in the suburbs. His extreme infirmity, and long-continued ill-health, had obtained him the privilege of remaining unmanacled; and habited in his gallows costume – one very similar to my own – he lay at full length in the bottom of the hangman's cart (which happened to be under the windows of the surgeon at the moment of my precipitation) without any other guard than the driver, who was asleep, and two recruits of the sixth infantry, who were drunk.

As ill-luck would have it, I alit upon my feet within the vehicle. W—, who was an acute fellow, perceived his opportunity. Leaping up immediately, he bolted out behind, and turning down an alley, was out of sight in the twinkling of an eye. The recruits, aroused by the bustle, could not exactly comprehend the merits of the transaction. Seeing, however, a man, the precise counterpart of the felon, standing upright in the cart before their eyes, they were of opinion that the rascal (meaning W—) was after making his escape (so they expressed themselves), and, having communicated this opinion to one another, they took each a dram, and then knocked me down with the butt-ends of their muskets.

It was not long ere we arrived at the place of destination. Of course nothing could be said in my defence. Hanging was my inevitable fate. I resigned myself thereto with a feeling half stupid, half acrimonious. Being little of a cynic, I had all the sentiments of a dog. The hangman, however, adjusted the noose about my neck. The drop fell.

I forbear to depict my sensations upon the gallows; although here, undoubtedly, I could speak to the point, and it is a topic upon which nothing has been well said. In fact, to write upon such a theme, it is necessary to have been hanged. Every author should confine himself to matters of experience. Thus Mark Antony composed a treatise upon getting drunk.

I may just mention, however, that die I did not. My body *was*, but I had no breath *to be* suspended; and but for the knot under my left ear (which had the feel of a military stock), I dare say that I should have experienced very little inconvenience. As for the jerk given to my neck upon the falling of the drop, it merely proved a corrective to the twist afforded me by the fat gentleman in the coach.

For good reasons, however, I did my best to give the crowd the worth of their trouble. My convulsions were said to have been extraordinary. My spasms it would have been difficult to beat. The populace *encored*. Several gentlemen swooned; and a multitude of ladies were carried home in hysterics. Pinxit [16] availed himself of the opportunity to retouch, from a sketch taken upon the spot, his admirable painting of the 'Marsyas Flayed Alive.' [17]

When I had afforded sufficient amusement, it was thought proper to remove my body from the gallows; this the more especially as the real culprit had in the meantime been retaken and recognised – a fact which I was so unlucky as not to know.

Much sympathy was, of course, exercised in my behalf, and as no one made claim to my corpse, it was ordered that I should be interred in a public vault.

Here, after due interval, I was deposited. The sexton departed, and I was left alone. A line of Marston's [18] 'Malcontent' –

> Death's a good fellow and keeps open house –

struck me at that moment as a palpable lie.

I knocked off, however, the lid of my coffin, and stepped out. The place was dreadfully dreary and damp, and I became troubled with *ennui*. By way of amusement, I felt my way among the numerous coffins ranged in order around. I lifted them down, one by one, and breaking open their lids, busied myself in speculations about the mortality within.

'This,' I soliloquised, tumbling over a carcass, puffy, bloated, and rotund – 'this has been, no doubt, in every sense of the word, an unhappy an – unfortunate man. It has been his terrible lot not to walk, but to waddle – to pass through life not like a human being, but like an elephant – not like a man, but like a rhinoceros.

'His attempts at getting on have been mere abortions, and his circumgyratory proceedings a palpable failure. Taking a step forward, it has been his misfortune to take two towards the right, and three towards the left. His studies have been confined to the poetry of Crabbe. [19] He can have no idea of a *pirouette*. [20] To him a *pas de papillon* [21] has been an abstract conception. He has never ascended the summit of a hill. He has never viewed from any steeple the glories of a metropolis. Heat has been his mortal enemy. In the dog-days his days have been the days of a dog. Therein, he has dreamed of flames and suffocation – of mountains upon mountains – of Pelion upon Ossa. [22] He was short of breath – to say all in a word, he was short of breath. He thought it extravagant to play upon wind instruments. He was the inventor of self-moving fans, wind-sails, and ventilators. He patronised Du Pont,[23] the bellows-maker, and died miserably in attempting to smoke a cigar. His was a case in which I feel a deep interest – a lot in which I sincerely sympathise.

'But here,' said I – 'here' – and I dragged spitefully from its receptacle a gaunt, tall, and peculiar-looking form, whose remarkable appearance struck me with a sense of unwelcome familiarity – 'here is a wretch entitled to no earthly commiseration.' Thus saying, in order to obtain a more distinct view of my subject, I applied my thumb and forefinger to its nose, and causing it to assume a sitting position on the ground, held it thus, at the length of my arm, while I continued my soliloquy –

'Entitled,' I repeated, 'to no earthly commiseration. Who, indeed, would think of compassionating a shadows? Besides, has he not had his full share of the blessings of mortality? He was the originator of tall monuments – shot-towers[24] – lightning-rods – Lombardy poplars. His treatise upon "Shades and Shadows" has immortalised him. He edited with distinguished ability the last edition of "South on the Bones". He went early to college and studied pneumatics. He then came home, talked eternally, and played upon the French-horn. He patronised the bagpipes. Captain Barclay,[25] who walked against Time, would not walk against *him*. Windham and Allbreath were his favourite writers – his favourite artist, Phiz.[26] He died gloriously while inhaling gas – *levique flatu corrupitor*,[27] like the *fama pudicitiæ*[28] in Hieronymus. He was indubitably a –'

'How *can* you? – how – *can* – you?' interrupted the object of my animadversions, gasping for breath, and tearing off, with a desperate exertion, the bandage around its jaws – 'how *can* you, Mr Lackobreath, be so infernally cruel as to pinch me in that manner by the nose? Did you not see how they had fastened up my mouth – and you *must* know – if you know anything – how vast a superfluity of breath I have to dispose of! If you do *not* know, however, sit down and you shall see. In my situation it is really a great relief to be able to open one's mouth – to be able to expatiate – to be able to communicate with a person like yourself, who do not think yourself called upon at every period to interrupt the thread of a gentleman's discourse. Interruptions are annoying, and should undoubtedly be abolished – don't you think so? – no reply, I beg you – one person is enough to be speaking at a time. I shall be done by-and-by, and then you may begin. How the devil, sir, did you get into this place? – not a word, I beseech you – been here some time myself – terrible accident! – heard of it, I suppose – awful calamity! – walking under your windows – some short while ago – about the time you were stage-struck – horrible occurrence! – heard of "catching one's breath," eh? – hold your tongue, I tell you! – I caught somebody else's! – had always too much of my own – met Blab at the corner of the street – wouldn't give me a chance for a word – couldn't get in a syllable edgeways – attacked, consequently, with epilepsis – Blab made his escape – damn all fools! – they took me up for dead, and put me in this place – pretty doings all of them! – heard all you said about me – every word a lie – horrible! – wonderful! – outrageous! – hideous! – incomprehensible! – et cetera – et cetera – et cetera – et cetera – '

It is impossible to conceive my astonishment at so unexpected a discourse; or the joy with which I became gradually convinced that the breath so fortunately caught by the gentleman (whom I soon recognised as my neighbour Windenough) was, in fact, the identical expiration mislaid by myself in the conversation with my wife. Time, place, and circumstance rendered it a matter beyond question. I did not, however, immediately release my hold upon Mr W.'s proboscis – not at least during the long period in which the inventor of Lombardy poplars continued to favour me with his explanations.

In this respect I was actuated by that habitual prudence which has ever been my predominating trait. I reflected that many difficulties might still lie in the path of my preservation which only extreme exertion on my part would be able to surmount. Many persons, I considered, are prone to estimate commodities in their possession – however valueless to the then proprietor, however troublesome, or distressing – in direct ratio with the advantages to be derived by others from their attainment, or by themselves from their abandonment. Might not this be the case with Mr Windenough? In displaying anxiety for the breath of which he was at present so willing to get rid, might I not lay myself open to the exactions of his avarice? There are scoundrels in this world, I remembered with a sigh, who will not scruple to take unfair opportunities with even a next-door neighbour, and (this remark is from Epictetus)[29] it is precisely at that time when men are most anxious to throw off the burden of their own calamities that they feel the least desirous of relieving them in others.

Upon considerations similar to these, and still retaining my grasp upon the nose of Mr W., I accordingly thought proper to model my reply.

'Monster!' I began, in a tone of the deepest indignation, 'monster! and double-winded idiot! – dost *thou*, whom for thine iniquities it has pleased heaven to accurse with a two-fold respiration – dost *thou*, I say, presume to address me in the familiar language of an old acquaintance? "I lie," forsooth! and "hold my tongue," to be sure! – pretty conversation, indeed, to a gentleman with a single breath! – all this, too, when I have it in my power to relieve the calamity under which thou dost so justly suffer – to curtail the superfluities of thine unhappy respiration.'

Like Brutus, I paused for a reply – with which, like a tornado, Mr Windenough immediately overwhelmed me. Protestation followed upon protestation, and apology upon apology. There were no terms with which he was unwilling to comply, and there were none of which I failed to take the fullest advantage.

Preliminaries being at length arranged, my acquaintance delivered me the respiration; for which (having carefully examined it) I gave him afterwards a receipt.

I am aware that by many I shall be held to blame for speaking, in a manner so cursory, of a transaction so impalpable. It will be thought that I should have entered more minutely into the details of an occurrence by which – and this is very true – much new light might be thrown upon a highly interesting branch of physical philosophy.

To all this I am sorry that I cannot reply. A hint is the only answer which I am permitted to make. There were *circumstances* – but I think it much safer upon consideration to say as little as possible about an affair so delicate – *so delicate*, I repeat, and at the time involving the interests of a third party whose sulphurous resentment I have not the least desire, at this moment, of incurring.

We were not long after this necessary arrangement in effecting an escape from the dungeons of the sepulchre. The united strength of our resuscitated voices was soon sufficiently apparent. Scissors, the Whig editor, republished a treatise upon 'The Nature and Origin of Subterranean Noises.' A reply – rejoinder – confutation – and justification – followed in the columns of a Democratic gazette. It was not until the opening of the vault to decide the controversy, that the appearance of Mr Windenough and myself proved both parties to have been decidedly in the wrong.

I cannot conclude these details of some very singular passages in a life at all times sufficiently eventful, without again recalling to the attention of the reader the merits of that indiscriminate philosophy which is a sure and ready shield against those shafts of calamity which can neither be seen, felt, nor fully understood. It was in the spirit of this wisdom that, among the ancient Hebrews, it was believed the gates of heaven would be inevitably opened to that sinner, or saint, who, with good lungs and implicit confidence, should vociferate the word '*Amen!*' It was in the spirit of this wisdom that, when a great plague raged at Athens, and every means had been attempted for its removal, Epimenides,[30] as Laertius relates in his second book of that philosopher, advised the erection of a shrine and temple 'to the proper God.'

Shadow – A Parable

Yea! though I walk through the valley of the *Shadow*.
Psalm of David

YE WHO READ are still among the living; but I who write shall have long since gone my way into the region of shadows. For indeed strange things shall happen, and secret things be known, and many centuries shall pass away, ere these memorials be seen of men. And, when seen, there will be some to disbelieve, and some to doubt, and yet a few who will find much to ponder upon in the characters here graven with a stylus of iron.

The year had been a year of terror, and of feelings more intense than terror, for which there is no name upon the earth. For many prodigies and signs had taken place, and far and wide, over sea and land, the black wings of the pestilence were spread abroad. To those, nevertheless, cunning in the stars, it was not unknown that the heavens wore an aspect of ill; and to me, the Greek Oinos, among others, it was evident that now had arrived the alternation of that seven hundred and ninety-fourth year when, at the entrance of Aries, the planet Jupiter is conjoined with the red ring of the terrible Saturnus. The peculiar spirit of the skies, if I mistake not greatly, made itself manifest not only in the physical orb of the earth, but in the souls, imaginations, and meditations of mankind.

Over some flasks of the red Chian[1] wine, within the walls of a noble hall, in a dim city called Ptolemais,[2] we sat, at night, a company of seven. And to our chamber there was no entrance save by a lofty door of brass; and the door was fashioned by the artisan Corinnos,[3] and, being of rare workmanship, was fastened from within. Black draperies, likewise, in the gloomy room, shut out from our view the moon, the lurid stars, and the peopleless streets – but the boding and the memory of Evil, they would not be so excluded. There were things around us and about of which I can render no distinct account – things material and spiritual – heaviness in the atmosphere – a sense of suffocation – anxiety – and, above all, that terrible state of existence which the nervous experience when the senses are keenly living and awake, and meanwhile the powers of thought lie dormant. A dead weight hung upon us. It hung upon our limbs – upon the household furniture – upon the goblets from which we drank; and all things were depressed, and borne down thereby – all things save only the flames of the seven iron lamps which illumined our revel. Uprearing themselves in tall slender lines of light, they thus remained burning, all pallid and motionless; and in the mirror which their lustre formed upon the round table of ebony at which we sat, each of us there assembled beheld the pallor of his own countenance, and the unquiet glare in the downcast eyes of his companions. Yet we laughed and were merry in our proper way – which was hysterical; and sang the songs of Anacreon[4] – which are madness; and drank deeply – although the purple wine reminded us of blood. For there was yet another tenant of our chamber in the person of young Zoilus. Dead, and at full length he lay, enshrouded – the genius and the demon of the scene. Alas! he bore no portion in our mirth, save that his countenance, distorted with the plague, and his eyes, in which death had but half extinguished the fire of the pestilence, seemed to take such interest in our merriment as the dead may haply take in the merriment of those who are to die. But, although I, Oinos, felt that the eyes of the departed were upon me, still I forced myself not to perceive the bitterness of their expression, and, gazing down steadily into the depths of the ebony mirror, sang with a loud and sonorous voice the songs of the son of Teios.[5] But gradually my songs they ceased, and their echoes, rolling afar off among the sable draperies of the chamber, became weak, and undistinguishable, and so faded away. And lo! from among those sable draperies, where the sounds of the song departed, there came forth a dark and undefined shadow – a shadow such as the moon, when low in heaven, might fashion from the figure of a man: but it was the shadow neither of man nor of God, nor of any familiar thing. And quivering awhile among the draperies of the room, it at length rested in full view upon the surface of the door of brass. But the shadow was vague, and formless, and indefinite, and was the shadow neither of man nor God – neither God of Greece, nor God of Chaldea, nor any Egyptian God. And the shadow rested upon the brazen doorway, and under the arch of the entablature of the door, and moved not, nor spoke any word, but there became stationary and remained. And the door whereupon the shadow rested was, if I remember aright, over against the feet of the young Zoilus enshrouded. But we, the seven there assembled, having seen the shadow as it came out from among the draperies, dared not steadily behold it, but cast down our eyes, and gazed continually into the depths of the mirror of ebony. And at length I, Oinos, speaking some low words, demanded of the shadow its dwelling and its appellation. And the shadow answered, 'I am SHADOW, and my dwelling is near to the catacombs of Ptolemais, and hard by those dim plains of Helusion[6] which border upon the foul Charonian[7] canal.' And then did we, the seven, start from our seats in horror, and stand trembling, and shuddering, and aghast: for the tones in the voice of the shadow were not the tones of any one being, but of a multitude of beings, and, varying in their cadences from syllable to syllable, fell duskily upon our ears in the well-remembered and familiar accents of many thousand departed friends.

Silence – A Fable

Ευδουσιν δ'ορεων κορυφαι τε και φαραγγες
Πρωνες τε και χαραδραι.

The mountain pinnacles slumber;
Valleys, crags, and caves *are silent*.

ALCMAN

'LISTEN to *me*,' said the Demon, as he placed his hand upon my head. 'The region of which I speak is a dreary region in Libya, by the borders of the river Zäire.[1] And there is no quiet there, nor silence.

'The waters of the river have a saffron and sickly hue; and they flow not onward to the sea, but palpitate for ever and for ever beneath the red eye of the sun with a tumultuous and convulsive motion. For many miles on either side of the river's oozy bed is a pale desert of gigantic water-lilies. They sigh one unto the other in that solitude, and stretch towards the heaven their long and ghastly necks, and nod to and fro their everlasting heads. And there is an indistinct murmur which cometh out from among them like the rushing of subterrene water. And they sigh one unto the other.

'But there is a boundary to their realm – the boundary of the dark, horrible, lofty forest. There, like the waves about the Hebrides, the low underwood is agitated continually. But there is no wind throughout the heaven. And the tall primeval trees rock eternally hither and thither with a crashing and mighty sound. And from their high summits, one by one, drop everlasting dews. And at the roots strange poisonous flowers lie writhing in perturbed slumber. And overhead, with a rustling and loud noise, the grey clouds rush westwardly for ever, until they roll, a cataract, over the fiery wall of the horizon. But there is no wind throughout the heaven. And by the shores of the river Zäire there is neither quiet nor silence.

'It was night, and the rain fell; and, falling, it was rain, but, having fallen, it was blood. And I stood in the morass among the tall lilies, and the rain fell upon my head – and the lilies sighed one unto the other in the solemnity of their desolation.

'And, all at once, the moon arose through the thin ghastly mist, and was crimson in colour. And mine eyes fell upon a huge grey rock which stood by the shore of the river, and was lighted by the light of the moon. And the rock was grey, and ghastly, and tall – and the rock was grey. Upon its front were characters engraven in the stone; and I walked through the morass of water-lilies, until I came close unto the shore, that I might read the characters upon the stone. But I could not decipher them. And I was going back into the morass, when the moon shone with a fuller red, and I turned and looked again upon the rock, and upon the characters – and the characters were "DESOLATION".

'And I looked upwards, and there stood a man upon the summit of the rock; and I hid myself among the water-lilies that I might discover the actions of the man. And the man was tall and stately in form, and was wrapped up from his shoulders to his feet in the toga of old Rome. And the outlines of his figure were indistinct – but his features were the features of a deity; for the mantle of the night, and of the mist, and of the moon, and of the dew, had left uncovered the features of his face. And his brow was lofty with thought, and his eye wild with care; and in the few furrows upon his cheek I read the fables of sorrow, and weariness, and disgust with mankind, and a longing after solitude.

'And the man sat upon the rock, and leaned his head upon his hand, and looked out upon the desolation. He looked down into the low unquiet shrubbery, and up into the tall primeval trees, and up higher at the rustling heaven, and into the crimson moon. And I lay close within shelter of the lilies, and observed the actions of the man. And the man trembled in the solitude; but the night waned, and he sat upon the rock.

'And the man turned his attention from the heaven, and looked out upon the dreary river Zäire, and upon the yellow ghastly waters, and upon the pale legions of the water-lilies. And the man listened to the sighs of the water-lilies, and to the murmur that came up from among them. And I lay close within my covert, and observed the actions of the man. And the man trembled in the solitude; but the night waned and he sat upon the rock.

'Then I went down into the recesses of the morass, and waded far in among the wilderness of the lilies, and called unto the hippopotami which dwelt among the fens in the recesses of the morass. And the hippopotami heard my call, and came, with the behemoth,[2] unto the foot of the rock, and roared loudly and fearfully beneath the moon. And I lay close within my covert, and observed the actions of the man. And the man trembled in the solitude; but the night waned, and he sat upon the rock.

'Then I cursed the elements with the curse of tumult; and a frightful tempest gathered in the heaven, where, before, there had been no wind. And the heaven became livid with the violence of the tempest – and the rain beat upon the head of the man – and the floods of the river came down – and the river was tormented into foam – and the water-lilies shrieked within their beds – and the forest crumbled before the wind – and the thunder rolled – and the lightning fell – and the rock rocked to its foundation. And I lay close within my covert, and observed the actions of the man. And the man trembled in the solitude; but the night waned, and he sat upon the rock.

'Then I grew angry and cursed, with the curse of *silence*, the river, and the lilies, and the wind, and the forest, and the heaven, and the thunder, and the sighs of the water-lilies. And they became accursed, and *were still*. And the moon ceased to totter up its pathway to heaven – and the thunder died away – and the lightning did not flash – and the clouds hung motionless – and the waters sunk to their level and remained – and the trees ceased to rock – and the water-lilies sighed no more – and the murmur was heard no longer from among them, nor any shadow of sound throughout the vast illimitable desert. And I looked upon the characters of the rock, and they were changed; and the characters were "SILENCE".

'And mine eyes fell upon the countenance of the man, and his countenance was wan with terror. And, hurriedly, he raised his head from his hand, and stood forth upon the rock and listened. But there was no voice throughout the vast illimitable desert, and the characters upon the rock were "SILENCE". And the man shuddered, and turned his face away, and fled afar off, in haste, so that I beheld him no more.'

Now there are fine tales in the volumes of the Magi [3] – in the iron-bound, melancholy volumes of the Magi. Therein, I say, are glorious histories of the heaven, and of the earth, and of the mighty sea – and of the Genii that over-ruled the sea, and the earth, and the lofty heaven. There was much lore, too, in the sayings which were said by the Sibyls; [4] and holy, holy things were heard of old by the dim leaves that trembled around Dodona [5] – but, as Allah liveth, that fable which the Demon told me as he sat by my side in the shadow of the tomb, I hold to be the most wonderful of all! And as the Demon made an end of his story, he fell back within the cavity of the tomb and laughed. And I could not laugh with the Demon, and he cursed me because I could not laugh. And the lynx which dwelleth for ever in the tomb came out therefrom, and lay down at the feet of the Demon, and looked at him steadily in the face.

The Man of the Crowd

Ce grand malheur, de ne pouvoir être seul.[1]

LA BRUYÈRE

IT WAS WELL SAID of a certain German book that '*er lasst sich nicht lesen*' – it does not permit itself to be read. There are some secrets which do not permit themselves to be told. Men die nightly in their beds, wringing the hands of ghostly confessors, and looking them piteously in the eyes – die with despair of heart and convulsion of throat, on account of the hideousness of mysteries which will not *suffer themselves* to be revealed. Now and then, alas, the conscience of man takes up a burden so heavy in horror that it can be thrown down only into the grave. And thus the essence of all crime is undivulged.

Not long ago, about the closing in of an evening in autumn, I sat at the large bow window of the D— Coffee-House in London. For some months I had been ill in health, but was now convalescent, and, with returning strength, found myself in one of those happy moods which are so precisely the converse of *ennui* – moods of the keenest appetency, when the film from the mental vision departs – the αχλυς ος πριν επηεν [2] – and the intellect, electrified, surpasses as greatly its everyday condition, as does the vivid yet candid reason of Leibnitz,[3] the mad and flimsy rhetoric of Gorgias.[4] Merely to breathe was enjoyment, and I derived positive pleasure even from many of the legitimate sources of pain. I felt a calm but inquisitive interest in everything. With a cigar in my mouth and a newspaper in my lap, I had been amusing myself for the greater part of the afternoon, now in poring over advertisements, now in observing the promiscuous company in the room, and now in peering through the smoky panes into the street.

This latter is one of the principal thoroughfares of the city, and had been very much crowded during the whole day. But, as the darkness came on, the throng momently increased; and, by the time the lamps were well lighted, two dense and continuous tides of population were rushing past the door. At this particular period of the evening I had never before been in a similar situation, and the tumultuous sea of human heads filled me, therefore, with a delicious novelty of emotion. I gave up, at length, all care of things within the hotel, and became absorbed in contemplation of the scene without.

At first my observations took an abstract and generalising turn. I looked at the passengers in masses, and thought of them in their aggregate relations. Soon, however, I descended to details, and regarded with minute interest the innumerable varieties of figure, dress, air, gait, visage, and expression of countenance.

By far the greater number of those who went by had a satisfied business-like demeanour, and seemed to be thinking only of making their way through the press. Their brows were knit, and their eyes rolled quickly; when pushed against by fellow-wayfarers they evinced no symptom of impatience, but adjusted their clothes and hurried on. Others, still a numerous class, were restless in their movements, had flushed faces, and talked and gesticulated to themselves, as if feeling in solitude on account of the very denseness of the company around. When impeded in their progress, these people suddenly ceased muttering, but redoubled their gesticulations, and awaited, with an absent and overdone smile upon their lips, the course of the persons impeding them. If jostled, they bowed profusely to the jostlers, and appeared overwhelmed with confusion. There was nothing very distinctive about these two large classes beyond what I have noted. Their habiliments belonged to that order which is pointedly termed the decent. They were undoubtedly noblemen, merchants, attorneys, tradesmen, stock-jobbers – the Eupatrids[5] and the commonplaces of society – men of leisure and men actively engaged in affairs of their own – conducting business upon their own responsibility. They did not greatly excite my attention.

The tribe of clerks was an obvious one; and here I discerned two remarkable divisions. There were the junior clerks of flash houses – young gentlemen with tight coats, bright boots, well-oiled hair, and supercilious lips. Setting aside a certain dapperness of carriage, which may be termed *deskism* for want of a better word, the manner of these persons seemed to me an exact facsimile of what had been the perfection of *bon ton* about twelve or eighteen months before. They wore the cast-off graces of the gentry – and this, I believe, involves the best definition of the class.

The division of the upper clerks of staunch firms, or of the 'steady old fellows,' it was not possible to mistake. These were known by their coats and pantaloons of black or brown, made to sit comfortably, with white cravats and waistcoats, broad, solid-looking shoes, and thick hose or gaiters. They had all slightly bald heads, from which the right ears, long wed to penholding, had an odd habit of standing off on end. I observed that they always removed or settled their hats with both hands, and wore watches, with short gold chains of a substantial and ancient pattern. Theirs was the affection of respectability; if indeed there be an affectation so honourable.

There were many individuals of dashing appearance, whom I easily understood as belonging to the race of swell pick-pockets, with which all great cities are infested. I watched these gentry with much inquisitiveness, and found it difficult to imagine how they should ever be mistaken for gentlemen by gentlemen themselves. Their voluminousness of wristband, with an air of excessive frankness, should betray them at once.

The gamblers, of whom I descried not a few, were still more easily recognisable. They wore every variety of dress, from that of the desperate thimble-rig bully, with velvet waistcoat, fancy neckerchief, gilt chains, and filigreed buttons, to that of the scrupulously inornate clergyman, than which nothing could be less liable to suspicion. Still all were distinguished by a certain sodden swarthiness of complexion, a filmy dimness of eye, and pallor and compression of lip. There were two other traits, moreover, by which I could always detect them – a guarded lowness of tone in conversation, and a more than ordinary extension of the thumb in a direction at right angles with the fingers. Very often, in company with these sharpers, I observed an order of men somewhat different in habits, but still birds of a kindred feather. They may be defined as the gentlemen who live by their wits. They seem to prey upon the public in two battalions – that of the dandies and that of the military men. Of the first grade the leading features are long locks and smiles; of the second frogged coats and frowns.

Descending in the scale of what is termed gentility, I found darker and deeper themes for speculation. I saw Jew pedlars, with hawk eyes flashing from countenances whose every other feature wore only an expression of abject humility; sturdy professional street beggars scowling upon mendicants of a better stamp, whom despair alone had driven forth into the night for charity; feeble and ghastly invalids, upon whom death had placed a sure hand, and who sidled and tottered through the mob, looking every one beseechingly in the face, as if in search of some chance consolation, some lost hope; modest young girls returning from long and late labour to a cheerless home, and shrinking more tearfully than indignantly from the glances of ruffians, whose direct contact, even, could not be avoided; women of the town of all kinds and of all ages – the unequivocal beauty in the prime of her womanhood, putting one in mind of the statue in Lucian,[6] with the surface of Parian[7] marble, and the interior filled with filth – the loathsome and utterly lost leper in rags – the wrinkled, bejewelled and paint-begrimed beldame, making a last effort at youth – the mere child of immature form, yet, from long association, an adept in the dreadful coquetries of her trade, and burning with a rabid ambition to be ranked the equal of her elders in vice; drunkards innumerable and indescribable – some in shreds and patches, reeling, inarticulate, with bruised visage and lack-lustre eyes – some in whole although filthy garments, with a slightly unsteady swagger, thick sensual lips, and hearty-looking rubicund faces – others clothed in materials which had once been good, and which even now were scrupulously well brushed – men who walked with a more than naturally firm and springy step, but whose countenances were fearfully pale, whose eyes were hideously wild and red, and who clutched with quivering fingers, as they strode through the crowd, at every object which came within their reach; beside these, pie-men, porters, coal-heavers, sweeps; organ-grinders, monkey-exhibitors, and ballad-mongers, those who vended with those who sang; ragged artisans and exhausted labourers of every description, and all full of a noisy and inordinate vivacity which jarred discordantly upon the ear, and gave an aching sensation to the eye.

As the night deepened, so deepened to me the interest of the scene; for not only did the general character of the crowd materially alter (its gentler features retiring in the gradual withdrawal of the more orderly portion of the people, and its harsher ones coming out into bolder relief, as the late hour brought forth every species of infamy from its den), but the rays of the gas-lamps, feeble at first in their struggle with the dying day, had now at length gained ascendency, and threw over everything a fitful and garish lustre. All was dark yet splendid – as that ebony to which has been likened the style of Tertullian.[8]

The wild effects of the light enchained me to an examination of individual faces; and although the rapidity with which the world of light flitted before the window, prevented me from casting more than a glance upon each visage, still it seemed that, in my then peculiar mental state, I could frequently read, even in that brief interval of a glance, the history of long years.

With my brow to the glass, I was thus occupied in scrutinising the mob, when suddenly there came into view a countenance (that of a decrepit old man, some sixty-five or seventy years of age) – a countenance which at once arrested and absorbed my whole attention, on account of the absolute idiosyncrasy of its expression. Anything even remotely resembling that expression I had never seen before. I well remember that my first thought, upon beholding it, was that Retzch,[9] had he viewed it, would have greatly preferred it to his own pictorial incarnations of the fiend. As I endeavoured, during the brief minute of my original survey, to form some analysis of the meaning conveyed, there arose confusedly and paradoxically within my mind, the ideas of vast mental power, of caution, of penuriousness, of avarice, of coolness, of malice, of blood-thirstiness, of triumph, of merriment, of excessive terror, of intense – of supreme despair. I felt singularly aroused, startled, fascinated. 'How wild a history,' I said to myself, 'is written within that bosom!' Then came a craving desire to keep the man in view – to know more of him. Hurriedly putting on an overcoat, and seizing my hat and cane, I made my way into the street, and pushed through the crowd in the direction which I had seen him take; for he had already disappeared. With some little difficulty I at length came within sight of him, approached, and followed him closely, yet cautiously, so as not to attract his attention.

I had now a good opportunity of examining his person. He was short in stature, very thin, and apparently very feeble. His clothes, generally, were filthy and ragged; but as he came, now and then, within the strong glare of a lamp, I perceived that his linen, although dirty, was of beautiful texture; and my vision deceived me, or, through a rent in a closely-buttoned and evidently second-hand *roquelaire* which enveloped him, I caught a glimpse both of a diamond and of a dagger. These observations heightened my curiosity, and I resolved to follow the stranger whithersoever he should go.

It was now fully nightfall, and a thick humid fog hung over the city, soon ending in a settled and heavy rain. This change of weather had an odd effect upon the crowd, the whole of which was at once put into new commotion, and overshadowed by a world of umbrellas. The waver, the jostle, and the hum increased in a tenfold degree. For my own part I did not much regard the rain – the lurking of an old fever in my system rendering the moisture somewhat too dangerously pleasant. Tying a handkerchief about my mouth, I kept on. For half-an-hour the old man held his way with difficulty along the great thoroughfare; and I here walked close at his elbow through fear of losing sight of him. Never once turning his head to look back, he did not observe me. By-and-by he passed into a cross street, which, although densely filled with people, was not quite so much thronged as the main one he had quitted. Here a change in his demeanour became evident. He walked more slowly, and with less object than before – more hesitatingly. He crossed and recrossed the way repeatedly, without apparent aim; and the press was still so thick that, at every such movement, I was obliged to follow him closely. The street was a narrow and long one, and his course lay within it for nearly an hour, during which the passengers had gradually diminished to about that number which is ordinarily seen at noon in Broadway near the park – so vast a difference is there between a London populace and that of the most frequented American city. A second turn brought us into a square, brilliantly lighted, and overflowing with life.

The old manner of the stranger reappeared. His chin fell upon his breast, while his eyes rolled wildly from under his knit brows, in every direction, upon those who hemmed him in. He urged his way steadily and perseveringly. I was surprised, however, to find, upon his having made the circuit of the square, that he turned and retraced his steps. Still more was I astonished to see him repeat the same walk several times – once nearly detecting me as he came round with a sudden movement.

In this exercise he spent another hour, at the end of which we met with far less interruption from passengers than at first. The rain fell fast; the air grew cool; and the people were retiring to their homes. With a gesture of impatience, the wanderer passed into a by-street comparatively deserted. Down this, some quarter of a mile long, he rushed with an activity I could not have dreamed of seeing in one so aged, and which put me to much trouble in pursuit. A few minutes brought us to a large and busy bazaar, with the localities of which the stranger appeared well acquainted, and where his original demeanour again became apparent, as he forced his way to and fro, without aim, among the host of buyers and sellers.

During the hour and a half, or thereabouts, which we passed in this place, it required much caution on my part to keep him within reach without attracting his observation. Luckily I wore a pair of caoutchouc [10] over-shoes, and could move about in perfect silence. At no moment did he see that I watched him. He entered shop after shop, priced nothing, spoke no word, and looked at all objects with a wild and vacant stare. I was now utterly amazed at his behaviour, and firmly resolved that we should not part until I had satisfied myself in some measure respecting him.

A loud-toned clock struck eleven, and the company were fast deserting the bazaar. A shopkeeper, in putting up a shutter, jostled the old man, and at the instant I saw a strong shudder come over his frame. He hurried into the street, looked anxiously around him for an instant, and then ran with incredible swiftness through many crooked and peopleless lanes, until we emerged once more upon the great thoroughfare whence we had started – the street of the D— Hôtel. It no longer wore, however, the same aspect. It was still brilliant with gas; but the rain fell fiercely, and there were few persons to be seen. The stranger grew pale. He walked moodily some paces up the once populous avenue, then, with a heavy sigh, turned in the direction of the river, and, plunging through a great variety of devious ways, came out, at length, in view of one of the principal theatres. It was about being closed, and the audience were thronging from the doors. I saw the old man gasp as if for breath while he threw himself amid the crowd; but I thought that the intense agony of his countenance had in some measure abated. His head again fell upon his breast; he appeared as I had seen him at first. I observed that he now took the course in which had gone the greater number of the audience; but, upon the whole, I was at a loss to comprehend the waywardness of his actions.

As he proceeded, the company grew more scattered, and his old uneasiness and vacillation were resumed. For some time he followed closely a party of some ten or twelve roisterers; but from this number one by one dropped off, until three only remained together, in a narrow and gloomy lane little frequented. The stranger paused, and, for a moment, seemed lost in thought; then, with every mark of agitation, pursued rapidly a route which brought us to the verge of the city, amid regions very different from those we had hitherto traversed. It was the most noisome quarter of London, where everything wore the worst impress of the most deplorable poverty, and of the most desperate crime. By the dim light of an accidental lamp, tall, antique, worm-eaten, wooden tenements were seen tottering to their fall, in directions so many and capricious, that scarce the semblance of a passage was discernible between them. The paving-stones lay at random, displaced from their beds by the rankly-growing grass. Horrible filth festered in the dammed-up gutters. The whole atmosphere teemed with desolation. Yet, as we proceeded, the sounds of human life revived by sure degrees, and at length large bands of the most abandoned of a London populace were seen reeling to and fro. The spirits of the old man again flickered up, as a lamp which is near its death-hour. Once more he strode onward with elastic tread. Suddenly a corner was turned, a blaze of light burst upon our sight, and we stood before one of the huge suburban temples of Intemperance – one of the palaces of the fiend, Gin.

It was now nearly daybreak; but a number of wretched inebriates still pressed in and out of the flaunting entrance. With a half shriek of joy the old man forced a passage within, resumed at once his original bearing, and stalked backward and forward, without apparent object, among the throng. He had not been thus long occupied, however, before a rush to the doors gave token that the host was closing them for the night. It was something even more intense than despair that I then observed upon the countenance of the singular being whom I had watched so pertinaciously. Yet he did not hesitate in his career, but, with a mad energy, retraced his steps at once, to the heart of the mighty London. Long and swiftly he fled, while I followed him in the wildest amazement, resolute not to abandon a scrutiny in which I now felt an interest all-absorbing. The sun arose while we proceeded, and, when we had once again reached that most thronged mart of the populous town, the street of the D— Hôtel, it presented an appearance of human bustle and activity scarcely inferior to what I had seen on the evening before. And here, long, amid the momently increasing confusion, did I persist in my pursuit of the stranger. But, as usual, he walked to and fro, and during the day did not pass from out the turmoil of that street. And, as the shades of the second evening came on, I grew wearied unto death, and, stopping fully in front of the wanderer, gazed at him steadfastly in the face. He noticed me not, but resumed his solemn walk, while I, ceasing to follow, remained absorbed in contemplation. 'This old man,' I said at length, 'is the type and the genius of deep crime. He refuses to be alone. *He is the man of the crowd*. It will be in vain to follow; for I shall learn no more of him, nor of his deeds. The worst heart of the world is a grosser book than the *Hortulus Animæ*;* and perhaps it is but one of the great mercies of God that *"er lasst sich nicht Iesen."* '

---

* The *Hortulus Animæ cum Oratiunculis Aliquibus Superadditis* of Grünninger[11]

Some Words with a Mummy

THE *symposium* of the preceding evening had been a little too much for my nerves. I had a wretched headache, and was desperately drowsy. Instead of going out, therefore, to spend the evening, as I had proposed, it occurred to me that I could not do a wiser thing than just eat a mouthful of supper and go immediately to bed.

A *light* supper, of course. I am exceedingly fond of Welsh rabbit. More than a pound at once, however, may not at all times be advisable. Still, there can be no material objection to two. And really between two and three, there is merely a single unit of difference. I ventured, perhaps, upon four. My wife will have it five; but, clearly, she has confounded two very distinct affairs. The abstract number, five, I am willing to admit; but, concretely, it has reference to bottles of brown stout, without which, in the way of condiment, Welsh rabbit is to be eschewed.

Having thus concluded a frugal meal and donned my nightcap, with the serene hope of enjoying it till noon the next day, I placed my head upon the pillow, and through the aid of a capital conscience, fell into a profound slumber forthwith.

But when were the hopes of humanity fulfilled? I could not have completed my third snore when there came a furious ringing at the street-door bell, and then an impatient thumping at the knocker, which awakened me at once. In a minute afterward, and while I was still rubbing my eyes, my wife thrust in my face a note, from my old friend, Doctor Ponnonner. It ran thus:

Come to me, by all means, my dear good friend, as soon as you receive this. Come and help us to rejoice. At last, by long persevering diplomacy, I have gained the assent of the Directors of the City Museum, to my examination of the Mummy – you know the one I mean. I have permission to unswathe it, and open it, if desirable. A few friends only will be present – you, of course. The Mummy is now at my house, and we shall begin to unroll it at eleven tonight.

Yours ever, PONNONNER.

By the time I had reached the 'Ponnonner,' it struck me that I was as wide awake as a man need be. I leaped out of bed in an ecstasy, overthrowing all in my way; dressed myself with a rapidity truly marvellous; and set off, at the top of my speed, for the doctor's.

There I found a very eager company assembled. They had been awaiting me with much impatience. The Mummy was extended upon the dining-table; and the moment I entered, its examination was commenced.

It was one of a pair brought, several years previously, by Captain Arthur Sabretash, a cousin of Ponnonner's, from a tomb near Eleithias, in the Lybian Mountains, a considerable distance above Thebes on the Nile. The grottoes at this point, although less magnificent than the Theban sepulchres, are of higher interest, on account of affording more numerous illustrations of the private life of the Egyptians. The chamber from which our specimen was taken, was said to be very rich in such illustrations – the walls being completely covered with fresco-paintings and bas-reliefs, while statues, vases, and mosaic work of rich patterns, indicated the vast wealth of the deceased.

The treasure had been deposited in the Museum precisely in the same condition in which Captain Sabretash had found it – that is to say, the coffin had not been disturbed. For eight years it had thus stood, subject only externally to public inspection. We had now, therefore, the complete Mummy at our disposal; and to those who are aware how very rarely the unransacked antique reaches our shores, it will be evident, at once, that we had great reason to congratulate ourselves upon our good fortune.

Approaching the table, I saw on it a large box, or case, nearly seven feet long, and perhaps three feet wide, by two feet and a half deep. It was oblong – not coffin-shaped. The material was at first supposed to be the wood of the sycamore (*platanus*), but upon cutting into it, we found it to be pasteboard, or, more properly, *papier-mâché*, composed of papyrus. It was thickly ornamented with paintings, representing funeral scenes, and other mournful subjects – interspersed among which, in every variety of position, were certain series of hieroglyphical characters, intended, no doubt, for the name of the departed. By good luck, Mr Gliddon formed one of our party; and he had no difficulty in translating the letters, which were simply phonetic, and represented the word, *Allamistakeo*.

We had some difficulty in getting this case open without injury; but, having at length accomplished the task, we came to a second, coffin-shaped, and very considerably less in size than the exterior one, but resembling it precisely in every other respect. The interval between the two was filled with resin, which had, in some degree, defaced the colours of the interior box.

Upon opening this latter (which we did quite easily) we arrived at a third case, also coffin-shaped, and varying from the second one in no particular, except in that of its material, which was cedar, and still emitted the peculiar and highly aromatic odour of that wood. Between the second and the third case there was no interval – the one fitting accurately within the other.

Removing the third case, we discovered and took out the body itself. We had expected to find it, as usual, enveloped in frequent rolls or bandages of linen; but, in place of these, we found a sort of sheath, made of papyrus, and coated with a layer of plaster, thickly gilt and painted. The paintings represented subjects connected with the various supposed duties of the soul, and its presentation to different divinities, with numerous identical human figures, intended, very probably, as portraits of the persons embalmed. Extending from head to foot, was a columnar, or perpendicular inscription, in phonetic hieroglyphics, giving again his name and titles, and the names and titles of his relations.

Around the neck thus ensheathed, was a collar of cylindrical glass beads, diverse in colour, and so arranged as to form images of deities, of the scarabæus, &c., with the winged globe. Around the small of the waist was a similar collar or belt.

Stripping off the papyrus, we found the flesh in excellent preservation, with no perceptible odour. The colour was reddish. The skin was hard, smooth, and glossy. The teeth and hair were in good condition. The eyes (it seemed) had been removed, and glass ones substituted, which were very beautiful, and wonderfully life-like, with the exception of somewhat too determined a stare. The fingers and the nails were brilliantly gilded.

Mr Gliddon was of opinion, from the redness of the epidermis,[1] that the embalmment had been effected altogether by asphaltum;[2] but, on scraping the surface with a steel instrument, and throwing into the fire some of the powder thus obtained, the flavour of camphor and other sweet-scented gums became apparent.

We searched the corpse very carefully for the usual openings through which the entrails are extracted, but, to our surprise, we could discover none. No member of the party was at that period aware that entire or unopened mummies are not unfrequently met. The brain it was customary to withdraw through the nose; the intestines through an incision in the side; the body was then shaved, washed, and salted; then laid aside for several weeks, when the operation of embalming, properly so called, began.

As no trace of an opening could be found, Doctor Ponnonner was preparing his instruments for dissection, when I observed that it was then past two o'clock. Hereupon it was agreed to postpone the internal examination until the next evening; and we were about to separate for the present, when some one suggested an experiment or two with the Voltaic[3] pile.

The application of electricity to a mummy three or four thousand years old at the least, was an idea, if not very sage, still sufficiently original, and we all caught it at once. About one-tenth in earnest and nine-tenths in jest, we arranged a battery in the doctor's study, and conveyed thither the Egyptian.

It was only after much trouble that we succeeded in laying bare some portions of the temporal muscle which appeared of less stony rigidity than other parts of the frame, but which, as we had anticipated, of course, gave no indication of galvanic susceptibility when brought in contact with the wire. This, the first trial, indeed, seemed decisive, and, with a hearty laugh at our own absurdity, we were bidding each other good-night, when my eyes, happening to fall upon those of the Mummy, were there immediately riveted in amazement. My brief glance, in fact, had sufficed to assure me that the orbs which we had all supposed to be glass, and which were originally noticeable for a certain wild stare, were now so far covered by the lids, that only a small portion of the *tunica albuginea*[4] remained visible.

With a shout I called attention to the fact, and it became immediately obvious to all.

I cannot say that I was *alarmed* at the phenomenon, because 'alarmed' is, in my case, not exactly the word. It is possible, however, that, but for the brown stout, I might have been a little nervous. As for the rest of the company, they really made no attempt at concealing the downright fright which possessed them. Doctor Ponnonner was a man to be pitied. Mr Gliddon, by some peculiar process, rendered himself invisible. Mr Silk Buckingham,[5] I fancy, will scarcely be so bold as to deny that he made his way, upon all fours, under the table.

After the first shock of astonishment, however, we resolved, as a matter of course, upon further experiment forthwith. Our operations were now directed against the great toe of the right foot. We made an incision over the outside of the exterior *os sesamoideum pollicis pedis*,[6] and thus got at the root of the *abductor*[7] muscle. Readjusting the battery, we now applied the fluid to the bisected nerves, when, with a movement of exceeding life-likeness, the Mummy first drew up its right knee so as to bring it nearly in contact with the abdomen, and then, straightening the limb with inconceivable force, bestowed a kick upon Doctor Ponnonner, which had the effect of discharging that gentleman, like an arrow from a catapult, through a window into the street below.

We rushed out *en masse* to bring in the mangled remains of the victim, but had the happiness to meet him upon the staircase, coming up in an unaccountable hurry, brimful of the most ardent philosophy, and more than ever impressed with the necessity of prosecuting our experiments with vigour and with zeal.

It was by his advice, accordingly, that we made, upon the spot, a profound incision into the tip of the subject's nose, while the doctor himself, laying violent hands upon it, pulled it into vehement contact with the wire.

Morally and physically – figuratively and literally – was the effect electric. In the first place, the corpse opened its eyes, and winked very rapidly for several minutes, as does Mr Barnes[8] in the pantomime; in the second place, it sneezed; in the third, it sat up on end; in the fourth, it shook its fist in Doctor Ponnonner's face; in the fifth, turning to Messieurs Gliddon and Buckingham, it addressed them, in very capital Egyptian, thus –

'I must say, gentlemen, that I am as much surprised as I am mortified, at your behaviour. Of Doctor Ponnonner nothing better was to be expected. He is a poor little fat fool who *knows* no better. I pity and forgive him. But you, Mr Gliddon – and you, Silk – who have travelled and resided in Egypt until one might imagine you to the manner born – you, I say, who have been so much among us that you speak Egyptian fully as well, I think, as you write your mother tongue – you, whom I have always been led to regard as the firm friend of the mummies – I really did anticipate more gentlemanly conduct from *you*. What am I to think of your standing quietly by and seeing me thus unhandsomely used? What am I to suppose by your permitting Tom, Dick, and Harry to strip me of my coffins, and my clothes, in this wretchedly cold climate? In what light (to come to the point) am I to regard your aiding and abetting that miserable little villain, Doctor Ponnonner, in pulling me by the nose?'

It will be taken for granted, no doubt, that upon hearing this speech under the circumstances, we all either made for the door, or fell into violent hysterics, or went off in a general swoon. One of these three things, was, I say, to be expected. Indeed each and all of these lines of conduct might have been very plausibly pursued. And, upon my word, I am at a loss to know how or why it was that we pursued neither the one nor the other. But, perhaps, the true reason is to be sought in the spirit of the age, which proceeds by the rule of contraries altogether, and is now usually admitted as the solution of everything in the way of paradox and impossibility. Or perhaps, after all, it was only the Mummy's exceedingly natural and matter-of-course air that divested his words of the terrible. However this may be, the facts are clear, and no member of our party betrayed any very particular trepidation, or seemed to consider that anything had gone very especially wrong.

For my part I was convinced it was all right, and merely stepped aside, out of the range of the Egyptian's fist. Doctor Ponnonner thrust his hands into his breeches pockets, looked hard at the Mummy, and grew excessively red in the face. Mr Gliddon stroked his whiskers and drew up the collar of his shirt. Mr Buckingham hung down his head, and put his right thumb into the left corner of his mouth.

The Egyptian regarded him with a severe countenance for some minutes, and at length, with a sneer, said –

'Why don't you speak, Mr Buckingham? Did you hear what I asked you, or not? *Do* take your thumb out of your mouth!'

Mr Buckingham, hereupon, gave a slight start, took his right thumb out of the left corner of his mouth, and, by way of indemnification, inserted his left thumb in the right corner of the aperture above mentioned.

Not being able to get an answer from Mr B., the figure turned peevishly to Mr Gliddon, and, in a peremptory tone, demanded in general terms what we all meant.

Mr Gliddon replied at great length, in phonetics; and but for the deficiency of American printing-offices in hieroglyphical type, it would afford me much pleasure to record here, in the original, the whole of his very excellent speech.

I may as well take this occasion to remark, that all the subsequent conversation in which the Mummy took a part, was carried on in primitive Egyptian, through the medium (so far as concerned myself and other untravelled members of the company) – through the medium, I say, of Messieurs Gliddon and Buckingham, as interpreters. These gentlemen spoke the mother-tongue of the mummy with inimitable fluency and grace; but I could not help observing that (owing, no doubt, to the introduction of images entirely modern, and, of course, entirely novel to the stranger) the two travellers were reduced, occasionally, to the employment of sensible forms for the purpose of conveying a particular meaning. Mr Gliddon, at one period, for example, could not make the Egyptian comprehend the term 'politics,' until he sketched upon the wall, with a bit of charcoal, a little carbuncle-nosed gentleman, out at elbows, standing upon a stump, with his left leg drawn back, his right arm thrown forward, with his fist shut, the eyes rolled up toward heaven, and the mouth open at an angle of ninety degrees. Just in the same way Mr Buckingham failed to convey the absolutely modern idea, 'Whig,' until (at Doctor Ponnonner's suggestion) he grew very pale in the face, and consented to take off his own.

It will be readily understood that Mr Gliddon's discourse turned chiefly upon the vast benefits accruing to science from the unrolling and disembowelling of mummies; apologising, upon this score, for any disturbance that might have been occasioned *him*, in particular, the individual mummy called Allamistakeo; and concluding with a mere hint (for it could scarcely be considered more) that, as these little matters were now explained, it might be as well to proceed with the investigation intended. Here Doctor Ponnonner made ready his instruments.

In regard to the latter suggestions of the orator, it appears that Allamistakeo had certain scruples of conscience, the nature of which I did not distinctly learn; but he expressed himself satisfied with the apologies tendered, and, getting down from the table, shook hands with the company all round.

When this ceremony was at an end, we immediately busied ourselves in repairing the damages which our subject had sustained from the scalpel. We sewed up the wound in his temple, bandaged his foot, and applied a square inch of black plaster to the tip of his nose.

It was now observed that the Count (this was the title, it seems, of Allamistakeo) had a slight fit of shivering – no doubt from the cold. The doctor immediately repaired to his wardrobe, and soon returned with a black dress coat, made in Jennings' best manner, a pair of sky-blue plaid pantaloons, with straps, a pink gingham *chemise*, a flapped vest of brocade, a white sack overcoat, a walking cane with a hook, a hat with no brim, patent-leather boots, straw-coloured kid gloves, an eye-glass, a pair of whiskers, and a waterfall cravat. Owing to the disparity of size between the Count and the doctor (the proportion being as two to one), there was some little difficulty in adjusting these habiliments upon the person of the Egyptian; but when all was arranged, he might have been said to be dressed. Mr Gliddon, therefore, gave him his arm, and led him to a comfortable chair by the fire, while the doctor rang the bell upon the spot and ordered a supply of cigars and wine.

The conversation soon grew animated. Much curiosity was, of course, expressed in regard to the somewhat remarkable fact of Allamistakeo's still remaining alive.

'I should have thought,' observed Mr Buckingham, 'that it is high time you were dead.'

'Why,' replied the Count, very much astonished, 'I am little more than seven hundred years old! My father lived a thousand, and was by no means in his dotage when he died.'

Here ensued a brisk series of questions and computations, by means of which it became evident that the antiquity of the Mummy had been grossly misjudged. It had been five thousand and fifty years, and some months, since he had been consigned to the catacombs at Eleithias.

'But my remark,' resumed Mr Buckingham, 'had no reference to your age at the period of interment (I am willing to grant, in fact, that you are still a young man); and my allusion was to the immensity of time during which, by your own showing, you must have been done up in asphaltum.'

'In what?' said the Count.

'In asphaltum,' persisted Mr B.

'Ah, yes; I have some faint notion of what you mean; it might be made to answer, no doubt – but in my time we employed scarely anything else than the Bichloride of Mercury.'

'But what we are especially at a loss to understand,' said Doctor Ponnonner, 'is, how it happens that, having been dead and buried in Egypt five thousand years ago, you are here today all alive, and looking so delightfully well.'

'Had I been, as you say, *dead*,' replied the Count, 'it is more than probable that dead I should still be; for I perceive you are yet in the infancy of galvanism, and cannot accomplish with it what was a common thing among us in the old days. But the fact is, I fell into catalepsy, and it was considered by my best friends that I was either dead or should be; they accordingly embalmed me at once – I presume you are aware of the chief principle of the embalming process?'

'Why, not altogether.'

'Ah, I perceive – a deplorable condition of ignorance! Well, I cannot enter into details just now; but it is necessary to explain that to embalm (properly speaking) in Egypt, was to arrest indefinitely *all* the animal functions subjected to the process. I use the word 'animal' in its widest sense, as including the physical not more than the moral and *vital* being. I repeat that the leading principle of embalmment consisted, with us, in the immediately arresting, and holding in perpetual abeyance, *all* the animal functions subjected to the process. To be brief, in whatever condition the individual was, at the period of embalmment, in that condition he remained. Now, as it is my good fortune to be of the blood of the Scarabæus, I was embalmed *alive*, as you see me at present.'

'The blood of the Scarabæus!' exclaimed Doctor Ponnonner.

'Yes. The Scarabæus was the *insignium*, or the "arms", of a very distinguished and very rare patrician family. To be "of the blood of the Scarabæus", is merely to be one of that family of which the Scarabæus is the *insignium*. I speak figuratively.'

'But what has this to do with your being alive?'

'Why, it is the general custom in Egypt, to deprive a corpse, before embalmment, of its bowels and brains; the race of the Scarabæi alone did not coincide with the custom. Had I not been a Scarabæus, therefore, I should have been without bowels and brains; and without either it is inconvenient to live.'

'I perceive that,' said Mr Buckingham; 'and I presume that all the *entire* mummies that come to hand are of the race of Scarabæi.'

'Beyond doubt.'

'I thought,' said Mr Gliddon, very meekly, 'that the Scarabæus was one of the Egyptian gods.'

'One of the Egyptian *what*?' exclaimed the Mummy, starting to its feet.

'Gods!' repeated the traveller.

'Mr Gliddon, I really am astonished to hear you talk in this style,' said the Count, resuming his seat. 'No nation upon the face of the earth has ever acknowledged more than *one god*. The Scarabæus, the Ibis, &c., were with us (as similar creatures have been with others) the symbols, or *media*, through which we offered worship to the Creator too august to be more directly approached.'

There was here a pause. At length the colloquy was renewed by Doctor Ponnonner.

'It is not improbable, then, from what you have explained,' said he, 'that among the catacombs near the Nile, there may exist other mummies of the Scarabæus tribe, in a condition of vitality.'

'There can be no question of it,' replied the Count; 'all the Scarabæi embalmed accidentally while alive, are alive. Even some of those *purposely* so embalmed, may have been overlooked by their executors, and still remain in the tombs.'

'Will you be kind enough to explain,' I said, 'what you mean by "purposely so embalmed"?'

'With great pleasure,' answered the Mummy, after surveying me leisurely through his eye-glass – for it was the first time I had ventured to address him a direct question.

'With great pleasure,' he said. 'The usual duration of man's life, in my time, was about eight hundred years. Few men died, unless by most extraordinary accident, before the age of six hundred; few lived longer than a decade of centuries; but eight were considered the natural term. After the discovery of the embalming principle, as I have already described it to you, it occurred to our philosophers that a laudable curiosity might be gratified, and, at the same time, the interests of science much advanced, by living this natural term in instalments. In the case of history, indeed, experience demonstrated that something of this kind was indispensable. An historian, for example, having attained the age of five hundred, would write a book with great labour and then get himself carefully embalmed; leaving instructions to his executors *pro tem.*, that they should cause him to be revivified after the lapse of a certain period – say five or six hundred years. Resuming existence at the expiration of this time, he would invariably find his great work converted into a species of hap-hazard note-book – that is to say, into a kind of literary arena for the conflicting guesses, riddles, and personal squabbles of whole herds of exasperated commentators. These guesses, &c., which passed under the name of annotations, or emendations, were found so completely to have enveloped, distorted, and over-whelmed the text, that the author had to go about with a lantern to discover his own book. When discovered, it was never worth the trouble of the search. After rewriting it throughout, it was regarded as the bounden duty of the historian to set himself to work, immediately, in correcting, from his own private knowledge and experience, the traditions of the day concerning the epoch at which he had originally lived. Now this process of rescription and personal rectification, pursued by various individual sages, from time to time, had the effect of preventing our history from degenerating into absolute fable.'

'I beg your pardon,' said Doctor Ponnonner at this point, laying his hand gently upon the arm of the Egyptian – 'I beg your pardon, sir, but may I presume to interrupt you for one moment?'

'By all means, *sir*,' replied the Count, drawing up.

'I merely wished to ask you a question,' said the doctor. 'You mentioned the historian's personal correction of *traditions* respecting his own epoch. Pray, sir, upon an average, what proportion of these Kabbala [9] were usually found to be right?'

'The Kabbala, as you properly term them, sir, were generally discovered to be precisely on a par with the facts recorded in the un-rewritten histories themselves; that is to say, not one individual iota of either was ever known, under any circumstances, to be not totally and radically wrong.'

'But since it is quite clear,' resumed the doctor, 'that at least five thousand years have elapsed since your entombment, I take it for granted that your histories at that period, if not your traditions, were sufficiently explicit on that one topic of universal interest, the Creation, which took place, as I presume you are aware, only about ten centuries before.'

'Sir!' said the Count Allamistakeo.

The doctor repeated his remarks, but it was only after much additional explanation that the foreigner could be made to comprehend them. The latter at length said, hesitatingly –

'The ideas you have suggested are to me, I confess, utterly novel. During my time I never knew any one to entertain so singular a fancy as that the universe (or this world, if you will have it so) ever had a beginning at all. I remember once, and once only, hearing something remotely hinted by a man of many speculations concerning the origin *of the human race*; and by this individual the very word *Adam* (or Red Earth), which you make use of, was employed. He employed it, however, in a generical sense, with reference to the spontaneous germination from rank soil (just as a thousand of the lower *genera* of creatures are germinated) – the spontaneous germination, I say, of five vast hordes of men, simultaneously upspringing in five distinct and nearly equal divisions of the globe.'

Here, in general, the company shrugged their shoulders, and one or two of us touched our foreheads with a very significant air. Mr Silk Buckingham, first glancing slightly at the occiput and then at the siniciput of Allamistakeo, spoke as follows –

'The long duration of human life in your time, together with the occasional practice of passing it, as you have explained, in instalments, must have had, indeed, a strong tendency to the general development and conglomeration of knowledge. I presume, therefore, that we are to attribute the marked inferiority of the old Egyptians in all particulars of science, when compared with the moderns, and more especially with the Yankees, altogether to the superior solidity of the Egyptian skull.'

'I confess again,' replied the Count, with much suavity, 'that I am somewhat at a loss to comprehend you; pray, to what particulars of science do you allude?'

Here our whole party, joining voices, detailed, at great length, the assumptions of phrenology and the marvels of animal magnetism.

Having heard us to an end, the Count proceeded to relate a few anecdotes, which rendered it evident that prototypes of Gall and Spurzheim [10] had flourished and faded in Egypt so long ago as to have been nearly forgotten, and that the manœuvres of Mesmer [11] were really very contemptible tricks when put in collation with the positive miracles of the Theban *savans*, who created lice, and a great many other similar things.

I here asked the Count if his people were able to calculate eclipses. He smiled rather contemptuously, and said they were.

This put me a little out; but I began to make other inquiries in regard to his astronomical knowledge, when a member of the company, who had never as yet opened his mouth, whispered in my ear, that for information on this head I had better consult Ptolemy [12] (whoever Ptolemy is), as well as one Plutarch *de facie lunæ*. [13]

I then questioned the Mummy about burning-glasses and lenses, and, in general, about the manufacture of glass; but I had not made an end of my queries before the silent member again touched me quietly on the elbow, and begged me, for God's sake, to take a peep at Diodorus Siculus.[14] As for the Count, he merely asked me, in the way of reply, if we moderns possessed any such microscopes as would enable us to cut cameos in the style of the Egyptians. While I was thinking how I should answer this question, little Doctor Ponnonner committed himself in a very extraordinary way.

'Look at our architecture!' he exclaimed, greatly to the indignation of both the travellers, who pinched him black and blue to no purpose.

'Look!' he cried, with enthusiasm, 'at the Bowling-green Fountain in New York! or, if this be too vast a contemplation, regard for a moment the Capitol at Washington, D.C.!' – and the good little medical man went on to detail, very minutely, the proportions of the fabric to which he referred. He explained that the portico alone was adorned with no less than four and twenty columns, five feet in diameter, and ten feet apart.

The Count said that he regretted not being able to remember, just at that moment, the precise dimensions of any one of the principal buildings of the City of Aznac,[15] whose foundations were laid in the night of Time, but the ruins of which were still standing, at the epoch of his entombment, in a vast plain of sand to the westward of Thebes. He recollected, however (talking of porticoes), that one affixed to an inferior palace in a kind of suburb called Carnac,[16] consisted of a hundred and forty-four columns, thirty-seven feet each in circumference, and twenty-five feet apart. The approach of this portico, from the Nile, was through an avenue two miles long, composed of sphynxes, statues, and obelisks, twenty, sixty, and a hundred feet in height. The palace itself (as well as he could remember) was, in one direction, two miles long, and might have been, altogether, about seven in circuit. Its walls were richly painted all over, within and without, with hieroglyphics. He would not pretend to *assert* that even fifty or sixty of the doctor's Capitols might have been built within these walls, but he was by no means sure that two or three hundred of them might not have been squeezed in with some trouble. That palace at Carnac was an insignificant little building after all. He (the Count), however, could not conscientiously refuse to admit the ingenuity, magnificence, and superiority of the fountain at the Bowling-green,[17] as described by the doctor. Nothing like it, he was forced to allow, had ever been seen in Egypt or elsewhere.

I here asked the Count what he had to say to our railroads.

'Nothing,' he replied, 'in particular.' They were rather slight, rather ill-conceived, and clumsily put together. They could not be compared, of course, with the vast, level, direct, iron-grooved causeways, upon which the Egyptians conveyed entire temples and solid obelisks of a hundred and fifty feet in altitude.

I spoke of our gigantic mechanical forces.

He agreed that we knew something in that way, but inquired how I should have gone to work in getting up the imposts on the lintels of even the little palace at Carnac.

This question I concluded not to hear, and demanded if he had any idea of Artesian wells; but he simply raised his eyebrows; while Mr Gliddon winked at me very hard and said, in a low tone, that one had been recently discovered by the engineers employed to bore for water in the Great Oasis.

I then mentioned our steel; but the foreigner elevated his nose, and asked me if our steel could have executed the sharp carved work seen on the obelisks, and which was wrought altogether by edge-tools of copper.

This disconcerted us so greatly that we thought it advisable to vary the attack to Metaphysics. We sent for a copy of a book called the 'Dial,'[18] and read out of it a chapter or two about something which is not very clear, but which the Bostonians call the Great Movement or Progress.

The Count merely said that Great Movements were awfully common things in his day, and as for Progress, it was at one time quite a nuisance, but it never progressed.

We then spoke of the great beauty and importance of Democracy, and were at much trouble in impressing the Count with a due sense of the advantages we enjoyed in living where there was suffrage *ad libitum*[19] and no king.

He listened with marked interest, and in fact seemed not a little amused. When we had done he said that, a great while ago, there had occurred something of a very similar sort. Thirteen Egyptian provinces determined all at once to be free, and so set a magnificent example to the rest of mankind. They assembled their wise men, and concocted the most ingenious constitution it is possible to conceive. For a while they managed remarkably well; only their habit of bragging was prodigious. The thing ended, however, in the consolidation of the thirteen states, with some fifteen or twenty others, in the most odious and insupportable despotism that ever was heard of upon the face of the Earth.

I asked what was the name of the usurping tyrant.

As well as the Count could recollect, it was *Mob*.

Not knowing what to say to this, I raised my voice, and deplored the Egyptian ignorance of steam.

The Count looked at me with much astonishment, but made no answer. The silent gentleman, however, gave me a violent nudge in the ribs with his elbows – told me I had sufficiently exposed myself for once – and demanded if I was really such a fool as not to know that the modern steam-engine is derived from the invention of Hero,[20] through Solomon de Caus.[21]

We were now in imminent danger of being discomfited; but, as good luck would have it, Doctor Ponnonner, having rallied, returned to our rescue, and inquired if the people of Egypt would seriously pretend to rival the moderns in the all-important particular of dress.

The Count, at this, glanced downwards to the straps of his pantaloons, and then taking hold of the end of one of his coat-tails, held it up close to his eyes for some minutes. Letting it fall, at last, his mouth extended itself very gradually from ear to ear; but I do not remember that he said anything in the way of reply.

Hereupon we recovered our spirits, and the doctor, approaching the Mummy with great dignity, desired it to say candidly, upon its honour as a gentleman, if the Egyptians had comprehended at *any* period the manufacture of either Ponnonner's lozenges, or Brandreth's pills.

We looked, with profound anxiety, for an answer – but in vain. It was not forthcoming. The Egyptian blushed and hung down his head. Never was triumph more consummate; never was defeat borne with so ill a grace. Indeed, I could not endure the spectacle of the poor Mummy's mortification. I reached my hat, bowed to him stiffly, and took leave.

Upon getting home I found it past four o'clock, and went immediately to bed. It is now ten A.M. I have been up since seven, penning these memoranda for the benefit of my family and of mankind. The former I shall behold no more. My wife is a shrew. The truth is, I am heartily sick of this life, and of the nineteenth century in general. I am convinced that everything is going wrong. Besides, I am anxious to know who will be President in 2045. As soon, therefore, as I shave and swallow a cup of coffee, I shall just step over to Ponnonner's and get embalmed for a couple of hundred years.

NOTES

The editor wishes to express his indebtedness to and admiration for the notes to the *Collected Works of Edgar Allan Poe*, Vols. II and III, edited by Thomas Ollive Mabbott, The Belknap Press of Harvard University Press, Cambridge, Massachusetts 1978.

THE GOLD BUG

1   The Motto is thought to have been written by Poe. The bite of a tarantula was believed to cause a mad paroxysm rather like a wild dance.

2   a prominent Huguenot family in Charleston. Huguenots were French protestants.

3   in Charleston Harbour: adjacent to Fort Sumter, where the American Civil War began

4   where Poe was a soldier from 1827 to late 1828

5   a seventeenth-century Dutch naturalist who had a special interest in insects

6   freed

7   mollusc with a shell of two halves joined by an elastic ligament

8   a kind of beetle; certain sorts of which were held sacred by the Egyptians

9   'human-head scarab'

10 cypher

11 whimsical fancy

12 leaps and half-turns

13 drunken figures in a festival in honour of Bacchus, the Greek god of wine

14 system of weights used in English-speaking countries

15 a blue pigment

16 a mixture of nitric and hydrochloric acids capable of dissolving gold

17 metallic part of a mineral separated in a crucible

18 saltpetre

THE FACTS IN THE CASE OF M. VALDEMAR

1   hypnotism; named after an Austrian and much in vogue at this time
2   'at the point of death'
3   John Randolph of Roanoke (1773–1833), a well-known Virginian statesman
4   pulmonary consumption
5   partly ossified
6   gristly
7   abnormal enlargement
8   the great artery

MS. FOUND IN A BOTTLE

1   'He who has only a moment to live no longer has anything to lie about.' Philippe Quinault (1635–88)
2   A view that nothing in human knowledge is certain. Pyrrho of Elis was a famous sceptic.
3   will-o'-the-wisps
4   off the coast of Java
5   a group of coral islands 200 miles west of Malabar on the Indian coast
6   coconut fibre
7   coarse brown sugar
8   buffalo-milk butter
9   East Indian coasting-vessels
10 a hot, suffocating sand-wind (did Poe mean *typhoon*?)
11 a stout sewing thread
12 a huge mythical sea beast
13 Old Age; the Olden Time
14 Baalbek in Lebanon
15 Palmyra in Syria
16 in Persia

A DESCENT INTO THE MAELSTRÖM

1   The motto is taken from Glanvill's *Essays on Several Important Subjects* (1676)
2   on the north-west coast of Norway
3   a group of islands off that coast
4   the author of *Geographia Nubiensis* (1619)
5   Atlantic Ocean
6   all these places are part of the Lofoten Islands. Poe's spelling is

sometimes his own. 'Stockholm' is 'Skarholm' and between Moskenesoy and Vaeroy ('Moskoe' and 'Vurrgh') whirlpools do exist.

7 See above; a large whirlpool off the west coast of Norway

8 author of *The Natural History of Norway* (1755)

9 fiery river in Hades

10 Athanasius Kircher (1602–80), a writer about the sea

11 between Sweden and Finland

12 Mahometans

13 Archimedes of Syracuse. Not unusually, Poe seems to have made up the reference.

THE MURDERS IN THE RUE MORGUE

1 a quotation from *Urn-Burial* (1658) by Sir Thomas Browne (1605–82)

2 Edward Hoyle (1672–1769) wrote about card games

3 Poe called his first collection of stories, *Tales of the Grotesque and Arabesque* (1840)

4 eccentricity

5 imaginative faculty. An important term in any discussion of Poe's work.

6 an idea which occurs in several Poe stories, including 'The Fall of the House of Usher' and 'William Wilson'

7 1714; a play by Prosper-Jolyot de Crebillon (1674–1762)

8 'all that sort of thing'

9 quackery

10 a brilliant constellation of stars in the southern part of the zodiac

11 John Pringle Nichol (1804–59), Regius Professor of Astronomy at Glasgow

12 Athenian philosopher (c. 300 BC) who believed that the highest good was pleasure. His view that everything material and spiritual is made out of atoms is mentioned by Poe in *Eureka*.

13 a form of masonry

14 'the first letter has lost its original sound'

15 an alloy used instead of silver

16 François-Eugene Vidocq (1775–1857), a thief who became a thief-taker and head of the first detective service in France

17 porter's lodge

18 perhaps, 'I humoured them with cautious respect'

19 excessive

20 an asylum

21 Georges Cuvier (1769–1832), a natural historian, most famous for *Règne Animal* (1817)
22 a large, long-armed ape, originally from Borneo
23 the fourth floor
24 Neufchâtel is a city in northern France
25 Botanical Gardens in Paris
26 staying power
27 Roman goddess of thieves; a head without a body
28 'to deny what is, and explain what is not'

THE MYSTERY OF MARIE ROGÊT

1 Friedrich von Hardenberg (1772–1801)
2 young working-girl
3 disturbances
4 favouring one side
5 a legal enquiry into a person's sanity
6 'William Landor' (Horace Binney Wallace) published the novel, *Stanley*, from which this quotation is taken, in 1838.
7 counter
8 small North American tree whose bark can be used in medicinal preparations. It does not grow on the banks of the Seine.
9 'and hence this anger'

THE PURLOINED LETTER

1 The motto means, 'Nothing is more hateful to wisdom than too much cunning': one of Poe's quotations whose derivation, despite his own statements, has never been confirmed
2 John Abernethy (1764–1831), a noted British surgeon
3 François de la Rochefoucauld (1630–80), French moralist
4 assumed to be a misprint for Jean de La Bruyère (1845–96)
5 Niccoló Machiavelli (1469–1527), Florentine writer on politics
6 Tomasso Campanella (1568–1639), Italian philosopher
7 'undistributed middle'. A syllogism with a part missing, leading to a false conclusion.
8 Sébastien-Roch Nicolas (1740–94), French cynic. The quotation means, 'It is fair to say that every publicly accepted idea, every received convention, is stupid, since it has appealed to the majority.'
9 'seeking office'
10 'superstition'
11 Cicero's term for supporters of his views
12 Jacob Bryant wrote a dictionary of mythologies in the late eighteenth century

13 schemer
14 boring-tools
15 'the force of inertia'
16 'the descent to Hell is easy' (*Aeneid*)
17 Angelica Catalani (1779–1849), an Italian opera singer
18 Prosper-Jolyot de Crébillon wrote *Atrée et Thyeste* in 1707. The quotation means, 'So deadly a plan, if unworthy of Atreus, is worthy of Thyestes.'

THE FALL OF THE HOUSE OF USHER

1 Pierre-Jean de Béranger (1780–1857). The quotation is from 'Le Refus': 'His heart is a suspended lute; whenever one touches it, it resounds.'
2 evidenced by a suspension of consciousness and a rigidity of the body
3 Karl Maria, Baron von Weber (1786–1826). Rather confusedly, 'The Last Waltz of Von Weber' was actually composed by Karl Gottlieb Reissiger (1798–1859)
4 Henry Fuseli (1741–1825) was an English painter of strange subjects
5 Poe's version of 'porphyrogenite', meaning 'born in the purple'
6 these are all actual books
7 this, however, is not an actual book

THE PIT AND THE PENDULUM

1 'Here the godless crowd, not satisfied, harboured a hatred of innocent blood. Now that our country has been preserved, and the cave of death destroyed, where horrid death has been, life and health show forth.'
2 'acts of faith'; the public burning of heretics
3 a town in central Spain, closely associated with the history of the Spanish Inquisition
4 saddle-strap
5 a person who refuses to submit to authority
6 the farthest possible point; see Poe's poem, 'Dream-Land'
7 an oriental, curved sword
8 an ecclesiastical tribunal of the Roman Catholic Church (thirteenth to nineteenth centuries) whose purpose was to discover and suppress heresy
9 The Comte de Lasalle did enter Toledo with the French army in 1808, but the English meaning of the general's name ('the room') seems to have been uppermost in Poe's mind.

THE PREMATURE BURIAL

1 All these are incidents involving great loss of life. Napoleon's army sustained considerable losses in crossing the River Beresina in Russia in 1812; well over 30,000 people died in the Lisbon earthquake in 1755; the Plague of London took many lives in 1665; and the mass murder of Huguenots in France occurred on St Bartholemew's Day, 1572. The English prisoners in Calcutta died in 1756.

2 small cog-wheels which engage with larger wheels

3 suspended animation due to a lack of oxygen in the blood

4 a favourite idea of Poe's; see 'Some Words with a Mummy'

5 see pp. 231–2

6 see p. 153

7 loss of consciousness due to a fall in the blood pressure

8 see Shakespeare, *Richard II* (Act III, Sc. 2, line 144)

9 William Buchan (1729–1805) published *Domestic Medicine* in 1769

10 a poem of 1742 by Edward Young which greatly influenced the development of the Gothic novel

11 Vathek's wicked mother in William Beckford's *Vathek* (1786)

12 the King of Turan in Persian epics

13 ancient name for the Amu Darya, a river in Russia

THE BLACK CAT

1 bizarre

2 the ruler of the infernal regions; see Poe's story 'The Imp of the Perverse'

THE MASQUE OF THE RED DEATH

1 manifestation

2 the central figure of Shakespeare's *The Tempest*, who similarly lived in isolation from society

3 extempore performers

4 adornments

5 a play (1830) by Victor Hugo (1802–85)

THE CASK OF AMONTILLADO

1 knowledge of precious stones

2 this is finer than ordinary sherry, but the two are, in some respects, one; rather like Fortunato and Montresor, whose names could be taken to mean the same thing

3 a knee-length cloak

4   torches which hang in brackets ('sconces') on walls
5   a French wine of reputedly therapeutic value
6   ' No one provokes me with impunity.'
7   large casks
8   a Bordeaux with a clearly intended pun
9   'Rest in peace.'

THE OVAL PORTRAIT

1   Ann Radcliffe (1764–1823) was one of the foremost English Gothic
      novelists. Her best-known work is *The Mysteries of Udolpho* (1794)
2   a portrait usually showing a head and shoulders against a shaded
      background
3   either Robert Sully (1803–55) or his uncle Thomas Sully (1783–
      1872), both American portrait painters
4   Moorish in style

THE OBLONG BOX

1   not known and probably made up by Poe
2   a fore-and-aft sail (one going in the direction of the length of the
      ship and set on the stern side of the mizzenmast, the mast nearest
      the stern in a three-masted ship)
3   a sail set on the section of the mast above the foretop, which is a
      platform at the top of the lower section of the foremast, that mast
      nearest to the bow of the ship
4   double-folded
5   kitchen on deck
6   raised side of a ship on the upper deck, on the left-hand side facing
      the bow
7   sail extended on a rope
8   on Pamlico Sound, North Carolina
9   side away from the wind
10   also on Pamlico Sound

THE TELL-TALE HEART

1   see Poe's poem, 'The Raven'

LIGEIA

1   this quotation has never been located and it is assumed that Poe
      made it up
2   a goddess in Greek mythology, possibly associated with fertility
3   a place in Greece containing statuary of Greek gods and goddesses
4   from the 'Essay on Beauty' by Thomas Bacon (1561–1626)

5   see Poe's poem, 'To Helen'
6   a Greek sculptor
7   the reference is to *The History of Nourjahad* by 'Sidney Biddulph' (Mrs Frances Sheridan)
8   dark-eyed maidens who inhabit the Mahometan paradise
9   fifth-century-BC Greek philosopher to whom has been ascribed the idea that Truth lies at the bottom of a well
10   Castor and Pollux
11   Epsilon Lyrae, near Vega
12   graphite
13   Mahometan angel of Death
14   insane
15   a powerful shape in the practice of the occult
16   a style of architecture in Western Europe in twelfth to sixteenth centuries
17   ancient Celtic art
18   in the style of Arabian/Moslem architecture
19   a place in Egypt where the ancient Pharoahs built a great temple
20   spiral/scroll-shaped parts

LOSS OF BREATH

1   see Poe's essay, 'How to Write a Blackwood Article'
2   see *Irish Melodies* of Thomas Moore (1779–1852)
3   Poe here refers to four great sieges, accounts of which will be found, respectively, in 'The Book of Kings', Diodorus, the *Odyssey* and Herodotus
4   the quotation from *Julie* (1761) by Jean-Jacques Rousseau (1712–78) means: 'The way of the passions has led me to true philosophy.'
5   pun on a ballet step
6   William Godwin (1756–1836) published *Mandeville*, a novel, in 1817
7   fifth-century-BC Greek philosopher who argued that there must be blackness in snow to produce dark water when it melts
8   a play (1829) by John Augustus Stone (1800–34)
9   *c.* 384–322 BC, a great Athenian orator
10   tyrant of Agrigentum, who roasted his victims alive in a brazen bull, *c.* 510 BC
11   fifth-century-BC Greek physician
12   a poem (1828) by Robert Montgomery, whom Poe disliked
13   Angelica Catalani (1779–1849), an Italian opera singer
14   another story in Herodotus. The Magian, after losing his ears, usurped the throne of Persia

15 Herodotus again. Zopyrus, a Persian patriot, cut off his own nose and ears and then pretended to the Babylonians that his own people had done it and as a result he had defected to the Babylonian side. He then betrayed Babylon to the Persians.

16 Latin for 'he painted'

17 a satyr who was punished by Apollo for presumption

18 John Marston (1576–1634) wrote *The Malcontent* (1603) but this line is from another of his plays, *Antonio and Mellida* (1600).

19 George Crabbe (1754–1832). A pun is intended here since crabs do not walk forwards.

20 spinning round on one foot/toe

21 a ballet step

22 in the *Odyssey*, the Giants try to pile Mount Pelion on top of Mount Ossa in order to reach the top of Mount Olympus

23 has not been identified; perhaps another of Poe's little fictions for the harassed editor

24 in which shot was made from molten lead being passed through sieves under water

25 Captain Robert Barclay-Allardyce is reputed to have walked 1,000 miles in 1,000 hours in 1809

26 the pen-name of Hablot K. Browne (1815–82), well known as an illustrator of the works of Charles Dickens

27 'greatly damaged by a slight breeze'

28 'reputation for modesty'

29 was a Greek Stoic philosopher (*c.* AD 60–120)

30 a reference to the section on Epimenides in the *Lives* of Diogenes Laertius

SHADOW – PARABLE

1 from the Greek island of Chios

2 possibly Ptolemais Theron on the Red Sea

3 not identified

4 an Ionian poet of the sixth century BC

5 Teos, an Ionian seaport where Anacreon was born

6 Elysium

7 the Styx, where Charon was the ferryman

SILENCE – A FABLE

1 the River Congo

2 elephant

3 Persian priests

4 prophetesses

5 a place in Greece

THE MAN OF THE CROWD

1   'This great evil, not to be able to be alone'
2   'the mist that previously was upon [them]'
3   Gottfried Wilhelm von Leibnitz (1646–1716) was a German philosopher and mathematician
4   Gorgias of Leontini was a statesman of the time of Plato
5   people belonging to very noble families
6   Lucian of Samosata, a second-century Greek satirist
7   from the island of Paros
8   (AD 160–230). A Carthaginian Christian theologian
9   Friedrich August Moritz Retzch (1779–1857) was a German painter
10 unvulcanised rubber
11 the title should begin, *Ortulus anime* . . .

SOME WORDS WITH A MUMMY

1   outer layer of skin
2   a mixture of bitumen, pitch and sand
3   invented by Allesandro Volta (1745–1827) and producing electricity by chemical action, like that old Poe stand-by, the galvanic battery
4   the sclerotic coat and the cornea
5   James Silk Buckingham (1786–1855), traveller, social reformer and temperance advocate
6   small bone in the big toe
7   any muscle which causes movement of a limb away from the mid plane of the body or from another part or limb
8   a celebrated comedian
9   mysteries
10 writers about phrenology
11 Franz Anton Mesmer (1733–1815) wrote on animal magnetism
12 Ptolemaeus was a second-century Egyptian astrologer
13 Plutarch (*c.* AD 46–120), a Greek biographer, wrote a treatise titled *On the Face of the Moon*
14 a Greek historian of the first century BC
15 an imaginary place
16 Karnak is a real place, on the upper Nile in Egypt, near the site of Thebes.
17 The Bowling Green Fountain in New York, first shown in 1843, was a laughing stock.
18 *The Dial* (1840–44), a quarterly magazine of literature and philosophy, was the voice of the New England Transcendentalists.
19 at will
20 an Alexandrian steam-engineer (*c.* AD 50–150)
21 a French steam-engineer (1576–1626)

WORDSWORTH CLASSICS

General Editors: Marcus Clapham & Clive Reynard

JANE AUSTEN

ARNOLD BENNETT

R. D. BLACKMORE

ANNE BRONTË

CHARLOTTE BRONTË

EMILY BRONTË

JOHN BUCHAN

SAMUEL BUTLER

LEWIS CARROLL

CERVANTES

ANTON CHEKHOV

G. K. CHESTERTON

ERSKINE CHILDERS

JOHN CLELAND

REX COLLINGS (*selector*)

WILKIE COLLINS

JOSEPH CONRAD

J. FENIMORE COOPER

STEPHEN CRANE

THOMAS DE QUINCEY

DANIEL DEFOE

CHARLES DICKENS

BENJAMIN DISRAELI

THEODOR DOSTOEVSKY

SIR ARTHUR CONAN
DOYLE

GEORGE DU MAURIER

ALEXANDRE DUMAS

MARIA EDGEWORTH

GEORGE ELIOT

HENRY FIELDING

RONALD FIRBANK

EDWARD FITZGERALD
(*translator*)

F. SCOTT FITZGERALD

GUSTAVE FLAUBERT

JOHN GALSWORTHY

ELIZABETH GASKELL

GEORGE GISSING

KENNETH GRAHAME

GEORGE & WEEDON
GROSSMITH

RIDER HAGGARD

THOMAS HARDY

NATHANIEL
HAWTHORNE

O. HENRY

JAMES HOGG

HOMER

E. W. HORNUNG

VICTOR HUGO

HENRY JAMES

M. R. JAMES

JEROME K. JEROME

JAMES JOYCE

RUDYARD KIPLING

D. H. LAWRENCE

SHERIDAN LE FANU

GASTON LEROUX

JACK LONDON

GUY DE MAUPASSANT

HERMAN MELVILLE

GEORGE MEREDITH

H. H. MUNRO

THOMAS LOVE
PEACOCK

EDGAR ALLAN POE

FREDERICK ROLFE

SIR WALTER SCOTT

WILLIAM SHAKESPEARE

BRAM STOKER

R. S. SURTEES

JONATHAN SWIFT

W. M. THACKERAY

TOLSTOY

ANTHONY TROLLOPE

IVAN SERGEYEVICH
TURGENEV

MARK TWAIN

JULES VERNE

VIRGIL

VOLTAIRE

LEW WALLACE

ISAAC WALTON

EDITH WHARTON

GILBERT WHITE

OSCAR WILDE

VIRGINIA WOOLF

P. C. WREN

Distribution

AUSTRALIA & PAPUA NEW GUINEA
Peribo Pty Ltd
58 Beaumont Road, Mount Kuring-Gai
NSW 2080, Australia
Tel: (02) 457 0011 Fax: (02) 457 0022

CZECH REPUBLIC
Bohemian Ventures s r. o.,
Delnicka 13, 170 00 Prague 7
Tel: 042 2 877837 Fax: 042 2 801498

FRANCE
Copernicus Diffusion
81 Rue des Entrepreneurs, Paris 75015
Tel: 01 53 95 38 00 Fax: 01 53 95 38 01

GERMANY & AUSTRIA
Taschenbuch-Vertrieb
Ingeborg Blank GmbH
Lager und Buro Rohrmooser Str 1
85256 Vierkirchen/Pasenbach
Tel: 08139-8130/8184 Fax: 08139-8140

Tradis Verlag und Vertrieb GmbH (Bookshops)
Postfach 90 03 69, D-51113 Köln
Tel: 022 03 31059 Fax: 022 03 39340

GREAT BRITAIN
Wordsworth Editions Ltd
Cumberland House, Crib Street
Ware, Hertfordshire SG12 9ET
Tel: 01920 465167 Fax: 01920 462267

INDIA
Rupa & Co
Post Box No 7071,
7/16 Makhanlal Street, Ansari Road,
Daryaganj, New Delhi – 110 002
Tel: 3278586 Fax: (011) 3277294

IRELAND
Easons & Son Limited
Furry Park Industrial Estate
Santry 9, Eire
Tel: 003531 8733811 Fax: 003531 8733945

ISRAEL
Sole Agent – **Timmy Marketing Limited**
Israel Ben Zeev 12, Ramont Gimmel, Jerusalem
Tel: 972-2-5865266 Fax: 972-2-5860035
Sole Distributor – Sefer ve Sefel Ltd
Tel & Fax: 972-2-6248237

ITALY
Logos – Edizioni e distribuzione libri
Via Curtatona 5/J
41100 Modena, Italy
Tel: 059-418820/418821 Fax: 059-280123

NEW ZEALAND & FIJI
Allphy Book Distributors Ltd
4-6 Charles Street, Eden Terrace, Auckland,
Tel: (09) 3773096 Fax: (09) 3022770

MALAYSIA & BRUNEI
Vintrade SDN BHD
5 & 7 Lorong Datuk Sulaiman 7
Taman Tun Dr Ismail
60000 Kuala Lumpur, Malaysia
Tel: (603) 717 3333 Fax: (603) 719 2942

MALTA & GOZO
Agius & Agius Ltd
42A South Street, Valletta VLT 11
Tel: 234038 - 220347 Fax: 241175

PHILIPPINES
I J Sagun Enterprises
P O Box 4322 CPO Manila
2 Topaz Road, Greenheights Village,
Taytay, Rizal
Tel: 631 80 61 TO 66

SOUTHERN & CENTRAL AFRICA
Struik Book Distributors
32 Thora Crescent
Wynberg, Sandton, South Africa
Tel: (011) 444 9473
Fax: (011) 444 9472

SLOVAK REPUBLIC
Slovak Ventures s r. o.,
Stefanikova 128, 949 01 Nitra
Tel/Fax: 042 87 525105/6/7

SPAIN
Ribera Libros, S.L.
Poligono Martiartu, Calle 1 - no 6
48480 Arrigorriaga, Vizcaya
Tel: 34 4 6713607 (Almacen)
     34 4 4418787 (Libreria)
Fax: 34 4 6713608 (Almacen)
     34 4 4418029 (Libreria)

UNITED STATES OF AMERICA
NTC/Contemporary Publishing Company
4225 West Touhy Avenue
Lincolnwood (Chicago)
Illinois 60646-4622
USA
Tel: (847) 679 5500 Fax: (847) 679 2494

DIRECT MAIL
Bibliophile Books
5 Thomas Road, London E14 7BN,
Tel: 0171-515 9222 Fax: 0171-538 4115
Order hotline 24 hours Tel: 0171-515 9555
Cash with order + £2.50 p&p (UK)